one

is not a lonely number

Evelyn Krieger

YM BOOKS

YM Books
An imprint of YALDAH
info@yaldah.com
www.yaldah.com/books

ISBN: 978-0-9841624-2-0

Copyright © 2010 by YM Books
Third edition December 2013

Cover design and layout by Leah Caras.

Manufactured in the United States of America

For my children,
Emily, Sam and Audrey,
who make three a lovely number.

*"One is the loneliest number
that you'll ever do."*

—Song by Three Dog Night, 1969

*"Who knows One? I know One.
One is God of the Heaven and the Earth."*

—Song from the Passover Haggadah, 1590

Eight is my favorite number. I think it's a beautiful number; it has two-way symmetry, it's an even number, it's in my birth date (September 18th), and it's the color of a blue sky. Okay, I know that last part must sound weird. But for me, numbers are not just squiggles on a paper or the stuff that makes your head ache in school. Numbers are… well, how can I say this? In my thirteen-year-old brain, numbers occupy a very special place. Numbers are alive. They have personalities, colors, and sounds. And since numbers are all around us (in case you haven't noticed), they keep me company. Numbers distract me from whatever is making me feel nervous, sad, or bored. So maybe it does sound odd, but it certainly makes life more interesting.

Take right now, for instance, as I walk home from school on a Friday afternoon. My watch says it's exactly 2:28 PM and up to this moment, it has been a pretty lucky day. I got a 96 on my Hebrew vocabulary quiz and an A- on my history project. Rabbi Lukins wasn't in school today, so I had a free period and finished the homework that I didn't do last night. My team won the volleyball game by eight points. My best friend Ruthie is once again talking to me after a pretty stupid fight. And, I have no zits on my face.

Crossing Fowler Street, I notice that the house with my favorite maple tree is number 314. (The numbers add up to 8!) Outside, the autumn air smells like damp leaves, and my black fleece jacket is soaking up the sun. Ahh… a perfect day.

My phone buzzes. There's a text from Mom:

Please set Shabbat table. 8 guests.

I groan. Even seeing my favorite number doesn't make me feel better about this message. I drop the phone into my pocket, and walk the four blocks to my house.

Now that I've told you a bit about The Numbers, I suppose I should tell you about The Guests.

Two

"**D**oris!" I call from our foyer. I drop my backpack, hang up my jacket in the front closet, then take off my sneakers and deposit them in the basket. The usual procedure. "Doris! Help! Do something!"

The sound of the vacuum cleaner stops, and Doris appears on the stairway balcony overlooking the foyer. She's dressed in her cleaning outfit: black stretch pants and a Boston Red Sox t-shirt.

"Hello to you, too," she says. "What you screaming about?"

"Doris, there are *eight* guests tonight. I can't take it anymore!"

"Yeah, yeah, and you say that last week?" she replies, lugging the vacuum down the stairs.

I follow Doris into the laundry room. "That's exactly my point. When is it going to stop? Can't we have one week without Shabbat guests?"

Doris hands me a stack of purple towels. "For your bathroom, princess."

"Doris, really. You know what I'm talking about. Can't you say something to my mom?"

Doris raises one eyebrow. "How long you lived in this house? Remind me." She shakes her head. "Your mother a saint. And your father, too, for that matter."

"What about me? Huh? Don't I get any sympathy? Week after week, sharing my house and meals with strangers!"

Doris opens the dryer and pulls out more towels. "You call your grandparents strangers, or the Loring family, or Mrs. Kastleman a stranger?"

"Okay, so maybe they're not all strangers, but it is getting annoying."

"Well, how about you try keeping your room clean for two weeks, then I'll try talking to your mom," she says, snapping a towel.

"Really?"

Doris laughs. "Yeah, really. And I'll tell her you don't want to go to school no more, and she should let you stay out until midnight on weekends, too!"

"Doris!"

She shoos me away. "Now, get going, sweetness. We got work to do."

I storm out of the laundry room carrying my stack of towels. "It's not fair!" I shout, stomping up the stairs. "The Sabbath is supposed to be a day of rest!"

When I open the door to my room, I immediately know it's Friday. Doris has put away my massive pile of clothes, made my bed, vacuumed the purple carpet, and neatened up my dresser and desk. I walk into my bathroom and hang up the towels. The sink is free of toothpaste goo, the mirror is shiny, and my dozen hair and skin products are all lined up neatly on a shelf.

I love Doris.

I feel a twinge of guilt for using her as a punching bag. She's used to it, I guess. Doris has worked for my parents since I was born. It wouldn't be an exaggeration to say she is like a second mother. She's here every day when I get home from school, and sometimes, she stays over when Mom and Dad are out of town. Doris even came to my Bat Mitzvah last year. It was one of the only times I remember seeing her in a dress. Even though there are just three people living in this huge house, it's Doris who keeps it running smoothly. Without her, something would have to change. And if there is one thing that I wish would change, it's my parents' guest policy.

Now, I'm all for the Jewish custom of *hachnasat orchim*, welcoming guests in your home. But, really, my parents take it to the extreme.

It's basically an open door policy around here. I never know who I'm going to run into in our hallway of guest rooms (yes, plural!), or in our study, or the kitchen. I can't remember the last time I ate a meal with just my parents. Imagine that. Or maybe you are thinking that would be a relief. But what if it meant sharing your table with people you didn't know (or didn't like), and listening to boring conversation and explanations of Jewish rituals you've done hundreds of times. *'Now, why is it you have two loaves of challah?'*

My parents never seem to tire of this. And that's where Doris comes in. Doris is the one who does most of the grocery shopping, laundry, table setting, and vegetable chopping while my mom's at work. I hate to say it, but without Doris, my mom would be going crazy trying to get ready for all our guests before candle-lighting at sundown, the time when all work stops for observant Jews. Without Doris I'd be stuck with even more chores. Like today, for instance: I'll set the Shabbat table (china, silver, goblets, cloth napkins in gold rings), slice the gefilte fish, and fill up the hot water urn. Not so bad. Doris, on the other hand, has already washed the floors, vacuumed, dusted, ironed, and polished Mom's candlesticks. She'll pick up the bakery order and the dry cleaning, prepare the guest rooms, make the salad, and warm up the soup, kugels, and chicken that my mom cooked last night. Then Doris will go home to her cozy apartment in Roslindale, where she lives with her sister and five-year-old niece. And my family gets to enjoy a peaceful twenty-four-hour Sabbath… with The Guests.

About an hour before Friday night candle-lighting, the guests will start to arrive. Some of them will come later with my dad on his way home from synagogue. And of course, I'll have to introduce myself and answer the same questions over and over again. *'So, what grade are you in?' 'Can you speak Hebrew?'* Maybe if I had cute little brothers and sisters, it wouldn't be so bad. The attention would be focused on them, and I could easily excuse myself from the table. 'Oh, time to put Ellie to bed,' or 'I think I hear the baby crying. I'll get her, Mom!' No such luck. And it doesn't look like that is going to change. I know I shouldn't say that. Miracles do happen. But now my mom is forty, and that might be too old. (Not that she ever talks to me about this.)

So it's just me, and my parents, and The Guests every Shabbat. Week after week.

My phone is ringing. Phew, it's Ruthie. Just the friend I needed to vent to about tonight's eight guests.

"So what else is new?" she says.

"Wanna come for dinner and keep me company?" I ask. Ruthie has five brothers. So she usually jumps at the chance to hang out at my house.

"Can't. It's Avi's birthday. We're celebrating tonight and I'm in charge of the baseball cake."

"Will I see you in shul tomorrow?" I ask.

"Yeah, if I can wake up in time." Ruthie is notorious for sleeping till noon and missing the Sabbath morning service in synagogue.

"It's Jeremy Schlossberg's Bar Mitzvah," I remind her. "They'll have a huge kiddush." Jeremy's parents own a catering business.

"Ooh. Then I'll definitely make it. I bet they'll have those chocolate éclairs they had at Shaina's Bat Mitzvah. Wear your purple skirt, Tal. We'll match."

"Sure. That is, if Doris washed it." Ruthie is really into clothes. And that's a good thing, because thanks to her, I have a clue about fashion.

"Gotta go," Ruthie says. "I still have to frost the cake before Shabbat. Good luck with your guests. Just chill. Everything will be fine!"

After Doris leaves, I finish my chores as fast as I can, so I still have some time alone in the house. I used to hate being alone, but now I kind of like it. There's no one nagging you, reminding you to do this or that, or to stop doing this or that. Our house is really big and orderly, with lots of fancy furniture, paintings, and breakable lamps and vases, which is pretty different than most of my friends' homes— especially the ones with lots of little kids running around. Which is the case with most of them. See, I'm the *only* kid in my school who doesn't have siblings, with the exception of Chana Friedman who was in the Only Club until her mom had a baby last year. On the other extreme, there is Rachel Greenbaum, who is the middle child of twelve kids! I can't even imagine that. Then there's me. The One and Only.

I suppose if I wasn't going to an Orthodox Jewish day school, I might not be so unusual. Religious Jews tend to have big families. You know, 'be fruitful and multiply.' If I ever get sulky about being an Only, I just have to go to Ruthie's and watch her five brothers climb all over each other like tiger cubs.

My friends love coming to my house, though, I guess because it's pretty, and because I have a cool game room in the basement. I get lots of compliments on my bedroom, since most of my friends have to share theirs with a sister (or two). I'm also the only one in the seventh grade with a backyard swimming pool. So, whenever we need a place for a surprise birthday party, girls' swim party, or Saturday night get-together, my house is usually the spot. That, I don't mind, because then *I* get to make the guest list.

One thing I like to do when I'm alone in the house is play the piano. We have a Steinway parlor grand that my father inherited from his father, my grandfather, Isaac Schumacher. (In case you didn't know, a Steinway is the Mercedes Benz of pianos.) It's in our living room, which is pretty formal. If it weren't for the piano, I'd probably never even go in there.

When I'm alone in the house I can play whatever music I like, and however I like to play it, without my dad (who happens to be a really good musician) giving suggestions or yelling "Ow!" when I hit a wrong note. I like making up my own tunes, which is pretty easy for me because I get the patterns in music. Music and math go together like peanut butter and jelly, which I also happen to love (and anything chocolate). My favorite number is the building block of music: an octave, eight notes, the distance from C to C, D to D, E to E, etc. Just another reason 8 is so perfect, in my mind at least.

And there goes the doorbell. Who could that be? My parents aren't even home yet. I close the piano and run to the front door. I peek through the hole (just like my mom taught me) and see an unfamiliar young woman with long dark hair, dressed in a multi-colored gypsy skirt and oversized ivory sweater. Maybe she's one of those fanatic missionaries who come around on Fridays. Then I see she has a suitcase. And it's pink! Yikes.

I hesitantly open the front door. The young woman smiles at me like I'm her long-lost relative. She's so thin she looks like she could blow away in the fall breeze.

"Hi there. This is the Schumacher house, right?" She has a southern accent, which surprises me.

"Yes… but my parents aren't home yet," I reply.

"Oh, am I too early? I wasn't sure how long it would take me to get here. I took a cab from the airport," she says, looking past me. "Wow. This is an incredible house."

"Are you staying for Shabbat?" I ask.

"That's the plan, and I'm really looking forward to it."

"Well… I guess you should come in." I hate when my mother does this to me. I'm letting a total stranger into the house.

She steps inside our entryway and gives it the once-over. "Whew," she whistles. "Someone really knows how to decorate. Beautiful taste."

"Thanks." I notice that her suitcase is pretty big for an overnight. And she's got a guitar case, too. "I'm Talia."

She extends her hand. "Nice to meet you, Talia. I'm Gabrielle Markus. Back home my friends used to called me Gabby."

I nod, wondering which name I should use. Now comes the awkward moment. What am I supposed to do with her? "Um, do you want something to eat or drink?"

"No, thank you. I had a sandwich on the plane. Where should I put my bag?"

I have no idea which room she is supposed to stay in, so I'll just guess. Doris must have forgotten to tell me. "Follow me." I lead Gabrielle up the staircase. "Have you met my parents before?" I ask.

"Not yet," she replies. "I've just talked to your mom on the phone and over e-mail. She seems like an amazing woman. It was really nice of her to invite me to stay, especially after the busy holidays," Gabrielle says as we head down the hallway to the guest room I figure would be best for a single girl. "Wow, those are some great paintings. That's Chagall, right?"

"Yeah." I don't bother telling her they are originals.

The guest room is across from my room, unfortunately. When I open the door, I smell the faint scent of lavender, a touch from Doris, no doubt.

"Here you are."

"What a beautiful room!" Gabrielle puts her bag down. "I'm used to crashing on my friend's couch. This is going to be a treat for sure." She surveys the room. "And my own bathroom, too. Hey, this is first-class hosting."

So I've been told.

"You're not from Boston, are you?" I ask her.

"My accent gives me away, huh? Well, actually, it's a long story. The short answer is no, but I'm here temporarily." She plops down on the bed. "Ooh, comfy. So, I was born in Texas. My family moved around a lot in the southern states—Georgia, Florida, I can't even remember them all. My dad is in the military. Eventually I ended up in the Big Apple." She opens her arms wide. "New York, New York!" she sings. "Well, that's a long story, too. And now, well, I'm in Boston for a while. Trying to find myself, you could say."

"Oh." The short answer would have been fine with me.

"How old are you?" she asks. "Twelve?"

"Thirteen."

"Ah, I remember thirteen." She says this as if she's holding a big secret. "I just turned twenty-three. A lot can happen in ten years. Hey, did you have your Bat Mitzvah this year?"

"Last year. We do it at twelve."

She snaps her fingers. "Right. Should have remembered that. I grew up Reform and they do it at thirteen. Not that I even had a Bat Mitzvah. My parents weren't into the synagogue scene. Matzah balls and bagels. That kind of stuff. Food Jews."

This is all getting too personal for me. "Well, I need to do a few things before Shabbat—"

"Oh, don't let me keep you." She jumps up from the bed. "Do you need any help?"

"No, uh, I'm all set. Thanks."

"Well then, I guess I'll take a shower and do a little stretching, if there's time," she says. "When is candle-lighting?"

"6:05," I say. "I'll tell my mom you're here. So… just make yourself at home." (That's what my mother always says.)

She gives me a big smile. "Thanks, Talia."

Stretching?

I go back to my room and fall onto my perfectly made bed. I hope Mom gets back soon. I do not feel like being Miss Hospitality to Miss Gabby. That's Mom's department. What could be taking so long? I glance at my clock radio. 5:03 PM. Five plus three…

Thirty minutes later, I hear the garage door open. Oops. Must have dozed off. I should already be dressed for Shabbat by now. I jump off my bed, quickly change into a stretchy black skirt and pull on a pink cashmere sweater. I brush my hair (medium length, wavy, boring brown) and put on a touch of cherry lip gloss. I check myself in the mirror. Not too bad. I can hear Mom's heels clicking on the kitchen floor as she starts the last minute prep. Fridays are usually frantic, especially in the winter, when Shabbat starts at four o'clock in the afternoon. I better get downstairs.

"Sorry I'm late," Mom says while dashing around the kitchen. "Terrible traffic. I've got to get out of work earlier." She gives me a peck on the cheek, then checks the crockpot. "How are we doing?"

"Fine, Mom. Who is this Gabrielle?"

She hits her forehead. "Oh, I almost forgot! Is she here?"

"Yeah, but you didn't tell me—"

"I think I'm losing my memory."

"I know that. Who is she anyway?"

"Shh. Not now. Where did you put her?"

"Across from my room. Who else is coming?"

She glances at her watch. "I better get ready."

"Mom, we need to talk—"

"I know, sweetie. We will, later tonight. Can you run down the checklist, while I change?"

"Me?"

Mom heads for the stairs. "Yes, you!"

I wish Mom would slow down. She's always saying she is going to leave work early on Fridays, and I can't remember the last time she actually managed to do it. Again, thank God for Doris.

I pour a few pitchers of water into the urn and plug it in, so we'll be able to have the essential after-dinner coffee and tea for the guests.

I set the kitchen timer so the warming tray will turn on tomorrow to heat up the lunch kugels. (In case you didn't know, observant Jews don't cook and turn on electrical things on the Sabbath. So we have to have everything ready in advance.) The chicken soup simmering on the stove wakens my appetite. I spot a bakery box of cookies on the kitchen table and am just about to sneak a few, when I hear our guest.

"Hello! Oh, don't you look pretty?"

"Thanks." Gabrielle is wearing a bright orange turtleneck and a skirt that looks like it was made from a bunch of men's ties. Pretty funky.

"Is your mom here?"

"Yeah. You just missed her. She's running kind of late. She'll be down in a few minutes."

Gabrielle looks around the kitchen. "Gosh, you guys have really got everything under control. I'm not very good at orchestrating Shabbat yet. I always seem to forget something, like putting the light timer on."

So I guess she keeps Shabbat. Lots of our guests don't. At least in the beginning. My parents have a knack for inspiring guests to explore Jewish traditions.

I feel stupid just standing here, so I walk into the dining room to check the candles. I'm pretty sure Gabrielle isn't married, but some single girls have the custom to light, too.

"Do you light your own candle?" I ask her, noticing Doris didn't set an extra one on my mom's silver platter.

"Yes, I do. I started last year. Just one. For now." She winks when she says this. (A married woman lights two candles; one for herself and another for her husband.)

I open the china chest and take out a single candle with a silver holder, and then place it next to my mother's three candlesticks.

Gabrielle moves closer to the table. "Do you light?" she asks me. "I know some girls wait until they're married."

I nod as I put a candle in the ivory holder my grandmother gave me.

"I just love lighting Shabbat candles," Gabrielle says, closing her eyes and breathing in deeply. "I feel so connected to all the Jewish

19

women of the world. Past and present. Know what I mean?"

Uh-oh. One of those touchy-feely kinds. "I guess." I never really thought about it. It's just something I do every Friday at sundown.

My mom walks into the room and rescues me. "Hello," she sings. "Welcome, Gabrielle. I'm Naomi Schumacher." Mom's dressed in a beige suit with matching heels and her special wavy Shabbat wig (she always covers her hair, like many observant Jewish women). I love seeing Mom finally relax every Shabbat, and the more carefree hairstyle completes the picture. I always tell her the Shabbat wig makes her look ten years younger than her everyday, down-to-business, straight, shoulder-length one.

Gabrielle shakes Mom's hand. "It's an honor to be here and finally meet you in person. I've heard so much about your extraordinary family."

Her comment makes me cringe. Why can't we just be *ordinary?*

After candle-lighting, Mom and Gabrielle go chat in the living room. I slip away to the study and curl up in the overstuffed blue chair with the mystery novel I started last week. I can hear Gabrielle going on and on about something or other. I'm sure I'll get an earful at dinner.

Normally, if the guests haven't arrived yet, Mom and I might have a little time to catch up... alone! Considering that I'm her only kid, you'd think that would be easy. But between her work, travel, committee meetings, Torah classes, and entertaining guests, it's actually hard to find time to talk. I mean, really talk. Not the how-did-you-do-on-your-history-test kind of talk. I'm proud of all my mom manages to accomplish, but once in a while I wish she were just a stay-at-home mom, like Ruthie's mother. Of course, with six young kids, Ruthie's mom has more reason to do that than mine does.

A little while later, the front door opens and I hear Dad call out, "Shabbat Shalom!" That's what he always does when he comes home from synagogue on Friday nights, and it always makes me feel good. I go to the entryway to meet him. The chilly night air brushes against my legs as Dad holds the door open for all the guests. My mother and Gabrielle come into the foyer.

"Welcome. I'm Naomi Schumacher," my mother says, taking

everyone's coats and handing them to me to hang in the closet.

I think I've heard my mother say that line a thousand times.

Everyone gathers in the hallway, making small talk. Looks like we've got two couples and four singles tonight.

"Please join us in the dining room," my mother says as she leads the way.

As we walk into the dining room, Dad puts his arm around my shoulder. "Did you have a good day?"

I tell him I did.

My mother shows everyone where to sit, and Gabrielle ends up next to me. My father stands at the head of the table, waiting for everyone to get seated. Then he says, "Welcome, everyone. It's not unusual for my family to have Shabbat guests, but it's not often that we have a table full of new faces. I'd like you to meet my daughter, Talia Bracha."

He's the only one who calls me by both names. My middle name means 'blessing,' which isn't bad. I smile, as if having eight pairs of unfamiliar eyes on me is the most natural thing in the world. That's just what I'm supposed to do.

"We'll have a chance for everyone to introduce themselves during the meal," Dad says. "And now, we start with the singing of *Shalom Aleichem*, a song to greet the Sabbath angels who accompany us on Friday night. You can find it in the little white booklet next to your plate, on page twelve, and there is transliteration for those of you who might not read Hebrew yet."

Oh no. Basic prayer explanations mean starter Jews. This is going to be a long dinner.

Luckily my father has a strong and pleasant voice. Gabrielle starts singing along a little too loudly and swaying side to side. I feel embarrassed for her. Hopefully the other guests won't think you're supposed to do that. I glance around the table to check them out. I like to guess something about each new guest, and then see how close I am when they actually introduce themselves.

There is a middle-aged couple who I bet is from out of town... another young couple, maybe newlyweds... a young guy, probably in college or grad school... and a woman of an uncertain age... thirty-five, maybe. She's wearing a white turban around her head. Hmm. Divorced, I suspect.

When Dad finishes singing, he tells everyone about the Jewish custom of blessing the children. "Maybe you saw this in *Fiddler on the Roof?*" he jokes. "Well, it's real and still around today in observant Jewish homes." He looks across the table at me, and then smiles. I get up and walk over to his side. Once again all eyes are upon me. Dad stands up and places both his hands on my head. He recites the blessing in Hebrew, then in English. "May God make you like our mothers, Sarah, Rebecca, Rachel, and Leah." Then he kisses me on the cheek.

This is one of those times that I wish I weren't an Only. At Ruthie's house all the kids line up for their blessing. It's really cute. Each one gets a special moment, but no one is singled out.

"That is so beautiful!" Gabrielle says, breaking the silence.

My father smiles and nods in agreement. "Another beautiful custom we have is for the husband to recite the *Aishet Chayil*, 'Woman of Valor.' A tribute to the Jewish woman—her strength, wisdom, and inner beauty." He bows slightly to my mother and begins singing. "*Aishet chayil, mi yimtza…*"

Gabrielle claps when he's done! What is wrong with her?

"Now, if a woman isn't married, can she sing it for herself?" Gabrielle asks.

My father laughs. "Sure. Everyone can sing it."

"It's such a gorgeous melody," she adds.

"You know," the lady in the white turban chimes in, "this is the first time I've heard that song, yet the melody is so familiar somehow. I can't think where I would have heard it before."

"Your soul must recognize it," Gabrielle says, seriously. She looks to my dad. "Right? I mean, I've learned that our souls were all present when the Torah was given at Mount Sinai, and that before we were born, our souls actually knew the whole Torah?"

At this rate, we're going to be here all night.

"Ah, I see you've learned a bit of Kabbalah," my father says. "Yes, we believe our souls existed before our conscious minds."

I am starving, so I hope Gabrielle can hold her comments until dinner.

Next, my father gives a brief explanation of the Kiddush. That's the special blessing over the wine on Friday nights. Dad asks everyone to stand, then he cradles the silver cup in the palm of his hands. A little wine spills over the brim as he recites the prayer. When I was little, he used to let me stand up on a chair next to him.

I glance over at Gabrielle. Her eyes are squeezed shut as if she's concentrating on his words. I guess I've been doing this so long that I sometimes don't even hear the words anymore, but I'm definitely not going to stand in front of everyone with my eyes closed. When he finishes, she sings "amen" a bit too loudly.

Dad passes a tray with little silver cups filled with sweet wine around the table. Some people might think it's strange for me to taste wine. For me, the tiny sip of wine goes along with Shabbat. I guess you could even say it is holy. Some of my friends only drink grape juice, mostly because they hate the taste of wine. It's just no big deal for me.

After everyone has their sips of wine, Dad gives the instructions for the ritual hand-washing before eating the challah, special Shabbat bread. Here we go again. I stand by the kitchen sink helping each guest pour a cup of water two times on each hand and then recite the proper blessing. Then everyone goes back into the dining room. It's always quiet as we wait because you're not supposed to talk between washing your hands and saying the blessing over the bread. But, almost always, someone doesn't know or doesn't remember this detail.

The lady in the turban asks my mother, "Do you actually make the holly?"

I smile to myself at this common mispronunciation which makes me think of that tune, 'Deck the Halls.' My mom smiles, nods, and holds up her just-a-minute finger. Dad lifts the two golden loaves of braided bread and recites the blessing. *"Baruch atah adonai, eloheinu melech ha'olam, hamotzi lechem min ha'aretz."* He slices the bread, puts it on a platter, and then passes it around the table. Everyone comments on how delicious the challah tastes. (They always do.) It really is. Even though Mom is crazy busy, she almost always manages to bake challah and freeze enough to last a few weeks.

"I enjoy making challah," my mother replies. "Now it's so much easier since I started using a bread machine for the dough."

"This is spectacular!" Turban Lady says, as she bites into the soft bread.

"Thank you. You know, baking challah is a special mitzvah for women," Mom adds.

"And mitzvah means 'a good deed'?" Turban Lady asks.

"Yes, in some ways, but it also means a commandment. A mitzvah is a way of connecting our actions to God."

"My wife is a wonderful baker and cook," Dad says, "but you should also know that the secret ingredient is Shabbat itself. All food tastes better when it is prepared for and eaten on the holy Sabbath."

"Ah, and that would be hard to bottle, I suppose," Gabrielle adds with a wink.

"Absolutely!" Dad slices up some more challah, which is my signal to start bringing in the gefilte fish plates. That's another downside of being an Only. No siblings to help with the serving.

Once I'm back at the table and everyone has their fish, Dad asks the guests to make introductions. "Please tell us something about yourselves," he says. "Especially about your Jewish journey, if you feel comfortable. I'll let my daughter start." He looks over at me and smiles.

Gee, thanks Dad.

Actually, I'm used to this, even though I really don't like introducing myself. "Hi. I'm Talia Schumacher. I'm thirteen and in the seventh grade at Hebrew Academy of Boston." Done. I force a quick smile and then look at Gabrielle on my right.

She takes a big breath. "Shabbat Shalom, everybody. I'm Gabrielle Markus. I'm twenty-three, new to Boston. I am in the process of moving from New York City where, up until a year ago, I had been dancing professionally with the New York City Ballet." She sighs, then looks up at the ceiling. "And as far as my Jewish journey goes, well, about two years ago I began taking classes with Rebbetzin Miriam Lowenthal at the Living Torah Center in Manhattan. I've just walked into, well, make that danced into, this amazing world of Torah and mitzvot and Jewish living. It is very exciting, but also a little scary, as I'm not sure where I'm headed with all this."

So she's a dancer. As far opposite from me as it gets. I'm always the one tripping over my feet at Bat Mitzvah parties. I wonder how Gabrielle hooked up with my parents.

It's Turban Lady's turn. "I'm Martha Sheffman. I live in the Back Bay. I haven't been at a Sabbath meal since my grandmother died when I was ten. I met Mrs. Schumacher at Beth Israel Hospital where I am undergoing chemotherapy, and was a bit surprised when she invited me for dinner, but I decided to give it a try." Her voice starts to crack. "And now, sitting here in the glow of the candles and listening to the beautiful prayers and tasting the holly, I feel like I just woke up. Like I've been missing out all these years."

Now I feel bad for calling Mrs. Sheffman Turban Lady, since she obviously lost her hair from chemo. I can't even imagine that.

My father lifts his Kiddush cup. "*L'chaim*, Martha! To life. You should have a speedy recovery."

My mother and I lift our cups, too, and say, "Amen."

Next comes Elana and Mark Rodman, married one year and new to the neighborhood. (I was pretty close on my guess.) Elana is beautiful, with wide-set dark eyes and perfect skin. (Sigh.) Her husband is pretty good-looking, too. They are thinking about joining a synagogue.

Okay, and we're moving on to Toby and Alan Miller, visiting from California for their fabric business. How in the world did they find my family? Mr. Miller has a gray ponytail. He makes a point of saying that he is president of their Reform temple in Berkeley and plays the accordion at the Friday night service. I've never heard of such a thing. Mr. Miller tries to crack a few jokes about the temple. His wife laughs like she has never heard them before. I give a fake laugh just to be polite.

The final introduction is the young guy, Jared Samuels from Babson College, who just started working part-time for my father. Well, that's news to me. He's wearing a blue-and-white knit kippah, which tells me he probably wears it more than once a week. So I wonder if my dad is trying to make a match with Gabrielle. That wouldn't be the first time something like that happened at our Shabbat table. Mom says that making a good marriage match is harder than splitting the Red Sea. After meeting some of the guests who show up at our house, I can believe it.

Now that the introductions are over, it looks like it's time for me to bring in the chicken soup. Hopefully I can manage without spilling.

Three

I wake up Saturday morning to the sound of someone humming outside my bedroom door. I check the clock. It's 8:00 AM. Good morning, lucky number. I lie in bed listening to the humming. Oh my gosh, I think it's her! *Ohhmmmm, ohhhmmmm.* What in the world?

I get out of bed, open the door, and peek out across the hall. The guest room door is shut, but I can hear the *ohhhhhmmmm* coming from inside. Then I hear steps on the floor and a few deep breaths. Then it sounds like she's trying to blow out a bunch of candles. *Whoo, whoo, whoo!* I tiptoe across the hall. I know I shouldn't be eavesdropping, but it almost sounds like she's having an asthma attack. What is she doing?

Then comes a crash. Yikes.

I tap lightly on her door. "Gabrielle?" Now it's quiet. Maybe she fell or something. Or fainted!

"Uh, just a minute." Her voice sounds strained.

"Are you okay?" I ask, more out of curiosity than compassion.

"Yeah... just had a little spill. You can come in."

I open the door and find Gabrielle on her knees, picking up pieces of broken blue glass. "I can't believe I did this," she cries. "Tell me it wasn't an antique, or a family heirloom."

"I think it came from Target, actually."

"Thank God," she says. "I am so embarrassed."

I'm not sure if she means breaking the vase or being seen in

Winnie the Pooh pajamas.

"You're not the first guest to break something."

"Thanks, but that doesn't make me feel better." Her face is all flushed.

I wonder what Doris would do. "Let me get something to clean it up with."

I go to the hallway closet where Doris keeps supplies. Sure enough, there is everything we could need for any kind of cleaning catastrophe. I return with a garbage bag, a rag, and a broom.

"Here you go. Be careful with the glass."

"Right," she says. "I don't want to bleed all over your floor, too." I can tell she feels bad. I stand there feeling kind of stupid. Should I offer to help?

"Don't worry about it," I tell her. "We can vacuum it after Shabbat."

"I was just doing my usual morning headstand," she says, as if this is the most normal thing in the world.

"Headstand?"

"Yeah. After my yoga and meditative breathing. It helps me to wake up."

I don't tell her that it woke me up, too. "Well, good morning. There's coffee cake and tea in the kitchen. Shul services start at nine if you're interested. There's a Bar Mitzvah today. You can probably walk over with my mom, but she usually doesn't leave until ten."

This information seems to brighten her mood. "Great. Thanks for the info. Oh, is the shul nearby?"

"Three blocks."

"Nice." She sweeps up the last of the glass pieces. "I lived a mile from the shul in New York. Well, at least the one I liked going to. Have you heard of the Lincoln Square synagogue?"

I shake my head.

"Wonderful rabbi. And they have this beginner service for people who don't know how to read Hebrew, or haven't been in a synagogue since who-knows-when. Anyway, that's the one I went to." Gabrielle ties up the garbage bag. "It's also a great place to meet a potential match, if you know what I mean. Of course that's probably the last thing on your mind. Huh?"

I just smile, but I have a feeling she is not going to stop talking unless I say something. "Yeah. Well, if you don't need anything else, I think I'll get dressed now."

"Thanks for your help!" she says, but her eyes don't quite match the cheerfulness of her voice.

"See you later," I say.

I go back to my room to wash up. When I look in the mirror, I see two zits on my cheek and my brown hair a frizzy disaster. Ugh. Time for the messy bun. While I put up my hair I start thinking about Gabrielle. There is something funny about her, but I can't quite put my finger on it. My friend Shifra says that people's body language sends all sorts of unconscious signals that other people pick up without even realizing. Shifra's really into analyzing people. I bet she'd be able to tell me something about Gabrielle after just one introduction.

I find my purple skirt hung up in the closet. (Thanks, Doris.) I match it with my new ivory sweater. I think I'll wear black tights since I'll be wearing my black Shabbat boots. I put on my silver hoop earrings and the Jewish star necklace my grandmother brought me from Israel.

Downstairs, I join my mom in the kitchen. She's reading *The Jewish Journal* and sipping tea. She sits smack in the morning sunlight, which she loves. Shabbat morning is the only time she lets herself relax a little.

"My, you're up early."

I decide not to tell her why. "I think I'll get to shul on time for a change."

"Oh, really?" Mom smiles. Guess she doesn't quite buy my reason.

I pour myself a glass of orange juice. "Mom? How do you know Gabrielle?"

She looks toward the entryway. "Shh. Now is not the time."

I sit down at the table. This is an answer I have heard many times before.

"Have some rugelach," she offers, pushing a plate of tempting pastries. "They're from the new bakery."

"Yum. Thanks." I lower my voice to a whisper. "I told her she could walk to shul with you."

Mom folds the newspaper. "Want to join us?"

I look at the wall clock. "Uh, I'll pass on that one. Ruthie's waiting for me. Oh, by the way, who are we having for lunch?"

Mom rattles off the guests. "The Selegmans, the Reingolds, and Gabrielle."

At least they're people I know, and the Selegmans have a daughter a couple years older than me.

"You can invite Ruthie if you'd like," Mom adds.

"Hmm. Maybe."

"Is there a Shabbat group this afternoon?"

"At Shifra's. Three o'clock."

Mom takes a sip of her tea. "You haven't hosted the group for a while."

"That's because you've been hosting a ton of people every week," I reply a bit too quickly.

Mom raises an eyebrow. "What does that have to do with having a Shabbat group here?"

I shrug. "I just thought you wouldn't want me to invite a bunch of girls over on top of all the other guests. It's kind of been like a hotel here, Mom."

"There is only one guest staying over this Shabbat, Talia," she says firmly.

"Okay. This Shabbat. But, I didn't even know that. Maybe you could give me some warning."

"Fair enough, but you know that I don't always know who is going to show up until the last minute."

I am tempted to say, *Well, why is that, Mom?* But I don't. I can't remember a time when we didn't have guests in our house, but only recently has it begun to bug me, and I don't qute know how to tell that to my parents.

"And," Mom continues, "it doesn't matter to me how many guests are here. Your friends are always welcome."

But it matters to me! "Thanks," I mutter. And speaking of guests… Gabrielle walks in wearing that tie skirt again with the same orange turtleneck. She has a beige fringed shawl draped around her shoulders.

"Shabbat Shalom!" she says, sounding like a morning news reporter. "Ah, I love a sunny kitchen. My New York kitchen didn't even have a window."

"That was my first requirement before we bought the house," Mom asks, getting up to set a plate for Gabrielle. "Did you sleep well?"

Gabrielle looks at me for a second. "Very well, thanks."

I stare at her purple feather earrings. Mom smiles. "Wonderful. We recently put in a new mattress."

"Sure beats the pull-out couch I slept on the past year," Gabrielle says, walking over to the window.

"Come have something to eat," Mom says, setting out a tea tray. "What a lovely skirt."

"Thanks," Gabrielle says, surveying our back yard. "I found it in a Greenwich Village shop."

I wonder if she's going to confess about the vase.

"Do you use your pool a lot?" she asks me.

"Sure, like around June through September."

Mom turns to our guest. "Now, do you want us to call you Gabby or Gabrielle?"

She squints like we asked her a hard math problem. "You know, I've always gone by Gabby, that is, with my friends, but now that I'm off to a fresh start, I think I'll return to Gabrielle."

Fresh start?

"It's a beautiful name," Mom replies, pouring Gabrielle some tea. "Did you know it had Hebrew origins? It means 'God is my strength'."

"Hey, I like that!" Gabrielle says. "Why didn't anyone tell me that?" She sips her tea, then winks.

I get up and put my plate in the dishwasher. "Gotta go," I say. "See ya in shul."

"Lookin' forward to it!" Gabrielle calls as I head for the door.

Outside, the sun is bright and it's a surprisingly mild morning for November in Boston. I barely need my coat. There are still piles of red maple leaves scattered around the neighborhood. On a day like this, I wish our synagogue was further away. I wouldn't mind walking a mile. (That would be 5,280 feet.)

Since I am early for a change, I decide to walk to Ruthie's house. I doubt she has left for shul yet. Ruthie lives five blocks from my house. I've known her since kindergarten, when her family moved from Baltimore. Since then, her mom had three more kids. We've had our ups and downs, but Ruthie and I have been best friends since third grade. I guess you could say we're opposites, but that just makes our friendship more interesting. Even though I'm kind of shy, Ruthie is loud and outgoing. She keeps me laughing. I think it would be boring if my best friend was as quiet as I am. (I recently took a personality test in a Jewish girls' magazine. I turned out to be introverted and a logical thinker. No surprises there.)

One thing I wouldn't mind would be having a good friend who also loved math. Our school is co-ed until fourth grade. When I was younger, I was the only girl in the highest math level. I hated the boys in my group. They had dirty fingernails and were always pulling each other's yarmulkes off. I was the only kid who could sit still and didn't feel the need to shout out the answers. One boy, Levy Rashinsky, who never combed his hair, would scribble over my math problems when the teacher wasn't looking. Now I am in honors math, and even that is pretty easy, but none of my good friends are in my class. But at least it's just girls now.

Ruthie's house is the blue one on the corner. It's not very big, and they jam pack a lot in there. It is overflowing with boy energy which can be kind of fun—that is, for about ten minutes.

I knock on the door, and a few seconds later, little Avi appears.

"Hi. Bye!" he says, still in his Batman pajamas.

"Hi, Avi. How come you're not in shul?"

He gives me one of his devilish looks. "I'm building a Lego spaceship."

"Oh, I see. I heard you had a birthday."

He holds up his little hand. "I'm five."

"Wow. Five is alive!"

Avi jumps up and down. "Yeah!" He runs away.

"Wait—" I poke my head in the door. "Hello?"

I hear Mrs. Braitman calling from upstairs. "Good Shabbos! Come on in, Talia."

I walk in the tiny entryway. There are boys' sneakers and Shabbos shoes piled near the front door. I overhear Sammy and Noam arguing about something in another room.

"Boo!" Avi jumps out from the family room. "Did I scare you?"

"Absolutely!" I feign.

"Come see my spaceship!"

I step into the family room. The first thing I notice is that the couch has been taken apart. All the pillows are on the floor and Avi is jumping from one to another.

"I know how to make the best spaceships. Better than Noam," he says.

"Hmm. I'm sure." I can't ever remember a time our family room was even half this messy. There are blocks scattered everywhere, books all over the coffee table, and I notice smashed Cheerios in the carpet. The Braitman family needs Doris.

I hear Ruthie bounding down the stairs. "Hi, Tal. I wasn't expecting you! Great, you wore the skirt."

She's wearing her purple skirt, too, but it looks much better on her than on me. In fact, everything looks good on Ruthie. She is five-foot-six, model thin, with mile-long legs. "Wasn't sure if you'd be up yet," I comment.

"That's because Avi pounced on me this morning. Sooo, I managed to get up after all. What are you doing so early?"

"Tell you later. Are you ready to go?"

"Sure. We'll get our choice of seats." Ruthie peeks in on her brother, but doesn't seem fazed by the mess. "Avi, go get dressed. Imma will take you to Shabbat playgroup," she says in her sisterly voice.

"No! I don't want to go to playgroup." He starts bouncing on the pillows. "I want to go with you."

Ruthie rolls her eyes. "Sorry, buddy. I'm going now and you are still in your pajamas. Do you want to go to shul in your PJs?"

"Wait for me!" he wails.

"Imma?" Ruthie calls upstairs. "I'm going now. Okay?"

"Can you wait for Avi?" she calls back.

"Imma! I'm going with Talia. We're all ready."

"Okay," Mrs. Braitman says. "Send him up."

Ruthie pats Avi's head. "Go, Avi. Imma wants you. I'll give you a lollipop in shul if you listen."

Avi crosses his arms. "Fine."

"See ya later," Ruthie calls as she heads for the door. She grabs my arm. "Let's get out of here!"

As Ruthie and I walk up Oak Street, I give her the guest report.

"He plays the accordion?" she asks incredulously when I tell her about Mr. Miller. "I've never heard of an accordion in shul."

"Me neither. It's not an Orthodox shul, obviously. They probably do a lot of things differently than we do."

"That just seems… weird."

I shrug. "It wouldn't seem weird if that's what we were used to."

"I guess."

Ruthie cracks up when I tell her about Gabrielle's headstand. "That is too funny. I mean, my brothers break things in our house practically every day, but somehow in your house that would really stand out. Imagine doing that after just meeting your hosts. So is she a klutz?" Ruthie asks.

"No! She's a ballerina. That's what makes it so funny."

"Cool. I always wanted to do ballet."

I give Ruthie a look. "Are you kidding?"

"You know I like to dance."

"Yeah, but not ballet."

"It's probably too late for me," she says, and then leaps over a pile of leaves. Ruthie starts walking backwards so she can face me. "So, do I get to meet her?"

"If you want. But, I'm telling you, there is definitely something odd about her."

"All the more interesting. Maybe she is a case for Shifra."

"That's exactly what I was thinking!"

We head up Grove Street and run into a pack of women and kids walking toward the shul. They must be going to the Bar Mitzvah.

"I heard Jeremy has a ton of cousins and out-of-town relatives coming," Ruthie says. "Good thing we got here early."

"I wish I had tons of cousins," I reply. "I mean, six is nice, but twelve would be even better. A dozen cousins."

"Don't start with your numbers," Ruthie jokes.

When we get to the shul, there is already a mass of strollers parked in front. A bunch of moms are talking while their little kids jump in leaves under the oak tree. I've been going to Young Israel of Greensborough all my life. I had my baby-naming there, which of course I don't remember, and my Bat Mitzvah. It's the biggest Orthodox shul (there are two other ones) in town. Greensborough also has one Reform and two Conservative synagogues, three churches, and a mosque, so besides being very Jewish, I guess you could say it's a pretty religious town.

Ruthie and I enter the lobby, which is filled with kids fooling around. You'd think it would be all hush-hush, but it's not. Never has been, and the rabbi is forever trying to solve this problem. Just outside the entrance to the women's section, Ruthie and I stop to look at a huge photo collage of Jeremy. Ruthie points to the picture of him getting his first haircut. "Oh, he was so cute!"

"Was?" I tease.

Ruthie elbows me. "Ha. Ha."

We both take a siddur from the bookshelf and go inside. The women's section is much more crowded than usual. Jeremy's family members fill the front row. Ruthie and I take a seat in the back where most of the teen girls like to sit. As talkative as Ruthie is, she's very good about davening and not talking (too much) during shul. I wish I could say that was true about most of the other girls. My mom would kill me if she saw me having a conversation during the service. When I was little, I always had to sit with my mom or go to a supervised playgroup. Even when all the other kids left during the rabbi's speech, Mom expected me to stay in. That's when I would open the siddur to a random page and do mental calculations with the page numbers. Yeah, I know it's nerdy, but it passes the time.

Just before the Torah reading, Mom and Gabrielle show up. That's one thing about our shul, people drop in throughout the service, which lasts a whopping two-and-a-half hours. I give Ruthie an 'over-there' look.

"Is that her?" Ruthie whispers. I nod. "Cool skirt. Are those neckties?"

"I think so," I whisper back.

Fortunately, Mom chooses a seat in the middle next to Mrs. Selegman, and Gabrielle joins her. Just then, I hear a deep voice chanting the blessings over the Torah. It's Jeremy. He used to be the smallest kid in my first grade class. Now he's as tall as his father standing at the bimah.

Jeremy starts the reading in a smooth, sing-song voice. He sounds a lot better than those Bar Mitzvah boys with squeaky voices. The shul is packed, but it is real quiet now. As Jeremy reads, I follow along in the Chumash. His Torah portion is *Chayei Sarah*, 'the Life of Sarah,' whose story really takes place after her death, but as my teacher Rabbi Weiss says, an influential woman lives on after death, so the emphasis is on how she lived. I like that idea.

This Torah portion has a lot of numbers in it. Sarah lived to 127, her husband Abraham lived to 175, and his son Ishmael to 135. Gosh, imagine living that long! This part of the Torah is also about finding a wife for Abraham and Sarah's son, Isaac, who ends up marrying the lovely and kind Rebecca. I guess you could call this the first romance in the Torah. There's even a matchmaker in the story. (When Ruthie and I were little, we used to act the whole thing out with Barbie dolls.) My parents met through a matchmaker right out of college. It's a pretty ordinary story. My mother always tells it so matter-of-factly. I kind of hoped for a little more drama.

By the time Jeremy finishes chanting the Torah portion and the additional Haftorah reading, says his speech (the typical Bar Mitzvah type), and begins Musaf, my stomach is growling. I hate to admit it, but this is the point when I usually show up. As I finish saying the silent *Shmoneh Esrei* prayer, I catch a glimpse of Gabrielle. She has the siddur close to her face and she is praying very intently. Then, with one hand, she pulls her shawl over her head! She sways back and forth, side to side. What in the world is she doing? Is that supposed to be her tallit? I've heard in Conservative synagogues some women wear prayer shawls like the men, but not here. A few of the ladies are staring at Gabrielle. My mother pretends not to notice. Again, I feel embarrassed for her. What next?

I look at Ruthie. She looks at Gabrielle, then at me. We are both trying not to crack up. She sits down and whispers, "I think you'd look great in one of those shawls!"

Four

Twice a month on Saturday afternoons, we have a neighborhood Shabbat group for seventh and eighth grade girls. It's run by two seniors from school. We take turns meeting at different houses within a mile radius. Mrs. Brody, the principal of our school, came up with the idea last year. She wanted to encourage the middle school girls to be less cliquey, and to spend part of their Shabbat doing something more meaningful than studying for an English test (which I never do), or gossiping with friends (which I sometimes do).

At first, the idea for the group was met with a groan from most of the girls. Those of us who live in the same neighborhood as our school just didn't want to do anything that seemed like "school" on Shabbat. Besides, we often got together ourselves, that is, in our own little groups, and we weren't thrilled about the idea of being supervised by high school girls. That was for little kids.

But here's how the whole thing took off. 1) Mrs. Brody convinced the two most popular seniors to run the group. 2) She made sure we had scrumptious snacks. 3) She gave us points for showing up, which could be redeemed for prizes like manicures and mall gift certificates.

Now the Shabbat group is called the Shabbat Club, and it's open to any local Jewish girl. This makes it easier for us to get to know girls who go to school at Bais Sarah, as well as a few from public school. And any girls from our school who don't live within walking distance are often invited for sleepovers, so they can come to the Shabbat

Club, too. This year's leaders, Gila and Baila, are awesome. They do fun activities and games. They also think up interesting topics to talk about, like *Should we care about what others think of us?* and *What kind of Jewish woman do you want to become?*

So this afternoon, after a long lunch of making polite conversation with the guests and listening to Gabrielle talk about her ballet days, I am ready to take a break and walk over to the Shabbat Club. That is, until Mom knocks on my bedroom door.

"Can I talk to you for a minute?" she asks, poking her head in.

I close my novel. "Sure."

Mom walks in and shuts the door behind her. She has already changed into her Shabbat robe, which means she'll probably take a nap soon. She sits down at the end of my bed and gets right to the point.

"Honey, I'd like you to take Gabrielle to the Shabbat Club."

"Are you kidding?"

"No. I think she'd enjoy it."

"But Mom, she's twenty-three."

Mom pats my leg. "Let's not be ageist."

"Mom, really. Why don't you take her to a women's class or something?"

"Well, for one thing, there isn't a class today. Mrs. Zindler isn't feeling well."

"How about the rabbi's class?" I suggest. I'm getting desperate.

"I just have a feeling that it would be good for Gabrielle to be with a group of lively young girls," Mom says.

"Can you at least tell me *why* you think that? I mean, what is her problem?"

Mom looks toward the door and lowers her voice. "Who said she has a problem?"

"She's...kind of strange."

Mom waves her hand. "You barely know her. She's interesting."

"Interesting? Mom, please. I just don't feel comfortable—"

"Talia, I'm not asking you to feel comfortable. I am asking you to make Gabrielle feel comfortable."

"But what is she going to do there?" I ask.

"That's not your worry. Leave that up to Gabrielle. You just need to walk over together and introduce her to the group."

Mom stares at me, waiting for an affirmative answer, no doubt.

I let out a long sigh. "Okay."

Mom gives me a thanks-for-cooperating smile. "She's reading in the library. Just let her know when you're ready."

"That was some Bar Mitzvah this morning," Gabrielle says as we walk up Oak Street. "Coffee cakes, fruit platters, noodle kugel, whitefish salad. I was in heaven. Did you try the chocolate cake?"

"Uh, no."

"It was divine. Now that I'm not dancing professionally, I've gone off my diet."

"You were on a diet?" I ask, noticing Gabrielle's trim figure.

"Ah, yes. A dancer always has to watch her weight. Not that I'm planning on getting fat. I'm just enjoying being able to eat and have dessert again and not think about the calories."

"Do you miss it?" I ask.

"Dieting?"

"No. Dancing."

Gabrielle looks toward the sky as if the answer is up there. "Well, yes and no. It's a tough life. You not only need tremendous physical stamina, but mental and emotional stamina as well. I know I'm not going to go back professionally, but I'd like to find a way to use it. I still practice, you know, the barre work, the stretches. I just got burnt out. And I don't ever want that to happen again…" Her voice trails off. She puts her hands in her pockets and is actually quiet for a couple minutes as we turn onto Huntington Street.

"Well, I stink at dancing," I say. "But I'm pretty good at eating. Especially if the first ingredient is chocolate."

Gabrielle laughs. "Ain't nothin' wrong with that! I read somewhere that eating chocolate lifts your mood. It releases some kind of chemical in your brain."

"Good to know," I reply.

The air feels colder, and I zip up my jacket. I am hoping I'll run into one of my friends on the way, so I don't have to continue this conversation. But there is one thing I am wondering about…

"So, why are in you Boston?" I ask casually.

Gabrielle looks at me. "That's what I'm trying to figure out."

I hate those kinds of answers.

Shifra lives at 19 Leroy Street in a Victorian that her parents are forever fixing up. As we walk toward her house, I run into Rina and Malki Sneiderman, twins from my class. They are wearing matching leather jackets.

"Hi, Talia," they say in unison.

"Hi. Love your jackets."

"Thanks," Rina says. "We just got them at Macy's. Great sale."

"This is Gabrielle," I say. 'She's visiting from New York City."

"Oh, hi, I'm Rina. I love New York."

"And I'm Malki. We're sisters, in case you didn't notice," she says, giggling.

Gabrielle just stands there staring at them, then finally manages a hello. What's with her?

"Don't bother trying to tell them apart," I grin.

We walk into Shifra's house. It smells of beef stew. Shifra's father and younger brother are sitting at the dining room table learning Talmud together.

Rabbi Polter looks up from his big book. "Good Shabbos, girls. Everyone is downstairs today. The basement is finally finished."

"Oh cool," Rina says.

And cool it is! Shifra's basement is completely redone with beige carpeting, track lighting, built-in shelves, a ping pong table, a couple of couches, and beanbag chairs. I smell the fresh paint on the walls.

"This is so nice!" I say to Shifra as she comes over to greet us. She's wearing her red hair up in a ponytail.

"Thanks!" she says. "I think I'm gonna move down here."

"Shifra, this is our Shabbat guest, Gabrielle Markus."

"Hi. Welcome," Shifra says in her usual pleasant way. "Have something to eat. I think my mom went overboard on the snacks."

I spot a coffee table spread with bowls of chips, cookies, candy, and fruit.

"Thanks, but I'm still stuffed from the Bar Mitzvah," Gabrielle replies.

"Right, the Schlossbergs'. I missed that one. Hey, guys," Shifra calls to the other girls. "Listen up."

Shifra introduces Gabrielle to the group leaders, Gila and Baila, and then the five other girls who are munching on the snacks.

Everyone looks up for a moment, says hi, and then goes back to chatting. I feel relieved. No one seems to be bothered that Gabrielle is here.

A few minutes later Ruthie arrives, followed by Hannah Finkelstein and her best friend, Esther Grubner—a rather annoying duo. Ruthie notices Gabrielle and gives me a what-is-she-doing-here look? So I just smile as if to say, *Tell you later.* (Ruthie and I are great at reading each other's expressions.)

"Okay, girls," Gila calls. "Let's get started."

"Don't mind me, Talia," Gabrielle says. "I'll just sit over here and breathe in the atmosphere."

"Sure. Whatever," I mutter.

Everyone gathers in a circle around the coffee table. Gila and Baila sit together on the beanbag chairs. "So, I want to begin by giving a big thank you to Shifra for hosting us this week in her fabulous new basement," Baila says.

We all give a cheer.

"Okay. We have a really cool activity today that is going to help you define what things you hold most important in your life. In our parsha this week, the Torah says that the life of Sarah was 100 years, 20 years, and 7 years. That's kind of a strange way of saying that Sarah lived to be 127, isn't it? And later in the story, when her husband Abraham dies, we are told that his days were 100 years and 75 years. Does anyone have an explanation for the way the Torah states their ages?"

My brain is firing. Add the digits of both their ages and you get 10 and 13, two really important numbers in the Torah, hinting at the 10 commandments and the 13 attributes of God. Add their ages together and get 302. Add those digits and you get 5—

"You're right, Esther," Baila says. "That's the explanation that the commentator Rashi gives."

Oops. I didn't even hear what she said.

"Any other ideas?" Baila asks.

Malki raises her hand. "I think that the Torah is just trying to say that Abraham and Sarah both lived their lives to the fullest extent. Like, they used their time wisely."

"That's an awesome answer, Malki. That, in fact, is one of the explanations our sages give. Abraham and Sarah made every day count. Imagine coming to the end of your life and feeling that you lived every one of your days to the best of your ability. While that might not be possible for ordinary people like us, we can still strive to follow Abraham and Sarah's example. Which brings me to our activity." Baila reaches into a paper bag and pulls out several plastic sandwich bags. "The way to spend your days fully is to know what is important to you. Like, if you care so much about what others think of you, you may end up not being true to yourself. If you are always trying to please others, then you might miss the time you need for you own development."

I glance at Gabrielle. She seems to be watching Malki and her sister intently.

"In the bags are six popsicle sticks," Baila explains, "with a particular value written on each. Each of you will get the same six sticks. Your job is to put the sticks in order according to what you think is most important in your life. For example, one of the sticks says 'Family.' So if family is more important to you than the other five values, then you'd put that stick on top. Get it?"

Baila tosses us each a bag. "I'll give you a few minutes to work on this. Don't be influenced by your friend. Try to figure out what matters most to you."

I spread out the six sticks on the floor, and then read them. Love, Money, Family, Learning, Friendship, Fun. Hmm. I switch them around a few times. This is harder than it sounds. Finally, the order I come up with is: *Friendship, Family, Learning, Love, Fun, Money.*

Gila asks us all to share our results, which we do. Amazingly, no one has put the sticks in the same order, not even the twins. On second thought... six sticks can be arranged in six-factorial ways,

6 x 5 x 4 x 3 x 2 x 1... wow, 720 different ways...

"One thing to keep in mind is that each value is important, yet there is no right order," Gila says.

Baila looks around at all the sticks, then says, "I think it's interesting that Talia is the only one who put money last."

"That's easy for her!" Hannah blurts out. "She doesn't have to think about money."

I feel my cheeks redden.

"That wasn't appropriate," Baila says to her.

"What? I'm just saying..." Hannah looks at me. "It's true, isn't it? Your family is rich, so maybe you don't think about what it's like *not* to have money."

I can't believe she said that. I want to get up and leave, pronto.

Ruthie comes to my rescue. "That's not really for you to say, Hannah. Maybe Talia just isn't so materialistic."

"No, maybe she isn't *realistic*. Money does matter," Hannah insists.

"So," Gila says, "Hannah, you put money first. And so did Katya. Anyone else?"

No hands go up.

"I put it second," Malki says.

"But without money, it's not going to be easy to have the other things," Hannah protests. "Think about it."

"I agree," announces Katya.

"Me, too," Esther chimes in.

"You don't need money for love," Ruthie adds.

Hannah rolls her eyes. "Maybe. But if you don't have money, you're not going to have a lot of time for love! And money can bring you opportunities and time to have fun, spend with your family, and learn. And by the way, Abraham was rich."

Esther laughs. "She's right!"

"Okay," Baila intervenes. "You can see how this exercise shows that we all agree money is important in life, but we don't agree *how* important."

Hannah shrugs. "Okay. So we agree to disagree. Right, Talia?"

I sigh, looking down at my sticks. "Right."

44

"So, now," continues Baila, "I'm going to ask you to do something a little harder. Try taking away three sticks. That is, if you had to narrow it down to just three out of six values that you think are most important in your life, what would they be?"

Hannah groans. "That's too hard."

I stare at the six popsicle sticks. I reconsider the money stick, but then decide to take it away. I leave friendship as number one and put love as number two, but I am torn between learning and family. I decide to stick with family.

"Okay," says Baila. "How many of you stayed with your top three choices?"

Most of the girls raise their hands.

"How many of you made a switch?"

Malki, Katya, and I raise our hands.

"Isn't it interesting what happens when you are forced to narrow it down?" Baila stands up, smoothing her black skirt. "Now, I'll leave you with this thought. Over the next two weeks, try to notice if the choices you make are in line with the order of your values. So if you say friendship is number one, is that reflected in how you treat your friends?" Baila collects the bags of sticks. "To be continued."

I look over at Gabrielle, surprised that she hasn't chimed in. I wonder which order she would choose.

"I feel some tension in the room, girls," Gila says. "I think we need some music." She picks up the song booklets and starts passing them out even though we know most of the songs by heart. "Any requests?" she asks us.

"How about *Ka Ribon*?" Rina suggests.

"You always pick that one," teases Malki.

"You've got it," replies Gila. "Page five."

All at once the room fills with the girls' voices. Gabrielle sits to the side of the group, smiling and singing along with us. It sounds pretty nice. It took us all a while to get comfortable singing together, but now everyone is really into it. And Gila is right—singing seems to melt some of the tension. I push Hannah's comment to the back of my mind.

"Can we do 'One Small Candle?' " Ruthie asks when we finish.

"I love that one."

> *All it takes is one small candle,*
> *One small, flickering, shining candle.*
> *That is all it takes to penetrate the dark.*
> *All it takes is one soft word,*
> *One soft, soothing, gentle word.*
> *That is all it takes to mend a broken heart.*
> *If we put our hearts and minds together,*
> *A thousand glowing candles burning bright.*
> *Then we become a force that can't be measured*
> *And together we can drive away the night.*
> *All it takes is one small tear,*
> *One small, salty, burning tear,*
> *That is all it takes to melt a heart of stone.*
> *All it takes is one bright smile,*
> *One sweet, caring, loving smile*
> *That is all it takes to know you're not alone.*

Gabrielle applauds. Baila looks over at Gabrielle. "Thanks. It's our Shabbat Club chorus."

"That was so beautiful!" Gabrielle says. "You guys sound really good together. Do you ever perform?"

Baila smiles. "No, but our school has a chorus that performs. Do you have a song you'd like to suggest?" Baila asks her.

Gabrielle looks like she just won a prize. "Oh, gosh, let's see." She flips through the song book. "Um, I don't see it in here, but how about *Hinei Ma Tov?*"

"Sure. That's really fitting for our group," Baila replies. "Togetherness, unity. Let's hit it, girls."

So we start the old camp standby and before I know it, Gila and Baila are swaying side by side. Even though it feels kind of corny, Ruthie and I do the same thing, moving closer together, putting our arms around each other. The rest of the group follows. Rina reaches her hands toward Gabrielle, who hesitantly joins in our circle. She sits between the twins, arm in arm, her eyes closed. *Hinei ma tov u'ma nayeem, shevet achim gam yachad.* How good it is when we all dwell in unity.

When we finish, Gabrielle opens her eyes and smiles. "Thanks," she says softly. "That was really nice." Then she quickly moves back to her seat.

That's when I notice the tears in her eyes.

Five

"Okay, so are you going to tell me why your guest was at the Shabbat Club?" Ruthie says as we walk back to her house.

"My mom insisted," I say. "Don't ask me why. I just hope Gabrielle found her way back to the house or my mom will kill me. I know I should have walked with her, but I didn't feel like going home yet."

"Well, she seemed to be having a good time."

"Well, I didn't."

Ruthie stops walking. "What's the matter?"

"I just can't believe Hannah said that," I say. "I mean, that takes chutzpah!"

"That's just Hannah being Hannah. Don't take it so personally."

The sun is low in the sky, and the wind has picked up. I put my hands in my coat pockets. "Do you think that about me?"

"Of course not! Come on, Tal. I've known you since first grade," Ruthie says, kicking at the leaves on the sidewalk. "But... why *did* you put money last?"

"*Ruthie!*"

"Don't get me wrong, I'm just curious. Money is important. Right?"

I sigh. "Okay, yeah, it is. Maybe I wasn't thinking that hard. I don't know. Baila didn't give us that much time, and money just didn't seem as important as the other five things."

Ruthie is quiet for a moment, like she is thinking this over. I spot a group of yeshiva boys walking toward us. The tallest one is wearing a black hat.

"Good Shabbos," the tall boy mumbles as he approaches.

After the boys pass, Ruthie whispers, "That was Meyer Feingold."

"Yeah, so? Don't change the subject."

"I'm not. His parents publish *The Jewish Journal* and they are pretty well-off."

"Duh. As if I haven't heard. What does it have to do with me?"

Ruthie shrugs. "I am just thinking. I heard he was a real mensch and the smartest boy in—"

"Are you a matchmaker now?" I laugh.

Ruthie slaps me on the arm. "Stop it! I'm just saying that coming from a wealthy family doesn't seem to have affected him in a negative way. I wonder what number Meyer would give the money stick?"

"I really don't care."

We turn onto Ruthie's street.

"Don't be mad, Tal."

"I wonder if other people think that about me."

"What Hannah said?"

"Yeah."

"They don't. Everyone was just as surprised as you were."

I want to believe Ruthie, but doubt is flooding my mind. At this moment, I don't feel sure of anything.

When we get to Ruthie's house she tells me not to make any noise. She carefully opens the front door and tiptoes inside. We quietly remove our shoes, and then run upstairs to Ruthie's bedroom before her brothers can see us.

"If I have to play another game of Battleship with Avi, I'll die," she says, closing, then locking, her door. "It's so boring!"

"I actually liked that game when I was little," I say, plopping down on Ruthie's canopy bed.

"You would!" she says, looking at herself in the mirror. She pulls her long, blond hair back and fastens it in a ponytail. "You always loved number games. Remember the game Life?"

"Oh, I forgot about that! I always wanted to be the banker."

"And," Ruthie reminds me, "you wanted to spin the spinner and guess the number instead of playing the real game."

I laugh. "Yeah, I was a weird kid."

"Was?" Ruthie teases.

I throw a pillow at her.

"Hey, speaking of weird… when is the ballerina leaving?"

"Probably after Shabbat, or tomorrow morning."

"Are you going to tell your mother about the vase?"

"Actually, I think I'll tell Doris. She could easily find a replacement. I remember once we had this old man staying with us. His hands were so shaky he kept dribbling the wine on our floor during dinner. It was so obvious but my parents didn't say a thing. Somehow Doris got the stains out of the rug. Another time we had this little boy pick up a glass paperweight and throw it. He wanted to see if it would bounce."

Ruthie laughs. "You always have funny guest stories."

"And some annoying ones, too." Outside Ruthie's bedroom window the sky is turning dark blue. Shabbat will be over soon.

"Want to come over tonight?" I ask.

Ruthie removes her crystal earrings and puts them in her jewelry box. "I'm babysitting for the Shankmans."

"Don't you get enough of little kids at your own house?"

"Yeah, but my mom doesn't pay me. And the Shankmans put their kids to bed before I even get there, and they leave me snacks. It's great."

"How come I never get any babysitting jobs?"

Ruthie shrugs. "Lots of competition. I'll put in a good word for you, though."

"I should work on my history project tonight," I say with a sigh. "Can I call you if I get bored?"

"Sure, maybe we—"

"Ruthie?" Avi calls outside the door.

Ruthie spins around then jumps on the bed next to me. She puts her fingers to her lips.

"Ruthie, are you in there?" Avi whines. "Ruthie, you promised you'd play with me!"

I cover my mouth to keep from laughing.

"I know you're in there, Ruthie. You better open up the door or

I'll zap you!"

Ruthie starts laughing, and I crack up too. Before we know it we are both laughing our heads off while Avi bangs on the door.

"I'll play with you right after Shabbat," Ruthie calls from her bed, trying to catch her breath. "Okay? I'll give you a special treat after havdalah."

The banging stops. "Bubble gum?"

"Sure."

"It seems like you are always bribing that kid with food," I say after Avi leaves.

"You're right. It's the only thing that works." Ruthie lies back on her bed. "It's so hard to get any privacy around here. That's why my dad installed a lock. Next thing I know they'll be trying to read my diary."

"Hey, that reminds me," I say. "You said you had something important to tell me."

Ruthie springs back up and looks at me, her eyes lighting up. "It's a secret."

"Ooh. All the better." I wait.

"I wasn't going to tell you…"

"Thanks a lot!"

"No, I mean, I wasn't *supposed* to tell anyone. Not yet, but I can't keep it inside anymore—"

"Just tell me!" I plead, leaning toward her.

"Maybe you should guess, then it would be like I didn't actually tell you."

"Oh, all right. What's it about?" I ask.

Ruthie grins. "My mom."

I think for a minute. "She's getting a job?"

"No. Why would that be a secret?"

"I don't know. Um, let's see…" Ruthie has that you-won't-believe-this look on her face and suddenly I know. "You're kidding!" I say, jumping off the bed.

"That was my response when she told me!"

"So… am I right to say that your mom," I lower my voice, "is pregnant?"

51

"How did you guess?" Ruthie squeals.

"Ruthie!"

"I know! I know! It has to be a girl!"

"Or you'll have *six* brothers," I announce as if she couldn't count.

"More like six monsters. I think I'll move in with you if that happens."

"Wow. That's pretty exciting. When are you allowed to tell people?"

"I guess when she starts showing. She's due May fifth."

"Five-five."

"Huh?"

"The fifth day of the fifth month, duh!"

"Oh, is that lucky or something?"

I flash Ruthie a smile. "Considering that I see the number five as a girl, I would say so."

It's Saturday night, and our house is quiet once again. Mom took Gabrielle to the Jewish Women's Circle. There is some well-known guest speaker named Leah Wellman who is giving a talk on women's spirituality. I wasn't interested, but Gabrielle acted like she was going to see a movie star.

I got back from Ruthie's house a half an hour before Shabbat was over. Gabrielle was reading in the family room. When I walked in she thanked me (again) for taking her to the Shabbat group. Before I knew it, she was chewing my ear off about one thing or another. That girl can really talk. I was listening politely, like Mom always tells me to do, but Gabrielle's chattering started getting on my nerves. Now, if Shifra were there, she would have been enthralled with Gabrielle's stories, but tonight I just wasn't in the mood.

I was rescued when my father came home from shul Saturday evening because it was time to say havdalah, the short prayer we say an hour after sundown, when Shabbat is officially over. We all stood in our dining room. Mom dimmed the lights while Dad filled his wine cup then lit the braided candle like he always does. Then Gabrielle asked him if *she* could hold the havdalah candle! I was like five years old the last time I did that. When Dad passed the spice box for us all to smell, Gabrielle closed her eyes and took a big whiff and said, "Ahhh. A scent for the soul!" I had to bite my lip to keep from laughing.

After Dad put out the candle, and wished everyone a good week, Gabrielle started telling us about this havdalah "ceremony" she once attended with a hundred people standing in the dark around a three-foot braided candle, all bidding the Sabbath farewell. She even acted it out for us, swaying back and forth, waving her hand. "Goodbye, Shabbat, goodbye," she sang.

Dad and Mom listened politely, as if they were truly interested, although I think they just wanted to turn on the lights and get on with their evening. That's when I expected Gabrielle to thank us for our hospitality and be on her way. No such luck. She and Mom started gushing about hearing the famous speaker. Next thing I knew they were both cleaning up in the kitchen together and talking like old friends. That's when I dashed upstairs to my room to call Liora, my second-best friend, who unfortunately lives an hour away in Hillsdale (also known as 'Hicksdale'). Liora's mother is the art teacher at our school. Every morning Liora and her brother drive in with their mom to school, just about the time I'm rolling out of bed. Liora also has an older sister, Alison, who is a freshman at the University of Chicago.

I told Liora about the wacky guests, the Bar Mitzvah, and the Shabbat Club. I was careful not to say anything about Ruthie's mom; even though I bet Ruthie won't be able to keep it a secret much longer.

Liora told me about her Shabbat (quiet) and how she wished her family could move to Greensborough so she could be closer to her friends and to school. "There's nowhere to walk to where I live, and no public transportation," Liora complained. Liora couldn't talk long because she was going out bowling with her family. They are always doing fun things together.

Liora is the only Chinese girl at our school, but with adoption becoming more common in the Jewish community, I suspect she won't be in that Only Club for long.

So now I'm sitting at my desk working on my history project, which is a pretty lame thing to be doing on a Saturday night. I hear a knock on the door. "Talia?"

It's Dad.

"Come in," I say.

Dad opens the door and glances around. "On your own tonight?"

"Yeah. Ruthie had to babysit. "

"Oh, well. Hey, your room looks real nice."

I smile. "Doris."

"Ah, our angel. Well, then, do you feel like a game of chess?"

"No thanks. I need to catch up on homework."

"That's a change," Dad says.

"Actually, it's just my history project. I'm researching women's jobs in the Middle Ages."

Dad steps into my room. "Sounds interesting."

"I guess, but I sure am glad I live in this era."

"Oh, I don't know, I wouldn't mind being a knight." Dad strikes a pose. "Just call me Sir David."

I laugh. "Right, Dad."

He walks over to my desk. "Need any help?"

"No thanks," I say, closing the book.

"Hmm. That's the problem with you getting older. You don't need my help anymore."

"I'll be sure to let you know when I do," I say.

"Glad to hear it. How was the Shabbat group?"

I don't say anything for a moment. "Okay."

Dad looks at me suspiciously. It's hard to hide anything from him. "Just okay, huh?"

I shrug. He puts his hand on my shoulder. "You're usually more enthusiastic about it."

I sigh. "Dad? Can I ask you a question?"

"You can always ask me a question. Shoot."

I fiddle with my pen. "Are we rich?"

Dad raises his eyebrows, and then he smiles. "What exactly do you mean by rich?"

"You know… tons of money."

Dad scratches his chin. "I don't know about *tons*, but we do have money in the bank. Thank God, I make a good living and so does your mother. We've made some good financial investments. Are we rich? I guess it would depend on one's standards." He pauses for a moment. "Where is this coming from, Talia?"

Hannah's comment echoes in my head. "It's just... well, I know we aren't poor, but I never really thought of us as rich, I mean, I don't know why, you and Mom really never talk about this stuff with me, but now that I think about it... there are other people who look at us on the outside..." I stop rambling. Dad waits for me to finish. Suddenly tears come to my eyes.

"Talia?" he says softly.

I tell him about the Shabbat Club activity and what Hannah said in front of all the girls.

Dad sits down at the end of my bed. "Sounds like you were caught off guard with that one."

I look down at my notebook, the words blurring on the page, and I nod.

"Actually," Dad continues, "I'm surprised that is the first time you've heard a comment like that."

I look up at him. "Really?"

"Well, unfortunately it is human nature to judge people, to make assumptions on what you see. So if someone has a huge house or drives a Porsche, or wears expensive jewelry, you might think he is rich. That person may or may not be. See, what it really boils down to, Talia, is how much money you have in your pocket at the end of the day. In other words, how much are you worth? And that is not so easy to tell just from the outside."

"But we do have a big house and you own a jewelry business!"

"And?"

"And you give a lot of donations to school and our synagogue."

Dad nods. "Giving charity is a mitzvah."

"But then other kids probably think of us the same way as Hannah does."

"I wouldn't worry too much about her comment, Tal. Kids make all kinds of silly statements."

"But it was embarrassing, Dad."

"Is it possible to take it as a compliment?" he asks. "Would you rather have been described as poor?"

"Of course not."

He folds his arms. "So, why is being rich embarrassing?"

I think about this for a minute. "I'm not sure, actually."

"If you don't flaunt your wealth, if you aren't spoiled by it, and you use it to do good things, then you have nothing to be embarrassed about. In fact, I'm pleased to hear that you put money last. To me, that means you value things that can't be bought."

I wipe my eyes. "Thanks. I wish I thought to say that this afternoon."

Dad puts his hand on my shoulder. "Hey, do you remember the Mishna we learned last summer when we read *Pirkei Avot*? Ben Zoma asks, 'Who is rich?' Do you remember his answer?"

I smile. "He who is happy with what he has."

"You got it. No matter how much money or stuff a person has, it's his nature to want more. Which brings unhappiness, because you think you never have enough. It's not easy to be satisfied with your lot."

"That's for sure," I say, thinking about some of the girls in school who always want the latest fashion or techno fad.

"And here's another thing to remember," my father says. "Every time you think about Hannah's comment, every time you let it bother you, you are giving her power over you."

I look at him, confused.

"Just try to let it go," he whispers.

I give him a hug. It's been a long time since I did that, but it feels good.

In bed that night I lie awake thinking. I wonder why Gabrielle got teary-eyed after the song. I wonder if Mrs. Sheffman will die from her cancer. I wonder if Hannah talks about me behind my back. Then I think about Ruthie's news and I imagine her holding a baby sister. I feel a lump in my throat. Then the tears come again, and I don't even know why. I let them fall on my pillow. In the darkness I hug my matted stuffed bear (Baba). No need to feel embarrassed. What's the matter with me? I should be happy for Ruthie, but the tears just keep coming until I realize I am not crying for her, but for me. I am sad that I may never be anyone's sister.

Six

Sunday. Surprise! Gabrielle Markus is still here.

Monday. She's still *here*.

Tuesday. She's *still* here.

Wednesday. *She's still here!*

Okay, it's not like we haven't had guests stay for longer than a weekend, but what is Gabrielle doing here, anyway? I haven't gotten a straight answer from my parents, and Doris doesn't know anything either. "She's a nice girl. What's your problem?" Doris said to me when I registered a complaint. Well, for one thing, there is her singing. Since my room is right across from Gabrielle's, I've had to listen to her sing and strum on her guitar every night. (My parents' room is conveniently tucked away on the third floor.) Gabrielle has that kind of twangy country-singer voice that I find annoying. Then there is her morning meditation/yoga sounds that you might think would be a quiet sort of thing. (At least she hasn't broken anything else.) And speaking of quiet, have I mentioned that this girl can really talk? No, make that *ramble*. I keep nodding while she blabs away, but really I'm thinking, *okay, what is your point?*

And this morning, as I finished my oatmeal, Gabby was gabbing away about this book my father gave her to read last night.

"I was up half the night reading it," she said breathlessly. "The words were jumping off the page, talking to me, saying, listen up Gabrielle, this is your life I'm talking about here!" She took a sip of orange juice, then shook her head. "Does that ever happen to you?"

"Uh, not really," I said, standing up to put my bowl in the dishwasher.

She sighed. "I feel like I have so much catching up to do. At least in Jewish learning. You're so lucky you go to a religious school."

Lucky? Never really thought about it that way. For one thing, our day is two hours longer than the public school day.

"Well, speaking of school," I said, trying to escape, "I have to get going now. Have a good day."

Gabrielle looked surprised. "Oh, you too, Talia. See you later, I hope."

I half expected her to ask if she could come along.

So, this is why I particularly enjoyed a few minutes of quiet as I walked to school. I arrived a little early, and just as I walked toward the school entrance, I noticed a bronze plaque on the outside wall.

Schumacher Building, 1982.

I have been through that door hundreds of times, and up until that moment, I'd never paid any attention to the plaque. But today the sun was shining on it, and for some reason I just stopped and stared. *Your family is rich so maybe you don't have to think about what it's like not to have money!*

I looked away self-consciously, as if someone else might be looking at the plaque, too. I watched Mrs. Riseman, our guidance counselor, walk through the front door, followed by a couple of sixth graders. Then I walked up to the entrance of Boston Hebrew Academy, opened the door, and entered the building my grandfather, Isaac Schumacher, helped build.

And now, I'm sitting in math class, waiting for the rest of the girls to finish their quiz. The afternoon sun is streaming through the second floor classroom window. I can see the towering oak trees in the distance. Dr. Janas' math class is my favorite. No surprise there, I guess, but it wasn't always like that. In the early grades I hated math class. It was like watching a movie in slow motion. When the teachers found out that I was really good at math, they just gave me more work, like twenty-five long division problems instead of fifteen. Now that's a good way to kill a kid's math enthusiasm.

Once, in first grade, Mrs. Miller was explaining to the class why you can't take 3 from 1. She wrote it on the board: $1 - 3 = 2$.

"Some of you have been writing your subtraction facts like this. Who knows what is wrong with this equation?"

Then a boy gave the answer she was fishing for. "You can't take a bigger number from a smaller number," he announced.

"That's right!" Mrs. Miller beamed.

Well, before I learned to keep my mouth shut around certain types of teachers, I raised my hand and said, "But that isn't right. You *can* take a larger number from a smaller number. It's just that you get a negative number. The answer would be negative two."

Mrs. Miller just stared at me. "Well, well. Someone has been visiting the seventh grade math class," she said sarcastically. "Are you purposely trying to confuse your classmates, Talia?"

"No, I just—"

"Do you want to be the teacher today?" she said, her hands on her hips.

The kids giggled.

I shook my head.

The funny thing is, I know I didn't mean to show off or to prove her wrong. I innocently believed that Mrs. Miller just hadn't been informed about negative numbers. After all, my dad was the one who told me about them.

That night, when my father tucked me into bed, I told him what had happened in class.

"You know, pumpkin, I forgot to tell you that the negative numbers are kind of a secret," he said. "Some teachers think that they are too hard for young kids to understand. So, they don't tell the kids about negative numbers until they are in about sixth or seventh grade."

I thought about this for a moment. "But what happens in the winter when the thermometer says minus ten?"

I'll never forget the look on my dad's face. He was quiet for a second, and then he started laughing and laughing. He gave me a great big hug. "Well… I guess they will be darn cold!"

Luckily, Dr. Janas appreciates my strengths. Her name is Bianca (don't you love it?) and she is about forty and really attractive. She has long, wavy, auburn hair, and wears fashionable clothes and high heels. You'd never think she was a math teacher, which is what I like about her, besides the fact that she is an amazing teacher and knows her stuff. I'm one of five kids in the honors math class. The boys' school has 12 students in honors, taught by Mr. Doring. (Rhymes with boring for a good reason, I hear.) The other 35 girls in my grade are either in regular or accelerated math, which includes all of my good friends.

"Time's up," Dr. Janas announces. The two girls still working groan, then reluctantly surrender their papers. "Your homework is just one problem today, which you can copy from the whiteboard. I expect you to spend a lot of time tinkering with it. I'll be looking forward to some creative solutions."

I start putting away my notebook and folder in my backpack when Dr. Janas calls my name. "Talia? Can we talk for a moment after class?"

Ordinarily, I would worry that I was in trouble, but I know Dr. Janas doesn't work that way. And I know I haven't caused any trouble in her class.

When the other girls have left the room, Dr. Janas closes the door and smiles. "Come sit down for a sec," she says to me.

I sit in the chair next to her desk. "First of all," she begins, "I want to tell you how much I enjoy having you in my class. You're the type of student that keeps me on my toes."

I smile. "Thanks."

She removes my quiz paper from her grade book. "You got a 98 on the quiz, which was pretty tough."

I'm relieved. I wasn't too sure about the last problem.

"I'm also happy to tell you that your score on the math team preliminary exam qualifies you to attend the regional competition this December."

"Really?"

Dr. Janas tilts her head. "Are you actually surprised?"

"Well, since you didn't say anything…"

"I didn't want to announce it in front of the class. I'm only

60

allowed to send three students from the girls' seventh grade division, so I wanted to check with you first. I'd love you to represent our school at the finals."

My heart jumps. "Wow. Um, who else would be going?"

"Hannah Finkelstein. You would compete both as a team and individually."

"Oh." I try not to look too disappointed. "Who's the third girl?"

Dr. Janas tidies the stack of papers on her desk. "Well, I wasn't planning on a third. There were several girls who scored just on the borderline. But this is a challenging competition, and you have to be willing to prepare for it. Since I am the official coach, I get to select the contestants. You and Hannah are not only the top math students, but you have what it takes to participate in this kind of competition."

The idea of preparing with Hannah Finkelstein really turns my stomach. I try to think of something to say.

Dr. Janas raises her perfectly groomed eyebrows. "So? What do you think?"

"Um, to tell you the truth, I'm not so sure Hannah and I would be the best match—at least for studying together."

"I see." Dr. Janas pauses. "Well, it is certainly better to prepare with a classmate, but I suppose it isn't necessary, except for our coaching sessions."

I really don't want Hannah as my sole teammate. It's going to take any fun out of the whole experience. "I think it would be better to have a third girl. I mean… three heads are better than two, right?"

Dr. Janas laughs. "Well, I haven't quite heard it put that way, but maybe, when it comes to problem solving." Dr. Janas leans back in her chair. "Let's see. I just don't know whom I would pick. Rina is on the volleyball team and doesn't have time. Julia hates competitions. And Shoshana and Lauren are still eleven. The rules say you have to be twelve."

"What about Liora Clark?" I blurt out.

Dr. Janas wrinkles her forehead. "I wasn't thinking outside the honors class."

"Yes, but Liora actually likes math and she's really motivated and disciplined. She likes contests. She's my good friend and I could help her."

Dr. Janas opens one of the grade books on her desk. "Hmm, let's think about that for a sec. I've got all the preliminary scores here. Liora…Clark. Well, yes, she did do quite well. But she'd have to be willing. Is this something you think she'd be interested in?"

"Oh, I know she would. I'd be happy to talk to her first, if that would be okay."

Dr. Janas looks out the window for a moment. I wait, my heart pounding. "I'm going to go with your inclination here, Talia. Let's leave it like this: you talk to Liora about the competition, and let her know that it is okay with me if she'd like to participate." Dr. Janas hands me a paper. "This flyer has all the info. If Liora is interested, have her come talk to me and I'll give her the study packet. Then we can schedule our first team meeting. Meanwhile, you can get started."

"Thanks, Dr. Janas," I say, taking my study packet. "I know we'll be a great team."

She nods. "It's nice to work with close friends, isn't it?"

"Definitely," I reply.

I suddenly remember the sticks from Shabbat Club. Where did I put friendship?

Dr. Janas stands up. "Thanks for reminding me. It's been a few years since I was thirteen."

I leave the classroom feeling triumphant. Now, I just have to convince Liora.

Seven

"Are you joking?" Liora says to me as we huddle in a corner of the courtyard during our afternoon break.

"No, I am not joking. She totally thinks you can do it," I half-lie to Liora after delivering the good news.

She looks confused. "But why didn't she say something to me?"

"She didn't know if it would be fair, I mean maybe there are other girls in the accelerated class who might want to be on the team. It has to come from you. You need to actually ask. That's why I said I would talk to you. And besides, you got a really good score on the preliminaries."

Liora runs her fingers through her jet black hair. "I just can't believe it," she says. "My mom is going to be *so* happy!" Then her face turns serious. "But… what if I'm not good? I mean, I'll be competing against you and Hannah, not to mention the boys and everyone else from the other schools. What if I come in last?"

"Liora! You are not going to come in last. We compete as a team, which means we get to solve the problem together, so even if you don't know the answer, then other team members get to help. And then you compete individually which I can help you on, and Dr. Janas will coach all three of us. Hey, this will give us a good excuse to have you sleep over at my house."

She breaks into a wide smile, and lets out a deep breath. "Okay. I'll do it."

I don't feel guilty about telling her a white lie. It's the power of positive thinking. Shifra once told me about this study where a kindergarten teacher was told her class was gifted, even though they really weren't. Turns out that the kids did really well that year and increased their skills, better than the other class where the teacher was told the kids had learning problems, even though they didn't. So, I figure it is the same thing with Liora. She wants to be on the math team, but she has to believe in herself first.

I give Liora a quick hug. "Thanks!" I say. "You and I will show Hannah Finkelstein a thing or two."

"Don't tell anyone yet," she says quickly, as Shifra and Ruthie walk across the courtyard toward us.

I wave to our friends.

Ruthie and Shifra are sharing a bag of potato chips. "You guys having a conference?" Shifra asks, approaching us.

"Yeah, I'm plotting how to get Gabrielle out of my house."

"The dancer?"

I nod. "She's still here."

"Doesn't she have a job?" Ruthie asks.

I shrug. "Who knows? She's just getting on my nerves."

"So what do you know about her?" Shifra asks.

"Not much. Let's see, she's from New York, becoming religious, used to dance professionally, and grew up in the South."

"Thought I detected that in her accent," Shifra says, offering me a potato chip.

"What I don't get is how she knows my parents."

"Everyone knows your parents," Ruthie replies.

"What's she doing in Boston?" Shifra asks me.

"That's what I've been trying to find out, but no one has given me a direct answer, including Gabbers herself."

Ruthie cracks up. "Gabbers?"

"Yeah, that's my nickname for her because she doesn't stop talking!" I make a gabbing hand motion with my fingers. "She's always telling stories and they aren't very interesting. She's very touchy-feely, too."

Shifra holds up her finger. "Wait a minute… this is sounding familiar."

Liora rolls her eyes. "Oh, here we go again. The amateur psychologist."

Shifra pops a potato chip into her mouth. "No… really. Listen. Remember that substitute we had, Mrs. Standish?"

"Oh, yeah," Ruthie says. "The one who talked all the time?"

"Exactly. I found out later that her brother died in a car crash."

Silence.

"That's sad," I say. "And what does this have to do with Gabbers?"

Shifra continues. "People who talk a lot often are trying to cover up something, some sort of pain. I noticed it with our neighbor Mr. Mortimer after his son died of cancer. Whenever he came to our house for Shabbat lunch, he'd go on and on talking."

"But Gabrielle seems really happy," I say.

"That's the point," Shifra replies. "Mr. Mortimer acted happy, too. So did Mrs. Standish. You don't really see it until you get to know them. Then you realize that something is a little funny… a little off."

Ruthie, Liora, and I consider Shifra's analysis. "Hey, that's like Mrs. Mellman, remember, our fifth grade music teacher?"

"That's right," Ruthie says. "She was so bubbly and talkative, even sort of nervous." Ruthie gasps. "She was the one who had the basement fire!"

Shifra nods. "Which killed her three cats."

"Ohh! That's terrible," Liora cries.

"I don't know," I say. "Gabrielle mentioned her parents. They're still alive. She's an only child—"

"Oooh, something in common," Ruthie teases.

"And that's about the only thing," I shoot back.

"Maybe Gabrielle had a tragic love affair!" Ruthie suggests.

I roll my eyes. "She's only twenty-three."

"So?" Ruthie says. "That's old enough. Maybe she was engaged and the guy didn't show up to the wedding? How traumatic is that?"

"I'd die," Liora says.

"I'd kill him," Shifra says.

"You have an overactive imagination," I sigh.

She smiles. "The best kind."

"Well, I'm giving it until Friday, and if she is still here, I'm just going to ask her directly."

"About the engagement?" Ruthie asks.

"No! I'll find out why she is here, and when she plans to leave."

"It's kind of mysterious," Liora says dreamily. "We never have any interesting guests at my house."

"Trade places with me any day, Liora," I say. "Be *my* guest."

The school bell rings. I spot Hannah Finkelstein and Esther Grubner sitting on a bench across the courtyard. Probably trying to calculate my parents' net worth.

"Maybe we could help you figure her out," Liora suggests.

"Ooh. Now there's an idea. You guys want to stay over this Shabbat?" I ask, feeling excited.

"That would be so much fun. We haven't had a foursome for a while," Liora replies.

"Do you think your mom will let?" Ruthie asks Liora. "I know she usually wants you home for Shabbat."

Liora gives me a knowing smile. "I have a feeling she will say yes to just about anything this week."

"What's that supposed to mean?" Shifra says, opening the school-building door.

Liora smiles. "You'll see."

Shifra stares at Liora. "Now you're the one being mysterious."

"I know. I'll fill you guys in later. And Talia—I'll call you tonight with the answer."

"Me too," Shifra adds.

"Me three," Ruthie says.

The hall starts to crowd with kids. "So, it'll be like the 'Four Investigators'?" I joke.

"Yeah. It'll be awesome. Gotta go!" Liora says, heading in the opposite direction. "See you guys in History."

After school, I walk home alone, since Ruthie takes Spanish on Wednesdays and Shifra has karate. My mind is spinning with the math problem Dr. Janas gave us for homework. What is the fastest way you can think of to add up the first 100 numbers: 1 plus 2 plus 3 plus 4, all the way through 100? I start to calculate, but the numbers get in the way. The colors start spinning. I see white number 1, skinny and friendless, standing alone next to 2 who is green and flirty and friends with mischievous 3, then 4 who is yellow and 5 which is turned around from the others, alive and purple… 6 is funny and 7 is brown… 8, my favorite, sky blue, peaceful, and cool… 9 is red and a loudmouth. By the time I get home I haven't even begun to figure out the homework problem.

When I walk into my house, I am surprised by the sound of the piano. I stop to listen, and quickly realize that it isn't Dad playing.

"Helloooo!" Gabrielle calls from the living room. "Talia?"

I dump my backpack and walk toward the living room. Gabrielle sits at the piano wearing pink sweatpants and a wrap-around fuzzy pink sweater. She looks like a bunny.

"Do you play piano?" I ask.

Gabrielle waves her hand. "Oh, I'm just a dabbler. I was trying to pick out that melody your father sang on Friday night, *Aishet Chayil?* It's so beautiful. I could imagine creating a dance to it. And this piano is marvelous." She closes her eyes. "I can sit here playing my little song and imagine I'm in Carnegie Hall."

"My grandfather Isaac played there," I say, bluntly. "And that was his piano."

She looks surprised. "You mean the man who started Schumacher Jewelers?"

"That's the one."

"Wow," she says, lightly running her fingers across the keys. "Do you ever feel his presence when you're playing?"

Her question stops me cold. I mean, what kind of thing is that to ask? I feel myself getting mad. "I think he'd be happy that I play," I manage to answer.

Gabrielle closes the piano top. "I wish I would have kept up my lessons years ago. But I was pretty consumed with dance and didn't have the time to take up another instrument on top of the guitar."

She stands up. One long pink thing. All she needs is a bunny tail. "So how was school?" she asks.

What, does she think she's my mother? "Good."

"I hated school, at least until I went to New York for dance. But

67

that's another story."

Spare me. "What did you do today?" I ask.

"I looked for a job."

"In Boston?"

"Yup. I tried the dance studios to see if they are hiring. I was thinking about trying something in Jewish education, but I don't have a teaching degree. I suppose I could go back to school, but I don't know if I'm up for all that academic stuff." She taps her forehead. "Kind of stressful."

Okay, this is too much for me to bear. I'm not waiting until Friday. "So, you're planning on staying in Boston?"

"That's the plan for now," Gabrielle grins.

I swallow hard, afraid to ask the next question. "Are you looking for an apartment?"

"Not for a while," she replies. "Your parents offered me the room here until I get settled. They are so generous!"

Eight

"Where were you yesterday?" I whine to Doris when she picks me up after school the next day. I slide into the front seat of her car and fasten my seat belt.

"Hello to you, too," she says, tossing me a brown paper bag. "I went home early. I have a life, you know."

I open the bag and take out an apple and a muffin. "Thanks," I say. Then I mumble a blessing and bite into the apple.

Doris pulls out of the school parking lot. "Besides, Gabrielle was there—"

"Oh, so she's my babysitter now?" I reply.

"You don't need no babysitter, Tali."

"Don't call me Tali. I'm not a baby anymore."

"No kidding," Doris says. "You used to be sweet."

"Did you hear that she is staying, indefinitely, at our house?" I ask.

"Ah, so that's what this is about?"

"Well?" I say.

Doris glances over at me. "Well what?"

"Doesn't she get on your nerves?" I ask.

Doris turns on Main Street, toward my orthodontist's office. "No. I think she's funny."

"Ha. Ha. Yeah, she really cracks me up." I peel off the muffin wrapper. "And I suppose this weekend Mom will invite another slew

69

of guests."

"I think you're onto something, sweetie."

"Doris?"

"Hmm?"

"Why do you think my parents want to have guests all the time?"

Doris is quiet. I wait for her to say something. "What I think," she says slowly, "is that they like to share their big house—to fill it up. You know that saying, 'the more, the merrier'?"

I think about Doris' answer. "So I'm not enough for them?"

Doris holds up her hand. "I never said that. Your parents love you. They spoil you terribly."

"They do not!" I hate when she says that.

"Hey, listen, princess. You try growing up in my country. I lived in a tiny house and shared my bedroom with a sister and a brother. No air conditioning or dishwasher. One pair of shoes." Doris looks at me. "And, my sister and me do all the chores."

She pulls up to the medical building. "And," she says as she parks, "my parents couldn't afford no fancy dentist to give me a perfect smile." She flashes her crooked front teeth.

"Okay, I get your point." I climb out of the car.

"And I get your point. You need to vent. That's okay with me." Doris pats my arm.

I love Doris.

Inside the orthodontist's office, there are several kids and parents waiting. A teenage boy stands at the video game machine, hitting the controls with the heel of his hand. The beeping and crashing sounds fill the small room.

"Hi, Talia," someone calls. I turn around and there is Hannah Finkelstein sitting by the window. "You go to Dr. Mavitz, too?" she asks, like it is some major coincidence.

"Yeah. You getting braces?"

She nods. "I'm so nervous."

"It's not so bad," I reply. I sit down.

Hannah's mother is furiously knitting away. "Haven't seen you in a while," she says to me. "How's your mother?"

"Fine," I say. Doris takes off her leather jacket and sits next to me. "This is Doris." I quickly try to think of how to introduce her. Nanny? No. Babysitter? Definitely not. "Our housekeeper."

"Nice to meet you, Doris. I'm Edith Finkelstein."

"Your housekeeper takes you to the dentist?" Hannah remarks.

Doris laughs.

"And isn't that a nice thing," Mrs. Finkelstein adds. "It's so hard to juggle all the children's activities and appointments with a full-time job. Does your mother work at the jewelry store?"

"No," I say. "She works for State Street Bank."

"Well, I'm sure she is glad to have your help, Doris," Mrs. Finkelstein says in a teacherly sort of way.

Doris smiles. "I always say every working woman needs a wife."

Mrs. Finkelstein stops knitting and just stares at Doris for a moment until she finally gets the joke. "Oh, of course! Yes, I couldn't agree more."

Hannah rolls her eyes.

"Talia Schumacher?" the dental assistant calls, saving me from this ridiculous conversation.

"See ya, Hannah. Good luck with the braces. Go for the yellow bands. They'll look great," I lie.

As I lean back in the dentist chair with that silly bib attached to my shirt, I start to worry that Mrs. Finkelstein might grill Doris in the waiting room. I had forgotten how nosy Hannah's mother can be. Once again, I'm thinking about Hannah's comment. I never gave any thought to Doris taking me to the dentist. She's been doing it for a while. It's not like my mom never takes me. Well, actually... I let my mind roll backwards to the last time my mom took me to an appointment, and I can't quite think of the day. Well, why should she bother leaving work? She has a very important position. She travels a lot. And it's not like Dad could take me either. Why did Hannah seem to think it was so odd for our housekeeper to take me to the dentist? Just the way she said it...

"You need to do a better job with hygiene, Talia," the assistant says as she lifts my lips with her latex-gloved fingers. "And, Dr. Mavitz is going to want to see you sooner. In three weeks."

Tell that to my mom, I think to myself.

That evening I have the pleasure of eating dinner alone with Gabrielle Markus. Doris left us a pot of chili, garlic bread, and a salad, and then abandoned me. Doris almost always stays when my parents have to work late. "You'll be fine," she said, giving me a wink as she headed out the door. Do I detect a pattern here?

So here I am sitting at the kitchen table across from Gabbers, who is dressed in a black, long-sleeved leotard, black stretchy skirt, black capris, and black flats. Guess she got tired of pink.

"This is delicious," she says. "I love home-cooked food. When I was living in New York, I almost always ate take-out, or made noodles and ketchup."

"There are a lot of kosher restaurants in New York, aren't there?"

"Oh yeah. But too expensive on a dancer's salary. So did Doris make this, or your mother?"

"To tell you the truth," I say, taking a bite of bread, "I'm not sure. But they're both good cooks."

"You are so lucky to have Doris," Gabrielle comments. "My mother never learned to cook well. I had this elderly babysitter named Mrs. Winters. I loathed her. She was an old grouch. She made the worst dinners that often included overcooked peas, which I detested. Anyway, one time, she insisted I eat the peas before I could leave the table. I knew I would gag if I had to put one more cold, mushy pea in my mouth. So, while Mrs. Winters was doing the dishes, I dropped the peas down my shirt."

I've just taken a drink of water when Gabbers says this. I burst out laughing and the water dribbles down my chin. I grab a napkin and wipe my mouth and the table.

"Sorry," I say, clearing my throat.

Then Gabrielle starts laughing, too. "Gosh, I haven't thought about that incident in a long time."

"I hate peas, too," I admit.

Gabrielle points her fork at me. "So, now you know a good trick!"

Later that night, I wait in bed listening for the sound of the garage opening. Dad is out at a school board meeting, and it's just Gabrielle and me in the house. I'm surprised that Mom isn't home yet. I didn't want to bother her by calling and asking, 'When are you going to be home?' That seems so childish. Still, I'll admit I do miss her when she comes home late.

Finally, I hear her car. Then comes the sound of the back door opening. Keys tossed on the mail table. High heels click on the floor. I hear her footsteps on the stairs, then down the hall. Then she knocks on my door.

"Come in," I say.

"Hi there. Sorry I'm so late." Mom closes the door behind her and walks over to my bed. "The meeting lasted three hours." She sits beside me; she smells of roasted coffee. "Didn't even have time to go to the gym." She sighs. "I'm exhausted. Did everything go well at the dentist?"

"Yeah. Doris made the appointment for December first, at four o'clock. Can you take me?"

"Doris can't take you?" she asks.

"Yeah, but… it's just that you haven't taken me in a while."

Mom yawns. "I'll have to look at my calendar. How was school?"

"Okay… oh, Dr. Janas asked me to join the math team for the finals!"

"That's wonderful. Do you want to do it? Will you have time?"

"Yeah, I'm gonna do it. Liora and I will be teammates."

"Perfect. Who else?"

"Hannah Finkelstein."

"That's it?"

"Dr. Janas can only send three girls."

"Well, that is certainly an honor." She pats my arm. "I'm proud of you." We sit in the dark for a few moments. "You had dinner with Gabrielle?"

"Yeah," I say unenthusiastically.

"I thought you might enjoy her company."

I sit up. "Why would you think that?"

"Well, why not? She's interesting. She's young."

"She's strange."

"Shh."

"And another thing," I whisper. "Why is she staying here?"

"She's been through a tough time and she doesn't have any family support right now," Mom says quietly.

"So we're adopting her or something?"

"Don't be silly."

"Why is it such a secret?"

"There's no secret, Talia. It's just her business. Not yours."

"But it's my house."

"No, it's our house. And our house—"

"—is an open house." I finish Mom's sentence.

"So you *have* been listening all these years."

I think of what Doris said about the guests filling up our house, but I don't have the courage to bring it up with Mom. "So who's coming this Shabbat?"

"Gabrielle will be here, if that's what you're getting at."

"Well, if I have to endure her strangeness, then could I at least have Ruthie and Shifra sleep over? And… maybe Liora, too?"

"Of course."

"Really?"

"Really."

"Thanks, Mom, because I kind of already asked them. And it's okay with their parents."

She kisses my cheek. "Good night."

"G'night."

That's one advantage of having an open house.

Nine

I am sitting in English class and fooling around with my calculator. I'm half-listening to Mrs. Wordsworth (yes, her real name!), who is explaining, for the third time, the difference between past and future participle. Why do so many kids not get grammar? It's just a bunch of rules. While I wait for my teacher to move on to something more interesting, I punch in 111 x 111 on the calculator, which equals... 12321. Hey, a palindrome! Let's try 1111 x 11. Answer is 12221. That works, too. Cool number. I try 1111 x 1111, which is... 1234321. Another palindrome. Hmm... 11,111 x 11,111 is 123454321. Wow, all the digits in numerical order. This would make a good mental math trick. What a crazy number 1 is. By itself it is so lonely, but if you—

"Talia?"

I look up to see Mrs. Wordsworth staring at me. "Well?" she says, crossing her skinny arms.

I drop the calculator on my lap. "Um, could you repeat the question?"

"I asked for the answer to number 12. Are you with us?"

I glance at my grammar book. "Sure... uh, that would be... *The car had been designed.* Past perfect participle."

Mrs. Wordsworth pinches her lips. "Thank you. Next. Rachel, sentence 13."

Mrs. Wordsworth is about the most boring English teacher

I've ever had. It's too bad, because I like reading and writing. But she has a way of dissecting a book to death. Mrs. Wordsworth also loves poetry—not the fun, easy-to-get poems you read in elementary school, but the kind that only make sense to the author and to English teachers. I never cared much for poems, especially ones that don't rhyme, and Mrs. Wordsworth sure hasn't helped change my mind.

"Grammar quiz Monday on chapter three," Mrs. Wordsworth announces just as the bell rings. "Along with your personification poem, which will be graded."

"Just great," I say to Ruthie as we head out of the classroom. "I haven't even started my poem, and I have no ideas either."

Ruthie swings her backpack over one shoulder. "Why don't you write about procrastination?"

"Very funny. I suppose you're done?"

"I am," Ruthie says, opening her locker. There are fashion pictures pasted all over the inside. "I personified my sewing machine."

"You're kidding, right?"

Ruthie smiles. "For real. I'll e-mail it to you."

"I have way too much to do before Monday," I groan. " W h a t should I write about?"

Ruthie shoves a notebook into her backpack. "Write a poem about your calculator."

I think about that for a second.

"I'm kidding, Tal!" Ruthie laughs.

"Actually—"

"Saw you punching numbers during English," Hannah Finkelstein calls out as she struts by. "Don't you think about anything else, Talia?"

"Sure. I think about how I'm going to win the math meet," I say, surprised at my own comeback.

Hannah grins at me, flashing her yellow braces. "You mean, how we're going to win?"

"Oh, you're planning to tie with me?"

"I was talking about the team challenge," she shoots back. "And by the way, I heard that your parents hired a private math coach. Can I get in on it?"

"That is so not true!" I say, my face reddening.

"And she is staying at your house."

Ruthie bursts out laughing. "Are you talking about Gabrielle?"

Hannah stands there waiting for me to say something. I start laughing, too. "You'd better check your sources, you know, like Mrs. Wordsworth always says? Gabrielle happens to be an out-of-town guest, and she's a dancer, not a mathematician."

Hannah shrugs. "Well, when are we going to start studying?"

"I'll call you."

Ruthie tugs at my arm. "Let's go. There's pizza."

"Later, Hannah," I sing, following Ruthie.

"I forgot about the pizza," I say when I catch up to Ruthie. "Doris even packed me a lunch."

"You could have sold yours to Hannah. Cheese gives her hives."

"I'll remember that," I say jokingly. "Seriously, I do not know how I am going to study with that girl."

"You don't have to study, Miss Math Whiz."

"Oh, yes I do. For this competition, at least. It's like a sport, I need to train."

"So you're a mathlete?"

I smile. "Yeah. You could say that."

The cafeteria has that warm smell of pizza. Every Rosh Chodesh, the Jewish new month, we have pizza, calzones, and Greek salad from Jerusalem Café, owned by Rina and Malki Sneiderman's parents. They absolutely get the Talia Schumacher award for best pizza (my favorite food after chocolate), and I have done quite a bit of taste-testing in my thirteen years.

"There's Shifra and Liora," Ruthie says, looking toward the back of the cafeteria. She waves to them and then gets in line with me. I decide to spice up my bag lunch with a slice of pizza with vegetarian pepperoni, a salad, and lemonade. Ruthie gets the Greek salad and seltzer.

"That's it?" I comment, looking at her pathetic lunch.

She shrugs. "I'm not that hungry."

"That's why you're so skinny."

"More like my brothers eat all the food before I can get to it."

I laugh. Ruthie has told me funny stories about her brothers' voracious appetites.

We head toward the back of the cafeteria.

"Hey," Liora calls to us. "Thought you'd never get here. This calzone is sooo good."

I sit down next to her. "Can I have a bite?" Liora pulls off a piece of the calzone and hands it to me.

Ruthie sits down next to Shifra. "Thanks for saving our seats."

"That's all you're eating?" Shifra asks, eyeing Ruthie's tray.

"Don't *you* start," Ruthie replies.

"You aren't worried about gaining weight, are you?" Shifra asks. "Because I saw this documentary on girls who try to starve themselves—"

"Oh, please," Ruthie says, almost choking on her salad. "I am not trying to starve myself."

"Why were they starving themselves?" Liora raises her eyebrow.

"They have an irrational fear of getting fat and a warped body image," Shifra replies. "It's a psychological disease. It got so bad that these girls had to go into a treatment center. There was a fourteen-year-old girl who weighed 60 pounds! And she kept on insisting she was fat."

"I don't think I'll ever get that disease," I say, biting into my pizza. "I love food. Gabbers was telling me how great it is being able to eat what she wants now that she isn't dancing professionally." I look at Ruthie's green salad and am reminded of Gabrielle's pea story. "Oh, and listen to this one." I repeat the story about her mean babysitter and we laugh so hard our stomachs hurt.

"That is so funny," Liora says. "My mom has tried about ten different ways to get me to eat tofu. Yuck." She makes a face. "The texture makes me gag."

Liora's mom is into health food big time. "Well, I promise not to serve any tofu on Shabbat," I reply.

"So you're coming for sure?" Shifra asks Liora.

"Didn't Talia tell you? My mom was so psyched about the math team news that she would have said yes to about anything I asked. And considering I brought my overnight stuff to school, I don't think she'll be changing her mind."

"Way to go!" Shifra says, slapping her five.

"Liora, I cannot believe you are doing the math team," Ruthie says, biting into a tomato slice.

Liora takes a sip of her soda. "Dr. Janas thinks I can do it."

I almost choke on my pizza. "Come on, guys," I prompt. "Liora needs your support."

"She needs your brain," Ruthie says to me.

"Thanks a lot," Liora replies. "But for your information, Talia and I will be working together."

"Hope you two aren't planning on talking math during our sleepover," Shifra chimes in.

I smile. "Wouldn't think of it."

"I heard the boys' school is competing, too," Shifra adds. "And the scores aren't separate."

"Ooh, I bet Meyer Feingold will be in it," Ruthie says. "You think you can beat him, Tal?"

Up until this moment, I had forgotten that the boys were included in the competition. "How should I know whether or not—"

Just then Mrs. Brody, our principal, walks to the front of the cafeteria and taps on a microphone. "Girls, may I have your attention, please? First, I want to wish everyone a happy Rosh Chodesh and extend a big thank you to the PTA and the seniors for helping out with our special lunch. Now, I will ask you to turn your attention to Maya Rubin, who will say a few words on the new month."

Everyone claps.

"Figures, she'd pick Maya," Liora mumbles.

Maya Rubin is in eighth grade and is about the most talented kid in middle school. She plays violin in the Boston Youth Symphony, and won first place in a music composition contest. (The Boston Pops even performed Maya's song.) If that wasn't enough to make a Jewish parent swell with pride, Maya's short stories have been published in magazines and last I heard she was writing a novel. To top it off, she's really modest and a nice person.

"Hi, everybody," Maya begins in her sweet voice. "We've just finished the month of *Cheshvan*, the month without any Jewish holidays. Now, in our new month, *Kislev*, we look forward to

Hanukkah. The days are now growing shorter. By the time Hanukkah comes, it will feel colder and darker. Then we will light the menorah and chase away some of the physical and spiritual darkness of the season. The Hanukkah candles, however, are supposed to be lit in a window or a doorway, so the light is brought *outside* our home.

"Jewish women have the special mitzvah of lighting Shabbat candles. Every Friday night we bring light into our home. We get to do this all year round. And, the first day of each Hebrew month is kind of like our day. Girls' day. Because the Torah tells us that the women did not participate in the sin of the Golden Calf. As a reward, God gave us a special day each month—*Rosh Chodesh.* So the message is to keep bringing the light into our lives and the lives of others. In other words, glow, girl!"

Everyone claps. Ruthie turns to me. "Exactly. I know you can beat the boys, Talia." She raises her seltzer can. "To girl power!"

Since it is Friday, we get out of school today at 2:15 PM (compared to 4:00 on the other days) so we have time to prepare for Shabbat. Sunset comes a little earlier each week. By December 21, the shortest day of the year, Shabbat rolls in at the crazy hour of 4:00 PM. Today candle-lighting is at 5:17 PM.

"You are so lucky to live close to school," Liora says on our walk home. "I'd be in the car for another thirty minutes, at least."

"I guess, except when it's freezing and Doris makes me walk home. Still, sometimes it would be nice not to live in a fishbowl," I comment.

"What's that supposed to mean?" Liora says, putting her hands in her pockets.

"Everyone knowing your business, people dropping by all the time. Sometime I think I'd like to walk down the street and not have anyone recognize me."

"Trust me, Talia. You wouldn't like it for long. My neighborhood is pretty boring, especially on Shabbat. I don't have any friends on my street."

"So why don't you guys move here? There's a house for sale on my block!"

Liora stops in her tracks, and looks at me like I'm clueless.

"Uh, because the houses here cost three times as much as they do in Hillsdale."

How could I say something that stupid? "Right. Forgot about that."

"I mean, it's not like my parents haven't looked," Liora says, kicking a stone on the sidewalk, "but at this point, we could just about afford a shack right on the main street."

Just as Liora finishes that statement, we walk up the driveway to my house, which for some reason looks even larger than it did this morning.

"I really hope Gabbers isn't around right now," I whisper. "I'm not in the mood."

"Hey, I want to meet this mystery guest."

"Don't worry—you will." I push open the door and see Doris washing the marble foyer floor. She seems surprised to see us.

"Hi, Doris!" I say. The house feels toasty warm.

"Oh, you girls home early!" she says, squeezing out the mop. "Watch out, it's wet over there."

"You remember Liora?" I say.

Doris smiles. "Of course I do. Haven't seen you in a while, though. Where you been? You got even prettier than the last time I see you."

"Thanks," Liora says, blushing. "Should I take off my shoes?"

"Yeah, just drop them in the basket," Doris says. "Just like Chinese do."

Doris.

I glance at Liora, but she just laughs, then slips off her flats.

"When the other girls coming?" Doris asks me.

"Probably just before Shabbat," I say, hanging up my coat. "They went home first to help out and get their stuff. We have the basement, right?"

Doris shakes her head. "Upstairs. All your friends sleeping in your room."

"But Mom said we could have the downstairs," I protest.

"That was until your father invited Mr. Jared."

"Who?"

"The nice boy that work for him. You know. He ate here once."

"Oh, him," I say, remembering the college student who came the Friday night Gabrielle arrived. "But he's only one person. He doesn't need the whole downstairs. You must have misunderstood my dad."

"No, I didn't," Doris says firmly. "Your father said Mr. Jared is not allowed to sleep on the same floor as all the girls."

"But that's the point. The four of us are supposed to be downstairs!"

"And what about Miss Gabrielle?" Doris asks, her hands on her hips.

I take out my phone. "I'm calling my dad."

Doris picks up the bucket. "Go ahead, princess. Now bring Liora's bag upstairs and offer her a snack like a good host."

"Doris!"

"It's okay, Tal," Liora says, "I really don't care where I sleep."

"I do! And my mom promised."

Doris lugs the bucket to the kitchen. "See you later, sweetheart."

I turn to Liora. "This always happens. Plans change day by day. I never know who is staying in my own house. And why does Jared whatever-his-last-name-is get priority over my friends?"

"It'll be cozy in your room," Liora says.

I know she is just trying to make me feel better. In school I made a big deal about us getting our own guest suite. Now Shifra and Ruthie will be disappointed. I feel the seed of a bad mood growing inside me.

"Let's go to my room. Then I'll call my Dad."

Liora follows me upstairs. I pause in front of the guest room. The door is closed and I can hear the shower running. I motion toward the room, and whisper, "She's in there."

Then I open my bedroom door. Doris has worked her Friday magic. Everything looks neat and smells fresh and lemony. There are three rolled sleeping bags next to my bed and a stack of pillows.

"I love your room!" Liora says. She points to the lava lamp. "Is that new?"

"Yeah. A birthday present from my grandmother. Isn't it cool? I like watching it in the dark when I'm trying to fall asleep."

She walks over to my bedside table and picks up a book. "*Magic Numbers?* Are you planning on putting a spell on someone?"

"Ha ha. Actually it's a really good book."

"If you say so. I'm the one who is going to need some magic numbers for the math team. Yesterday I tried a couple practice problems that were in the booklet. I got them all wrong." Liora sits down on my bed. "I still can't believe Dr. Janas recommended me."

I feel a stab of guilt. "Liora, you have to believe in yourself first. Be more confident."

"You sound like Shifra."

"But it's true. You'll never win if you think you're gonna lose." I can hear Mom in my own words.

My phone rings. It's my father. I launch my complaint about the sleeping arrangements. Dad apologizes but says it is important that Jared stays over for this Shabbat. He doesn't say why, of course. My parents never tell me anything about our guests. Dad reminds me that it wouldn't be proper for him to sleep on the same floor as Gabrielle and my friends.

"But he's going to leave right after Shabbat," Dad says, trying to console me, "and you girls may use the basement Saturday night, and if it's okay with their parents, your friends can sleep over, too."

This idea lifts my spirits. "Okay. Thanks, Dad." I hang up and then tell Liora the news.

"I doubt my mom will let me sleep over two nights in a row," she says, flipping through the math book.

"What if... we say we're going to have our first study session?"

Liora's face lights up. "For real?"

"Sure. I mean, not the whole night. Shabbat ends early. We'll have lots of time to hang out." I hand Liora the phone. "First ask your mom how her day was. Then tell her about school, and then ask her about sleeping over."

I sit next to Liora while she talks to her mom, or rather, answers all her mom's questions. Liora's mother is just about the most overprotective mom on the planet. And when it comes to school, she is expected to bring home a report card decorated with A's. Liora's phone conversation is all one syllable words.

"Yes... no... no... yes... fine... great... ok... sure... of course... no... I know..."

Then she brings up the math team.

"It will give us a jump start on the competition," Liora says into the phone.

I give her the thumbs up.

"Of course they're going to be home. It was her dad's idea," she says, a hint of exasperation in her voice.

She is silent for a moment. "Okay. Right. I will. Yes, thanks so much, Mom. Have a great Shabbat!"

She hangs up the phone. "Wahoo!"

"Sounds like you had to pass a test," I say.

"No kidding, and if it wasn't your family I doubt she'd have said yes." Liora leans back on my bed. "Your bed is so comfy. I could fall asleep right now."

"Oh, no you don't!" I pull the pillow out from under her head.

"Stop it!" she laughs.

One thing about Liora is that she never gets enough sleep at night. She's always dozing off during class. "And if you fall asleep on us tonight, prepare for the consequences!" I say, pointing my finger.

Liora groans and sits up. "Okay, maybe I'll take a shower now."

Shifra and Ruthie arrive half an hour before Shabbat. I quickly brief them on the sleeping arrangements as we head upstairs to my room.

"That's cool with me," Ruthie says. "I hope I can get out of babysitting my brothers Saturday night, though."

"You've got to," I say. "When else do we get to do this?"

"You're right."

Liora greets us in a gray and black sweater with silver sequins on the neckline. Her hair is still wet from the shower.

"Hi, guys," she says to Ruthie and Shifra. "Did you hear the good news?"

"Absolutely," Shifra replies, dropping her overnight bag. "Nice going. A two-nighter."

"Okay, I set the timer on my lamp to go off at midnight," I announce.

"Fine with me," Ruthie says. "But Liora will never stay awake that late."

Shifra laughs. "That's just what I was thinking!"

"Very funny," Liora says as she combs her perfectly straight black hair. "You guys don't have to get up at six o'clock every morning."

Ruthie checks herself in my dresser mirror. "Can you tell I'm wearing blush?"

We all study her face. "Nope. Looks natural to me," I reply.

"My mother won't let me wear a trace of makeup," Liora says. No one is surprised.

"You don't need it," Ruthie says. "You have a perfect complexion."

"I look so pale," Shifra says, bending over. "I tried blush once, but ended up looking like a clown."

"It probably was the wrong shade," Ruthie replies. "And you have to know just where to apply it." She sucks in her cheeks. "It goes on the—"

There is a knock on my door.

"Hi, y'all!" Gabrielle says when I open the door. She is wearing a blue bathrobe. "Heard you were having a powwow this Shabbat." I notice the skirts hanging over her arm.

She catches me off guard. "Uh, yeah. My friends—"

"Hi!" Ruthie calls out. "I met you at the Shabbat Club. Ruthie Braitman."

"Right, and—" Gabrielle looks behind me. "You're Shifra? The group was at your house?"

"That's right," Shifra says. "And this is Liora. She wasn't there that Shabbat. She lives kinda out there."

"Nice to meet you," Liora says. "I live in Hillsdale and it's not so out there."

"I'm Gabrielle. What school do you go to?"

"I'm in Talia's class," Liora replies.

Gabrielle's face registers a hint of surprise. Guess she hasn't met many Jewish Chinese girls.

"Her mom's our art teacher," I add.

"You girls are so lucky to go to a Jewish school," Gabrielle says. "I had to do the post-high-school crash course." She laughs at her own joke. "Anyway, I am really looking forward to another Shabbat here. Talia's mom is the greatest cook. Well, I suppose you guys have eaten here before. Her parents have been so welcoming to me. I don't know

85

if Talia told you, but I'm on leave from a New York City dance career. Kinda starting over, you could say. Looking for a job. This is my first trip to Boston. I'm from the South in case you couldn't tell from the accent."

Gabrielle looks at the skirts hanging on her arm. "Oh, I almost forgot why I knocked! This afternoon I went shopping at a consignment store on Hartford Street—what a place! Anyway, I picked up these skirts, but now I'm just not sure, I mean, I really wished I had a friend along to help me." Gabrielle goes on about the lady in the store who sold her the skirts. Shifra, Ruthie, Liora, and I just stand there waiting for Gabrielle to take a breath. "And so, I was wondering if you guys will be honest with me—"

Ruthie jumps up from my bed. "That's my department!"

"Definitely," Shifra adds. "Ruthie is our fashion queen."

"Oh, thank you so much," Gabrielle says, stepping further into my room. "Now you have to be honest. I love unique clothing, but sometimes I get a little carried away." She holds up the first skirt, a purple and brown paisley one that flares out.

"Okay, that is really stylish," Ruthie says, "but I have to see it on you to know for sure."

I stifle my laugh. Ruthie can be very dramatic.

"Do I have time to try it on before Shabbat?" Gabrielle asks me.

I check the clock. "We've got fifteen minutes."

"I'll be quick," she replies, and then dashes across the hallway.

Liora is covering her mouth to keep from laughing out loud.

"Wow, Talia, you were right." Ruthie makes a gabbing sign with her hand. "This is gonna be fun."

Gabrielle comes right back and twirls around in the doorway.

"Stunning," Ruthie gasps.

I hope Ruthie is telling the truth. I'm not so sure.

"I totally agree," Shifra says.

"Me, too," Liora says, giggling.

"I think this is my favorite," Gabrielle says. "Okay, next one." And she's off to change again.

The second skirt is black leather with silver studs around the hem and a thick chain belt. "Now I know this is a little off-beat," Gabrielle says, "but, it kind of called out to me."

All four of us just stare. I don't know what to say.

"Uh, that one kind of calls out 'punk rocker'," Ruthie says honestly. "Maybe better in Manhattan than Greensborough."

Gabrielle looks down at herself. "Oh. Yeah, I see what you mean." For a second I think she is going to cry. "I know every Jewish community has its dress standards... Then she looks up, her eyes bright, and smiles. "Well, I asked you to be honest. The lady said I have a week to return it." She takes a deep breath. "Skirt number three coming right up."

"I hope this one is better than number two," I say as we wait.

"I can't believe you said that."

Ruthie throws her arms up. "What? I'm going to let her go to shul wearing that?"

"She *is* strange," Liora whispers.

Skirt number three is brown suede with small fringes on the hem.

"Ooh. Retro," Ruthie exclaims. "I like it. Turn around."

"Do you think it's too tight?" Gabrielle asks.

Ruthie re-examines the skirt. "No, you're skinny enough to make it work."

The skirt *does* look good on her, but I know my mother wouldn't let me wear it. Then again, I'm not twenty-three years old.

"Well, two out of three's not bad," Gabrielle says. "I'm so glad I didn't get the other seven. Thanks again. See y'all downstairs." Then she closes the door.

Ruthie looks at me. "Was she serious?"

Ten

I love Shabbat when my friends sleep over. I love sitting at the dinner table with them and pretending they are my sisters. I know this probably sounds weird, but if you're an Only, I bet you understand. I've always wanted a sister or two, and if it is God's will that my mother only give birth once, why couldn't I have had a twin?

Tonight, when Ruthie, Shifra, and Liora stood beside me while I lit my Shabbat candle, I said a silent prayer asking for a sibling (or two). I used to do that all the time, but after a while I sort of gave up. When I was little, Mom used to tell me that the heavens were open when we lit Shabbat candles, and that I should pray for people who are sick or in need of something. I remember looking up at her as she stood in the glow of the candles, her hands covering her face. I'd wait there a moment for her to finish praying. Once I asked what took her so long. She told me she was praying for all the ladies who were wishing for a baby. It was only later that I realized she was also praying for herself.

My dad brought home just one guest from shul tonight. What a relief. Mr. Delinski is a nice man who is like ninety years old. He is seated next to Dad at the head of the table. Next to Mr. Delinski is Jared Samuels, who is sitting across from Gabrielle. My mom is in charge of seating. I think some match-making is going on here. Gabrielle is wearing her new paisley skirt with a purple turtleneck and feather earrings (weird). Her hair is swept up in a loose bun. I notice she is wearing makeup and lip gloss. Dressed to impress, perhaps? I'm sitting on the other side of my dad, across from Mom and next to Liora, Shifra, and Ruthie.

I know my friends are all watching Gabrielle, who is providing a lot of entertainment. Between singing *Shalom Aleichem* and the first course of the meal, she must have asked my dad twenty-five questions. Then Jared starts asking her about the New York City Ballet and we all get an earful of wacky stories. Ruthie, Shifra, Liora, and I are trying real hard not to crack up, relying on our communication mode of knowing looks, smirks, and under-the-table kicks.

After dinner my father walks Mr. Delinski to his apartment. My friends and I help clear the table and rinse the dishes. Wow, it is so much more fun to clean up with friends. Jared and Gabrielle retreat to the living room. Oh boy.

Ruthie whispers in my ear as I brush the crumbs off the tablecloth. "I am dying to know what they are talking about."

I give Ruthie the 'watch out, my mom is nearby' look. I have to admit, I'm kind of curious, too. I sure hope this is one of those quick matches so that Gabrielle will be on her way soon. My cousin got engaged after five dates. Can't quite imagine doing that, but it does happen. Pretty common among the very religious Jews. They get right down to business once they want to get married. Hmm... eight dates seems lucky.

"Thank you, girls," Mom says, as we carry the last dishes to the sink. "It's a treat to have all this help."

"Anytime, Mrs. Schumacher," Ruthie replies. "The brisket was delicious, by the way."

"And so were the lemon squares," Shifra adds.

"Thank you. There's plenty left over for tomorrow, and I've made some apple muffins for the morning. I'll leave them on the table. Why don't you girls go upstairs and get changed?"

"But it's only nine o'clock," I say. "Can't we hang out in the family room?"

"Actually, I'd prefer if you went upstairs. You don't have to go to sleep yet."

My mother gives me one of her looks, and then I get it. She doesn't want us down here while Gabbers and Jared are on their "date." This is really going too far. But, I decide not to push the matter, since I won the basement for tomorrow night.

I look at my friends, who are waiting politely for my direction. "So… you guys want to get in our pajamas early and hang out in my room?"

"That sounds cozy," Mom says, smiling.

Okay, I get the hint.

"My mom would kill me if she knew I was sleeping on the floor," Liora says, once we are all settled in my room for the night.

I sit up in my bed. "Why?"

"Dust mites in the carpet," she replies.

"You're joking," Ruthie says.

"She thinks it will make my asthma flare up."

"I didn't know you had asthma," Ruthie fluffs her pillow.

Liora sighs. "I don't. Well, I did, but that was when I was four."

"You should have told me, Liora," I say. "I'd have gotten Doris to blow up the air mattress before Shabbat. Do you want to sleep in my bed?"

"No, thanks." She turns on her side. "I'll live dangerously."

"You? Fat chance," Ruthie replies.

"I'll give you the air mattress tomorrow night."

"I thought my mom worried a lot, but your mom gets the worry award," Shifra says. "But it's just because she loves you, Liora dear."

The way Shifra says this makes us all crack up. "People who worry about things are usually control freaks," she adds.

Liora laughs. "Yup, that's my mom."

"It's very common in firstborns," Shifra says, matter-of-factly.

"Bingo," Liora replies.

"Is your mom an only child?" I ask Liora.

"No. The oldest of three."

"Hey, Shifra," I say, "if I'm the oldest and the only child, what's my personality supposed to be?"

"Firstborns are usually very intelligent, independent, perfectionistic, high-achievers," Shifra rattles off like she's reading from a textbook. "Same for only children, although they tend to be somewhat egotistical."

I laugh. "Well, I guess that describes me."

"Where do you read this stuff?" Ruthie asks.

"My dad's *Psychology Today* magazines."

"There must be a lot of worrying, perfectionistic, high-achievers in China," Liora says. "Parents are only allowed to have one child."

"Are you kidding?"

"No, for real. Didn't I ever tell you that? China was once overpopulated and people were starving. So their government made a one-child-per-family law in certain parts of the country. And it worked. It isn't so overcrowded now."

I'm shocked. "What if someone has two kids?" I ask. "What, do they take it away or something?"

"They stop giving government benefits like free school, and they charge you huge fines and make life hard. Plus, they make you feel really ashamed. They kind of brainwash people into believing one-child families are best and the right thing for the country. That's why I was abandoned as a baby."

"Abandoned? Because you were number two?"

"I'm not sure if I was number one or number two. What stinks is that most parents want to have a boy, because boys are more valued and carry on the family name. It's an old cultural thing."

"That makes no sense!" Ruthie exclaims. "Girls rule!"

"Not in China," Liora says.

"So that's how you ended up in an orphanage?" Ruthie asks.

"Yup, and I would still be there if I hadn't been adopted."

We are all quiet as we consider that. I'm curious if Liora knows anything about her birth mother, but that might be too personal, or make her feel bad in case she doesn't know a thing. It occurs to me that in China, maybe one is not a lonely number.

"Gabbers is an only child," I say. Then suddenly we are all cracking up again, just thinking about her.

"Did you notice how loud she talks?" Ruthie says.

"And how much?" I add.

"I told you, guys," Shifra said. "She is hiding some trauma."

"Maybe she got booed during a dance performance?" Ruthie says, which sends us into hysterics again.

"Shhh, you guys," I say, trying to stifle my laughter. "She might hear us."

Ruthie lowers her voice. "I bet she's still talking to Jared. Let's listen for her to come upstairs and then ask her how the date went."

I throw a pillow at Ruthie. "No way! My mom would *not* approve of that."

Ruthie throws the pillow back at me. "I'm just curious. I bet she did most of the talking."

"I wouldn't be surprised if she tells us all about it in the morning," Liora says. "That is, if we kind of just asked her a leading question."

"You guys are nosy," Shifra says.

"Why honey, we're just *curious*," Ruthie replies, imitating Gabrielle's southern accent.

"Do you guys ever wonder who you're gonna marry?" Liora blurts out.

"Are you hinting something?" Ruthie teases.

"No! Just, you know, the person you are going to marry is somewhere in the world right now. Right? So, like, don't you ever wonder what he is doing at this very minute?"

We are all quiet for a second, pondering Liora's question.

"What if he lives right here or goes to our shul?" Shifra says.

"Or the boys' school," I add.

"That is too weird," Liora laughs.

"Oooh, I'm getting a vision!" Ruthie says, excitedly. She stands up on her sleeping bag. "It's Liora's future husband. He's lives far, far away… and it's now Shabbat morning and he's getting ready to go to shul. He's eating rice for breakfast and he's holding… chopsticks!"

Everyone laughs at Ruthie.

"Very funny," Liora says. "I seriously doubt I'll find a Jewish Chinese guy to marry."

"There must be a lot of men in China if they are giving away all the girls!" Ruthie exclaims.

"I'm sure you want to have more than one kid."

"Definitely," Liora says. "How many kids do you want, Tal?"

"At least four."

"And she'll give them numbers for names," Ruthie laughs.

Liora yawns. "Ohhh, I... think three is nice."

"Hey!" Ruthie says, hitting Liora on the head with her pillow. "No falling asleep on us yet!"

"Stop! I can't help it. As soon as I lie down—"

There is a soft knock on the door. Probably Mom telling us to be quiet.

"Talia?"

Yikes, it's Gabbers! Everyone starts giggling.

"Quiet, guys!" I whisper. "Uh, yeah?" I call from my bed.

"Can I come in for a sec?"

"Sure."

Gabrielle opens the door halfway and peeks her head in. "Hi, y'all. Sounds like you're having a fun slumber party." Her cheeks are flushed.

"Oh, were we too loud?" Ruthie asks earnestly.

"No, no. I just heard you as I came upstairs and was reminded of the sleepovers I used to go to, and how we stayed up till three AM talking and giggling."

"We'll go to sleep soon," I say. "Got to get up for shul. We'll try not to make any more noise."

"Don't worry about it," Gabrielle says, waving her hand. "Girls' laughter is a happy sound. For me at least. Well, good night, sleep tight, and don't let the bedbugs bite." Then she closes the door, and we all collapse with laughter once again.

Eleven

It's Sunday afternoon, and I've finished all my homework for tomorrow, except for the dumb personification poem I'm supposed to write for English, but I'll get back to that tonight. I'm waiting for my mom to get home from her sisterhood meeting so I can ask her to drive me to the mall to get new sneakers. If my mom isn't at work, entertaining guests, or at the gym, she's in a meeting. I don't even know where my dad went. Maybe to the store. So, it's one of those rare moments when I'm alone in my own house. Gabrielle is out visiting someone named Ashley, an old dancer friend who now lives in Back Bay. Maybe Ashley will ask Gabrielle to move in with her.

Last night Shifra, Ruthie, Liora, and I had so much fun. We found an old home video of our fourth grade Chanukah play and just laughed and laughed at how little we looked (and how big we thought we were). We made popcorn, brownies, and root beer floats. Then Ruthie said we had to burn off the calories, so we played tennis on the Wii and then did Dance Dance Revolution, which my friends like a lot more than I do. Anyway, around eleven o'clock Mom came downstairs to tell us it was time to go to sleep. That's when Liora had a panic attack. She suddenly remembered that we hadn't studied any math, and that was the whole reason she was supposed to be sleeping over Saturday night, and now she would get in big trouble for lying.

Ruthie said that Liora's mom would never know whether or not she really studied. Liora insisted she would know. "I just can't lie to

94

her," she told us.

Shifra said Liora suffers from a guilt complex. I decided to solve the problem by getting up early Sunday morning to do some math practice with her. Well, this solved the problem of being truthful, but now there is another problem. Liora doesn't seem to get the math. And I don't get why. I mean, she does great in her class, and Dr. Janas even said her score on the preliminary exam was good. Maybe she's just nervous or not used to these kinds of problems. One thing is for sure. Liora's going to need more prep time than I thought.

I hear my mom open the front door. I jump up from my desk, and head downstairs.

"Hi, Mom!"

"Got your homework done?" I get the vibes that Mom's not in the best mood.

"Ninety percent. I'm ready for a break, and I was really hoping you could drive me to the mall. I need sneakers."

"Talia, I really don't feel up to shopping right now. The last time I took you shoe shopping you didn't like anything, and it took six stores until we found a pair."

"That was for Shabbat shoes, Mom. Sneakers are much easier to find."

"How about next week?" She hangs up her coat.

"But I only have one pair that fits, and they're falling apart."

Mom sighs and drops her keys on the table. "I'm pretty tired."

Tired? My mother tired in the middle of the afternoon? "Are you feeling okay?"

"Just been doing too much, probably. I think I'll just take a quick rest."

"And then can we go?" I push.

Lo and behold, Gabbers walks in the door interrupting this important moment. She's wearing a denim jacket with rhinestones and a swirly black skirt.

"Hi there!" she sings.

My mother immediately perks up. "Did you have a good time with your friend?"

"It was wonderful!" Gabrielle practically shouts. "I still can't believe I found Ashley. She trained at City Ballet with me, and now she's teaching at the Boston Ballet School! So lucky." Gabrielle starts talking faster. "And, she married someone from the company. Alex Forrest. Fantastic dancer and incredibly handsome. They have a cute little apartment and a poodle named Balanchine, you know, after the famous choreographer? Anyway, it was so nice to see someone from my past. Someone I actually know in this city. And she said we could get together again. I might even take her adult ballet class."

"Well, I'm so glad it worked out for you," Mom says. "Maybe you can invite them over for a Shabbat meal."

Oh, great.

"Wow, that's very nice of you," Gabrielle says. "But they're not Jewish."

"That doesn't matter," Mom replies. "Any of your friends are welcome here."

Mom looks at me. Oh, no. She has that look on her face. "Gabrielle, are you busy right now?"

Gabbers shakes her head. "Nothing planned. Can I help you with something?"

"Actually, Talia is dying to get to the mall for new sneakers, and I'm a bit tired right—"

"Oh, I'd love to!"

"Great. You can take my car. It's only a few miles away. Talia can direct you, I'm sure." My mother reaches in her purse and pulls out a wad of cash, then hands it to me. Put this in your wallet. Let's keep it to sixty dollars. Sound reasonable?"

"Thanks. Do you care which brand I get?"

"You're the one who has to wear them."

I am not thrilled about going with Gabbers, but I guess it's better than not going at all. Mom always looks at everything in such a practical way, but she just doesn't get that I want to spend some time with her. And I can't exactly say that at the moment.

"Okay. I'm ready when you are," I tell Gabrielle.

The Brookside is my favorite mall. They don't play loud, annoying music or have mini shopping stands all over the place. There's a huge skylight and a white grand piano on the lower level with someone actually playing show tunes, jazz, and classical music. When I was little, I always tried to count the number of steps on the mall escalator. After I turned twelve, Mom started letting me go to the mall with my friends, as long as we stayed together and had a cell phone. Liora's mom doesn't let her go to the mall with her friends unless an adult is with them at all times. That kind of misses the point.

Anyway, Gabbers still hasn't stopped talking the whole time since we got into the car, parked, and rode up the glass elevator to Macy's. While I'm trying on a pair of Nikes, she is checking out the ankle boots on display. These are pretty comfortable sneakers, but kind of boring. I mean, I really don't care, but suddenly I am thinking of what Ruthie would say. She always looks for a fashion flair in every piece of clothing she wears. Then I spot some Skechers, which come in a few colors. Hmm. Maybe not the best sneakers, but they do look pretty cool. So I try those on and they fit great.

"Hey, those are funky," Gabrielle says as I check out my feet in the mirror.

I shrug. "Not sure they are practical. At least for gym."

"Practical? Hey, do you like them? Do they make you smile? Let's see you jump. Come on."

I look around me to make sure no one is watching and then I jump.

"Run around a bit!" Gabrielle urges me.

"In here?"

"Why not? If the shoe fits, run in it!"

I roll my eyes, and then I start walking across the carpeted area as fast as I can.

"They look great!" Gabrielle hollers.

A few customers turn to look at her. My cheeks redden.

I circle around where she is standing. "Okay, I'll get these," I say, hoping to make a quick exit.

Gabrielle picks up the same pair in orange. "But which color?"

"Not orange, that's for sure, but... I like the pale blue." I look down at the white ones I'm wearing. "Do they have size six?"

Gabrielle starts going through the stack of boxes. "Got it!"

"I'm not sure which one to pick," I say.

"Get 'em both," Gabrielle gushes. "A girl can never have too many shoes."

I smile. "Tell that to my mom."

"But these are only thirty dollars. You have sixty to spend. What a great deal. Two for the price of one."

I consider her logic. "Maybe I will. I can wear one for gym and the other for everyday."

"Oh, now, wait a minute…" Gabrielle opens another shoebox. "They also come in lime… and… here's a lavender one…"

"Hmm, that's nice. Maybe I'll get lavender instead of the blue."

But Gabrielle doesn't stop going through the shoes until she has collected five other pairs of Skechers in size six of different colors.

"Will you look at that?" she says, hands on her hips. "They've got a color for every day of the week."

"Well, I think these two will be enough—"

Her green eyes widen. "I say, get them all!"

I smile. "Right." I look around. "Where do we pay?"

Gabrielle starts putting the shoes back in the boxes. "It will be my treat. You've been so nice to me. I'm sure it isn't easy having so many guests all the time."

I can't believe what she is saying. "No really, that's too much. You don't have to do that. These two pairs are fine—"

"Don't be silly, Talia. I've got a charge card. Hey, do any of your friends wear size six? You could lend them out, rent them for a day! Or heck, give them away if you want!" Her voice is getting louder. "Any birthdays coming up? A color for every outfit—"

"Gabrielle, really, um, I don't need that many, and I think my mom would get mad at me."

She looks at me as if I said something that made no sense. "Don't you worry. It's my idea, my gift. And, tell you what. We won't spring them on her all at once. Come on. Let's go!"

I watch her head toward the checkout counter, balancing the stack of five boxes in her arms. I quickly pick up my white and blue pairs, and then go after her. A nervous feeling hits my stomach.

"Wait!"

But she doesn't seem to hear me. She is already chatting with the cashier.

"A pair for every day of the week! Isn't that something?" Gabrielle says, handing over her credit card.

I tap her arm. "Gabrielle, you don't have to—"

"And this young lady here is going to buy Sunday and Monday with her own money," Gabrielle announces, her Texas accent sounding very strong.

The cashier looks at me, smiling politely. "Aren't the colors great?" she says. "I think you are the first customer to buy seven pairs."

I smile. Seven. Heaven. The color of a rainbow.

Twelve

"She bought all *five* of them?" Shifra whispers to me across the table Monday afternoon.

"And all in size six," I say. We are huddled at a table in the back of the library during study hall. "And I haven't told my mom yet."

"That is so cool," Ruthie says.

"More like crazy," I whisper.

Shifra nods. "I agree."

"Can I have the lime pair?" Ruthie asks.

"You're not taking this seriously," Shifra says.

"What?" Ruthie whispers. "She's a shopaholic. Who cares?"

Shifra chews on the end of her pen. "I think it's more than that."

"Maybe that's just her way of being nice," Liora suggests. "You know, southern hospitality."

"But I wish you could have seen her," I say to my friends. "She acted like it was the most normal thing in the world."

Shifra leans forward. "I suspect mania."

"What's that?" Liora whispers.

"It's when your brain gets all fired up, and you become hyper, and you have tons of energy, and you think you can do anything."

"Sounds great to me," Ruthie says.

"It's an illness, stupid," Shifra replies. "And you don't always make good decisions when you're having an episode."

Ruthie shrugs. "Still, I could use some mania. Is it contagious?"

Liora and I start cracking up. Hannah Finkelstein appears at our table, her arms crossed. "Can you guys be quiet? Some of us are trying to study."

"Give me a break, Hannah," Ruthie says. "Like you don't talk during study hall."

"We have a grammar quiz next period, in case you've forgot."

"Forgotten, you mean," I say, flipping open my grammar book.

Ruthie laughs. "Since when do you need quiet? Seems like you always have something to say."

Hannah huffs and walks away.

"Seems like she could use some mania," Ruthie comments.

I put my head down and try not to laugh. "You're gonna get us kicked out of the library."

Liora starts giggling which gets Shifra going, too.

"Okay, girls. Tone it down," the librarian calls out. "Final warning."

I see Hannah look up from her textbook. She glares at us triumphantly.

Shifra opens her notebook and writes something in big letters, then holds it up for us all to see:

TO BE CONTINUED...

English is the last period of the day. Mrs. Wordsworth reads us a short poem by Carl Sandburg called "Fog." It's supposed to demonstrate good use of personification, which, if you didn't know, is describing a non-living thing by using characteristics of a person. Like, *the sun's fingers touched my shoulder.* Hey, I just made that up! Not bad.

Last night, before I went to bed, I wrote my personification poem, and I think it is pretty good. So, I plan to do something I don't usually do in English class: volunteer to read my own writing.

"Talia?" Mrs. Wordsworth asks the second she sees my hand go up. I can tell she is trying not to act surprised.

I hear a soft giggle from Hannah Finkelstein, but it doesn't faze me. I walk up in front of the classroom, holding my paper. I wait until I have everyone's attention (something my mom always told me to do in public speaking) and then I begin. As soon as I read the title, a warm confidence glows inside me.

One

The number One stands alone,
Tall and thin, disappearing amongst the crowd.
A shapeless entity.
The color white.
The taste of air.
One is the sound of silence.
Its voice barely audible until it stands next to another.
Number One yearns to unite with the others.
One is a lonely number.

The class is quiet when I finish. Then Ruthie claps and a few others follow.

"Kind of weird," Hannah mutters.

"We don't use that language when responding to a poem," Mrs. Wordsworth snaps. "Hannah, can you think of another way to phrase your reaction?"

Hannah looks up at the ceiling, trying to keep a straight face. "Uh, how about, *strange?*"

Mrs. Wordsworth purses her lips. "Anyone else?"

Malki Sneiderman raises her hand. "I really liked it. I mean, I've never thought about a number in that way, but since I am a twin I've always known doubles of things. And I think it would be really lonely to be just one."

Mrs. Wordsworth nods in agreement. "An excellent observation, Malki. Poetry can help us look at something in a way we never would have considered before." Mrs. Wordsworth smiles at me as I sit down at my desk. "And Talia, I must say that in all the years of my giving this assignment, you are the first student to personify a number. That was a very original poem."

I look over at Ruthie. She smiles knowingly and gives me the thumbs up.

After school, Hannah, Liora, and I sit around Dr. Janas' desk for the first math team practice. It feels rather awkward.

"So, girls, how have your preparations been going?"

Liora bites her lip and doesn't say anything. I don't know what to say, but Hannah does, of course.

"Is there any rule against having an outside tutor?"

I think I'm going to strangle her.

Dr. Janas raises her eyebrows. "Well, no, of course not, but I highly doubt any of you would need one."

Hannah looks at me.

"She's not my tutor!" I blurt out.

"Prove it."

"I don't have to—"

Dr. Janas interrupts. "Talia, can you clue me in?"

"Hannah has this crazy idea that the person staying at my house is my math tutor."

Dr. Janas frowns. "Hannah, there are no regulations against outside coaching—"

"But she's not my coach! She's just a guest."

Dr. Janas holds up her hand. "Fine. I believe you, but frankly what matters right now is teamwork and I'm getting an uneasy feeling that you girls are not functioning as a team." Dr. Janas leans back in her chair. "Well?"

"I've been studying with Talia," Liora says quietly.

"See? They don't even include me!" Hannah complains.

I look at Hannah. "We just got started. There's plenty of time."

"And that is just what we are wasting right now," Dr. Janas says, crossing her legs. I can't help noticing her navy pumps. I wonder if she has them in other colors. "Let's get a few things straight, shall we?" Dr. Janas says. "First of all, the more you three work together, the better chance you will have on the team part of the competition. As far as the individual test goes, well, each of you will have to decide what works best. Hebrew Academy has not won the team competition for eight years." My ears perk up when she says that number. I see eight wearing a gold crown. "Two years ago Aaron Zweiler placed second in the individual, and last year, Yosef Samuels came in third."

Hannah frowns. "No girls?"

"Not in the top three, at least since I've been here." Dr. Janas folds her arms. "So, does that bit of info motivate you girls to put aside the pettiness and get to work?"

Hannah looks down at her contest booklet and nods her head.

Dr. Janas looks at me and Liora.

"Yeah. Sure, I'm ready," I say.

Liora lines up three colored pens on her desk. "Me, too."

Dr. Janas stands up and walks to the whiteboard. "Okay, then, here's a problem from last year's test." She picks up a green marker and starts writing. "I want you to copy this on your paper. Sometimes the act of rewriting the problem jump-starts your brain, and you are less likely to miss an important detail, like a square or negative sign."

$$975 \times 935 \times 972 \times (?) =$$

What is the smallest number you can substitute for the question mark, if you want to get an answer (product) with the last four digits as 0?

Dr. Janas sits down in her swivel chair. "And now, girls, I'm going to be a fly on the wall. I'll listen and observe how you approach and solve the problem, but I won't say a thing until you're done." She looks at her gold watch. "You've got ten minutes."

At first we all just sit there, staring at the problem. Liora twirls her hair. Hannah starts writing. I stare out the window, letting my brain take over.

"Well?" Hannah says to me.

"I'm thinking."

"You're supposed to think out loud."

"That's not how I work, just give me a second."

Hannah sighs and then goes back to her calculations. Liora looks at me with a worried expression, which makes me lose my train of thought. I really wish Dr. Janas weren't sitting here watching. I mean, it's kind of intimidating. I hope she doesn't have second thoughts about Liora. I look at the problem. Those nines are chocolate brown which makes me hungry.

After a couple of minutes, Liora seems to have an inspiration. She picks up her pen and starts scribbling. I go back to my thoughts and let the numbers wrap around my brain.

"Are you spacing out or something?" Hannah says.

Gosh, she's annoying. "Would you stop? I told you, I'm *thinking*."

"But we're supposed to work together, and how are we going to know what you're thinking? And we only have ten minutes—"

"Shut up!" As soon as the words escape my mouth, I want to take them back. I can't believe I said it.

Hannah throws her pencil at me. Liora groans. Dr. Janas taps her manicured fingernails on the desk and just stares at us. And so, our first practice session gets off to a great start.

I walk out of the school building with Liora, neither of us saying anything. Liora's mom and brother are parked outside waiting for her. Mrs. Clark lowers the car window and smiles at us.

"Hi, Mrs. Clark," I say, trying to sound cheerful.

Her face is full of expectation. "How did it go?"

"Okay," Liora says, opening the car door.

Liora's eight-year-old brother, Adam, is sitting in the back seat engrossed in his Gameboy.

She turns to me. "I'll call you, Tal."

I force a smile. "Yeah. Later."

As I watch them drive away, I get that nervous feeling in the pit of my stomach. It's that uh-oh feeling that you can't quite name. Except this time I know what it is, because I not only got myself into it, but Liora, too, *and* her mother. I remember that her mom and her brother have to stay longer on math practice days. They probably won't get home until six.

I walk home alone. The November chill and gray sky match my mood. I look at the addresses on each house I pass, and multiply the digits, then look for patterns. This keeps my mind off Hannah. Let's see… 21, 25, 47, 67. All odd. One square number so far. Add up the digits and get 3, 7, 11, 13. Four primes in a row. I always thought it was interesting that 1 isn't a prime number.

At least I can vent to Doris, I think as I unlock the front door.

"Hey, Doris!" I take off my coat and shoes and lug my backpack over to the stairs. "Doris?" The stillness of the house surprises me.

I walk into the kitchen. Everything is clean and shiny. I see a note on the table.

Talia, Sorry I couldn't stay. Your dad be home at 7 and mom at 8. Miss Gabrielle at dance class. Tuna casserole for dinner to warm up and salad in fridge. Please put away your clean clothes I left upstairs. Okay? Be good, sunshine. Love, Doris.

I stare at the heart Doris drew next to her name. I bite my bottom lip and suddenly I am crying. I feel so alone, like the number One. Hey, I am alone. There is no one around to talk to. Not even Gabbers. It's not like this hasn't happened before. But today things are just different, and I don't feel like being alone right now.

I pour myself a glass of chocolate milk and sit down at the table. I am in no mood to do my homework. I think about calling Ruthie. Maybe she can come over and keep me company. That's when I see the message light on our phone blinking. Doris usually takes the messages. Probably another guest request.

I walk over to the phone and push the play button just in case. *Hi, Mrs. Schumacher. Jared Samuels. Just calling to thank you for a wonderful Shabbat. I really appreciate it.*

Yeah, yeah. Next.

This is a courtesy call for Naomi Schumacher from Mass General Department of Obstetrics confirming your appointment with Dr. Freeman tomorrow, Tuesday, at 1:30 PM.

I replay the message and listen more carefully. Obstetrics? *Obstetrician.* That was one of Mrs. Wordsworth's vocabulary words. It means a doctor who cares for pregnant women, who delivers *babies!* Why would my mother need an obstetrician? Unless… Then I remember her saying she was tired and couldn't drive me to the mall, and her moodiness, and her… oh my gosh, she had a stomach ache Shabbat morning. Just like Ruthie told me about her mom. She called it morning sickness. My hands are shaking. Do I erase the message? No. I'll just leave it. I won't say anything. I'll just wait… wait for her to tell me herself. Excitement buzzes in my head. I run upstairs to my room. I've got to call Ruthie.

Thirteen

"You're absolutely sure it was the obstetrics department, and not like, the gastric department or something?" Ruthie asks when I call to tell her the news.

"Positive."

"Wow, Tal. This is really exciting!"

"Our moms could both be pregnant at the same time!" I say, my voice low, even though no one else is in the house.

"That would be so awesome. Still, you better not get your hopes up. You don't know for sure. Maybe she wants to have a baby, but isn't pregnant yet."

"Yeah, I thought of that, but, just the fact that she is going to a baby doctor means something, doesn't it?" I say, looking out my bedroom window.

"Definitely. So you should watch for the symptoms. If you hear her throwing up in the bathroom you can be pretty sure."

"Eew."

"My mom threw up her breakfast every morning for three weeks," Ruthie replies.

"What else?"

"Tiredness. My mom says she can hardly keep her eyes open around three in the afternoon."

"I get the picture."

"And, be on the lookout for baby books, like *What to Expect*

When You're Expecting."

"How about her stomach. Is your mom getting bigger?" I ask.

"Uh, that doesn't happen until around four months. You'll notice her wearing looser clothing. My mom's given up belts."

"Oh." My mind is spinning, trying to think what my mom has been wearing the past week.

"Listen, Tal, I wish I could come over, but I have to babysit now. Call me pronto if you find out anything else."

"Okay. One more thing. Don't tell anyone. Not even Shifra—"

"Duh, like I would do that. Don't worry. Just be nice to your mom, even if she's cranky. Talk to you later."

I lie back on my bed and start imagining a little baby in our house. I don't care if it is a girl or boy. I'll take either one. (Although a sister would be especially nice.) Let's see, if Mom really is pregnant then the baby would be born... when? Seven more months? I'll still be thirteen. Hmm. Thirteen years older than my little sister. That means when I'm eighteen, she'll only be five, and then I'll probably spend a year in Israel, and then college.... I'll hardly see her! When she is thirteen, I'll be twenty-six, probably married, and then she'll be the only child in the house. This thought squeezes my heart. Well, who cares? I'll take whatever kind of sibling relationship I can get, even if we don't do much growing up together. Maybe she could come stay at my house every summer and help out with my kids. I could take her on trips with my family. I'll be the big sis, showing her the world.

I hear the front door open. I jump up from my bed, hoping to see Dad or Mom. I open the door and walk to the top of the stairs. "Dad?"

"Just me," Gabrielle calls out.

I am only slightly disappointed to hear that it's her. Mom's secret is swirling inside me, making me feel hyper.

"Hi," I say, walking downstairs.

Gabrielle closes the front closet. "Howdy." She's wearing a gray warm-up suit. Her hair is in a sleek bun, which makes her look taller. "First ballet class in a while. Whew. I'm wiped. It's amazing how quickly you get out of shape."

"Out of shape?" I gasp. "That's hard to believe."

Gabrielle laughs. "Well, maybe that is an exaggeration. But, I had been dancing four to six hours a day. I do feel a bit rusty."

"So you went to your friend's ballet school?"

"Yup. The Boston Ballet, where she teaches. I navigated the train system and didn't get lost, either. So much easier than New York." She sits down in the middle of the foyer and stretches her legs out, then bends forward at the waist. "Oh, do I need a good stretch." She grabs her feet, practically folding herself in half!

It hurts just watching her in that position. "Wow. You're really flexible."

"Took many years," she says, letting out a deep breath. "It's important to breathe when you stretch. You know?"

"I guess I don't do much stretching."

Gabrielle pops up like a jack-in-the-box. "Want me to show you some good ones?"

"Um, maybe another time."

"Oh. Okay." She looks down at my stocking feet. "Hey, did you show off your new sneakers?"

I nod. "I wore the blue today. Ruthie wants the lime pair." I jump down over the last stair step. "My friends couldn't believe how carried away you got."

Gabrielle stares at me and for a split second she looks confused. She picks up her silver dance bag and slings it over her shoulder. "I think I'll go shower."

"Doris left a casserole if you're interested," I say, as Gabrielle heads up the stairs. "Want me to warm it up later?"

"Uh, sure." Gabrielle looks back at me. She has a strange, faraway look. "That would be nice. Thanks."

I wait until 6:45 PM to start getting stuff ready. I figure I might at least be able to eat with Dad for once during the week. I preheat the oven and then set out four place settings on the kitchen table. I even remember the napkins. I put out two different kinds of salad dressings. Outside the kitchen window the sky is already dark. Last month at this time, I was playing basketball in the backyard. The only good thing about the days getting shorter is looking forward to Hanukkah and school snow days.

Even though Doris left us dinner, I decide to add my own touch. I open the pantry and scan the choices; maybe tomato soup would be good tonight. A can of black olives catches my eye. From the freezer I pull out a loaf of Italian bread. I defrost it in the microwave, slice it open, and slather on some butter. Then I sprinkle garlic powder. I wrap the loaves in tin foil and put them in the oven. Voilà!

"Something smells good," Gabrielle says when she comes back downstairs. She has her hair in a towel turban and her cheeks are flushed. "I'm famished. Can I help you?"

I shrug. "Want to get the drinks?"

I hear the front door open. "My dad's home." I look at my watch. "Right on time." I feel proud taking care of the dinner on my own.

"Hiho!" Dad calls. That's his trademark 'hello.'

I walk into the entryway. "Hi, Dad!"

He puts down his briefcase. "How's my girl?"

"Great."

I give him a quick hug. His shirt smells of the cool outside air. "I've got dinner all ready," I tell him proudly.

He looks surprised. "Where's Doris?"

"She had to leave early, but I've got everything under control."

"That's what I like to hear. Wish I could say that about work."

"Something happen? A robbery?"

Dad laughs. "No, not that bad."

"You didn't sell enough jewelry?"

He waves his hand. "It's a little more complicated. But hey, I'll try to park my business woes at the door." He sniffs the air. "What's for dinner?"

"Come see," I say, leading the way to the kitchen.

I don't quite understand what Dad means when he talks about having a tough day at work. He's in charge of two branches of Schumacher Jewelers. The stores are beautiful and quiet inside. What could go wrong besides a robbery or not selling enough watches or rings? Maybe one day he'll explain it to me.

Gabrielle chitchats with Dad as I get the garlic bread out of the oven, trying not to burn myself. My ears perk up when she says something about an interview tomorrow, but I don't catch the details.

Just as Dad, Gabrielle, and I are about to start eating dinner, the garage door opens. "Mom's home?" I ask.

Dad sips his soup. "Guess so."

"But it's only 7:15."

"She must have finished up early," Dad says. "Would you pass the salad?"

My heart is thumping. Should I say something about the message now? What if she plays it while we are all sitting here?

I stare at my soup, unable to eat. I hear the back door open.

"Math team practice today. Right?" Dad asks.

"Yeah."

"Feeling confident?"

"What?"

"I said, are you feeling confident?"

I nod. "So far, so good."

Then Mom walks into the kitchen. "Hi, Mom!" I say a bit too cheerfully.

"Hi, sweetie." She puts her keys and cell phone on the kitchen desk, then looks over at us. "Smells good." She is wearing her navy skirt and white silk blouse. No belt.

"Come join us," Dad says.

"You're home early, Mom."

"Yes, I decided to call it a day. I've just been so tired lately."

My stomach drops.

"Well, I'm glad you did," Dad says, pouring water into the glass next to Mom's plate. "It's a rare weekday night we can all eat together."

All?

"I don't know how you do so much," Gabrielle comments. "I thought I had a lot of energy."

Mom smiles. "Maybe my age is catching up with me." She washes her hands at the kitchen sink. "These days I really understand the morning blessing we say, you know, thanking God for giving strength to the weary?"

"Right," Gabrielle says, removing her towel turban. "I'm still

111

learning the morning prayers, but that is a good one for sure."

Mom joins us at the table. It's hard for me to look at her. I'm afraid my face will tell everything. I decide not to mention the phone message.

"Talia pulled dinner together," Dad tells Mom.

"Well, that was nice of you," Mom says, surveying the food. "Everything looks great."

"Tastes great, too," Gabrielle says, lifting a spoonful of soup.

Mom puts her napkin on her lap. "So, how was school?"

I shrug. "The usual." I try to avoid the math practice topic. "Mrs. Wordsworth liked the poem I wrote. I think I'll get an A."

"I thought you didn't like poetry," Mom says, surprised.

I tell everyone about the English assignment.

"So, once I found the right topic, it was pretty easy."

"That's fascinating," Gabrielle says. "Could I read it?"

"Sure."

"So you really think the number one is lonely?" Dad asks.

I almost choke on a piece of garlic bread. I look at Mom who is staring at me, waiting for my answer.

"Well, yeah. Don't you guys think so?"

Dad's forehead wrinkles. "I'll have to think about that one."

"I suppose it's how you look at it," Mom says thoughtfully. "I mean one could also mean unity or wholeness, right?"

Before I can say anything, Gabbers jumps in. "I think I know what Talia means. It's like that song from the sixties." Gabrielle looks at my parents. "You probably remember it from your youth." Then she starts to sing. *"One is the loneliest number...* remember?"

I feel my cheeks redden.

"Oh, of course!" Mom says and she sings another line. "One is the loneliest number, whoa, worse than two..."

"I didn't know you listened to rock music, Mom."

She shakes her head, smiling. "A 1969 classic. I was a kid when that came out."

"Never heard of it," I mutter.

"You're dating yourself, Naomi," Dad jokes. "Anyway, Talia has always had an original way of looking at numbers."

"That's for sure," Mom says.

"I remember when she first counted all the keys on the piano," Dad says. "She was about four. She threw her hands up and began chanting, 'eighty-eight, eighty-eight, great, great, great.' "

Gabrielle laughs.

I roll my eyes. I think it's time to change the subject.

Mom smiles at Dad. "Do you remember the magnetic numbers we had on the fridge?"

Oh, no. I feel an embarrassing childhood story coming.

Mom turns to Gabrielle. "Talia loved playing with those numbers, lining them up in different formations. She must have been about three at the time. Well, just before Passover, Doris cleaned the entire fridge, including the sticky magnets. She stored them in a plastic bag. Talia just threw a fit. When Doris tried to show her that the numbers were now in a new place, Talia said, 'But they need to live on the fridge because numbers get hungry, too!'"

Gabrielle, Mom, and Dad all laugh. I just smile, feeling really glad that none of my friends are here right now.

I can't fall asleep. I keep thinking about Mom and the tiny life that might be growing inside her. A life that is related to me. I wanted so badly to ask her tonight before I went to bed, but I knew it wouldn't be right. It's her secret. Then I start thinking of Gabrielle and what secret she might be hiding. I can't ask her, either. Just like Mom. I'll either have to read the clues or wait for Gabrielle to say something, to finally tell me why she is here. Or enlist the help of my friends as detectives.

I turn over in bed for the tenth time. My alarm clock glows 11:15 PM. One plus one plus one plus five. *Eight. Eight, eight, eight is great.* I chant this silly rhyme until I drift off to sleep.

Fourteen

It is 1:45 PM on Tuesday, and I know right now Mom is at the obstetrician's office. Sitting in the back of Rabbi Cohen's class, I can barely concentrate. Maybe today will be the day she tells me the good news. Rabbi Cohen is reading the class a news story in Hebrew and we are supposed to be jotting down the key ideas. I hope it has something to with babies because that's the only idea on my mind.

I look over at Ruthie who is drawing dress designs in her Hebrew notebook. She's the type who can listen and draw at the same time. Hannah Finkelstein sits three desks up on the left. I can see her surreptitiously dropping her pencil and a crumpled paper, which of course is a note for Esther Grubner who is sitting behind her. Sure enough, Esther quickly retrieves the paper. She hunches over to read it. I see her shoulders moving, like she is smothering her laughter. Then Esther leans toward Hannah and whispers something to the back of her head. Hannah slinks down in her chair and puts her hand over her mouth, then whispers something to Esther. Hannah glances back at me. Then she starts whispering to Esther again.

I feel my cheeks flush.

"*Sheket!*" Rabbi Cohen says to them. Then he asks Hannah a question about the news story, which of course she can't answer because she was too busy writing something mean about me.

I guess Hannah is still mad about what happened at math practice—as if she never loses her temper! I was even ready to apologize, but now I'm not so sure. The problem is that Hannah Finkelstein is not someone you want as your enemy. The past few school years I have learned to just tolerate her, but sometimes she gets out of hand.

I'm tempted to write Ruthie a note, but decide not to risk it. Rabbi Cohen is now yelling at Malki Sneiderman to pay attention. Sigh. What is the Hebrew phrase for: "*Can you perhaps teach in a more interesting manner?*" Last year, we had Morah Siegal for *Ivrit*. She was so cool. We did a whole unit on food and she let us set up a class restaurant where we practiced ordering everything in Hebrew. Morah Siegal also told us really interesting stories about when she served in the Israeli army. We saw pictures of her next to an army tank. I loved her native accent, too. Now she is on maternity leave, so we have to suffer with Rabbi Cohen.

After class I rush to my locker to check my phone on the remote chance that Mom sent me a text saying *Good news*, or *Call me right away*. No such luck. Not even one missed call from her. I grab a granola bar from my backpack and head off to math class.

I'm really dreading seeing Dr. Janas after what happened yesterday. Thinking about my behavior reminds me of the book *Anne of Green Gables*, which I read last year. The main character, Anne, is always getting herself into some trouble. She consoles herself by saying, "Tomorrow is always fresh, with no mistakes." After a particularly humiliating school incident, Anne's beloved teacher, Miss Stacey, reminds Anne of her own wise words. I really liked that scene. I hope Dr. Janas believes in this saying, too.

I take my seat, then pull out my homework from my folder. Dr. Janas is busy writing on the whiteboard. She's wearing a soft green sweater and a tweed skirt. Most people look bad in green, but she looks fabulous. I see Hannah stride into the classroom and plop her backpack on the desk next to me. I decide at this very moment to start fresh.

I take a deep breath. "Did you figure out the homework?" I ask Hannah, as if nothing ever happened.

She stares at me for a moment then shrugs. "It was easy."

"It took me a long time," I say, opening myself up for an insult.

She flips back her brown hair. "Well, maybe you need to learn the shortcut."

I look over my paper and bite my tongue. "Probably."

I turn my attention to Dr. Janas. On the board she has written: **WHAT IS A POLYNOMIAL?** followed by a bunch of mathematical sentences. Then she starts handing out a paper.

"Good morning, mathematicians. Today I thought we'd start with a little team building." Dr. Janas eyes me for a second. "With the person sitting next to you, please look over the examples on this paper and try to come up with the definition of a polynomial. I'll give you five minutes."

I can't quite avoid working with Hannah, so I scoot my desk a bit closer to hers and look over the handout. Dr. Janas has given five examples that are polynomials and five examples that are not.

Hannah begins. "Okay, polynomials don't have square roots."

"And no negative exponents," I add.

Hannah nods. "Seems like they are sums of a few numbers with variables."

Though we're opposite in many ways, Hannah and I both like a challenge. Pretty soon we forget the personal stuff and just talk the language of math. Dr. Janas calls on us to give our ideas, and to my surprise, we are pretty close.

"Sure I could stand up here and recite a definition for you," Dr. Janas says, "but when you attempt to discover it yourself, you are more likely to remember it." She scribbles a few key words on the board: coefficient, degree, leading term. "And while most of you were on the right track, you were missing some math vocabulary to actually describe what you found." Dr. Janas turns around and writes a typical polynomial on the board.

$$5x^2 + 4x + 8$$

"In this polynomial there are three terms: $5x^2$ is the first term, $4x$ is the second term, and 8 is the third term. This expression doesn't have one answer—one value. You know that, right? You have to know what x is to evaluate it. The value of x could be 3, 10, or negative 6, or anything else. In each case you get a different value for the expression."

Dr. Janas starts working out the polynomial, showing us how you can get different answers. "Still, there is one term in the polynomial that never changes no matter what the value of x," she announces. "Which is it?"

I raise my hand. "Eight." (Hey, there's my number again.)

"That's correct," Dr. Janas replies. Since 8 never changes no matter what x is, 8 is called a constant."

I look at the polynomial on the board and the numbers start to jump out at me, their colors blending. I begin to see them as a sort of number friendship. The first friend, $5x^2$, is the leader; the others follow. New friends might join. The friendship might change over time, depending on what x happens to be (like maybe, a misunderstanding), but the constant is the true friend, the one who is always there, unchanged. Hmm. I like that. Popular Polynomials...

"Earth to Talia!" Hannah says, tapping me on the shoulder.

"Huh?" I look around and everyone is paired up again.

Hannah rolls her eyes at me. "We're supposed to figure it out." She points at the whiteboard.

I pick up my pencil and start copying the problem. "Oh, sorry. Let's see…"

After math class, I have a short break until gym. I head toward the library to use the computer, and that's when I see her. At first I think it must be a coincidence, but then who else has that colorful tie skirt? Gabbers! I stop in the middle of the hall and just stare. She is walking toward the school office. For a second I think she is here to deliver a message to me. I feel my heart pound. Through the office window I see our principal, Mrs. Brody, come out to greet her. She is shaking Gabrielle's hand. What is going on here? Then the two of them disappear into her office.

Fifteen

"What could she possibly be doing here?" I say to the group at our lunch table the next day.

"The mystery unfolds," Shifra says dreamily.

"I bet she's applying for a job," Liora says, taking a sip of her yogurt drink. "You said she was looking for one, right?"

"A job here?" I say incredulously. "She's not a teacher. She hasn't even been to college." Then I remember Gabrielle saying the word *interview* last night at dinner, which makes me nervous.

Ruthie starts giggling. "I know, maybe Mrs. Brody is starting a ballet program!"

Everyone laughs but me. "First my house, now my school. I'm afraid she's moving into my life."

Ruthie gives me a knowing look. I haven't had a chance to talk to her alone about my mom's secret. Then she says, "Come on, Talia, it's not like she's coaching your math team."

"Or replacing Doris," Shifra adds.

"That is so not funny," I say, peeling an orange. "My parents should charge her rent. She gets a guest suite to herself, takes a shower every day—I know because I hear it—eats our food, uses our computer, and even borrows my mom's car! And I have to listen to her guitar-playing while I'm trying to study."

Shifra zips up her lunch bag. "But it's such a big mitzvah that your parents do, having all those guests. I know it gets on your nerves, but I think it counts as a mitzvah for you, too."

"Thank you very much, Rebbetzin Shifra, for your comment," I reply sarcastically. I really hate when anyone says that to me, as if I don't know my parents are doing a big mitzvah. But how big does the mitzvah have to get? What's next, Hotel Schumacher, where everyone stays for free?

Shifra just shrugs and smiles. (Thankfully she isn't easily insulted.) "Just ask her, Talia. When you get home tonight, tell Gabrielle you saw her at school. See what she says."

"That's another thing," I say. "My parents are always telling me that a guest's business is not my business. My mom really gets on my case if she hears me asking them 'personal' questions."

"So don't ask, just comment," Shifra replies. "You have to carefully pull the info out of her."

"Was Gabrielle wearing your new sneakers?" Ruthie asks, which makes me smile.

"Seriously," Liora says. "You have to tell us the minute you find out. I'm dying of curiosity."

"Me, too," Shifra adds. "Let's all chat tonight."

"Can't," Liora says. "My dad turned off the internet."

"*What?*" all three of us gasp.

"Just temporarily," Liora explains. "My parents think I'm spending too much time online and want me to concentrate on preparing for the math contest."

Ruthie groans. "Oh, I get it."

"*But...* if I do well on the contest," Liora says, her eyes brightening, "they'll get me my own laptop!"

A sick feeling invades my stomach.

"Ooh, you're so lucky," Shifra says. "I'll inherit my brother's."

"How well do you have to do to get the laptop?"

"They didn't exactly say..."

Whoa. "Maybe you should stay over this Shabbat. You can come to the Shabbat Club in the afternoon and we can study Saturday night—"

"That didn't go so well last week," Liora says, making a face.

I put my hand over my heart. "I promise. This time we'll really study. No sleepover party."

"Don't worry, we won't bother you," Ruthie says, "or invite you to go ice skating with us."

"You're so mean!" Liora laughs.

"It's bad enough we have so much homework," Ruthie sighs. "Why anyone would want to take on more math is beyond me."

"Don't you know Talia by now?" Shifra asks, putting her arm around me. "Miss Numbers here does this stuff for fun!"

"Maybe I'd do it for a laptop," Ruthie considers.

"It's not winning that counts," I hear myself say.

"Are you joking?" Liora replies.

Shifra shakes her head. "Did Gabrielle tell you that?"

After school, before I even go inside the house, I decide to shoot a few baskets in the side yard. I put on my stretchy gloves first, trying to keep my hands from freezing. There aren't many days left when I'll be able to play basketball outside. It gets dark so early now, and before I know it, the snow will be here. Shooting hoops is one way I unwind after a stressful day. I like the rhythmic sound of the ball dribbling and seeing how many shots I can make in a row. Ruthie used to come over and play with me, but lately she's lost interest and seems more worried about breaking a fingernail.

After about twenty minutes, my body feels warmed up. I've managed seven shots in a row, and then comes her voice.

"Yoo-hoo?"

And there she is—the mystery girl herself. Gabbers walks up to the court wearing a leather jacket over her tie skirt.

"You look pretty intense there. Can I join you?"

"Sure." I toss the ball to her.

"Oops," she says, leaning over to retrieve the ball. She aims at the basket, then shoots. "Darn. I was never good at basketball."

"Too busy dancing?" I tease.

She tries again and misses. Yikes—she has terrible form.

"I guess so. That's the downside of being so single-focused. I missed out on sports and other things. I always had to be careful not to injure my knees and ankles doing other activities like skiing and running track."

Gabrielle tosses the ball back to me. I dribble, then make a jump-shot from the corner.

"Hey, you're good!" she says.

Okay, I admit to showing off.

"You have to hold the ball correctly, for one thing," I tell her. "Then, you push it forward, like this."

"Oh. It must look a lot easier than it is," she says.

"Here, give it a try."

I coach her through the steps, until she actually makes a basket.

"Score!" Gabrielle shouts and jumps up and down like a kid.

I dribble some more, not looking at her. "Hey, I saw you at my school today."

"Really? I didn't see you. I wanted it to be a surprise."

"Surprise?" I stop dribbling and stare at her.

"Yeah," she grins.

"What kind of a surprise?"

"I'm not supposed to say anything yet. You'll hear about it soon enough."

I feel like throwing the ball at her head. "Oh."

She rubs her hands together. "It's pretty chilly out here. I think I'll go in now. Maybe I can help Doris get dinner ready."

Oh, great, so now she wants to be our cook.

"Thanks for the lesson," she says.

The sun is setting and my hands are cold, but I don't want to go inside yet. Not with her, anyway. *Surprise.* Why does everything have to be a secret around here?

Then I get another surprise. I hear the garage door opening and see Mom's car pull up the driveway. What is she doing home so early on a Wednesday?

"You're home early again," I say, greeting Mom in the foyer.

"That I am," she sings. "I just finished a major account, so I thought I'd take a little time off." She hangs her coat in the closet.

"Really? Like a vacation?"

Mom laughs. "Not exactly. Just cutting back hours for the next couple weeks."

I follow her into the kitchen. "Are you feeling better?"

"Actually, I'm feeling pretty tired. Probably just stress. Thanks for asking, though." Mom smiles at me. "Besides, I rarely get to see you after school."

That's for sure. "So… what's new?"

Mom raises an eyebrow. "What do you mean?"

I shrug. "I don't know, um… at work and stuff."

Mom opens the fridge and takes out a lettuce, peppers, and a cucumber. "Well, we're hiring a new credit specialist. A really sharp young woman from the North Shore. And Stacey, our office assistant, is going on maternity leave."

My ears perk up. "Oh, that's good news. I mean… for her."

Mom nods, then starts washing the lettuce. "Yes, but she's a tough one to replace. In fact, I wouldn't be surprised if she decides not to come back."

"Why?"

"It's her first child and six weeks' maternity leave is a very short time. You can't predict how you're going to feel. I've seen it happen enough—new moms cutting back hours or just quitting to stay home with their baby."

"Did you do that, with me?"

Mom starts peeling the cucumber. "I took off two years, and then joined a new firm. Then we got Doris."

Right, my second mom.

She slices the cucumber and offers me a piece.

"Do you think you'll ever quit?" I ask, leaning on the counter.

"Why would I do that? I love my job."

Now I am really confused. "I mean, like if you had more kids." I can't believe I just said that.

Mom chops the pepper, not looking at me. "Then I suppose I'd consider part-time for a while."

Right smack in the middle of this important conversation, Gabbers walks in. "Hi, Naomi. Can I help you?"

"Sure," Mom says. "If you can just take out the salmon steaks in the fridge, the mustard, and the Italian dressing. Talia, would you set the table, please?"

I open the cupboard and remove five plates. Before I know it,

Mom and Gabrielle are chatting away. *Aargh.*

"So everything went well today?" Mom asks her.

"Perfect. I'm very excited." Gabrielle removes the plastic wrap from the fish. "I'm supposed to keep quiet about it until the announcement." Gabbers looks over at me. "So, I just told Talia that I have a surprise."

"Oh, of course," Mom says sheepishly. "Didn't mean to spill the beans."

I slam the silverware drawer shut. Why am I the last to know everything around here?

"Hello, sweetheart," Doris calls to me as she walks into the kitchen carrying a broom in one hand. "Naomi, I thought I heard you. What are you doing home?"

Mom brings the salad bowl to the table. "Gee, I didn't think coming home early would warrant such attention around here." She smiles at Doris. "Just decided I wanted to see my girl."

Doris pats my back. "That is nice. I think she like that. Right, Miss Talia?"

I roll my eyes, even though I feel glad that Mom said she came home for me. "I guess."

"You guess!" Doris says. "How many times you complain to me your mama not home enough?"

"*Doris.*" I give her one of my please-be-quiet looks.

"That's okay, Talia," Mom says apologetically. "You have a right to complain."

I do?

"Maybe I should've been a teacher," she replies. "Better hours."

Doris puts the broom inside the kitchen closet. "So, I got the basement made up already."

"Oh, thank you. They're supposed to be here early Friday," Mom says as she puts the fish pan into the oven.

"Who?" I ask.

"Rabbi and Mrs. Birnbaum. They're coming from Brooklyn for a wedding Saturday night."

"And they're staying Shabbat?"

"Of course," Mom says.

"But, do you think they should, I mean, you haven't been feeling well—"

"For heaven's sakes Talia, I'm fine. They're the only guests this weekend."

"For now," I mutter.

"I'll be happy to help with anything, Naomi," Gabrielle offers. "Errands, cooking..."

"Thank you. I appreciate it."

"I was going to have Liora over again, Mom. We need to study."

"No problem," she says. "Besides, I think you are going to like the Birnbaums."

"Sure, Mom. If you say so."

"I'm not kidding. In fact, I believe you know Rabbi Birnbaum."

"I do?"

"Yes, but I'm not sure you'll recognize him now."

"What, was he my preschool teacher or something?"

Mom laughs. "No, you'll see. For now, I'll keep it a surprise."

I plop down in my chair. I've had enough.

"How exciting," Gabbers comments. "A little mystery."

Sixteen

The houses on Math Street have addresses in order starting with 1, then 2, 3, 4, and so on. Talia lives in one of these houses. There are between 1 and 20 houses on the street. The sum of all the addresses less than Talia's address equals the sum of all the addresses greater than hers. How many houses are there on Math Street?

"I just don't get it," Liora says.

Hannah makes a face. "Draw a picture."

Liora scowls back at her. "Easy for you to say."

The three of us are attempting another Thursday after-school math practice with Dr. Janas. So far, I'd rate our team spirit as negative one.

"Girls, there won't be time for bickering," Dr. Janas sighs. "You'd probably have seven minutes for this type of problem. Think aloud, but support each other."

Hannah opens her mouth to say something, then closes it.

"Any ideas, Talia?" Dr. Janas asks me.

I smile, thinking about all the house numbers I've played with on my way home from school. "I guess I'd make a table. And then look at all the possibilities."

"Great strategy. Why don't you demonstrate," she says, handing me a dry-erase marker.

On the whiteboard I draw a stick house, and label it 'Talia' with a question mark inside. On the left side of the house I write, 'Beginning of Math Street.' To the right of the house I write, 'End of Math Street.'

"So, I'd use the guess-and-check method. Let's guess Talia's house is number 5." I write down 5 underneath the stick house. "We know that all the house numbers before Talia's house add up to the same number as all the house numbers after Talia's house."

"Oh, I get it." Liora looks relieved. "Thanks for translating."

"Liora," Dr. Janas asks. "What would you do next?"

Liora takes a deep breath and looks at the board. "Okay. So to see if Talia's address is 5, you'd add up the street numbers before 5. Since they are in order it would be 1 plus 2 plus 3 plus 4, which equals 10."

While Liora is thinking out loud, I jot down the numbers on the board underneath the column that says, 'Beginning of Math Street.'

"Now we add up the house numbers after 5," Liora continues, "which is "6+7+8+9+10+11+12+13+14+15—"

"Wait!" Hannah blurts out. "You don't have to go that far. Once you realize the sum of 6 plus 7 is bigger than 10, you try another guess. The sums on each side of her house are supposed to be equal."

Liora face reddens. "Oh."

"That's correct," Dr. Janas says. She goes on to explain this to Liora.

Liora nods, twirling a strand of her black hair.

"Since this is a timed test, you don't want to waste any minute." Dr. Janas smiles at Liora. "So how about another guess for Talia's house number?"

"How about 15?"

"Go ahead," Dr. Janas prompts.

"So, you add up the houses before 15... that's..."

I make a mental note to show Liora the shortcut for adding numbers in a series. Good thing I made plans to go home with her after school today.

"...106," Liora concludes.

"No, 105," Hannah says, rolling her eyes.

"Don't do it in your head," Dr. Janas tells Liora gently. "Write everything down. Now what?"

Liora starts writing down the numbers. Then she slowly explains her problem-solving method. "This could take forever," she complains.

"Well, now you have the strategy, so use your intuition and number sense to finish the chart." Dr. Janas raises her hands in the air as if expecting something. "So? Get to work!"

A few seconds later Hannah cries, "Got it! Talia's house number is 6, which means there are eight houses on Math Street."

"Prove it," Dr. Janas says, grinning.

Hannah confidently starts to prove her answer, but Liora cuts her off. "But how did you know how many houses there are?"

"Let me finish," Hannah says impatiently. She rattles off the strategy. "Since we added up the numbers 1 through 5, and then 7 and 8, there must be eight houses. Eight houses on the block."

As soon as Hannah says 'eight,' I see a flash of blue in my head. Gosh, does this happen to anyone else?

Liora sits there looking frustrated.

What do I say now? "If you do the problem all over again on your own, it will help," I suggest.

"Good idea," Dr. Janas says. "There are several variations of this type of problem. So when you encounter something like this on the test, you'll say, 'Oh, yeah, this is like the street address problem.'"

Liora sighs and puts her head down on the desk.

"All right then, I think we've done enough," Dr. Janas says. "Keep on reviewing all the problems in the packet. Study the solutions. Make time to practice alone as well as together." She closes the briefcase on her desk. "Okay? See you on Monday. Oh… Liora, could I just have a word with you before you leave?"

I stand outside the classroom, waiting for Liora. I try to eavesdrop, but the band practice down the hall makes it hard to hear anything. I imagine the worst—Dr. Janas telling her she shouldn't compete—but no, Dr. Janas wouldn't do that. Liora is good with calculations, but word problems seem to give her trouble, and if I don't help her, our team will be in trouble. Thank goodness her mom said she could sleep over this Friday night. Shabbat ends early, so we'll have time to study Saturday night and do something fun with Ruthie and Shifra.

The door opens and Liora and Dr. Janas walk out. I scan Liora's face for signs of distress. She looks okay.

"Bye, girls," Dr. Janas says. We hear her clicking down the hallway in her heels.

I turn to Liora. "What did she say?"

"She offered to meet with me at lunch or during my free period."

This is good news. "Really?" I feel relieved. "I mean, that's great. Will you do it?"

"Sure." Liora grins. "I really want that laptop."

We start walking down the hall together. "But, you won't be too disappointed if… you don't get it?"

"What do you think? Of course I will!" Liora stops at her locker to get her coat. "I'm going to really work hard. I don't expect to beat you, but I want to be up there in the top ten."

"Top ten of our school or *all* the schools?" I ask, feeling a bit desperate.

"Out of our school, duh."

We walk through the empty hallway, past the teachers' offices, and into the entryway. A few high-school girls are gathered around a table working on a poster of some sort. The November chill hits us as we step outside.

"There's my mom," Liora says, heading toward the traffic circle. "See ya!"

"Don't forget to bring your sleepover stuff to school tomorrow!" I call to her.

Seventeen

Last night, while checking out one of the math sites Dr. Janas recommended, I clicked on a link for mental math tricks. I found a video of Dr. George Welland, a *mathemagician*. (Isn't that a cool word?) Besides having two Ph.D. degrees, and being a university math professor, he performs amazing math tricks for audiences around the country and on television. He can multiply three-digit numbers in his head and tell you what day of the week you were born on just by knowing the date. Dr. Welland is very funny, and he throws in a few regular magic tricks (hat and wand) as well. I can't wait to get his book, *Mental Math and More!* I wrote down one of his tricks in my private notebook ("Tali's Tricks") which I've been keeping since third grade.

I kind of got carried away watching Dr. Welland's show, and stayed up too late, which is why right now I am struggling to keep my eyes on my siddur. Each school day the seventh through twelfth graders meet in the main sanctuary at 8:05 AM for morning prayers, otherwise known as davening. We have assigned seats, which is supposed to keep us from talking. The high-school girls take turns leading the service. Some parts we say silently, some we sing or recite together. It's not easy to keep your mind on what you're saying, especially since we go pretty fast and basically say the same thing every day. The whole thing takes about 45 minutes. I sit on the end of a middle row, next to Esther Grubner, one of Hannah's fans, and we never have much to say to each other. For me, davening is kind of like brushing my teeth: I do it twice a day, some days more thoroughly than others, and don't think too much about what I'm doing. That's not how it's supposed to be. Some girls, like Maya Rubin, seem to really get into it—even day after day.

Gabbers also gets into davening. When we sing the Grace after Meals on Friday night, she says every word carefully. And I guess that's because it's all new to her. I've been singing that prayer in the lunch room each day since I was three years old. I wonder how you keep things fresh when it comes to daily prayer obligations.

Today is Friday, which means that after davening, our principal, Mrs. Brody, will talk to us about the weekly Torah portion. I think she knows that most of us are still waking up, so she tries to be lively and even manages a joke or two.

"Girls, this week we have such a beautiful Torah portion," Mrs. Brody says, standing in front of the podium. "It is the famous story of our forefather Jacob fleeing his home from his twin brother, Esau, whom he fears will harm him."

My mind starts to wander. What if my mom had twins? If so, I sure hope they'd get along better than Jacob and Esau. Twins are popular these days. I heard there are four sets in this year's first grade class. 4 times 2 is 8. Malki and Rina Sneiderman are the only twins in the middle school. They do everything together. I try to imagine having an identical, but I can't. Not that it wouldn't be fun.

"Then comes the famous story of Jacob's dream," Mrs. Brody continues. "The Torah tells us that he took twelve stones to use for a pillow. Doesn't sound very comfortable, does it? Let's think a moment about the number twelve..."

Twelve has a beautiful sound to it. Twelve is very long and straight. *In an old house in Paris all covered with vines, lived twelve little girls in two straight lines...* Hmm, how many girls are in here today? Maybe eighty? I start to mentally count the girls in my row, then the next, and the next. I get to 65 when I hear Mrs. Brody say, "And before you head off to class, I have exciting news to share."

That gets my attention.

"As you know, we all look forward to Hebrew Academy's high

school production each spring. It is not only a fundraiser, but a wonderful showcase for the talent, creativity, and spirit of our girls. I am pleased to announce that this year we are offering the first middle school production, slated for February."

The room fills with cheering. "Yes!" Esther Grubner says, punching the air.

I am not cheering—yet.

"Now, all you actresses, writers, artists, dancers, musicians, organizers, and technical whizzes are invited to participate in this exciting event. And, thanks to a generous grant from the Jewish Arts Council, the production expenses will be covered. This means the proceeds from ticket sales and program ads will go directly to the middle school activities budget."

Another round of applause from everybody. Okay, that sounds nice, but what is it going to mean for me?

"Best of all," Mrs. Brody says with a big smile, "we are now able to hire a production director to help us make this show the very best. I am pleased to announce that I have found a wonderfully creative and talented young woman for the job of production director—Miss Gabrielle Markus from New York City."

A jolt of alarm shoots through my body. Oh, no. I slink down in my seat. Mrs. Brody is beaming. "You will have a chance to meet her today during lunch. I am sure you will all be very welcoming to Miss Markus, who is new to our community. And girls, let's extend a thank you to the Schumacher family for hosting Miss Markus during her stay in Boston."

I see heads turn to look at me. My cheeks burn. Hannah Finkelstein flashes me one of her smirks. This cannot be happening.

After Mrs. Brody dismisses us, there is the hum of murmuring as the girls file out into the hallway. Ruthie catches up with me, grabbing my arm.

"Well, I was half-right!" she says.

I keep on walking. "Just don't say anything," I snap. "I don't want to talk about it. Or even think about it."

She moves closer to keep up with my stride. "Oh come on, Tal. It won't be so bad—"

I spin around. "Forget it. You don't understand." I run down the hallway to the bathroom and hide inside a stall.

A few seconds later I hear the bathroom door swing open. "Talia?"

"Leave me alone," I mutter, surprised at my own words.

"What did I do?" Ruthie knocks on the stall door. "I'm on your side, remember?"

I feel a tear trickle down my cheek. "I hate being singled out like that."

"She didn't single you out," Ruthie says gently. "Mrs. Brody was talking about your parents."

"Right. Exactly. Why can't I be from an ordinary family, not someone with their last name on the school building?" I open the door. "And don't you see what this means? Gabbers is going to be staying a while—at least through February?"

"Is she really so bad?" Ruthie asks me.

I shrug. "I guess not. Just kind of annoying. But now, who knows what it will be like? I mean, maybe she'll want to hold practices at my house!"

"Think of it all as part of the mystery we're trying to solve... *The Mystery of Miss Markus,*" Ruthie announces dramatically, sweeping her arm in the air.

I feel a little smile creep up. Everyone needs a friend like Ruthie.

Ruthie glances at her watch. "Come on. No time for sulking, Tal. We'll be late for class."

Later, during American history, I start thinking about what Ruthie said. This inspires me to write something in my notebook.

Interview Questions for G.M.
-Are you ever going back to dancing?
-Do you have a best friend?
-Do you get along with your parents?
-Have you ever been in love?
-Why did you come to Boston?
-When are you leaving?

When we start partner work, I show Ruthie my notebook. She grins, and scribbles something on the bottom of the list, then gives it back. I laugh quietly as I read her addition.

132

What are your favorite tunes to sing in the shower?

I love Ruthie's sense of humor. No matter what happens, she always looks on the bright side. She's everyone's cheerleader.

Last year, at my Bat Mitzvah party, I spilled water all over my dress during the meal. It looked like I wet my pants! Before I knew it, Ruthie dumped some water on her dress, and then on other girls who sat next to her. "Let's match Talia!" she said. I thought they would scream, but everyone just cracked up.

Mr. Connors writes the homework on the board. **Quiz on the Declaration of Independence tomorrow.** I'll have no problem with that one; Dad has been reading it aloud to me every July Fourth since I can remember. Life, liberty, and the pursuit of happiness. Amen.

When lunch rolls around, I start feeling that nervousness in my stomach. Shifra and Liora have already saved a table and they are dying to talk to me. Ruthie and I hurry at the washing stand.

"You got front row seats," Ruthie says, sitting down. "Thanks."

I sit down and take out the corned beef sandwich Doris made.

Shifra leans toward me. "Did you *know?*"

"Are you kidding? This must be the surprise Gabbers was talking about. I had no idea. Not in a million years."

Shifra's eyes narrow. "And your mom knew?"

"Don't remind me," I say. I open my water bottle. "And, according to my mom, I have another surprise tonight. Has to do with our Shabbat guests."

"That's me!" Liora says.

"That's besides you. Some rabbi and his wife from Brooklyn, who I'm supposed to know, are also coming."

"Do I know them, too?" Liora asks me.

"You will tonight."

Ruthie opens her diet soda. "How many others are coming?"

"Last count, that was it. But, I never know. We get last-minute calls all the time. And, my dad has a habit of bringing people home from shul who don't have a place to eat."

Shifra shakes her head. "Your dad's a tzaddik."

I'd have to agree, my dad is a pretty righteous person. "Once he

133

brought home a bum. He really smelled bad. Well, I shouldn't really call him a bum, but he was homeless, and, believe it or not, Jewish."

"That's so sad!" Ruthie exclaims. "How did he end up out on the street?"

"I think he had a drinking problem. Anyway, I've had about all the surprises I can take today."

Shifra looks around the cafeteria. "So where is Miss Markus?"

"Who knows?" I say. "Hanging out in Mrs. Brody's office?"

Ruthie munches on a carrot stick. "I wonder what kind of show it will be."

Liora taps my arm. "Look. There she is."

Gabrielle walks into the cafeteria with Mrs. Brody, who grabs the microphone. "May I have your attention, please?"

Everyone quiets down when they see Gabrielle. She is wearing a long-sleeved black shirt that says *New York City Ballet* across the front, with a swirly denim skirt, and black ankle boots. Her dark hair cascades over her shoulders.

"She is model skinny," Ruthie whispers.

"Girls, I'd like to introduce our new production director, Miss Gabrielle Markus."

Gabbers stands there grinning ear to ear.

"Miss Markus brings a professional background in dance, music, and drama to our school production. Please welcome her."

Everyone applauds. Mrs. Brody hands Gabrielle the mike, and the room hushes.

She pauses and takes a deep breath. Is she nervous?

"Thank you so much," she begins with her southern drawl. "I've only been in Boston a few weeks and everyone in this community has been so welcoming to me. I'm thrilled to have this job. Honored, really. Hebrew Academy seems like an amazing place. Soon you'll be receiving a notice about the play, information on tryouts, and other opportunities for involvement. I really want your input, so don't be shy about sharing your ideas and suggestions."

I can think of a suggestion: *quit now.*

"So, I look forward to getting to know y'all and well, that's about it. Have a great Shabbat!"

The rest of the school day passes in a blur. I keep thinking about Mom. I'm worried about how Liora will do on the math team. I can't decide whether or not to invite Hannah to practice with us Saturday night. And, I just don't know what to say to Gabbers. (I'm sure she'll have plenty to say to me.) I am definitely not trying out for this play. Count me in for the audience.

At 2:15 the bell rings for our early Friday dismissal.

"TGIF," I say when I meet Liora at my locker. (Thank God it's Friday!)

"It's raining out," she groans. "My bag is gonna get soaked."

"Don't worry. I can call Doris."

Ruthie runs up to us. "Hey guys, did you see this?" she says, waving an orange flyer.

"Haven't been to my mailbox yet," I say, closing my locker. "What is it?"

"It's a notice from Miss Markus!"

I take the note from Ruthie.

MIDDLE SCHOOL PRODUCTION TRYOUTS
Miriam's Song
Actors Singers Dancers Musicians
Please prepare a two-minute audition piece.
4:15 PM , Dec. 3
Auditorium
For questions or to sign up:
miriamssong@HebrewAcademyofBoston.com

"Who is Miriam?" I say, zipping my backpack.

Ruthie laughs. "Are you kidding? Remember baby Moses?"

I slam my locker shut. "Oh, right." I shake my head. "I'm so stressed, I can't think straight." It would make sense that Gabrielle would pick Miriam, sister of Moses. She knew how to dance.

It's half an hour before sundown and the usual pre-Shabbat rush is in full force at our house. Mom is dashing around the kitchen with last-minute food preparations. Gabrielle is in the shower. The

Birnbaums, whom I haven't even seen yet, are still downstairs in the guest suite. Dad just walked in the front door carrying his suit from the dry cleaners.

"Hi, Dad," I call from the dining room, where Liora and I are setting the Shabbat table.

"Hi there," he says, quickly taking off his coat. "Running late. I forgot to tell Doris to pick up the dry cleaning."

"Well, we're all ready," I announce.

Dad looks over at us. "Oh hi, Liora. Great to have you again." Dad walks to the dining room and kisses me on top of my head. "So did you meet Rabbi Birnbaum?"

I sigh. "No, Dad, I didn't. They've been downstairs."

"Well, he'll be going to shul with me soon. I'll introduce you then." He winks at me, then glances at his watch. "I'd better get dressed."

"Anyone else coming?" I ask as he heads toward the stairs.

"Don't think so. Check with your mother."

"Wow," Liora says. "How can you not know if you're having guests?"

"That's just the way it is around here." I place my father's cup on his plate. "People call on Friday afternoon looking for a place to eat or sleep."

"We don't have guests stay over for Shabbat very often," Liora says. "When we do, my mom always stresses out, trying to make everything perfect."

"Doris does most of the stressing," I say, folding a cloth napkin into a fan.

Liora picks up a napkin. "Hey, where did you learn to do that?"

"From my mom. Here, I'll show you."

While Liora and I finish preparing the table, my mom calls out a hundred requests from the kitchen. *Talia, please take out another challah from the freezer. Talia, bring the towels upstairs. Talia, fill the hot water urn. Talia, call Bubbe to wish her a Shabbat Shalom.*

Finally, Gabbers appears in the nick of time to help out in the kitchen. "What a stylish dress," I overhear Mom say to her.

"Thanks," she says. "Bought it this afternoon in celebration of my new job."

I motion to Liora and we peek our heads into the kitchen. Her ruby dress has a cinched black belt and looks like something out of the 1950s. I wonder if she bought it at an antique store. Liora gives me a look, and I smile back.

"Hi, girls," Gabbers says cheerfully.

"We're delighted for you," Mom says, plugging in the hot water urn. "Talia must be thrilled."

Thrilled? Does Mom not get it? I haven't even had a second to talk to her about the situation, especially with Liora here.

A few minutes later, I hear Dad in the entryway talking to the Birnbaums, who have finally come up from the basement.

"Talia?" he calls.

I dutifully appear, smile on face, with Liora by my side.

"Talia, I'd like you to meet Rabbi and Mrs. Birnbaum."

"Hi. Nice to meet you," I say politely. "This is my friend Liora."

Rabbi Birnbaum is dressed in a black suit with a white shirt and red suspenders over his pot belly. He gives me a huge smile.

"It's a pleasure to meet you," he says in a booming voice. His blue eyes are sparkling. Yes, he looks vaguely familiar.

"I'm sorry we didn't come up sooner," Mrs. Birnbaum adds. "We needed a rest after the long drive. So much traffic on the turnpike."

She also has a warm smile and kind eyes. I admire the cut of her blonde wig.

"Is there anything you need before Shabbat?" I ask them, like my mother taught me to do.

"I think we're all set," she replies. "Everything is so pleasant downstairs."

Hotel Schumacher, I think.

"How about a pair of sunglasses for you?" Dad asks Rabbi Birnbaum, who smiles and nods. I can tell that's supposed to be a joke, but I don't get it.

After Dad and the rabbi leave for shul, Mom, Gabrielle, Mrs. Birnbaum, Liora and I assemble in the dining room to light the Shabbat candles. As I cover my eyes and say the blessing, I add a silent prayer. *Please, God, bless my mother with a baby. A girl or a boy…*

or one of each.

Gabrielle stands there for another minute. We all wait politely. I wonder what she is praying for.

"Shabbat Shalom!" Mom says and lets out a sigh of relief that her work is done. At least for the next twenty-four hours. "Please, come sit down."

I really want to go upstairs with Liora, but I decide to be social for at least a few minutes.

"That is a magnificent piano," Mrs. Birnbaum exclaims as she follows Mom into the living room.

"It was my father-in-law's, Isaac Schumacher," Mom says. "He studied at the Boston Conservatory."

"And do you play, Talia?" Mrs. Birnbaum asks, sitting down on the white sofa.

I nod. "But not nearly as well as my grandfather did. He was really amazing."

Gabrielle sits down across from me. "Talia doesn't give herself enough credit," she says. "I've heard her play. She definitely has a good ear."

Well, thank you, Miss Markus.

"It's in the genes," Mrs. Birnbaum says, smoothing out her navy skirt. "All of our children picked up a bit of my husband's musical talent."

"Is he a musician?" I ask.

My mother grins and looks at Mrs. Birnbaum. "I'm afraid Talia didn't recognize him," Mom says.

Mrs. Birnbaum waves her hand. "She's a big girl now, and he's changed over the years."

"Oh my gosh, I know him!" Liora blurts out.

My mother laughs. I look at Liora, then at Mrs. Birnbaum.

"Am I missing something?" Gabrielle says.

"Me, too," I say.

"Talia," Mom says. "Rabbi Birnbaum is *Uncle Yussie*."

I stare at her. I don't believe it! Yes, that booming voice. It *is* Uncle Yussie. I didn't recognize him without his goofy hat and purple pants.

"I knew it!" Liora cries. "Just wait till the kids see him in shul."

The real Uncle Yussie, in my house, going to my shul? What if the kids come banging at our door? Tell me I'm dreaming.

Gabrielle looks confused. "Uncle Yussie?"

"My husband is a famous Jewish children's entertainer," Mrs. Birnbaum explains. "Think Barney without the dinosaur costume."

I am still recovering from the shock when my mom says, "Talia adores Uncle Yussie. I think she still has all his videos downstairs."

My cheeks redden.

"Which one is your favorite?" Mom asks me. "Isn't it 'I'm So Proud to Be Jewish?' "

"Mom, that was when I was *four*."

"I liked that one, too," Liora admits.

Mrs. Birnbaum smiles. "The older fans are so surprised when they run into him. Last week he performed at Children's Hospital and one of the young doctors got all excited, saying, 'I remember seeing you in concert when I was a little kid.' "

"I'm afraid I missed out," Gabrielle adds. "I grew up on Raffi."

"Who's that?" I ask, and then the adults are all laughing again.

Later that night, Liora and I exchange memories from our early childhood. I guess Uncle Yussie's arrival kind of started it all.

"It was weird seeing Uncle Yussie dressed normally," Liora says as we lie in the dark.

"Well, minus the red suspenders," I say.

Liora laughs. "His beard got grayer."

"Actually, I think my grandfather wore black suspenders. Hey, I kind of forgot that."

"He was the one who donated our school building?"

"Yeah, he's the one."

"Do you remember him?"

"Sure. I remember that he always gave me bubble gum, which my mom didn't want me to have. He was really tall—well, at least it seemed that way to me. He would teach me things about the piano, like how to play a tune just on the black keys. And I loved watching him play. He introduced me to the piece *Rage over the Lost Penny*."

"That's a funny name," Liora says.

"It's by Beethoven and it really does sound like someone is furious. My Zayde would play it super-fast while I'd run in circles. Then he'd make up a story to go with the song which always involved a penny." As I tell Liora this, I feel a knot in my stomach. "He died the day after Yom Kippur, when I was five."

Liora is quiet for a moment. "How old was he?"

"Seventy-nine. I remember being really upset about him not living until eighty. I remember crying about that."

"That's understandable. You just wanted him to live longer."

"Well, sort of. I really think it had more to do with the number. Seventy-nine, yuck. It's an ugly number."

"What are you talking about?"

"That's just how I see it. And eighty, well, besides having my favorite number in it, eighty is beautiful. And it rhymes with Zayde."

Liora cracks up. "You are so weird!"

I lie on my back staring at a thin line of light across the ceiling. "I know it sounds weird. I can't help it. That's just my brain."

Liora rolls over in her bed. "How did your grandfather make so much money?"

Her question makes me flinch as I remember Hannah's remark. "In the jewelry business and the stock market. He was very generous, though. He gave tons of money to Jewish charities, especially education. And the money is still getting used to build libraries and schools. Schumacher Charitable Trust Fund."

"That's so great, Tal. It's like your grandfather is still alive in a way. You know what I mean?"

I consider Liora's idea. "Yeah. You're right." We lie quietly for a few minutes. My throat feels lumpy. "I really miss him."

"I'll never know my biological grandfather, so I can't really miss him," Liora says sleepily.

And as she drifts off, I'm left to ponder all the one-kid families in China. That's one place where I wouldn't stand out.

In the morning as I sit with Liora, Ruthie, and Shifra in shul, I suddenly remember this crazy dream I had last night. I was at an Uncle Yussie concert and he called me up on stage to help with a magic trick. I was all excited until I got up there and remembered that I was thirteen, not three. Then I realized I was wearing my pajamas! Hannah Finkelstein was in the audience. She stood up and threw water balloons at me. Then everyone else did the same. What a nightmare.

I close my eyes and see Hannah's mocking smile.

"What is the significance of Jacob's dream?" the rabbi asks the congregation.

Gosh, for a second I could've sworn he said *Talia's* dream.

"So much has been written about this famous biblical dream," Rabbi Gordon says from his podium. "It was a vision with angels going up and coming down a ladder, which stretched from earth to heaven. God appears to Jacob in the dream and promises that the very land upon which he is sleeping would be given to him and his descendants. God then promises to protect Jacob on his journey. And what does Jacob do when he awakes? He says, 'God is in this place and I did not know it!'"

Lots of kids go out to the hallway during Rabbi Gordon's speech, but I never do. My mother always made it clear that we sit quietly during the rabbi's speech. But, I really do like his speeches, now that I'm old enough to understand them. They aren't the usual stuff, and he always adds an interesting twist. I glance at my friends. They seem to be interested, too.

"I ask you to consider this: How many of us go through our lives, day after day, going about our business, keeping busy, without noticing the hand of God, without feeling His presence? What is it that will cause us to wake up and say, 'God was in this place, and I did not even notice?' Our sages suggest that Jacob is expressing regret. Perhaps, if he had realized that the ground upon which he slept was holy, that he was in the Divine presence, then he would have stayed awake all night!"

I think what Rabbi Gordon is talking about happens after you grow up. Kids notice everything that is going on around them. They live in the here and now. They don't rush all the time like adults. This makes me think about the guest we had the Shabbat Gabrielle came, the turban lady. The one who had cancer. She said she hadn't been to a Shabbat dinner since she was a kid. *I feel like I just woke up. Like*

I've been missing out all these years.' I don't ever want that to happen to me—to wake up one day and feel like I missed the important stuff.

After the service, Ruthie, Shifra, Liora and I move through the crowded sanctuary and out toward the social hall for the kiddush buffet. My stomach is grumbling. Hope they have those chocolate wafers.

"My brother's dying to meet Uncle Yussie," Ruthie says, as she puts her siddur back on the bookshelf.

"How does he even know he's here?" I say, feeling panicky.

"My dad told us when he came home from shul last night. He said Uncle Yussie gave out lollipops to the little kids who were there."

"So that was your mom's surprise?" Shifra asks.

"Yeah. Let's hope it's a better one next time."

"Talia didn't even recognize him," Liora says to Ruthie.

Shifra scans the crowd. "Where is he?"

"Follow me. And don't expect me to introduce you," I say, maneuvering past Meyer Feingold and his friends.

I see Meyer looking at me. He mumbles "Shabbat Shalom." I look the other way.

"Come on," I say to Liora. "Let's go stake our place at the pastry table."

She whispers in my ear. "Dr. Janas says Meyer's a math whiz."

I shrug. "So I've heard. I wonder what he's doing here. His family belongs to the Woodland Street Synagogue."

"Maybe—"

"Hey, look," Shifra interrupts, pointing to the back of the social hall. "There he is! Juggling!"

Sure enough, it's Uncle Yussie, juggling three balls with a crowd of excited kids closing in on him.

"Uncle Yussie!" a little boy cries.

"Can I try?"

"Are you gonna sing?"

The knot of kids keeps getting bigger. They start jumping up and down. I overhear a woman say, "He's staying at the Schumachers'."

Uncle Yussie tosses the balls to the kids. Big mistake. In a second they're all fighting for them.

"Oh, there's Avi," Ruthie says. "I hope he doesn't get crushed."

Uncle Yussie reaches into his tallis bag and starts giving out candy. "Remember to say a blessing!" he says in his famous, jolly voice.

I feel a hand tap my shoulder. I turn to see Hannah Finkelstein grinning at me. "Did Uncle Yussie give you a private show?"

I wish a Divine ladder would appear right now so I could climb out of this nightmare.

I made plans with Ruthie to meet her after Shabbat lunch, but right now Gabbers is asking Uncle Yussie a million questions about his performing career. Everything he says reminds Gabbers of some event in her life which she of course shares with all of us. I bet Liora is thinking the same thing as I am: when is this going to end? Mom seems to pick up on this and finally excuses me and Liora. Hurray!

We make our getaway and Liora and I head over to pick up Ruthie for the Shabbat Club. The afternoon sun warms my cheeks on this crisp November day. The maple trees are bare now but look less gloomy in the sunshine.

Ruthie bounds out of her house as soon as we approach the walkway. She's wearing a cute beige sweater coat. "Rescue me!" she cries, running toward us. "What took you guys so long?"

"Uncle Yussie sang a long encore," I joke. I catch a glimpse of her brothers Avi and Noam banging on the living room window.

"It's an insane asylum in there," Ruthie says, exasperated.

From what I've witnessed over at Ruthie's house, she's probably not exaggerating by much.

"What happened?" Liora asks as we head up Oak Street together.

"First Avi came home from shul singing Uncle Yussie's song, 'Saturday's My Day of Rest' at the top of his lungs, which set Noam off because he doesn't like Avi's singing."

I cringe hearing that Uncle Yussie set things off.

"Then, Noam was upset because he didn't get to see Uncle Yussie. Then they started tackling each other and Noam threw a toy car and hit Avi in the head. That was all before lunch. Then after I coaxed Benny for fifteen minutes to take his antibiotic, he spit it out on the kitchen floor." Ruthie takes a big breath. "At lunch, Sammy started whining about how my father favors Jake just because my dad let Jake drink the last of the grape juice. He left the table crying. And to top it off, my mom is throwing up all day long."

"And I thought my house was lively on Shabbat," I say, stepping over a smashed pumpkin on the sidewalk.

"It's like this every day," Ruthie says. "I can't imagine what's going to happen when the baby comes."

"Maybe your parents will hire help," I say.

"Yeah, and you're looking at her," Ruthie replies.

"But what about when you're in school?"

Ruthie shrugs. "I think my grandmother will come then. At least for the first few weeks."

Ruthie often complains about how much she has to help out around the house. The truth is, I think Ruthie really likes being the big sister. Her brothers do get annoying, but you can tell they think Ruthie is the best. Still, it would be nice if her parents hired a housecleaner.

Esther Grubner is hosting the Shabbat Club this week. By the time we get there, the girls are all gathered around Esther's family room munching on snacks. "Hey, Shabbat Shalom everyone," Gila, the group co-leader, says as we take off our coats. "So glad you guys could make it."

"I thought maybe you'd bring Uncle Yussie along," Hannah calls out to me. All the girls crack up.

"No," I say, "but I did arrange for an autographed picture just for you, Hannah."

"And no selling it on eBay," Ruthie adds, which makes everyone laugh again.

"Come on, sit down," Baila, the second leader, says. "We were just getting started."

After the usual shmoozing and singing, we recite Psalms together for Israel and then for people who are sick. Then Baila says she has something on her mind that she'd like to share.

"Last time we met, we talked about the role of money in our lives. I know some of the comments hit a sore spot in a few of you, and I don't want to rehash that right now. What I do want to do, is to share an interesting idea related to that topic. I came across it when I was studying this week's Torah portion."

Baila puts her hands together. "So, we all know the story about the dream of Jacob's ladder."

Oh, here we go again.

"Well, I learned that the Hebrew word for ladder is *sulam*. The numerical value for the letters in that word equals 136."

My ears perk up.

"It so happens that the Hebrew word for money, *mammon*, and for poverty, *oni,* also equal 136."

"Cool," I say.

Baila smiles. "Yeah, I thought so, too. But I started to wonder how the words ladder, money, and poverty are related."

Esther chimes in. "It's kind of obvious with money and poverty. The words are sort of opposite. But I don't get how ladder fits in."

"I'm not sure they are opposite," Liora comments. "Wealth would be the opposite of poverty. Money can take away poverty."

"Absolutely," Gila says. "So what about the ladder?"

We're all quiet for a moment, then Shifra jumps in. "Oh, I get it. Maybe the ladder represents climbing to a higher place, like a career ladder. Each step you climb might get you more money. So money can take you to higher places."

"Okay," Gila replies. "You're definitely onto something. Now how about a ladder and poverty?"

Shifra tries again. "Are you saying that if you don't use money correctly then you go down the ladder, and you'll become poor?"

Baila tilts her head. "Well... that's a possibility. What I got out of the commentary was that a ladder takes us up or down. And if the ladder symbolizes money, then the money we are blessed with can do the same. It is all how we use it. If we use our money to help others, to better our communities and our schools, to live a Jewish life, which by the way is pretty expensive—then we are going upward toward God. We're growing spiritually."

"But I still don't see what poverty has to do with it," Liora says.

"Just like wealth can lead to corruption, so can poverty," Alison Leber suggests.

"You might be tempted to steal and cheat?" Hannah asks.

Gila nods. "That's right. So, girls, whether money is number one on your value list or at the bottom is not important. What matters is whether you use the money to ascend the ladder to good things or descend the ladder to bad things."

"I like that," Shifra says.

"Good. So now after this lofty idea, let's have some fun and play the ladder letter game. You have sixty seconds to put yourselves in alphabetical order by first name. Go!"

I don't see Gabrielle all Shabbat afternoon. When I ask my mother where she is, she just says, "Oh, I think she's visiting."

Visiting who? It's not like she knows that many people around here. Maybe she has another date with Jared Samuels in someone else's living room. Or they might have gone for a walk in the park.

By four o'clock the house is quiet. Everyone seems to be taking a Shabbat nap except for Gabbers, wherever she is, and Liora and me. Upstairs in my room, I open my desk drawer and take out my math notebook.

"This is the notebook I told you about."

She looks at the cover. "Tali's Tricks. Cute stickers."

"I was eight when I started it. You know, the sticker phase?"

"I like the little drawings, too." Liora flips through my notebook. "Wow, you were really serious."

"Not serious," I object. "More like… obsessed with tricks. I had fun playing around with numbers."

Liora looks at me. "Playing around?"

I take the notebook back. "Here. Let me try this one. Pick a secret number, but don't tell it to me."

"Okay. Got it."

"Now add 7 to your secret number."

"Yeah."

"Multiply your answer by 2."

Liora nods.

"Subtract 6… and divide that by 2."

"Um… okay."

I close the book. "What number did you end up with?"

"Eighteen."

"Your secret number is 14," I say triumphantly.

Liora nods. "You're right. But I don't think you're going to wow the talent show."

"What's cool is how it works. It's just basic algebra."

Liora flops down on the trundle bed. "I'll take your word for it."

"Okay, that trick is pretty lame, but how about this one—"

"Spare me, Talia!" Liora groans. "Can we wait till after Shabbat for the math lesson?"

"Sure...I wasn't trying to teach you anything."

"I know. It's just that... you can get a little carried away with math."

"Hmm. So I've been told."

After havdalah, Liora and I clear off the Shabbat table and load the dishwasher. Then we bake brownies to be savored after our math study session. Liora brought up the idea of asking Hannah to come over, but I didn't want to chance it. I'm really enjoying the time alone with Liora for a change, and I was pretty sure Hannah would spoil things.

Mom said it would be okay to use the library. Even though I prefer studying sprawled on my bedroom floor, I thought the library would put us more in the mood for work. It has paneled walls, built-in bookshelves, a computer, and a big mahogany table with leather chairs.

"This is a nice room," Liora says, walking around the library. "So many books!"

I start setting up our papers and stuff on the table. "No kidding. My parents are huge book collectors. And so was my grandfather. We have a Passover Haggadah from 1743."

Liora runs her hand across the leather-bound Talmud volumes.

"Impressive."

I sit down and pat the seat next to me. "Okay, ready for Tali's tricks?"

First, I review some basic things like decimals, percentages, and fractions, just to make sure Liora is strong in that department. So far, so good. Then I show her some shortcuts for different types of calculations. Finally, we start to tackle the contest booklet. That's when the trouble begins.

"This doesn't make sense," Liora says, throwing her head back.

"Okay. Just try working through it backwards," I coax. "See if that helps."

We trudge through more problems.

Not including numbers with zeros, how many three-digit numbers have digits that add up to 6 (example: 330)?

Liora looks up at me, worried. "Does Hannah know this stuff?"

"Don't worry about Hannah! She'll be able to help us in the team part. It won't matter if you don't know what to do."

I immediately regret my words.

Liora's dark eyes widen. "So I'm just supposed to sit there like I'm stupid?"

"No, that's not what I meant. It's just… well, that's why it is a team. Not everyone can contribute fully for every problem. Three heads are better than one."

Liora drops her pencil. "I think you mean *two* heads."

I decide to try a different approach. I ask Liora to watch me while I solve a problem and think aloud.

"So then, the last step is to find the square root of 136. Get it?" I ask hopefully.

Liora rubs her eyes. "Yeah, I think so. Can we have some brownies now?"

Mr. Clark picks up Liora at 9:30 PM. That's considered late for Liora's parents. He thanks me for all the help I'm giving his daughter. He says he always knew Liora had what it takes to do something like this, and that she just didn't have enough confidence. That was what I thought when I came up with the idea. Now I'm not so sure.

Right after Liora leaves, Ruthie calls asking me to cover for her babysitting job tomorrow afternoon at the Shankmans. Her mom needs her at home. I am more than thrilled because I rarely get calls to babysit. My parents give me an allowance, but I'd like to earn my own money for a change. I also like being in other people's homes to see how they run their household, and how they treat their kids. And besides, if I'm going to be a big sister, I need some practice.

After a game of chess with Dad, I go upstairs to bed. As I get to my room, I hear Gabrielle humming. Her door is opened slightly. I decide to knock. She doesn't answer. I knock again. She's still humming. I open the door a little. She's sitting on her bed wearing headphones and typing furiously on her laptop. She is still dressed in her Shabbat clothes.

"Gabrielle?"

She looks up, startled. "Oh, you scared me!" She pulls off the headphones. "Sorry, I didn't even see you there, I was so engrossed in this music. Did you ever listen to Avital Miller? She's an Israeli singer. Gorgeous voice. I only wish I could sing like that. Her songs put me in a trance. Hey, I'm working on the play right now—you know, the script for the production? Can I ask your input on a few things?"

I'm not sure which question to answer. "Uh, yeah. I guess. I was going to bed, actually—"

"It will only take a sec." She waves her hand. "Close the door, come on in." She pats the end of her bed. "Here, sit down. I'm really excited about this. I think it's going to be good. Last night I could barely sleep. My mind was spinning with ideas. Does that ever happen to you?"

"Sometimes when—"

"Well it happens to me a lot. You know, the creative type. Anyway, Mrs. Brody told me I should just go with it—plan the whole thing and then present it to the girls. At first I wanted to make them a part of it, you know, so they wouldn't feel like I was imposing it on them. I wanted them to embrace the idea. But Mrs. Brody said it would take forever, and the girls wouldn't be able to agree, so it was just best to bring a planned production. To tell you the truth, I'm a little nervous about that. What do you think?"

Think? Does she really want to know? I decide to be honest. "Mrs. Brody is probably right," I tell her, "but the girls might give you a hard time. It depends. I only saw the title, but what's it really about?"

Gabrielle closes the laptop and gets off the bed. "Okay, picture this." She spreads her hands into the air. "Miriam as a child. Miriam the big sister. Miriam the midwife. Miriam the prophetess." Then suddenly she is swaying her body, her hands fluttering in the air. "Miriam, who crossed the Red Sea, leading the women in song."

"So… it's about Miriam?"

"Yes! All the faces of Miriam. Everything we know about her from the Torah, the commentators, and the Midrash." Gabrielle starts pacing back and forth. "We'll tell her story through drama… dance… song… art." She spins around, her eyes wide with excitement. "What do you think?"

I'm skeptical, but I don't say this. "I think it's a good idea."

Gabrielle looks as if I just said I loved her or something. "Oh, thank you!" Her voice gets all soft. "*Thank you*. I really wasn't sure. I'm new to this. I needed to get a girl's opinion." Suddenly her expression shifts. "So, what part would you like?"

"Me? I don't know, really. I mean, I'm not a dancer or singer or anything—"

"But you can play the piano!"

How do I get out of this?

"I'll have to think about it. But, right now I'd better get to bed before my dad comes upstairs."

Gabrielle blinks. "What time is it, anyway?"

"Probably a little after eleven."

Gabrielle hops back on the bed, and opens the laptop. "Don't let me keep you. I'm going to finish this up." She smiles at me. "'Night."

"See ya," I say, closing the bedroom door behind me. I guess it's nice when you finally get to go to bed when you want to.

Later that night, I wake suddenly from some bad dream that I can't even remember. My heart is pounding in my rib cage. The clock glows 3:35 AM. Ugh. I remember that it's Sunday and feel relieved. Then I hear a faint clicking sound. I roll over and look toward my open door. Who opened it? Mom? Dad?

I get out of bed and step into the dark hallway. I see the light beneath Gabrielle's door. I hear the clicking of the computer keys. Then she starts to hum.

Eighteen

"Did you bring the toy bag?" Rebecca Shankman asks me as I walk in the front door. She is chewing on her blonde pigtail. "Ruthie always brings a toy bag."

Thanks for the heads-up, Ruthie.

"Come on in," Mrs. Shankman says. "Let me take your coat. Rebecca, sweetie, this is Talia."

"Did she bring it, Mommy? Did she?"

Mrs. Shankman is all dressed up in an elegant floral skirt. I wonder if she bought her pearl necklace at my dad's store.

"Rebecca is very fond of Ruthie," Mrs. Shankman explains. She turns to her daughter. "I'm sure Talia has lots of games to play with you."

I do?

Mrs. Shankman gives me a tour of the downstairs, while Rebecca tags along peppering me with questions.

"Give Mommy a minute, sweetie. I need to show Talia where everything is, okay?"

Mrs. Shankman goes through the afternoon schedule, the house rules, and emergency numbers. Then Mr. Shankman comes into the kitchen carrying a little boy who looks like he just woke up.

"There's my sweetie pie," Mrs. Shankman sings. "Dan, you remember Talia Schumacher."

"Sure. And this is Dovi," Mr. Shankman says. Dovi takes one

look at me and buries his head on his dad's shoulder. "He's a little shy, especially with new sitters."

"And we haven't had one for a long time," Mrs. Shankman adds. "The kids are so fond of Ruthie, and Rebecca was very disappointed to hear she couldn't make it." Mrs. Shankman lowers her voice. "Rebecca doesn't adapt well to change."

That's nice to know.

Mrs. Shankman opens the fridge. "I have their dinners all prepared, so you don't have to do a thing but stick the plates in the microwave for 45 seconds. Here are some cups of sliced grapes and apples. If they eat well they can have an oatmeal-raisin cookie for dessert. Rebecca gets straight juice and Dovi's is half water. But don't let him see you put the water in. The sippy cups are in the dairy cupboard. Let's see… what else?"

Mrs. Shankman is making me nervous. "I think I'll be fine," I say confidently.

She peers at me for a second. "Have you babysat before? Ruthie wasn't sure."

I feel my neck grow warm. "Uh, yes, a few times. I have little cousins that come over now and then."

"It's a lot of responsibility, caring for a preschooler and a toddler. That's why we prefer girls who have younger siblings. You can understand that." Her worried face brightens. "But Ruthie highly recommended you, so, I guess we can relax."

I nod and force a smile.

"Well then, I think we're all set," she announces.

As soon as Mr. and Mrs. Shankman pull out of the driveway, Rebecca starts to cry.

"What's wrong?" I ask.

"I want my mommy."

"She'll be back soon. Want to play a game?"

Rebecca frowns. "I don't like you."

I'm insulted. "What did I do?"

Oops, wrong question. This only makes her cry harder. Then Dovi toddles into the family room. At least he is smiling.

"Hi, Dovi. Do you want me to read you a book?" I say in my best babysitter voice.

Dovi stares at his whimpering sister. Then his face crumbles. Oh, no. He plops down on the rug and wails. Why didn't Ruthie warn me about this? And what do two- and four-year-olds like to do, anyway? I consider texting Ruthie, but then decide to figure it out on my own.

I start going through their toy box, pulling out a ball, a naked doll, a fire truck. "How about this?" I ask, holding up an animal puzzle.

Nothing stops their crying.

Then I spy the television. Hmm. Mrs. Shankman didn't say anything about that. I open the cabinet. Bingo. They've got a whole mess of kiddie DVDs.

"Hey, Rebecca, Dovi, want to watch a show?"

My words are magic. Both kids stop crying and crawl over to the TV. "Let's see," I say, browsing through the choices. On second thought... I turn to Rebecca. "Do you have a favorite show?"

Rebecca's blue eyes light up. "Uncle Yussie!"

Nineteen

In school the next morning after davening, Mrs. Brody announces that instead of our usual Community Meeting, Miss Markus will meet with us to go over the production details. I am looking forward to this about as much as I look forward to the usual Community Meeting. Every other Monday we have Community Meeting when each grade meets with the dean, principal, and guidance counselor to discuss various school matters like dressing modestly, peer pressure, stress relief—you know, the kind of stuff teachers like to talk to us about.

Everyone but me seems to be excited about the production. I never was much of a performer, so what is there to be excited about? I'm also a little worried about how Gabrielle will act. I mean, it's not like she's related to me, but just the fact that she is now connected to my family opens the door to embarrassment.

During History, my mind drifts off to what Hannah said. Maybe I should have listened to Liora and invited her. It's true that we don't have much time left before the competition. One way or another we need to practice together. I am hoping that our school practice threesomes will be enough.

At lunch I tell the gang about Gabrielle's all-nighter.

"How could she write a whole play in one night?" Liora asks, stirring her yogurt cup.

"I think she worked on it all day Sunday, too."

"Uh-oh," Shifra says, leaning toward me. "Sounds manic."

"Sounds intense," Ruthie says while sketching a dress in her sketchbook. "I mean, I sometimes get caught up in a sewing project, but I never stayed up all night to do it."

"But it was more than that," I say. "It was like she was in another world."

"She was!" Ruthie says. "Miriam's world."

We all laugh.

"We'll definitely be seeing a lot of Miss Markus now," Shifra says, "which should give us more clues to the mystery."

"We'll have more chance to get to know her," Ruthie says, adding a belt to the dress.

"Has anyone forgotten that I have to live with her?" I whine.

"I thought she was fun," Liora said. "C'mon, Tal. You have to admit she's entertaining."

"Yeah, Gabrielle *and* Uncle Yussie. That's enough entertainment for a while," I say, crushing my milk carton.

"I bet things are going to get a lot livelier around school," Liora adds. She licks the yogurt off her spoon. Then she nudges my elbow. "Here comes Hannah."

Hannah is wearing a smug look on her face. She stops at our table and stares at me for a second. "How come I was left out of the math study last night?" she asks, hands on her hips.

She catches me off guard. Did Liora tell her?

"What's the big deal?" I shrug. "We don't have to study together all the time."

She squints her green eyes. "Do you not know the meaning of the word *team*?" she says.

"And do you not know the meaning of *mean*?" I shoot back.

"I am not mean!"

Ruthie jumps in. "You mean you don't mean to be mean."

"That's not what I mean!" Hannah replies, which makes us all crack up. She bites her lip. "You guys are so immature." Then she turns on her heels and walks away in a huff as usual.

"Sorry," Liora says to me. "It just kind of slipped this morning when she pounced on me asking if I did problem set six."

I sigh. "I asked you not to tell her, Liora."

"Sorry, I'm not good at keeping secrets."

Shifra zips up her lunch bag. "I just don't get it. Since when is math study so secretive?"

"Talia doesn't like studying with Hannah," Liora blurts out.

"Who does?" Ruthie says.

"That's not the point," Liora says. "We're supposed to be a team."

I feel a sliver of guilt creeping up. "I think we needed our time together last night. Don't you? Look at how much you learned," I say, trying to convince myself as much as Liora. "Hannah just felt left out. You'll see. We'll get a lot done when all three of us work with Dr. Janas."

After everyone in the cafeteria sings the Grace after Meals, Mrs. Brody tells us there will be a meeting in the student lounge.

"How are we all supposed to fit in there?" Ruthie remarks as we leave the lunchroom.

"I bet Gabbers asked for a cozy meeting place," I reply. "Maybe she is planning on doing some yoga with us. Can't you imagine fifty girls doing headstands?"

The student lounge is a carpeted area just outside the library with a skylight, comfy chairs and couches, a snack machine, game shelf, and mini-tables. On the partition separating the lounge is a small gold plaque that says: *A gift from the Schumacher family.* My parents donated the lounge in honor of my Bat Mitzvah (thankfully they didn't say that on the plaque!) and it has become a popular hangout for anyone who actually has a free moment during school.

Gabrielle is standing beneath the skylight. Her skin looks pale against her black turtleneck. She's wearing an orange gypsy skirt with her hair pulled back in a single braid.

"C'mon in everyone," she says with that huge smile. "Find a place to sit. On the floor is fine."

Surprisingly, we all fit snugly in the lounge. I settle down next to Ruthie and Malki Sneiderman. Everyone is still talking while Gabrielle stands in front of us. She waits, and finally the whispering stops. Then Gabrielle closes her eyes and takes a deep breath.

"There is energy flowing here right now. Can you feel it? It's girl

156

energy. Creative energy."

Ruthie stifles a laugh.

"There is power in this energy," Gabrielle says in a whispery voice. "Let's all close our eyes a moment. Don't say a thing. Just feel the energy."

Here we go. I feel only one thing—I'm getting uncomfortably hot. I hear a few giggles.

"Shh. Please, girls," Gabrielle says softly. "Just focus on the energy. Let go of your thoughts, your self-consciousness. Just be."

By some miracle, all the girls manage to keep quiet for a few moments. I feel really stupid doing this.

"Ah, that was nice. Wasn't it?" Gabrielle says, her eyes wide. Then she starts to describe the theme of the production. "Miriam's life begins with an act of love, as she places her baby brother's basket into the Nile and waits and watches until he reaches the safety of the Pharaoh's daughter. Our production will explore all the roles of this Jewish leader, from big sister, to midwife, to prophetess, and finally, as a wise elder. We will use our creative feminine energy to bring Miriam to life." Gabrielle's dramatic voice has captured the students. I glance around. No one is laughing. At least not yet.

"There will be plenty of roles for each of you to choose from," she says, looking around the room. "In addition to the main characters, we are going to need a chorus, a music ensemble, dancers, costume and set designers, ticket sellers, and a few other odds and ends. I've made a special place for notices regarding the production on the middle school bulletin board. Please check this frequently. Tomorrow, you'll be able to pick up a copy of the play in the office. Any questions?"

While Gabrielle answers questions, I start plotting how I can get out of all this. I remember Mrs. Brody saying she expected everyone to be involved. I wonder if hosting the production manager counts. Maybe I could just sell tickets. That doesn't sound too time-consuming.

"I can't decide," Ruthie says to me after the meeting as we head toward our lockers. "Costume design or dance?"

I reach for my phone. "Maybe you should do both," I say flatly. "Hang on a sec. There's a text from my mom." I scroll down the message. "No way!"

"What?"

I look up at Ruthie. "My mom wants to take me out for dinner. Tonight."

"Yeah, so?"

"She never does that, especially on a weeknight. Listen." I look down at the message and read it out loud.

Let's have mom/daughter time. Something I want to talk about. Shalom China. 6:30.

Ruthie's eyes widen. "Do you think—"

"Yes!" I start jumping up and down. "She wants to tell me the good news. I just know it!"

Ruthie hugs me. "Maybe she has cravings for Chinese food."

I am in a good mood the rest of the day. Even Mrs. Wordsworth's poetry reading sounds good. And when Hannah Finkelstein gets the highest score on the math quiz, I am actually happy for her.

Twenty

Mom picks me up after work. I hop in the car and give her a kiss on the cheek.

"Well, that's nice," she says, pulling out of the driveway. "Hungry?"

"Yeah." I am grinning ear to ear.

It's only a five-minute drive to the restaurant. Greensborough has one kosher pizza shop, two bakeries, a dairy restaurant, a deli, a steakhouse, an ice cream parlor, and Shalom China, my favorite.

Mom tells me that she heard Mrs. Sheffman's cancer is in remission. For a split second, I think this might be what she wanted to talk about, then I realize she wouldn't be taking me out to dinner for that. Whew.

"That's great news, Mom." I glance over at her.

"It made my day, that's for sure. Thank God."

There is soft Chinese music playing as we enter the restaurant. The hostess escorts us to a table in the middle of the dining room.

"Do you have something more private?" Mom asks.

My stomach flutters.

"Of course," she replies politely.

Mom and I follow the hostess to a small booth in the back. I take off my coat and slide onto the leather seat. Mom asks the hostess for tea. A small lantern glows on the tabletop. I unfold the stiff white napkin and place it on my lap, showing Mom that I do remember my manners.

"Well, this is different," I say. "I mean, good different."

She smiles. "Sometimes it's good to do something out of the ordinary."

"Is Dad coming, too?" I ask.

Mom shakes her head. "No, just the two of us tonight." She opens her menu. "Egg rolls?"

"Sure. With duck sauce. Can we get pan-fried dumplings, too?"

After we order, she starts asking me about school. It's not what I want to talk about, of course, but I go along. I tell her about Gabrielle's production meeting (keeping positive), and how I think I'll sell tickets.

Mom raises her perfectly groomed eyebrows.

"That's all?"

"I'm not into dance, Mom. Or singing. Or acting for that matter."

"What about musical accompaniment? I have inside information that Gabrielle would really like you to play the piano."

Oh, no. Looks like Mom and Gabbers are in this together. I fish for a good excuse. "I'm pretty busy. There's the math team—"

Mom waves her hand. "Talia, you are ahead of the game. And besides, the competition is a few weeks away. The production isn't until mid-February."

"Why does it matter what part I do, anyway?" I ask, trying not to show my annoyance.

Mom sips her tea. "I just think you should take a more active role. Use your talents." She gives me one of her Mom looks. "Your grandfather would be very proud of you."

I feel the pressure coming on. Why does she have to bring my grandfather into this?

"I'll think about it," I reply with forced cheerfulness.

A pretty Chinese waitress brings the Kung Pao chicken. Seeing her reminds me of China's one-child rule. I wonder if the waitress has any siblings or if she is in the Only Club, too. Then I almost forget why I am sitting here with my mother! That nervous feeling returns to my stomach. I can barely eat.

After more chitchat with Mom, I can't wait any longer. "So, what did you want to tell me?" I say, trying to sound casual.

"Well," Mom says, dragging out the word. "I have good news."

I take a deep breath.

Her eyes are gleaming. "I got a promotion."

I swallow. "A what?"

"A job promotion. My title is now Senior Tax Manager."

I feel a copper taste in my mouth. I can't speak. I move a bit of rice around my plate.

Mom raises her glass. "Hey, that's good news, in case you didn't realize it. Aren't you going to wish me a mazel tov?"

"Congratulations," I mumble.

"Well, maybe it doesn't sound very exciting to you now, but the good news is that I won't have to travel! And… I can work more from home. It's called flex-time." Her words seem to be coming from the bottom of a well. "Is something wrong, sweetheart?"

I try to push the tears back. "Can we go home?"

She reaches her hand toward mine. "Are you feeling sick?"

I shake my head. *How could I have been so stupid?*

"Talia, please tell me what's wrong."

I look across the restaurant, hoping not to see anyone I know. "I can't talk about it now. Please, let's just go."

"But we just got started."

I don't know what to say. Mom stares at me while I pick at my egg roll. She waits a moment, then signals the waitress and asks her to wrap our food.

Thankfully, she doesn't say anything more during the ride home. I sit in the cold silence of our car thinking about what I'm going to say to Ruthie.

As soon as I walk into the house, I go right up the stairs to my room and close the door.

"Talia?" I hear Mom call. "Can we talk?"

I fling myself onto the bed and bury my face in my pillow.

A moment later Mom is knocking. "Talia, honey, please. Did I say something wrong? I think I at least deserve an explanation. Please, talk to me. Whatever it is, you can tell me."

I hear her open the door. I can no longer hold in my tears.

"Talia?"

She walks over to the bed and sits down. "I have this feeling that you were expecting me to say something else. Is that it?"

"Yes," I manage to say in between sobs.

She waits.

Do I make something up or tell the truth? I take a deep breath. "I feel stupid telling you this... but I really thought you were going to say—"

Mom waits again. "Say what?"

"Say... say that... you were quitting your job."

Did I really just say that?

Mom sighs deeply. "Oh, Talia. I'm so sorry, honey. We had this conversation, didn't we? About my staying home? I guess I didn't take you seriously. But I don't need to quit my job in order to spend more time with you. Things will be better without all the business trips and night hours. You'll see."

I hug my pillow. "Yeah, I guess."

"You probably thought a promotion meant more work, hmm? Well, it usually does. This is more of a job change. I took it so things would be less hectic."

"Oh. I get it now," I say, trying to sound like I feel better.

Mom rubs my back. "Look, let's see how it goes. And if there is some school event you want me to be part of, or someplace you want me to take you, then you'll let me know. Okay?"

What am I getting myself into?

"You know..." she says thoughtfully, "we should take a trip together. Just the two of us. Maybe during the December break. We could go to New York, go shopping, see a Broadway show. How does that sound?"

I smile through my tears. "Sounds good, Mom."

She leans over and kisses my forehead. "How about we go downstairs and have some of those fortune cookies?"

I imagine the message in mine: *You are a fool.*

Twenty-One

Ruthie is waiting for me in the doorway of her house. "Bye, Mom! Have a good day," she calls, stepping outside. Her long blonde hair is still damp from the shower. Ruthie searches my face and immediately knows that I do not have good news.

"Let's go," I sigh. I start walking toward school.

Ruthie follows me. "Tell me what happened," she says, buttoning her jean jacket. "Ooh, it's getting cold."

"Nothing to tell, except that I was way off."

"Your mom's not pregnant?" she asks surprised.

"The only part I got right was the letter *p*. She's not pregnant, she got a *promotion*."

"Oh, Tal, you must have been so disappointed!"

"No kidding." We turn onto Fuller Street. "I still can't believe it."

"How did you act when she told you? Did you tell her what you thought?"

"No way." Even though Ruthie is my best friend, I don't want to tell her the full truth. "I just pretended to be real happy. It *is* good news, you know. My mom won't have to travel anymore."

"That's some consolation, I guess."

"But what I don't get is why she went to the obstetrician," I say.

"There must be other reasons for going to that kind of doctor," Ruthie replies.

"Maybe. She even got fatter around the waist."

"Don't tell her that," Ruthie warns.

We walk for a few minutes without talking. I can tell that Ruthie is trying to find a silver lining to my disappointing news.

"Hey, just because it didn't happen now doesn't mean it still couldn't," Ruthie says, right on cue.

I shake my head. "I seriously doubt it. I think I just fooled myself because I wanted so badly for it to be true. Looks like I'm going to be a lifelong member of the Only Child Club, after all."

"Do you think your parents would ever adopt a baby?" Ruthie asks. "You know, like Liora's parents."

"Now, there's an interesting idea. I've never heard my mom say anything about adopting."

"My mom knows a lady who adopted a baby from Kazakhstan," Ruthie says. "I don't even know where the heck that is, but the baby is adorable. And, then, about a year later, the lady got pregnant! Liora told me that her mom thought she couldn't have any more children, but after they adopted her, they had Adam a few years later."

For a second, I imagine having a cute Chinese baby sister. Then I realize how far-fetched the idea is. Ruthie looks over at me. "You never know, Tal."

We get to school just after the school bus arrives. "You won't tell anyone, right?" I ask her before the bus unloads.

Ruthie puts her arm around my shoulder. "Your secret is safe with me."

"Thanks. Let's catch Shifra before davening."

She slaps her head. "Oops, I almost forgot. I was supposed to meet with Rabbi Cohen before school. I better go. See you at break!" Ruthie dashes off.

As I walk to my locker, I see the sign on the music room door: *Middle School Production Headquarters, Miss Markus, Director.* Mrs. Brody must have given Gabbers a workstation in the music room. I expect she'll be hanging around school most of the day planning her big show. I'm sure to run into her in the hallway. What if she stops to gab? I sure hope she doesn't try to walk home with me after school. Which brings me to another concern—that Gabbers is going to talk, talk, talk, about the play at home, and maybe drag me into the whole planning thing. And, if I end up playing piano for the ensemble, she'll want to practice with me in the living room. Tryouts are next week. I'll have Thanksgiving break to think about it, but from what my mom said last night, I don't think I have much choice. There's likely to be no escape from *Miriam's Song*.

It's raining during morning recess, so Shifra, Ruthie and I decide to head over to the student lounge. Looks like everyone else got our idea. I spot Hannah and Esther on the bean bag chairs poring over some magazine. Maya Rubin and Rina Sneiderman are huddled together at the table in the corner.

"Did you read this?" Maya Rubin calls out as soon as we walk in. She waves Gabrielle's script in the air.

I'm not surprised Maya likes it, considering her musical talent. I walk over to her table. "No, I haven't read it, but it's on my list—after *Moby Dick*."

"Seriously, Talia. It is amazing," Maya gushes.

I turn to Shifra. "Have you reviewed this masterpiece?"

"I started reading it during science," Shifra admits. "I really liked it. It's a great play."

Rina Sneiderman joins in. "Me too! I love the songs. Are you trying out for the chorus?" Rina asks Shifra. Everyone knows Shifra has a gorgeous voice.

"Definitely. I'm trying to convince Talia to join me."

"Yeah, right," I say. "I'm selling tickets."

"Miss Markus seems really nice," Maya adds. "I think it's so cool that she is a professional dancer."

"Make that *was*," I say.

"Still, New York City Ballet? That's not small stuff," Maya says. "So why did she come here?"

"You're asking the wrong person," I reply.

"That's classified information," Ruthie jokes.

"What's she like?" Maya asks.

I glance back to see if Hannah is eavesdropping. I refrain from outright gossiping, but offer a tantalizing tidbit. "I happen to know that the talented Miss Markus wrote this script in just two days."

"No way!" Rina exclaims. "That's impossible."

"You mean she didn't *buy* the script?" Maya asks incredulously.

"Nope. What you have in your hands is an original," I say. "Just like Miss Markus."

Ruthie laughs at my inside joke. "I'm trying out for the dance."

"Cool. There are a lot of dances," Maya says, turning the pages of the script.

"I don't get it," Rina says, looking at the cast page. "Who is supposed to play Moses and Aaron?"

"How about Rabbi Cohen?" Ruthie suggests. "Isn't his first name Moshe?"

We all laugh at the thought of our Hebrew teacher acting with a cast of girls.

Just then Hannah Finkelstein pops up from the bean bag chair. She walks right over to us. Can she ever stay out of our business?

"Did you help write the script, Talia?" she asks in her usual mocking voice.

I roll my eyes. "That's not my department."

Hannah grins. "Well, after that lonely poem you wrote, I thought you might have penned a few songs. I suppose you'll get to play Miriam?"

"Why on earth would I want to do that?" I reply.

She folds her arms. "We all know you want to be numero uno. Plus, your parents have the pull around here, and they're hosting Miss Dancerina."

Ruthie huffs. "Hannah, you are so way-off, it isn't funny."

I feel the anger rising in my chest. "For your information, I have no interest in that part. So go ahead and try out if you want. I really don't care."

"Well, that's a surprise," Hannah says with a shrug. "I think I will try out, after all."

"Great to hear," I say just as the bell rings.

Hannah runs her fingers through her hair. "Well, see you in Math, then," she says to me. I watch her confidently strut back over to Esther. "C'mon."

Rina stands up. "Ugh, she can be so annoying. I didn't want to mention it, but Hannah's going to be competing against me and my

166

sister."

"Really?" I say. "You and Malki both want to be Miriam?"

Rina nods. "We're used to competing against each other."

"Won't you feel disappointed if Malki gets the part?" I ask, wondering how this kind of thing works with twin sisters.

"A little, but I'll be happy for her, too," Rina says, heading out of the lounge. "So, either way, I kind of win." She waves. "See ya!"

Rina's comment reminds me of my phantom sibling, and I feel a tug in my heart.

"Hannah suffers from delusions of grandeur," Shifra says as we head down the hallway.

"Translation please?" Ruthie says.

Shifra stops by the drinking fountain. "It means that Hannah thinks she can do anything. Basically a big shot."

We all crack up. "Right on," Ruthie says.

After school, in the privacy of my bedroom, while Doris is downstairs ironing, I sprawl on my bed and start reading the script.

The stage is dark. The elderly Miriam stands alone in the spotlight facing the audience.

Miriam: I have lived a full life. I have seen our redemption from Egypt. I have traveled the desert with my people. I have witnessed God's miracles. I am the daughter of Yocheved and Amram, sister to Moses and Aaron, mother of Hur, ancestor of King David. My name means Bitter Sea. I am Miriam.

Music begins. Spotlight on chorus. Song: Looking Back.

I read it straight through. The story goes back and forth between the old Miriam and her younger self. There are six dances, and nine songs. (Couldn't she have made it an even number?) The crossing of the Red Sea looks cool. So do the scenery descriptions. I have to admit, the play sounds pretty good.

There's a knock on my door. "Talia?"

Yikes, it's Gabbers. What is she doing home already? I hide the script under my pillow.

"Come in."

She pokes her head in the door. "Hi there! Don't mean to bother you, but I was just wondering if you had a chance to read my script?"

Is she a mind reader or something? "Yeah, actually I have."

She looks relieved. "Can I come in for a sec?"

Oh boy. "Sure."

Gabrielle sits on the edge of my bed. A little too close for comfort. "So? What do you think?"

I tell her the truth.

She turns into a little kid. "Oh, I'm so happy! I mean, I thought it was good, but you know how you just sometimes need validation? I poured my heart and soul into this, and we haven't even begun the rehearsals! Wow." She lets out a deep breath, then looks at me with her eager green eyes. "Do you have any suggestions?"

"Me?"

Gabrielle pats my knee. "Yeah, you. Anything I should add or take out?"

"Um, not really. It's good. And everyone at school seems to like it too. I heard a lot of kids read it during class," I say. "Did you really write this in two days?"

"Yeah, just about," she says, her eyes gleaming. "Right now my head is just bursting with ideas for choreography and music."

"You're writing the songs?" I ask incredulously.

"Just the words. I'm setting it to Jewish melodies, except for 'Miriam's Song.'" She looks at me as if she's revealing a secret. "That one is my baby. I'm working on it now."

"Wow, I didn't know you wrote music, too."

She gives me a bashful look. "Well, when I'm inspired. Sometimes I become like a vessel and this creative force just flows through me. That's how it was writing the play. It felt as if Miriam was standing right next to me telling me her life story." She catches my doubtful expression. "Sound strange?"

"Kind of," I admit. "I can't say I have ever felt a biblical character visit me, but I guess that would be pretty amazing if it happened."

"I think it comes from my dance training," Gabbers continues. "In a performance you totally immerse yourself in the movement and the music. You can't be thinking about anything else. You *are* the dance. You become one."

"One?" I ask.

She puts her hand over her heart. "Whole. Complete."

What in the world is she talking about?

"It's an amazing experience when it happens," Gabrielle says dreamily. "But it takes a lot of hard work."

I pull my knees up to my chest. "Oh."

"So… I'm hoping you can help me?"

Uh-oh. "How?"

"By listening to my composition and telling me what you think."

"I guess I could do that," I say, relieved she didn't ask me to be one of the dancers.

"Great! Thank you so much." Gabrielle bites her bottom lip. "There is one more thing… would you consider trying out for the piano ensemble?"

I feel my cheeks flush. "Did my mother put you up to this?"

Gabrielle shakes her head. "No. No, she didn't. Really. I had you in mind from the very beginning. I mean, I know I have to be fair with the tryouts, but I think you would be great. Mrs. Brody thought so—"

"You talked to Mrs. Brody about me?" I say, my voice rising.

Gabrielle holds up her hand. "Don't get nervous. Mrs. Brody wanted to go over the parts and since I didn't know the students she made a few suggestions, that's all. She thought Maya Rubin would be the first choice for violin."

"Of course," I mutter. "How could she not be?"

"Oh, do you play the violin, too?"

"No," I snap. "I am just saying that I don't want it to look like you or Mrs. Brody are playing favorites."

Gabrielle looks confused. Then I realize that she probably doesn't understand about my family connection to Hebrew Academy.

"What I mean is… see, some kids think I get extra perks because of my family." I check Gabrielle's face for understanding. "Like last year during the public menorah lighting on the Boston Common, I was chosen to represent our school and light the first candle. I was really excited about it, but then I found out some girls were saying I got picked just because of my family name."

"Hmm. I think I see where you're coming from." Gabrielle seems to consider this for a moment. "But you know, Talia. This is a little different. It's about talent."

"Maybe, but some kids won't believe it."

The comment Hannah made at lunch today replays in my head. "They'll say you chose me because my parents are hosting you."

She nods her head. "I get it."

"So that's why I think it would be better if I just sold tickets, which I am really good at."

Gabrielle smiles. "Of course you can sell tickets, but anyone can do that. How many girls can play piano accompaniment?"

I shrug. "A few."

"My point exactly. You can't worry about what others are going to say when it comes to being an artist. There will always be naysayers and nosy-bodies. It just comes from their insecurities and envy. Believe me, I experienced this a lot in dance. It's a very competitive world." She looks up at the ceiling as if remembering something. "When I was just sixteen, I got the part of the Sugar Plum Fairy in the Nutcracker. A more experienced dancer who had also auditioned for the role got really ticked off that I landed it instead of her. She started a rumor that I got the part because I was dating the choreographer, which was totally not true!"

"That's horrible. What did you do?"

"I simply ignored her. I focused on dancing my very best. The rumor eventually died, and I earned the respect of the other dancers."

"Because they saw you really did deserve to be the Sugar Plum Fairy?" I ask.

Gabrielle nods. "Exactly. Which is why I hope you will never hide your talents because of what others might do or say." She pauses. "So, how about trying out next Tuesday?"

I rest my chin on my knee. "Can I have some time to think about it?"

"Of course. That's the right thing to do. So when would be a good time to listen to 'Miriam's Song'?"

I mentally run through my homework and phone plans. "Uh, how about after dinner?"

Gabrielle jumps up from my bed. "Fantastic! Oh, I really appreciate this." She points a finger at me. "I'll repay the favor sometime. Okay?"

I can't quite imagine what favor Gabrielle could do, other than getting her own apartment. "Okay. It's a deal."

Gabrielle reaches her arms upward and stretches her long body. "Ah, that feels better."

Just in the nick of time my phone rings.

"Oh, I once danced to that ring tone!" Gabrielle says, twirling toward my door. "Catch you later."

"Hey," I say, answering Liora's call. "You rescued me from Gabbers," I whisper.

"My mom invited you to come home with me tomorrow!" Liora announces.

"On a school night?"

"She made an exception for math team study."

"But I'd have to sleep over."

"It's fine," Liora says. "You haven't been to my house in ages."

She's right. "Okay, I'm pretty sure I can. Let me check with my mom. Unless I text you, assume that I'm coming."

"Do you think Hannah will get mad?"

"She doesn't have to know," I say. "We can plan a threesome after Thanksgiving break."

After we hang up, I sit on my bed thinking about whether staying over at Liora's is a good idea or not. I hope her mom doesn't think I'm going to tutor her or something. I feel that funny feeling in my stomach again. And then I hear the piano downstairs. I listen for a couple of minutes. It's Gabbers picking out a sad-sounding melody.

Twenty-Two

"Whoa, I've never seen a purple kitchen before," I say as Liora opens the fridge to get us a snack.

"My mom painted it this summer. She likes change. And color."

No kidding. The Clarks' living room walls are the color of salmon and the couches are a deep purple.

Liora takes out a bowl of cut-up fruit. "Do you like yogurt dip?"

I don't tell her that I'd prefer chocolate-chip cookies, my favorite. I'm not sure Mrs. Clark even keeps them in the house.

"Sure." I sit down on the bright yellow chairs that are stenciled with bird designs. Then I notice a bird mobile hanging from the ceiling, and carved wooden birds along the windowsill over the sink.

Liora's brother Adam comes in and sits down across from me. "Can I have some, too?" he asks.

"Of course," says Liora, putting out some toothpicks for the fruit. "Here. I'll get you a plate. Did you wash your hands?"

Adam nods.

I am always impressed at how well Liora and her younger brother get along. The whole car ride home they didn't fight once. Ruthie ought to find out Liora's secret. (Or is it having *one* brother instead of five?)

Adam takes a toothpick and stabs a chunk of melon. "I'm good at math, too," Adam says to me.

I smile. "Great. Then you can join the boys' math team in a few years."

"Do you get a prize if you win?"

"Uh-huh," I say, munching on an apple slice. "There are winners in different categories."

"Do you win money?" he asks, his blue eyes widening.

"Not at this contest. I think you get a trophy."

"Cool."

Liora pours us each a glass of cider.

"Thanks," Adam says to her. Then he looks at me. "I hope my sister wins."

I glance at Liora. She grins and pats her brother's shoulder. "He's my biggest fan."

After we finish our snack, I follow Liora to the "study station." (That is just what they call it.) It's basically the Clarks' den transformed into homework central. There is a long wooden table and a hutch filled with school books and supplies. In the corner is a computer table, a file cabinet, and a globe. There is even a whiteboard on the wall.

"You could have your own homeschool in here," I say as I unzip my backpack.

Liora starts taking out her binders.

"So you don't study in your room anymore?"

Liora shakes her head. "My mom thinks it's important to have a set place to work, so you develop an association. I used to fight her, but now I'm used to it. Anyway, I've got everything here and this way I don't lose things."

I follow Liora's lead and start my homework. A little while later, Mrs. Clark pokes her head into the den. "Is Adam's violin playing bothering you girls?"

Liora shrugs. "I don't even hear it anymore."

"Talia's probably used to a quieter house—"

"I'm fine, Mrs. Clark." Why does everyone assume my house is so quiet? Don't they realize how much noise guests can make?

"Well, you just let me know if it does," Mrs. Clark says. "He can always practice later." She looks over at our books and papers spread over the table. "So, do you think you'll have time for math practice?"

"That's the plan," Liora replies, clicking open her binder.

"I'm so thrilled that Liora gets to participate in this," Mrs. Clark says, smiling at me. "She usually doesn't go for the competition."

My stomach lurches.

"*Mom.*"

"She wouldn't even let me enter her painting in the Youth Arts Festival," Liora's mother says with dismay.

"That's because you were on the committee, Mom."

"There were no rules against that—"

"Can we not get into this?" Liora taps her pen.

Mrs. Clark waves her hand. "Sorry! Won't bother you two. Let me know if you need anything, okay?"

Liora throws back her head when Mrs. Clark leaves. "She just can't let go of that art competition."

"But you are a really good artist," I say.

Liora scowls. "Don't you start."

"Sorry." It's not like my mom has never pressured me to compete. "I think I know how you feel. My mom really wanted me to try out for the ensemble."

Liora nods. "I just wasn't sure my painting was good enough, and it's not like my mom is unbiased."

"Don't you think she'd tell you if your painting wasn't good enough?"

Liora hesitates. "She's my mom."

"Yeah, but she's an art teacher, so she would know, right?"

"Unless she's in denial, as Shifra would say."

For a split second I consider telling Liora that I was the one who recommended her for the math team, not Dr. Janas, but then the second turns to a minute, and she pulls out the contest packet.

"I get mixed up with the triangle names," she says, flipping to the geometry section.

You're kidding, I think to myself.

So, I pull out my bag of tricks. I write the word *isosceles* on a piece of paper. "See how the word has two letters made from straight lines?"

Liora nods.

"That can remind you that an isosceles triangle has *two* sides with the same length. And an equilateral triangle is easy to remember because all three of its sides have *equal* lengths. The right triangle is obvious—it has one right angle, and that just leaves the scalene, the odd one out, with no sides the same length. Get it?"

Liora stares at the triangles I've drawn. "Yeah, thanks. That's what I need—little memory tricks."

After half an hour of practice problems on triangles, I ask Liora if we can take a break. Geometry doesn't excite me as much as number problems. So I watch while Liora feeds dinner to her two parakeets, two hamsters, and 21 goldfish.

"My dad says we can get a dog this summer," Liora tells me as she peers in the fish tank.

"Oh, you're so lucky! What kind?"

"Don't know yet. My dad wants Adam and me to research different breeds and learn about dog care first. That's why we have to wait. I'm leaning toward a goldendoodle, though."

I tell Liora about my mother's dislike of furry things. "And she thinks one of our guests may be allergic."

"I'd get a cat if I could, but my sister is allergic to them. I thought maybe once she went away to college Mom would let me, but no." Liora's face brightens. "But when I turn thirteen, I can volunteer at the animal shelter on Sundays. Then I can spend time with all those lonely kitties."

Before we go to bed (at the late hour of nine o'clock), Liora hangs up her uniform skirt in the closet. She pauses for a moment, staring at the closet shelf. "Want to see my baby box?"

"Sure."

Liora stands on her tiptoes to reach the top shelf, then pulls down a red velvet box.

"That's so pretty," I say, as she gently sets it down on her bed. I sit down next to her. She lifts the cover.

"This is the stuff my parents brought back from China when they picked me up at the orphanage." Liora picks up a yellow plastic rattle and shakes it. Then she takes out a tiny white undershirt. "This is what I was wearing in the orphanage." Next she pulls out a small blue blanket. "This is what I was wrapped in when my mother left me next to the police station."

Before I can even absorb the idea of little Liora abandoned, she says, "Oh, and here's the note my mother left."

I stare at a folded piece of paper with Chinese scrawled on it.

"It says my name, Li Mei."

"So your Chinese mother gave you a name?"

Liora nods. "It means 'pretty rose.' At the orphanage they called me Mei-Mei." Liora giggles. "I think it's common for Chinese babies to be called a nickname until they go to school."

"Why did your parents change it?"

"They wanted to give me a Hebrew name, so they used Li, in Liora, which means 'my light' in Hebrew. And my middle name is Shoshana, for 'rose.'"

I smile. "That's nice."

She folds the paper and puts it back in the box. "And here is the photograph they took of me with the other seven babies who were adopted that day. See, there I am with the purple headband."

I look at the picture of eight Chinese babies squished on a red couch. "I think you're the cutest," I remark. "And the luckiest."

Twenty-Three

I should have known better than to think we could go away for Thanksgiving break. Mom insisted that we stay home because there were three Harvard students from Israel who needed a place to stay. She said the college empties out over the weekend and it would be very lonely for these students to stay on campus. I just don't get it. Couldn't she find them someplace else to go? Why do we have to be their home away from home?

So Mom hosted my Bubbe and Zayde, Aunt Lisa and Uncle Joel, Aunt Tzippy and Uncle Yaakov, and my younger cousins, Daniella, Ian, Seth, and Dov for Thanksgiving. I love hanging out with my relatives, but it is also fun to visit them for a change. It's not too often that *I* get to be the guest. Last year, we all met at Aunt Tzippy's in Connecticut for Thanksgiving weekend. Sigh.

The big surprise was that Gabbers went home to visit her parents in Texas. She told us that her great aunt's 100th birthday was on Thanksgiving and the family was throwing a big celebration. (Can you imagine living to a three-digit number?) I noticed that Gabrielle didn't seem too excited about visiting her family. I overheard my mom advising her on how to deal with her mother's not-kosher kitchen. Mom really got down to the nitty-gritty details. I half-expected her to give Gabrielle a freeze-dried kosher turkey to pack in her suitcase.

When my parents were out of hearing distance, I asked Gabrielle when the last time she saw her parents was. She had to think about it for a few seconds. She guessed it was a year ago. Then she remembered that her parents came to see one of her dance performances last spring.

"It's usually better for all of us if they meet me on my turf," Gabrielle said. I wanted to ask her what she meant by that, but my mother came back into the room.

When I told this to Shifra later, she said, "Sounds like a dysfunctional family." That made me more curious. Ruthie says that most families are dysfunctional, including hers. Even though Ruthie's family members are pretty hyper, I know Ruthie is just kidding. I wonder if parents who make their house a free hotel would be considered dysfunctional. Even so, I can't imagine not wanting to come home to visit. As Shifra says, "There must be more to the story."

The tryouts for *Miriam's Song* were yesterday. Ruthie and Shifra both got on my case about not trying out, so I caved. Ruthie had a great suggestion for an audition piece—"Matchmaker" from *Fiddler on the Roof.*

"You don't want to play your usual Mozart sonata," Ruthie advised me. "This is more like a Broadway musical." Then Ruthie gave me her devilish grin. "Besides, I bet marriage is definitely on Gabrielle's mind. That song will put her in a good mood."

"You mean in the marriage mood," Shifra laughed.

So that's what I played. Gabbers started swaying back and forth to the music. I tried to keep my eyes on the notes so I wouldn't look at her and start cracking up. She clapped when I finished.

"Talia, I love that song! And you played it with such spirit. Would you just play it one more time while I sing along? That way I can be sure you can accompany the chorus."

I was in real danger of a laugh attack, so I counted the beats in my head while Gabbers belted out the song. *Matchmaker, matchmaker, make me a match, find me a find, catch me a catch!* I was sure everyone waiting in the hallway could hear her singing.

Shifra got to skip the tryout since she is already a member of the school chorus. Ruthie reported that the dance audition was actually a lot of fun. Basically, Gabrielle put all the wannabe dancers on stage, taught them a short routine, and then watched as they performed it.

"You could definitely tell Gabrielle is a pro," Ruthie said after the audition. "Would you believe she can do the splits?"

"Yes, I would," I replied. "She can stand on her head, too."

Ruthie and I both laughed, remembering the vase incident.

According to Rina and Malki Sneiderman, Gabrielle was more serious during the acting tryouts. She sat in the front row of the auditorium while each girl read a section of the play. Rina said that Gabrielle kept her on stage quite a while, asking her to do the part over and over again. Ruthie, Shifra, and I all agreed that we hoped Gabrielle doesn't pick Hannah, even if she is a natural actress. It would definitely go to her already swelled head.

On top of all the excitement over the production, everyone is getting ready for Hanukkah, which begins tomorrow night. Even though it doesn't come during winter break this year, we'll still have a lot of fun in school. For one thing, we get out an hour earlier each day, and there is no homework. The seniors and PTA always plan a special holiday program, activity, or field trip. This year my grade will help the second graders make beeswax candles. The fourth and fifth graders are having a menorah design contest. The sixth grade gets an olive oil–making demonstration. The eighth grade will deliver gifts to kids in Children's Hospital, and the middle-school chorus will perform for Hebrew Senior Center.

After lunch, Liora and I walk to math class together. "Only two weeks left till the contest," she sighs. "I don't know if I'm ready."

"I bet everyone feels that way," I say, opening the classroom door. I see the girls gathered around Dr. Janas' desk.

"Hey, Talia, check this out," Hannah calls to me. "It's right up your number alley."

I walk over to the desk. Hannah is examining a glass jar full of jellybeans.

Dr. Janas smiles at me. "Want to try the MaccaBean challenge? The closest estimate wins the jar."

I smile at Dr. Janas' pun on the Maccabees, the Jewish army that fought the Syrians in the Hanukkah story. "Sure. I love jellybeans."

Hannah hands me the jar. "No eating, no cheating."

I turn the jar around and mentally count the number of jellybeans I see on the bottom layer, and multiply it by how many rows there are, just to give me a starting point. Then I let my number intuition take over. I write my name and the number 269 on the slip of paper, and put it into the little box Dr. Janas made for the guesstimates.

Liora goes next. She tilts the jar to one side. "I stink at these kinds of contests."

Dr. Janas puts the jar back on her desk. "Okay, girls, it's Hanukkah math today, so grab a paper and a partner, and problem-solve away."

Suppose we celebrated Hanukkah for 16 nights instead of 8. On each night you still light an additional candle, plus the shamash, the helper candle. Assuming you let the candles burn down each night, how many candles will you need for the 16-day holiday?

The bell rings and Dr. Janas tells us we'll go over the answers tomorrow. She lifts up the jellybean jar. "So, our winner appears to be a great guesstimator." She walks over to my desk and hands me the jar. "You were short three, Talia. There were 272."

"Ah, figures!" Hannah calls out. "I guessed 355."

"That's because you always exaggerate," I reply, opening the lid. "Here, want some?"

After class, Dr. Janas asks Liora, Hannah, and me to stay.

"Here are the permission slips for your parents to sign so you can travel to the competition site in Wellesley," she says, handing out three papers. "I realize that during Hanukkah there is a no-homework policy, but I hope you will find some time to work on a few practice problems. We won't be having any after-school practices this week. It's really up to you girls."

I see the panic in Liora's face. "What about my study session?"

"I'll try to squeeze it in," Dr. Janas replies, "but with all the holiday programming going on, I'm just not sure."

"Well, I guess we should all get together, then," Hannah says matter-of-factly, as if it were the most natural thing in the world.

I bite my tongue.

Dr. Janas smiles knowingly. "That's just what I had in mind."

As soon as we leave the classroom, I spot a bunch of girls crowding around the bulletin board outside the music room.

"They must have posted the parts!" Hannah squeals. Then she hurries down the hall. We quickly follow her.

"You're Batya!" Esther Grubner shouts as Hannah approaches. "Someone just told me."

I'm relieved. Better that Hannah should be Pharaoh's daughter than Miriam, the star of the show.

"Congratulations, Hannah," Liora says. "You get to be a princess after all."

"Who is Miriam?" Hannah asks, straining to see over Esther's head.

"Me!" Rina says, spinning around in front of us.

Malki taps Hannah on the shoulder. "And me!"

"What?" Hannah says, moving her way through the mob of girls as they check out the sign. "Two Miriams? Oh, I get it. Miss Markus picked them 'cause they're twins. It makes sense. Very cute."

Of course Hannah would find a way to explain her defeat.

There are small cries of excitement as each girl finds her role. Finally, I make my way to the bulletin board.

MIRIAM'S SONG CAST

Elder Miriam – Rina Sneiderman

Younger Miriam – Malki Sneiderman

Yocheved – Katya Berichevsky

Amram – Tamar Eisenberg

Aaron – Hindy Abrams

Grown-up Moses – Leah Bridman

Pharaoh's Daughter (Batya) – Hannah Finkelstein

Ensemble – Talia Schumacher, Maya Rubin, Shanie Cole, Elyse Stein, Jessica Reber

Dancers – Ruthie Braitman, Rebecca Stevens, Adelle Krauss, Chava Seligson, Shonnie Myers, Devorah Ernstoff, Batsheva Kowalski, Chanie Feldman, Esther Grubner, Madeline Halpern, Orna Duvani, Zehava Teitlebaum, Yael Haber, Aliza Schwartz, Faith Goodman

Set Design – Galit Bronstein, Shira Cohen, Liora Clark, Sarah Jacobs, Heidi Roberg, Leah Klein

Costumes – Ruthie Braitman, Hindy Abrams, Miriam Matz, Julia Lightman

Chorus – Shifra Polter, Tanya Goldman, Dina Michaelson, Freida Shuman, Laurie Shiner, Sophie Epstein, Lisie Weisman, Shoshana DelaRosa, Ayelet Greenburg, Alison Moskowitz, Nina Josephs, Bayla Walker, Sara Davidson, Hadassah Hirsch, Danielle Fine, Audrey Simons, Mariasha Zuroff

Program Design – Rochel Rosen

I have to admit, the idea of picking Rina and Malki as the two Miriams is pretty clever. Next to the cast sign is a flyer listing all the practice times for each committee. Boy, Gabbers sure has been busy. Looks like the dancers have a lot of rehearsals. Lucky for me, Mrs. Berman, our music teacher, will be directing the ensemble.

"Hey, everyone," Ruthie announces as we study the cast. "Miss Markus forgot to pick someone for baby Moses!"

Twenty-Four

In our living room window, our silver menorah is polished and filled with enough oil for the first night. On a table nearby, my own menorah is ready, too, with a purple candle for the *shamash* and a white one for the first night. Dad made me this menorah for my eighth birthday. Using those colorful number magnets, he glued a row of one through eight on a rectangular mirror. On the top of each number he glued a silver bolt for the candleholder. Then he painted my name in Hebrew script on the mirror. It is one of the most special presents I've ever gotten.

After we light the menorah and sing *Ma'oz Tzur*, Gabrielle looks like she is going to cry.

"It's so beautiful," she says softly. "The oil menorah is different. I like it better than candles."

"Closer to the original," Dad says.

Gabrielle's eyes look misty. "The flame is so quiet. And still."

Just like our house tonight, I think, with just the four of us. But it won't be quiet for long—Mom invited half of Greensborough over to celebrate on the other nights of Hanukkah. She's also planned a party, a toy drive, and a candy menorah-making activity.

Dad tells Gabrielle that we are only allowed to gaze at the Hanukkah lights, not to use them for any other purpose, like for reading or lighting the fireplace. "Nowadays we might not think about this, but before electricity, you'd have to make sure another candle was burning," he says, as we all stand by the window. "That's why we have the *shamash*, the extra candle we use to light the others. So if you want to light your gas stove, you can use that one."

"Interesting," Gabrielle says. "I never knew that."

"And to honor Judith, a Hanukkah heroine, women are not supposed to work while the candles burn," Mom adds, standing next to Gabrielle. "I think that's a pretty smart custom, don't you? Otherwise, we'd be running back to the kitchen to fry the latkes."

"Speaking of latkes..." I hint.

"Don't worry," Mom says to me. "Doris picked up the order from Hillers. All I have to do is heat them in the oven."

"You didn't make them from scratch?" I kid her.

Potato pancakes are the one food item Mom never makes herself. She almost burned down the house one Hanukkah while trying to fry a batch for twenty guests. Doris was cleaning grease off the kitchen walls for a week.

"I'll save that job for you, sweetie," Mom replies.

"How about some music?" Dad says. He sits down at the piano and starts playing the dreidel song.

"That's really original, Dad," I remark, plopping onto the leather couch.

"How about this?" Dad starts making up kooky variations on the song. "And here's Beethoven's version."

I laugh. "Now that's more impressive."

Then Dad serenades us with a few more songs while Gabrielle just stands by the window staring at the menorah. This is the quietest I've seen her since she arrived.

Suddenly a feeling of boldness comes over me. "Gabrielle?"

She turns to look at me. "Hmm?"

"Did your family give you gifts or gelt when you were a kid?"

She looks away for a moment. "Gifts."

Well, that's about the shortest answer she's given so far. I wait for more and then ask, "What was your favorite?" I hope Mom won't consider this a personal question.

"Oh, let's see." She twists up her long hair and lets it fall again. "Probably tickets to see the Kirov Ballet perform *Swan Lake*. I was only nine, but I was simply mesmerized. That's when I knew I wanted to be a dancer." Gabrielle returns to her candle-gazing.

So that's it? No rambling story tonight? Maybe she is taking Dad's comments about the menorah a little too seriously.

Dad stops playing piano and turns around on the bench. "Isn't it time for the Dreidel Quiz?" He stands up and reaches in his pocket. "I've got some crisp dollar bills here and a few silver coins."

"Dad, I'm too old for that," I groan. Actually, I'm just half-kidding because I really like the game.

"Come on. It's a family tradition," he says, walking over to the coffee table. He reaches in my box of dreidels that I've collected over the years and pulls out my favorite one, made from red glass. This seems to catch Gabrielle's attention.

"Oh, that's a pretty dreidel," she says, coming closer for a good look.

Dad started the Dreidel Quiz when I was five. Basically, I spin and Dad asks me a question related to Hanukkah. If I get it right, I get the money. If the dreidel lands on the Hebrew letter *shin*, Dad asks me a question about the Hanukkah story. Letter *nun* gets a math question. Letter hey is a *halacha* (Jewish law) question. If I spin a *gimmel*, I get double my age in quarters without having to answer a question.

Tonight I spin a *nun* first.

Dad taps his forehead. "Okay... answer in ten seconds. How many candles are in 11 boxes of Hanukkah candles?" Dad asks.

I grin. "484."

"That's my girl!" He hands me a dollar bill.

"Dad, that was too easy!"

"How'd ya do that so fast?" Gabbers asks.

"There's a simple trick for multiplying a two-digit number by 11," I reply. "There are 44 candles in one box, so the problem is 44 times 11. Just add the digits together—4 plus 4, that gives you 8. Now put the 8 between the two digits. Answer is 484. So, 23 times 11 is 253. Get it?"

"That's handy," Gabbers says. "But I'm not sure I'd remember it when the time came for me to use it!"

Mom laughs. "I know what you mean. Accountants like calculators."

I spin again. It lands on *shin*.

"Okay..." Dad says, thinking up his question. "So that was too easy, huh? How about this? In which year on the secular calendar did the Hanukkah miracle take place?"

"Simple. 139 B.C.E."

Dad hands over another bill. "Right again."

By the end of the game, I've won twenty-four dollars and fifty cents. As I count the money, my brain bursts with colors.

"I think it's latke time," Mom announces as the first night's menorah flames sputter out.

Gabrielle gets up from the couch where she watched our game. "Please don't be insulted, Naomi, but I think I'll pass tonight."

Mom looks surprised. "Are you not feeling well?"

Mom always thinks not wanting to eat dinner means you're getting sick.

Gabrielle says, "I'm just not hungry now, and I've still got a lot of preparation to do for the rehearsals."

Mom looks disappointed. "Well, feel free to come back down later and have the leftovers."

Gabrielle smiles weakly. She looks kind of pale. "Thanks. I think I'll go upstairs now."

Well, that's a little weird.

Just when it seems that I will finally have dinner alone with my parents, the doorbell rings. It's Mrs. Guryev, the elderly lady across the street. She hands my mother a basket of fruit and thanks her for the box of Hanukkah candles. So, of course, Mom invites Mrs. Guryev to dinner.

Twenty-Five

"Absorb the music, girls!" Gabbers exclaims, her hands motioning wildly as she moves across the stage. "In your muscles, in your bones, in your heart. Feel the rhythm!"

I am sitting at the keyboard waiting for the cue to play the song again (seventh time) while Gabbers gives the dancers a pep talk. The ten girls just stand there, panting, looking at Gabbers like she is speaking a foreign language. Even usually-hyper Ruthie looks exhausted.

Gabbers' face is all flushed. "This is 'Miriam's Song,' the highlight of the show. Imagine that you have just crossed the Red Sea." She spins around, her purple skirt swirling with her. "You've witnessed God's greatest miracle. You're so thankful to be alive!" She sweeps her arms toward the ceiling. "So. Let's try it again. And this time, I want to see energy!" Gabbers steps to the side of the stage, then snaps her fingers. "Music, please!" Her pink-slippered foot starts tapping. "And-a-one, and-a-two, and-a-three... begin."

I know the song by heart already. This is the only dance number that has live music, which is turning out to be a good thing, as I really don't want to sit through all those dance rehearsals, especially when Gabbers makes them do it ten times. This is our third rehearsal. Yesterday the whole ensemble practiced with the chorus. Mrs. Berman, our music teacher, took things under control. I have to say, the singers are much better than the dancers. Maybe it is just because they are more experienced and have performed a lot. Our school offers Israeli dancing, but nothing like what Gabbers is trying to get the girls to accomplish.

"Stop, stop," she calls out, waving her hand in the air. "Okay. That was better, but the two girls in the back—Faith and Yael—you're supposed to glide to the right, opposite of the three girls in front of you. Get it?"

Faith and Yael nod.

"Okay. One more—"

All the dancers groan.

Gabbers stops. "What's the matter?"

Esther Grubner speaks up. "Miss Markus, we've been standing on the stage for an hour after a whole day of school. We're tired."

Gabbers looks surprised. She checks her watch. "Time flies, huh?" She puts her hands on her hips. "Tell you what. I'm gonna call it a day. When you go to sleep tonight, I want you to mentally rehearse the dance. Visualize yourself doing each step perfectly. "

A couple of girls start giggling.

"I'm not joking," Gabbers says. "Professional athletes do this all the time. Golfers, ice skaters, basketball players—they imagine themselves making the perfect move over and over again. It has been scientifically proven to work."

"So, can we just skip the rehearsals, then, and practice in our sleep?" Ruthie asks. Everyone laughs.

Gabbers smiles. "If only it were that easy." She puts one hand on her head and the other on her chest. "Mind and body, girls."

It's already dark by the time we leave rehearsal. Doris is waiting in the traffic circle, and I offer Ruthie a ride home.

"Where's Miss Gabrielle?" Doris asks as I open the car door.

I shrug. "Was she supposed to come home with us?" I say, getting into the back seat. I didn't even think to ask her.

"Your mother say she might need a ride."

Ruthie slips in beside me.

"Gabrielle never said anything about needing a ride," I say. "I bet she's going to her ballet class."

"Okay. Never mind. I just try to do my job."

I buckle my seatbelt, and Doris drives away from the school. "I thought Mom would pick me up today," I say to Doris.

Doris glances in the rearview mirror. "What, you don't like me no more?"

"You should be home by now. That's all." I lay my head back. I think I could fall asleep.

"I go home when I go home. That's all," Doris replies.

"My legs are killing me," Ruthie gripes. "I never thought Gabrielle would be such a slave driver."

"Well, the story does take place in Egypt," I say.

"One thing is for sure—she is a really good dancer. Did you see her do that leap? How in the world does she expect us to do something like that?"

"*Visualize!*" I say dramatically.

Ruthie laughs. "Yeah, right."

"So did you meet about the costumes yet?" I ask.

"That's next week." She thinks for a minute. "Hey, isn't that when the math contest is?"

"Yup. Next Tuesday."

"You ready?"

"Sure," I say. "I just hope Hannah cooperates with Liora and me during the team part."

"You'd better beat the boys."

"Okay, Ruthie, enough pressure."

"Oh, that reminds me," Ruthie says excitedly. "My mom's ultrasound is tomorrow!"

I feel a slight twinge of envy. "Are you going to find out if it's a girl or boy?"

"Would you believe my mom wants to be surprised? After five boys you'd think she'd be dying to know."

"Maybe she doesn't want to be disappointed, like if she wants another girl and it's a boy...."

"I *know* she wants another girl. So do I. Can you blame us?"

Doris pulls up to Ruthie's house. "To be continued," Ruthie says to me as she gets out of the car. "Thanks, Doris!"

Doris waves. "No problem, honey."

I watch Ruthie open the front door to her house. Avi practically jumps into her arms.

"Hey, Doris," I say, "you're kind of psychic. Ruthie's mother is pregnant. What do you think she'll have?"

"A baby."

"Doris, really."

"Okay, it gonna be a girl. No doubt."

I look out the car window. I love Doris.

By 9:30 PM Gabrielle still hasn't returned. I'm sitting in the kitchen wearing my cozy pajamas and sipping hot cocoa with Mom. I was just telling her all about the rehearsal when Gabrielle barges in.

"Hi y'all!" She's wearing a beat-up leather coat and a red floppy hat. "Whew, it's getting nippy out there." She's holding a bunch of shopping bags.

"Doris thought you were coming home with us after school," I say. "Where did you go?"

"Oh, I had loads more to do," Gabbers says. "I've been running around town looking for odds and ends for the show." She drops her bags on the kitchen floor. "I guess I got a little carried away. Wait till you see the fabric I found for the Nile."

"I would have been happy to let you borrow the car," Mom says, sounding a tad worried.

"Oh, that's so nice of you, but I don't mind walking," Gabbers says breathlessly. "It helps me learn the bus and trolley system. And I don't have to worry about parallel parking."

"Did you walk all the way back from Fuller Street?" Mom asks, surprised. I mentally calculate that to be 2.5 miles.

Gabrielle nods. "I was in the mood for a brisk walk. Helps clear my head."

"How about some hot cocoa?" Mom offers. She walks over to the stove. "It'll warm you up."

Gabrielle takes off her coat and hat, then sits down at the table. "Talia, you were great today. You're a natural, really."

I shrug, pretending not to care, but inside I feel good.

"I know I worked the dancers hard," she says looking at me. "But

190

you'll see, when they really get it, they're gonna soar. Sunday, I've got the day divided up by scenes and dances so no one will have to stay longer than necessary."

"Talia tells me you're using the Sneiderman twins for Miriam?" Mom says, lifting the hot water kettle.

"They're amazing!" Gabrielle gushes. "Just perfect for the part. I think it was meant to be."

Mom brings the steaming mug to the table. "Whipped cream?"

"No thanks. I'll save the calories."

"Could you imagine having two of me, Mom?"

She smiles and joins us at the table. "All the more to love." She looks at Gabrielle. "You're right though, those Sneiderman girls are gems. I don't think I've ever seen them not smiling."

"Except on the first day of kindergarten," I add. "I remember it! Rina was in my class, and Malki was across the hall with Miss Cindy. Rina started crying at naptime because she wanted her sister. Wow, I forgot all about that."

Gabrielle's face gets serious all of a sudden. She takes a sip of cocoa. She has that faraway look in her eyes again.

"Well, it sounds like you're off to a great start, Gabrielle," Mom says. "Just make sure to give yourself some downtime. You and I are both high-energy types. Sometimes we don't know when to stop."

"That's for sure," I say, squirting another puff of whipped cream in my drink.

Gabrielle doesn't say anything.

"What I mean is," Mom continues, "I don't want to see you get overloaded."

Gabrielle blinks, like she's coming out of a trance. "Hmm?"

"You still have weeks to go. Pace yourself."

Gabrielle nods and gulps her cocoa. "Mind if I leave the bags in the front hallway? I need to schlep them to school tomorrow."

Mom looks confused. "Sure. That's fine."

Gabrielle checks her watch. "Gosh, where did the time go? I still have some song editing I wanted to get done." She stands up and takes her coat and hat. "Well, thanks for waiting up. See you tomorrow, Talia. Sleep tight."

Mom sits quietly with me for a few minutes after Gabrielle goes upstairs.

"She does have a lot of energy," I whisper.

My mother nods. "Exuberance."

"Hey, that was one of our vocab words last week. Adjective. Filled with or characterized by a lively energy and excitement," I recite.

"It can be a good thing, especially when you hit middle age," Mom says.

"I think Gabrielle sometimes stays up all night."

Mom's eyes narrow. "And how would you know that?"

Oops. "Well…. sometimes I just wake up in the middle of the night, and I hear her guitar playing."

"Maybe you're dreaming," Mom says.

I don't tell her about the time I heard popcorn popping in the microwave or the shower going or her weirdo New Age music.

"Anyway, Gabrielle is an adult," she says, gathering the mugs. "You, my dear, are thirteen. Time for bed."

Twenty-Six

It's Sunday afternoon and our school is buzzing with production practice. I just finished rehearsing with the chorus. Maya Rubin is sensational on the violin; I think she may steal the show. I feel inadequate playing next to her. I guess that's the difference between a gifted musician and a competent one like me. Sometimes I wonder what my grandfather would think of my playing. Mrs. Berman was very complimentary, and I don't think she'd be one to say nice things just to make me feel better.

There's a break until *Miriam's Song* practice, so I head over to the art room to see what Liora and the scenery team are doing.

"Hey, Talia," Liora calls to me as I peek in. Israeli music fills the room. "Check out my pyramid." Liora, Heidi Roberg, and Galit Bronstein are gathered around a giant mural hanging on the wall.

I look over Liora's shoulder at the ancient Egypt scene in progress. "You guys are good."

"Thanks," Heidi says, dipping her brush in the sand-colored paint. "Mrs. Clark gave us pictures to get us started. Hope Miss Markus likes it."

"Oooh, my favorite song!" Galit says when "Pure Heart" comes on. She starts singing along as she sketches another pyramid.

Liora's mother is in the back of the room washing paintbrushes.

"Hi, Mrs. Clark," I say as I walk to the sink. "Nice of you to come in on a Sunday."

"My pleasure. Look how much we've done already!" Mrs. Clark wipes her hands on her smock. "These girls are terrific."

"Need any help?" I offer.

Mrs. Clark motions for me to come closer. "Are you as nervous about the math meet as Liora?" she whispers.

My stomach starts fluttering again. "I guess." This is half-true since I am nervous *for* Liora.

"She's been working so hard." Mrs. Clark pats my arm. "Thanks to you."

I can barely look in her eyes, but I feel that I need to say something. But what? "Dr. Janas told us it's going to be really hard, but that the experience of just competing is valuable."

Mrs. Clark nods. "Oh, of course. Math is so important for your future."

I suddenly get this picture in my mind of Mrs. Clark, her heart full of hope, plucking a Chinese baby from the orphanage.

"I think Liora just needs to relax a bit," she says.

"Mom!" Liora calls over the music. "Are you talking to Talia about the contest?"

Mrs. Clark winks at me.

"She doesn't stop," Liora groans.

I'd like to tell Mrs. Clark to just relax herself and stop putting the pressure on Liora. But I don't.

A half-hour later I'm back at the keyboard in the auditorium. Apparently, the visualization exercise has not helped the dancers interpret "Miriam's Song." Everyone is getting frustrated. After the fifth try, Gabbers sits down on a stool at the side of the stage. She closes her eyes and starts breathing deeply. The girls just stare. Oh, no. I hope she's not going to make those noises!

After what seems like eternity, Gabbers says calmly, "Girls, for some reason I am not communicating my vision to you. It is not your fault." She breathes in again. "I'm trying to release any negative energy that may be interfering with my teaching."

"Uh, Miss Markus? Can I say something?" Ruthie attempts.

Gabbers sits up. "Of course."

"I think it would really help if you danced with us. I mean, you're the professional dancer, right? And you created this dance." Ruthie looks back at the other girls for support. "We need a guide."

"That's a great idea!" Chava exclaims.

"Yeah," Batsheva adds. "And our mistakes would be less noticeable with all eyes on you."

Gabbers stands up. "Hmm. An interesting proposition." She puts her hands on her hips and looks off into space.

"We could use it as a selling point on the poster." Ruthie's voice gets dramatic. "Boston Hebrew Academy presents *Miriam's Song*, featuring Gabrielle Markus of the New York City Ballet!"

The girls clap. Gabbers' face is beaming. "Wow. It never even occurred to me… okay, then. I'll do it!"

Everyone cheers. Gabbers holds up her hand. "But first, I'll need to check with Mrs. Brody." She smiles. "Thank you, Ruthie. I appreciate your out-of-the-box thinking."

Ruthie curtsies. "My specialty."

Ruthie's power of persuasion impresses me. Her grand idea may just transform the show.

Twenty-Seven

It's the first snow of the season, December 18th, which should be a lucky day. I watch the fat flakes falling on the windshield of Dr. Janas' Toyota Camry. Hannah, Liora, and I sit squished in the back. The leather seats feel cold under my uniform skirt. Dr. Janas is playing a CD of ambient music to help us keep calm.

"A relaxed mind is an alert mind," Dr. Janas says to us from the driver's seat. "A mind that's open to problem solving."

We are headed to Wellesley Middle School for the math meet. Hebrew Academy is one of nineteen schools participating.

"Shouldn't we be studying or something?" Liora asks.

"You've got to be kidding," Hannah laughs as if Liora is the dumbest person in the world.

"That wouldn't be wise at this point, Liora," Dr. Janas says gently. "It's time to clear your mind. Nothing else."

I look out the car window and watch the snow falling. I count the cars that pass by. Anything to keep me from punching Hannah. Then I think of the first few prime numbers… 2, 3, 5, 7, 11, 13, 17, 19. I can't say why but 17 looks to me like it is dressed in white fur and 19 shimmers like an emerald stone. I'm feeling better already.

What's cool is that 5 and 7 are twin primes because they are only separated by one number. If you subtract them, you get 2. Then, 11 and 13 are twin primes, and 17 and 19. But 23 and 29 are prime, and their difference is 6. The prime numbers keep going on and on. No one knows for sure how many twin primes there are. Mathematicians have been debating it for years.

When we pull up to the middle school, I see a big banner hanging across the entrance welcoming the contestants. Dr. Janas parks and we quickly walk across the snowy parking lot. Then she escorts us through the crowded lobby to the registration table. We all get a contest t-shirt that has a big square-root sign on the front. Next, we follow the kids and coaches down the hallway to the cafeteria.

There are long tables with desktop dividers set up. Colorful balloons float near the ceiling.

"I'm so nervous," Liora says as we enter.

Hannah looks around. "I think we're just supposed to find seats."

"There's Mr. Doring," Dr. Janas says, pointing.

Mr. Doring, the boys' team coach, waves at us. He is sitting in the fourth row of tables with the boys.

"That must be our school's spot," Dr. Janas says.

Unlike Dr. Janas, Mr. Doring's appearance screams 'Nerdy Math Professor.' He's actually wearing a bow tie. Dr. Janas introduces me, Liora, and Hannah.

Mr. Doring squints at me. "Schumacher. Any relation to the jewelry store?"

I nod. "My dad owns it."

Mr. Doring smacks his knee. "Whaddya know! I bought my wife's engagement ring there many moons ago."

I smile politely, hoping he's not going to ask any more questions about our family business.

"I hear you girls make a pretty tough team," he says, scratching the bald spot on his head.

Dr. Janas puts her hand on my shoulder and the other on Liora's. "You betcha."

"This is the *crème de la crème* of the boys division," Mr. Doring says, patting Meyer on the back. "Meyer Feingold, Daniel Rashinsky, and Alex Kahn."

The boys mumble a hello. I glance at Meyer. He's wearing a white dress shirt and black pants, which makes him stand out in the crowd of blue jeans and t-shirts.

Mr. Doring points to the sign on the table. *#15 Boston Hebrew Academy Boys Division/Girls Division.* "So this is our station. For the individual rounds you guys will work behind the dividers. I'm not sure how they handle the teams."

Dr. Janas frowns. "Seems like it could get noisy in here. Last year they held it in a library."

After we chitchat with Mr. Doring for a few more minutes, the room quiets. "Better take a seat, girls," he says.

Mr. Oakley, the contest coordinator, stands on a small stage at the front of the cafeteria. He taps on the microphone. "Welcome, everyone, to this year's Massachusetts Regional Math Meet."

After a nice introduction, he goes over the rules and procedures, which Dr. Janas has already prepped us for. Round One is individual—thirty questions to answer in forty minutes—no calculators. For Round Two we're each given two problems at a time to solve in six minutes. There are a total of eight problems and we get to use calculators. The Team Competition is Round Three. Liora, Hannah and I will have twenty minutes to solve ten problems. Our team can only submit one answer for each problem.

"The top four teams," Mr. Oakley says, "and the four top-scoring individuals will advance to the State Contest in May. The state winner will go on to National Championships in Orlando, Florida this July." There's a murmur among the crowd of kids. Liora is sitting next to me and biting her fingernails.

Mr. Oakley looks around the cafeteria. "Pretty exciting, huh? But let's remember that all of you here today are winners. You've worked hard, you've earned your spot here, and you have chosen to challenge yourself. So before we get on with the competition, let's everyone give a big round of applause for the awesome group of mathematicians."

Then Mr. Oakley asks the coaches to wait in the hallway during the test. "We've got a nice refreshment table set up for you."

Dr. Janas smiles as she leaves. "Good luck, girls!"

The room gets very quiet as the tests are passed out for Round One. Liora is sitting next to me, but of course, we're not allowed to talk to each other.

"At the count of three, you may turn over your paper," Mr. Oakley announces. "One. Two. Three. Please begin."

Dr. Janas told us to scan the test and then do the problems we feel most sure about first.

Penelope bought a pair of sneakers on sale for $63.10. The original price was $76.00. What percent discount did the store offer?

I decide to solve this easy one first. Next.

How many numbers from 1 to 1000 are not divisible by 2 or 5?

I know this! As I start writing, the numbers suddenly turn blue and orange. I blink, then try again. This time the numbers start wiggling around, which is very distracting. I must be nervous or something. It's usually not this bad.

I take a deep breath and close my eyes. *Focus, Talia.* I see all the odd numbers lining up. I start mentally crossing out the numbers that end in 0 or 5. Before I know it, the room seems to disappear. I'm sailing through the test. It's just me and the numbers.

Next thing I know, I'm finished! I look up, and the room is still hushed. Then the timer buzzes.

"Not too bad, huh?" Hannah brags when we exit the cafeteria for our ten-minute break.

"The one about calculating the train's arrival time really threw me," Liora says, her voice panicky. "Did you get 2:30 AM, Tal?"

The answer was 2:30 PM.

"Let's not talk about it now, okay? Just relax." I move toward the refreshment table. "Want a soda? It'll keep your brain awake."

"My brain is already aching. We've still got two more rounds." Liora groans.

Dr. Janas comes over to greet us. Thank goodness she doesn't ask how it went.

"I just checked, and the chips are kosher," she says, biting into an apple. "So enjoy."

"Look at the boys pigging out," Hannah comments. "They could at least chew with their mouths closed."

"Keep your eyes to yourself, Hannah," I tease.

After a trip to the bathroom, I settle down for Round Two. I set out three sharpened pencils and my favorite calculator on the table. This time, the problems are projected on a huge screen, two at a time.

Mr. Oakley reads them out loud. We have six minutes.

There are a bunch of socks stuffed in a laundry bag. There are 80 white socks, 60 black socks, 40 blue socks, and 20 green socks. If you close your eyes and reach in the bag, what is the fewest number of socks you can take out in order to guarantee that you have at least one pair of socks with the same color?

Hey, I think I saw the mathemagician do something very similar to this! It's the old sock drawer problem. I get right to work.

By the time the last problem set shows up on the screen, my head is bursting.

I let out a deep breath. I can't believe I did them all. I glance over at Meyer. He's already done.

Everyone gathers again in the hall for a break. Dr. Janas takes us aside. "Let's see if we can find a quiet spot for a moment."

We follow her down a hallway. She spots an open classroom and pulls us inside. "Sit down for a moment, girls."

"I'm exhausted," Liora says. "I'm sorry, Dr. Janas, I really didn't get enough sleep last night."

Hannah scowls. "Why don't you get some coffee at the refreshment table?"

"Girls, we only have a few minutes. I just want to review your team strategy. My sense is that the boys have spent a lot more time working together than you three have."

I stare at the tile floor. Liora was right. I should have invited Hannah to practice with us.

"But I don't want to discourage you. Now is the time to rise above your differences. Each of you has a strong area and a weak area. Hannah, you're a whiz at geometry. Talia, you're a quick calculator. Liora, you're good at spotting careless errors and remembering formulas. I'd like you to take a couple minutes to plan your strategy."

Dr. Janas leaves us alone in the classroom. I listen to her heels click down the hallway.

"Okay, so I think I should tackle the geometry problems," Hannah announces, "and Talia, you do the rest."

"What am I supposed to do? Sharpen your pencils?" Liora says.

"You can be the checker," Hannah suggests cheerfully.

"The checker?"

"That's a good idea," I chime in. "We can work on the problems while you're checking them."

Liora considers this for a second. "Okay. But isn't that a lot of responsibility?"

Hannah sighs. "Of course it is! But you're good at that."

My stomach is churning again. I feel terrible for dragging Liora into this.

The loudspeaker announces that it's time for the Team Competition.

"Well, this is it," Hannah says. "I really want to beat the boys."

I shake my head. "Give it a rest, Hannah. They're a part of our school."

"Still…" she says, tossing her hair back. "Come on, let's roll."

A polygon has 19 sides. Find the sum of the measures of the polygon's interior angles.

"Got it," Hannah says. "19 minus 2, times 180. Answer, 3060."

Our strategy is to read each problem, one at a time, silently. The first person to say "got it" works through the problem out loud. Then we respond by saying either "disagree" or "next." So far we've gotten through five of the ten problems. When I say *we*, I mean Hannah and me. Liora can't even check the math fast enough. But there's no time to build her confidence or calm her nerves. The wall clock is ticking. My heart is pounding, and I want to win.

"Next!" I call after we solve the ninth question.

What is the sum of the first 100 numbers? 1 + 2 + 3 + 4 + 5 …

"I know this! 5050."

"Are you sure?" Hannah asks me. "We'll get points off. Let's leave it blank." She glances at the clock. "There are only a few seconds left."

Liora starts scribbling away. "Hold on a sec…"

I feel a surge of energy. "Dr. Janas gave it for homework! Remember? Gauss' formula?"

Dr. Janas told us a story about the famous mathematician whose first-grade teacher (back in the 1780s) gave his class busy-work by telling them to add up all the numbers from 1 through 100. Meanwhile, the little genius Carl Freidrich Gauss figured out a quick way to do this by devising a simple formula.

I wouldn't forget the answer. 5050 is a beautiful number.

"Trust me on this, guys," I say.

Mr. Oakley's voice comes over the loudspeaker, announcing that we have ten seconds left. Liora puts down her pencil in defeat. "I trust you."

I write down the formula and 5050 on the answer sheet. Then the buzzer rings.

It's now 2:15 in the afternoon, and we're back in the cafeteria awaiting the final results of the competition. All the contestants and coaches are watching a DVD about careers in math while the judges are scoring. It's one of those jazzy documentaries that are supposed to appeal to kids. Hannah, sitting on my right, is totally absorbed. Dr. Janas is sitting next to Hannah and Mr. Doring. I steal a glance at the boys. Meyer is playing a game on his phone.

"At least we got to miss school," Liora whispers.

"The state championship is all day!" I whisper back.

Liora grins. "Fat chance."

"I'm glad you're here."

Liora gives me a thumbs up.

"Shush, you guys," Hannah says.

Liora rolls her eyes.

There's an African-American woman on the screen talking about how she uses math in her job of designing roller coasters. Now that's pretty cool.

After the video ends, the lights go on, and Mr. Oakley comes in to announce that the scores have been finalized. You can just feel the nervous energy bouncing around the room. Liora squeezes my arm. After a little pep talk (you know, the "everyone is a winner" speech), Mr. Oakley says he'll be announcing the top five winners in each category starting with the team results. The room is quiet again.

Well, this is it.

His voice booms across the cafeteria. "This year's top-scoring team is… Newton Academy!"

The cheering begins as the four members of the team (all boys) make their way up to the front of the room, giving each other high-fives. Mr. Oakley drapes a medal around each boy's neck, while a photographer takes pictures. I bet their coach is pretty happy right now. Of course, I didn't even imagine that our team would place first, but I hope we get in the top ten.

Second place goes to Wayland Middle School, third to St. Paul's, and fourth, Concord is tied with Stevenson. My stomach is doing somersaults.

When Mr. Oakley calls our school next, my heart jumps. I can't believe it! I stand up, but Dr. Janas tugs at my arm. Then I see Meyer, Alex, and Daniel proudly marching up to the front. Oh. I must have missed the words *boys' division*. I look over at Dr. Janas who is clapping her perfectly manicured hands.

I start clapping, too, even though I'm disappointed. I know I should be happy that Hebrew Academy placed fifth, but why couldn't it have been the girls? I feel like I let Shifra and Ruthie down.

I glance at Liora. She's biting her nails again.

Mr. Oakley tells us to check the contest website tomorrow to see the rest of the results for the team competition. The top ten teams will get a plaque. I guess there is still hope that our team made the top ten, although at this point, I'd be happy with the top twenty.

Next, Mr. Oakley starts talking about the individual competition and how challenging it is. A perfect score is 65. Nice number. Kind of an orange-yellow.

"So we'll do this a little differently by calling our fifth-place winner first," he says. "And that would be… Hau Wong from Coolidge Middle School!"

Hau looks like he's about nine years old. He has quite a cheering squad. I notice there are a lot of Chinese kids around here. I wonder if that makes Liora feel proud.

Danny Yee comes in fourth. Evan Aronovsky from Framingham is third. I can feel the place growing tense as Mr. Oakley is about to announce the second-place winner.

When he calls Meyer Feingold's name, Dr. Doring almost falls off his chair. Meyer, looking rather serious for a winner, walks up to the podium and stands next to the other three winners. He's about a foot taller than all of them. Mr. Oakley shakes Meyer's hand and presents him with a trophy.

Nice.

"This is wonderful!" Dr. Janas gushes.

"Congratulations, Meyer," Mr. Oakley says in a booming voice. "You should be very proud of yourself. You're keeping up your school's terrific reputation."

The camera lady snaps Meyer's picture.

"And now, we come to the first place winner of the Regional Math Competition." Mr. Oakley gives a dramatic pause. "With a perfect score, ladies and gentlemen, please give a round of applause for... Talia Schumacher of Boston Hebrew Academy!"

Dr. Janas screams over the clapping. "Perfect score!" She gives me a hard hug.

Liora and Hannah both jump out of their seats. "Go girl!"

And then I am walking toward the podium, my knees shaking.

Perfect score?

"Talia, you blew us away!" Mr. Oakley says as I take my place next to Meyer.

"Mazel tov," Meyer says.

I feel my cheeks turn red.

"On behalf of the entire Mathematics League we are pleased to present you with a trophy and a one-hundred-dollar savings bond," Mr. Oakley booms. "You, and the other four winners, are invited to compete in the Massachusetts State Championships. Congratulations and best of luck."

There's so much going on that my mind hasn't fully absorbed the news. Cameras flash, Mr. Oakley continues talking, and all I can concentrate on is making sure my knees don't buckle.

The lady with the camera is snapping away. She steps toward me. "Talia, can you hold up your trophy for me? That's great, honey. Hold it right there."

I run my fingers over the gold number one atop the trophy. It stands tall and proud, and not a bit lonely.

By the time Dr. Janas drops me off at home, Mom, Dad, Doris, and Gabrielle are all waiting for me. "Congratulations!" they yell as I walk through the front door. I'm shocked to see them. Dad gives me a hug, then Mom, then Doris. I feel great.

"Oh, she so smart," Doris beams. "I always say that, huh?"

I am in such a good mood that couldn't care less when Gabrielle grabs my hand and spins me around the entryway.

"Phenomenal!" She eyes my trophy. "How does it feel to be number one?"

"Pretty good, actually."

Dad puts his hand on my shoulder. "Your hard work paid off, Talia. We're very proud of you."

"I still can't believe I got everything right."

I look at Mom. Do I see tears?

"Feels like a dream, doesn't it?" she says. "I wish I could have been there to see you."

"Uh, that's okay, Mom."

Everyone laughs.

"And what about Hannah and Liora?" Mom inquires.

"They don't get their individual scores until tomorrow," I say. "It'll be posted on the website."

Mom takes my hand. "Well, I think this calls for a celebration. Step into the kitchen, my dear."

Dad, Gabrielle, and Doris follow. On the kitchen table, there's a chocolate cake. *Mazel Tov, Talia* is written in white icing across the middle. All around my name are colorful number candies.

"Wow! When did you have time to get that?"

"As soon as I got your text, I left the office and stopped at the bakery," she says proudly.

"Really?"

"Well, of course!" she says, as if she does this every day.

"She work real fast," Doris adds, winking.

Just then the doorbell rings.

"Why don't you get that?" Mom says, putting out the plates.

I run back to the entryway and am thrilled to see Shifra and Ruthie at the front door. "Mazel tov!" they both exclaim.

We exchange hugs. "Thanks, guys."

"Got the message during last period," Ruthie says. "I could barely keep myself from running home."

"Everyone is so psyched," Shifra adds. "Mrs. Brody announced it to the whole school just before dismissal."

"Invite them in, for heaven's sake, before they freeze," Doris calls from the kitchen.

"Oh, right. Come join me for cake," I say. "Have you talked to Liora?"

"Yeah, she seemed really happy for you and relieved that it's over," Shifra answers, stomping the snow off her boots. "She's dying to get her score."

"So how did Hannah behave, after all?" Ruthie asks as we walk to the kitchen.

"She was fine. She really rose to the occasion. I'm sure she placed in the top ten."

"I hope so," Ruthie says, "or we'll never hear the end of it."

"Hi, girls," Gabrielle says to Ruthie and Shifra. "Isn't this just wonderful?"

Ruthie sits down at the table. "That it is! Awesome. Fantastic!"

"Girls rule!" Shifra says.

"Talia, you're so lucky to have supportive friends," Gabrielle says wistfully.

"Amen," Dad says, putting out the paper cups.

"I just remember a lot of back-stabbing in junior high." Gabrielle shakes her head as if trying to get rid of a memory. "I've really been impressed with the level of consideration I've witnessed among the students."

"Really?" Ruthie asks.

Shifra laughs. "We're not perfect, Miss Markus."

I immediately think of Hannah.

Gabrielle waves her hand. "Oh, I know that, but you girls have something special. You may not realize it now. Trust me on this one."

Mom slices the cake. "I agree with you, Gabrielle. I think generally the girls at Hebrew Academy have excellent *middos*."

"Translation?" Gabrielle asks.

"Character traits—like honesty, kindness, humility. Of course, girls will be girls. But generally, they look out for one another. Don't you think, Tal?"

I feel a dull ache in my stomach. I think that is true. I want to believe it's true. "One for all and all for one," I say, and then take a bite of the cake. It's fudgy and delicious. "Yum."

Then the doorbell rings. "Gosh, Mom, you didn't invite my whole class, did you?" I ask, half-joking.

Mom heads toward the front door. "Wouldn't think of it."

"I have a sneaking feeling Mrs. Brody is planning something in school tomorrow," Gabrielle says.

Shifra licks the frosting off her fork. "Definitely."

"As long as I get a heads-up, I don't mind—"

"Well, isn't that nice," Mom says, walking back to the kitchen and holding a bouquet of flowers. She smiles at me, then reads the card. "Mazel Tov, Talia, on your fantastic victory. Fondly, the Feingold family."

Ruthie's eyebrows shoot up. "*He* sent you flowers?"

"His *family!*" I practically shout.

"Who?" Gabrielle asks.

Shifra cracks up. "The Feingolds."

"Talia beat their son," Dad explains. "And they're showing good sportsmanship."

"I didn't beat him, Dad. I just got a higher score. We're both going to the state championship."

Dad laughs. "And you'll be wearing a shirt with number one on the back."

That night, I am tossing and turning. I can't fall asleep. I'm still hyper from the excitement of the day. My mind is racing. How did Liora do on the Individual Round? How did our team do? Will Liora be able to get her new laptop? Is Hannah jealous of my winning? (She did seem really happy for me.) And what about Meyer? Did he expect to get first place?

One thing is for sure. I may have studied hard, but I never expected to be first! Dad always tells me to make a plan for success. "Expect the best, make a plan, and enlist God's help." That's what my grandfather did when he started Schumacher Jewelers in 1952. He started with nothing. I don't think I made the best plan about getting Liora into the competition. In fact, there wasn't any plan at all—just a spur-of-the-moment idea to save me from being stuck with Hannah. And maybe that's why our team didn't place higher.

But the Individual Round was different. I was able to block out everything and completely focus on my goal. Somehow that was enough to finish all the problems and get them right.

Then suddenly it hits me. I remember what Gabbers said about performing. *You can't be thinking about anything else. You are the dance. You become one.*

Twenty-Eight

"Girls, break is over. Get to class," the school librarian says to us as Liora, Hannah, and I huddle around the computer the next day.

Hannah tries to log on to the site. "We're just trying to check our math scores, Mrs. Jacobs. Just one sec," Hannah pleads.

"Hurry," Liora urges her.

"Here!" Hannah clicks on the Massachusetts Regional results.

"Go to 'team results,'" I say, clenching my fists.

Liora and I hold our breath.

"We're sixth!" Hannah shouts.

Liora jumps up and down. "Oh my gosh!"

Hannah slaps me five. "Way to go."

"So we'll be getting a plaque," I say. "I wonder if Dr. Janas knows yet."

"Girls! Pipe down," Mrs. Jacobs nags.

"We're almost done," Hannah says. "This is so awesome. I've got to call my mom."

"My mom is going to be so happy," Liora says. "Check the individual scores!"

"Yeah, there she is at number one," Hannah announces dramatically. "Talia Schumacher."

I smile seeing my name in red, above Meyer's.

"Okay, where am I...?" Hannah whispers. She scrolls down.

"Come on, come on. Yes! I'm tenth!"

"You just made it!" I shout. "Congratulations!"

Hannah jumps and does a little victory dance. "Oh, yeah!"

I am genuinely happy for her.

"Where am I?" Liora asks anxiously.

Hannah jumps back to the computer. We peer over her shoulders as she scrolls down the list. By number thirty, Hannah says, "Hmmm, maybe there's a mistake."

"Keep going," I say, as a sinking feeling settles in my stomach.

"You can see how close the scores are," Hannah says, obviously trying to comfort Liora.

"I don't see my name at all—"

"There you are!" Hannah says.

We all stare at the screen.

"That's it?" Liora says, her voice rising. "I'm at the bottom?"

Hannah checks the screen. "Uh, number 71."

"I came in last?"

"Actually you tied with Henry McLure."

Liora looks at me. Her face starts to crumple. "I came in last with some boy I don't even know."

"Well, someone has to be last," Hannah says.

Bad choice, Hannah.

"And it had to be *me*? They couldn't have just listed the top twenty-five or something? Now everyone has to know I'm a failure!"

"That's not what it means, Liora," I say, reaching for her arm. "You're not a failure—"

But it's too late. She's already run out of the library.

"That's enough, girls," Mrs. Jacobs snaps. "Out."

"This stinks," Hannah says, slinging her backpack over her shoulder. "I thought you studied with her."

"I did! So did Dr. Janas. What more could I do?"

"She wasn't ready. I could tell," Hannah says smugly.

"So what was I supposed to do? Tell her to drop out? That's not my job. And besides, her score was 38. It's not so bad." I follow Hannah out of the library and into the hallway.

She looks back at me. "No, it's not a bad score. Except that 69 kids all scored higher. How would you feel?"

I probably wouldn't feel worse than I do right now, which is pretty miserable.

Suddenly, my Number One status doesn't seem so wonderful. In fact, I'd give it up just to have Liora score in the top twenty. She may not be in honors math, but I never dreamed she'd come in last. Could I really have been that far off about her ability? And what is Dr. Janas going to say?

Liora avoids me the rest of the day. When Shifra and Ruthie ask me what's up, I don't have the guts to tell them. I'm sure they'll find out soon enough. At lunch, Maya Rubin, the middle school newspaper editor, interviews me for an article about the math contest. I try to focus on the team effort. Still, my heart isn't in it.

Math is last period. Dr. Janas has hung a banner over the door: *Congratulations, Talia, Hannah, and Liora.* Thank goodness she didn't single me out. She brought in popcorn and fruit punch for our class. The other girls bombard me with questions, but I don't feel much like talking—or celebrating.

"Should we call Liora to join us?" Dr. Janas says brightly.

"Negative," Hannah replies. "She is majorly upset about coming in last."

Dr. Janas looks concerned. "Oh, dear. That's too bad. I really hope she is not taking this too hard."

"She is," I reply, slumping in my desk.

"That's exactly why I didn't want to compete," Julia says. "This school is enough of a pressure-cooker."

Dr. Janas sighs. "Girls, let's talk about this for a moment. There are simply going to be times in our lives where we have to perform under pressure..."

As Dr. Janas goes off on a tangent about performance anxiety, my mind starts to drift. I can't get the number 71 out of my head. It's a muddy color. It's thick like molasses. Number 71 starts to fill up my brain until it hurts—

"Talia?"

I look up. Dr. Janas is looking at me expectantly. "Would you agree?"

I have no idea what she just asked, but for some reason I just nod in agreement.

"So, what is your trick for handling performance anxiety?"

"Me?" I glance around at my five classmates. "It's a matter of mind and body." Then the words just fall out of my mouth. "I block out everything else and become one with the problem."

The girls start to giggle.

"Good advice, Miss Markus," Hannah says sarcastically.

Dr. Janas smiles. "I think that is good advice. And it takes a lot of practice to be able to relax and open your mind. The psychologists call that state 'flow.'"

And at that moment I realize what happened to Liora. She choked! My nail-biting, anxiety-prone best friend panicked under the pressure of the ticking timer and all those smart brains in the room. She wasn't under-prepared… she was over-pressured.

As if reading my mind, Dr. Janas says, "I suspect that Liora's nerves hindered her performance."

"Like stage fright?" Julia asks.

"Exactly. You're in the school play, and once you step in front of the audience, you forget the lines you memorized."

"Lucky Liora doesn't have a speaking part in *Miriam's Song,*" Hannah blurts out.

I wonder if Gabbers ever got stage fright. It's hard to imagine.

Dr. Janas sits on the desk and crosses her long legs. "I used to be a nervous test-taker myself."

I'm amazed. "Really?"

"Absolutely. I'd get stomach aches, headaches. Sometimes my mind would go blank and I'd forget the multiplication tables!"

"What did you do?" Hannah asks, munching a handful of popcorn.

Dr. Janas smiles. "I had a wonderful guidance counselor— Mrs. Jennings. She taught me a form a self-hypnosis. It didn't work overnight, but with practice I gradually learned to relax and to conquer my fear."

"That's cool," Julia says. "Maybe Liora and I can take lessons."

"Unfortunately, I didn't realize Liora was so nervous," Dr. Janas says regretfully.

"Can you talk to her, Dr. Janas?" I ask. "She won't talk to me."

"Absolutely." She picks up the classroom phone. "Hi, can you send Liora Clark down to see me in Room 414? Great. Thanks."

Dr. Janas looks up at the class. "Okay, girls, I'm going to dismiss you early so I can meet with Liora. Consider it a reward for your hard work."

I take my time packing up while the others dash out the door.

"Talia, would you like to wait here for Liora?" Dr. Janas asks after they leave.

I suppose I could just go home and avoid the situation altogether—well, at least until tomorrow. No, that wouldn't be right. I've got to win Liora back, especially since I'm the one who got her into this predicament.

"Thanks," I reply. "I hope she doesn't mind."

I wonder whether Liora told her mother yet. Most likely she'll sulk the whole ride home and then tell her tonight. I can just see Mrs. Clark's face when she hears the news. *But I thought you studied with Talia?* Maybe Mrs. Clark will think I purposely led Liora astray in order to increase my odds of winning. That thought makes my stomach hurt. No, she wouldn't think that... would she?

A minute later Liora appears at the door.

"Dr. Janas?"

Her eyes look swollen, like she's been crying.

"Come in, come in. I'm sorry you missed our little party." Dr. Janas lifts the pitcher. "Care for a drink?"

Liora shakes her head. "No, thanks. I wasn't in the mood for celebrating anyway." Liora looks at me. "What are *you* doing here?"

"Waiting for you," I reply, trying to sound cheerful.

"Oh."

"Liora, you have every right to celebrate even if you are unhappy with your score," Dr. Janas says.

Liora folds her arms across her chest. "I'm supposed to celebrate coming in last?"

I stand awkwardly by my desk, pinning all hope on Dr. Janas' words of comfort.

"Liora… you know about the Boston Marathon, right?" Dr. Janas says.

Liora nods.

"You have to qualify just to run in the race. Last year there were over twenty-three thousand entrants. Two percent of them weren't able to finish. Yet almost everyone who entered the race knew he or she would not be in the top one hundred." Dr. Janas pauses. "So, why do you think they bothered entering the race?"

"For the challenge, I guess," Liora replies.

Dr. Janas nods. "Exactly. It's an accomplishment just to finish the 26 miles. Each runner has a personal-time goal as well."

Liora sighs. "So what does this have to do with math?"

"Everything. You see, the top one hundred finishers were all amazing runners. Yet, someone still had to finish last among the top. Do you see what I mean?"

"Kind of," Liora says meekly.

Dr. Janas looks at me. "Talia, can you guess what the time difference was between the women's division first-place winner and the second-place winner in the marathon?"

"Uh, like a minute?"

"Try one second. And the difference between number 99 and 100 was six seconds."

"Wow," I reply. I like this analogy.

Dr. Janas waits for this to sink in. "You see, Liora, you're among the elite finishers because all of the students were the top. You didn't drop out of the competition. You didn't score a zero on the test. You earned a respectable score."

Liora lets out a big sigh. "I wanted to do better, though…" Her voice trails off. I hope she doesn't start crying.

Dr. Janas walks over to Liora and says very gently, "You were pretty nervous, weren't you?"

Liora hangs her head down. "Yeah."

"I was, too."

Liora looks up, confused. "What do you mean?"

Dr. Janas tells Liora all about her bad case of nerves in junior high school. "And it wasn't only tests that gave me the jitters. I felt like I was going to throw up at the start of every race."

"You were a runner?" I blurt out.

Dr. Janas smiles. "A sprinter. Later on I went for distance. Much less nerve-wracking."

Liora looks interested in this bit of info. "Did you run the Boston Marathon?"

"Four years ago. I was number 963 overall."

"So, you were in the top five percent?" Liora asks. "That's pretty good."

"I was happy with it," Dr. Janas says.

"You got over your nervousness?"

"I did. And you will, too, with some effort and practice." Dr. Janas pours herself a glass of punch.

"Okay," Liora says. "I get your point, but please don't ask me to enter another math competition!"

"That's completely your choice. If it wasn't for Talia volunteering you, I wouldn't have even thought to ask."

Oh, no. Liora's eyes grow wide.

"But I'm glad I did," Dr. Janas continues. "And I thoroughly enjoyed coaching you."

Liora's eyes well up. "Thanks, I need to go now." Then she dashes out of the room.

Dr. Janas looks perplexed. "Am I missing something?"

I grab my backpack. "I'd better go, too. Bye." I head toward the door. "Thanks for the snacks."

Girls start to spill into the hallway from another classroom. I call Liora's name, even though I don't see her. I start to run.

"Hey, Tal, congrats!" Gila says as I pass her.

"Thanks! Gotta go."

Where is Liora? I imagine she's getting into her mom's car right now, probably crying and telling her what an awful friend I am.

"Liora!" I spot her standing by the entrance doors. "Wait up!"

I run toward her. She turns and faces me, her eyes tearful.

"Liora, please let me explain—"

"You lied!"

Ouch. "Not exactly."

"What's that supposed to mean? I thought it was Dr. Janas' idea all along. No wonder I came in last!"

"Liora, just listen—"

"I don't want to hear anything you have to say." She turns around and pushes the door open.

I step outside after her. I feel the cold breeze through my sweater. "Can I call you, at least?"

I watch Liora walk down the traffic circle to her mom's car.

"Liora?"

She doesn't look back.

"Yoo-hoo!" I hear Gabbers' voice behind me. I turn around and there she is, all smiles, carrying a huge bag of stuff.

"Heading home?" she asks.

"Uh, yeah. Soon." I am really not in the mood to walk with her.

"You okay?"

"Yup. Just fine."

"You don't look fine."

Leave me alone. I look away. Liora's car is gone.

"Well, I'm off to dance class," she says. "Got to keep in shape if I'm going to be in the show."

I put on my jacket. "So you decided?"

Gabbers nods. "Mum's the word, though. I'm not telling the girls until tomorrow's rehearsal."

"I'm good at keeping secrets," I say. My own words surprise me, and I get a dull ache in my stomach.

"Me, too," Gabbers says.

Esther Grubner bounces down the front steps. "Hi, Miss Markus! Nice boots."

"Why, thank you," she says with that Texas drawl. "See you tomorrow, right?"

"Definitely. And congratulations, Talia. Amazing win."

I force a smile. "Thanks, Estie."

Gabbers gives me one of her dreamy looks. "Everyone must have been all over you today. I get chills just thinking about it. Number One."

Why does she have to be so dramatic? "Yeah, everyone is pretty excited," I say, hoping she'll leave me alone.

"Hmm… you don't sound so excited."

I shrug. "I'm just tired, I guess."

"Of course you are! That was a mental workout. You just need to decompress."

I'm not even going to ask what that means.

"Have you ever had a massage? It does wonders for the immune system, not to mention stress relief. I used—" Gabbers squints. "Hey, isn't that Doris?"

I look across the traffic circle. "Yikes, I totally forgot. I've got an orthodontist appointment. Gotta go."

"See you later tonight, then?" Gabbers says. "Hey, can I show you my idea for the parting of the Red Sea?"

I head toward Doris' car. "Yeah, sure."

"Wonderful," she says. "Toodleloo!"

Twenty-Nine

Did you ever wish you could rewind a scene from your life? That's what I was wishing by the end of this week. Liora is still not speaking to me. Last night she ignored me online. Today she ate lunch with Hannah instead of our usual group. Shifra and Ruthie say I should just give her time to cool off, but even these past four days feel like an eternity.

I keep replaying Dr. Janas' innocent comment. That's the scene I want to rewind. Just before she made that fateful remark, I sensed a softening of Liora's sadness, like she realized that her score really wasn't so terrible after all. She was simply on the bottom rung of an elite ladder of mathletes.

I guess I was pretty dumb to think Liora wouldn't find out the truth. But is the truth really so bad? That's what I am having trouble figuring out. Ruthie says she doesn't think it is such a big deal and that Liora is overreacting. Shifra thinks I did the wrong thing, but since I had good intentions, it's not too bad. I think Liora would have never tried if I hadn't stretched the truth. Of course, without Liora, I would have been stuck working with Hannah. Now I wonder if that would have been as bad as I had imagined.

It's hard to be in a good mood when your good friend is mad at you. A little irritation turns into a big deal. I just about bit off Doris' head when she asked me to put away my laundry. I blew off Gabbers when she asked me to listen to her latest idea. I slammed my bedroom door after Dad told me to get off the computer and go to bed. On Friday morning I yelled at Mom when she nonchalantly mentioned we were having an Israeli family of seven staying for Shabbat.

"Why do you need advance notice?" she asked me. "What difference does it make?"

What difference? Why is she so clueless? I just want to know what is going on around here, like for starters: how many people are going to be sleeping in our basement suite or guest rooms or eating at our Shabbat table, or shmoozing in the kitchen Saturday morning? I'd like to know if they speak English, Hebrew, or French. I'd like to know if they are staying the weekend or moving in for a while. I'd like to know if I can come downstairs in my pajamas or if I'm going to bump into Uncle Yussie in the hallway.

Tonight, Ruthie asked me to go ice skating with her and Shifra. I said no. Usually, I would jump at the chance to go out on a Saturday night, but I just didn't feel like being social. Mom drove the Israeli family to the airport. Gabbers is out on a date, though I'm not supposed to know that. Dad is running a boys' Torah group at our shul. So I, for once, have the house to myself. You'd think that would be enough to cheer me up. First, I tried playing the piano, but I just couldn't get into it. Then I went back to the computer to see if Liora was signed on. She wasn't. So I went to the mathemagician's website, thinking that might cheer me up. I started watching his performance on *Good Morning America* where he demonstrated how to figure out on which day of the week someone was born by just knowing the year and month. He knew instantly that October 5, 1952, fell on a Sunday. Then I remembered—Liora's birthday is December 27, next week, during our winter vacation. And I guess that is the reason I am sitting here crying while Dr. Welland is wowing his audience.

I quickly wipe my tears on my sleeve when I hear the garage door open. A minute later Dad is calling me.

"In here," I call from the library, trying to make my voice sound normal.

"You all by your lonesome?" Dad leans against the door frame.

I blink. "Didn't feel like doing anything."

"Aha." Dad gives me a long look.

"I'm watching the mathemagician." I look back at the screen.

Dad waits there, like he is expecting me to say something. "You mean you haven't had enough math this week?"

I know he means to be funny, and I start to laugh, except it comes out as a cry. Before I know it, my tears are falling again. I cover my face and sob. Funny thing, Dad doesn't move from the doorway. He doesn't even speak. Mom would have been firing questions at me.

"Feel better?" Dad asks.

I wipe my eyes and nod.

Then he walks toward the computer desk and puts his hand on my shoulder. "You've been sitting on something, haven't you?"

My voice comes out hoarse. "Yeah. How did you know?"

"Hmm… let's see… my usually easygoing daughter turns into a grump after winning first place in a math competition." Dad makes the sound of an alarm. "Beep, beep, stress-detector going off!"

I shake my head and sniffle. "It's not stress."

He sits down in the leather chair next to me. "Okay… then do you want to tell me about it?"

So I do. I tell him the whole big mess. When I'm finished, I feel surprisingly lighter, like a brick fell off my head. I'm also relieved that Dad doesn't appear angry. In fact, he's not saying anything.

"Well?" I prompt.

Dad folds his arms and looks across the room, as if he is trying to spot something on the wall. Then he says in Hebrew, *"Lifnei iver lo teeten michshol."* Dad looks at me and raises his eyebrows.

"Before the blind…" I shrug. "Not sure."

Dad completes the translation for me. "Do not put a stumbling block. You remember this Torah prohibition?"

I'm confused. "Kind of. Who is blind?"

Dad waits, then says, "Anyone who is weak, vulnerable, or misinformed."

I think I get where he's going. "I guess that would be Liora?"

Dad slowly nods his head. "We are not supposed to give others bad advice."

I open my mouth to object, but then close it.

"It happens every day in business," Dad says. "Misleading

advertising. Shady money managers. Basically, it means profiting from someone else's ignorance." Dad leans toward me, and whispers, "Taking advantage of a friend for your own benefit."

Shame creeps up my skin. "But it wasn't like I planned for her to fail. I really thought she would do well."

"Are you sure?"

"Okay, maybe I thought that I could help her do well. Or maybe I didn't think much at all. I just wanted her to be in the contest." I look to Dad for sympathy, but there doesn't seem to be any coming.

"Do you know what the rest of the saying is?"

"No."

"You should fear God, I am your Lord," he answers. "It's the Torah's way of teaching us that the so-called blind person doesn't know what is in your mind and heart. Only God does."

I stare at my screensaver of dancing numbers. I can't think of anything to say.

Dad stands up. "Let me demonstrate." He walks across the study to the oak cabinet on the wall. I watch him open its door and then reach in toward a small safe. I hear the beep of the buttons as he pushes them. He reaches into the metal box and pulls out a blue velvet pouch. He brings the bag to me.

"Imagine you are getting engaged," he says.

I roll my eyes. "*Dad.*"

He holds up a finger. "Just listen, Talia. Your fiancé takes you into a jewelry store to buy a diamond ring. The sales person shows you these." Dad removes four diamonds of similar sizes from the velvet pouch. They are beautiful. "Here," Dad says, "hold one."

I smile and pick up the diamond, holding it to the desk light. "Wow."

"So the salesman asks you questions about what kind of setting you like and finds out how much the guy wants to spend. Right? And the guy says, two thousand dollars. But the salesman quickly figures out that the customer doesn't know much about diamonds. He's just in love and wants to buy a gorgeous ring for his fiancée."

"So… he could trick him?" I ask.

"Exactly."

I give the diamond back.

Dad places it next to the others on top of the velvet pouch. "One of these diamonds is only worth six hundred dollars. The others are much more valuable. Can you tell which one?" he asks.

I examine each diamond, but they really look the same to me. "I have no clue."

"So, if you can't tell, and they all look pretty good to you, what difference does it make? I could charge you two thousand and give you the six hundred dollar one. You'd never know."

"But that would be cheating."

"Yes, it certainly would. And according to Jewish law, it would also be *lifnei iver.*"

I think this over. "I need to apologize to Liora."

Dad nods. "That would help."

"Do I have to tell Mom?"

"I'll leave that up to you."

"But are you going to tell her? She'd be really mad at me."

Dad closes his eyes for a moment. "If Mom asks me what's been bugging you, I may just have to tell the truth. Or at least direct her to you."

"Okay." I look at the diamonds. "Which one is the cheapest?"

Dad picks up the third diamond. "This one."

"But how can you tell without examining it?"

"I have a trained eye. But that doesn't mean I can tell any diamond's worth. I still need my professional tools. Do you know that the lighting in some jewelry stores is so bright, that even poorly cut diamonds look gorgeous?"

I take a closer look at the diamond. "Gosh, it must be so easy to get ripped off."

"It sure is, but not at Schumacher Jewelers!" He recites the store's motto, "we pride ourselves on the highest integrity and service."

I smile. "Thanks, Dad."

He puts the diamonds back. "Feel like getting a snack at Milk and Honey?"

"Sure. I just need to do something first."

Dad leaves me alone in the study. I click off Dr. Welland and open my e-mail. I wait for a second to see if Liora is online. No luck. So I start writing.

Hey Liora,

I don't blame you for being mad at me. I guess you figured out why I did what I did. But the truth is, Liora, I really thought you would like being in the competition. I thought it would build your confidence. And I really liked studying with you! I am soooo sorry things turned out the way they did. If I could take it all back, I would. We've never been in a fight before, Liora. Would you please, please forgive me? Your BFF, Talia

Thirty

Adults like to say, "Time heals all wounds." I don't know if this is true or not, but as far as what happened between me and Liora goes, I'm hoping that the winter break is enough time. Ruthie told me that Liora visited her aunt and uncle in Maryland. Maybe a change of scenery will change her mind about me being a rotten friend.

And me? Mom actually pulled through and planned our trip to New York—with just one glitch: Gabbers had to come along for the ride! Needless to say, Mom and I didn't get much talking time on the way there. At least Gabbers didn't share our hotel room. Thanks to Mom's generosity, Gabbers had her very own suite. Fortunately, she had other plans during the day, like seeing dancer friends and some mysterious person she needed to "check in with". So Mom and I got to hang out together. And that was really nice even though it was freezing outside. My favorite part was the horse and carriage ride through Central Park. Mom and I huddled under the woolen blankets. We just sat back and enjoyed the wintery tour. I kept thinking how much fun it would have been if Liora came along, too.

We also took a backstage tour of Carnegie Hall, where my grandfather once gave a piano performance many years ago. The view from the concert stage was amazing. I tried to imagine myself sitting down at that shiny grand piano in front of a full house. No chance. Then I remembered what Dr. Janas told us about stage fright. And that made me think about Liora. Again.

On our last night in the city, Mom treated me and Gabbers to dinner at a kosher French restaurant. Gabbers, of course, tried to speak French with the waiter which made for a pretty hilarious scene. Her request for fish, *poisson*, came out as *poison*—like the stuff that kills you.

We got back to Boston today, just as the sun was setting and the sky turning a peachy color. Gabbers slept the whole way home which made Mom wonder if she was getting sick. Even though we had some peace and quiet, I didn't feel so much like talking.

Now I'm home and anxiously waiting for Shifra and Ruthie to arrive. At seven o'clock the doorbell rings and I jump up from the couch to greet them. We exchange hugs as if we haven't seen each other in months.

"Your hair!" I scream when Ruthie steps inside.

She smooths her chin-length, blond bob. "You like it?"

I cannot believe she cut off her long hair. "It looks great!" And that is the truth. Of course, just about any hairstyle would look good on Ruthie with her high cheekbones and enormous blue eyes.

"She surprised me, too," Shifra says, taking off her down jacket. "Even my brother did a double-take."

"I needed a change," Ruthie says. "I can always grow it out for the summer."

"So how was Kansas?" I ask. Ruthie's family went there to visit her grandparents. I've never even met anyone from Kansas.

"Awesome," Ruthie says, checking out her figure in our entryway mirror. "My grandparents gave us the Wichita tour. My brothers went nuts over the World War One Air Museum."

Ruthie's mom converted before she got married, so all her relatives on that side aren't Jewish. I've always been kind of curious about that.

"What did you do for Shabbat?" I ask.

"We got invited to stay with this really nice family about half an hour from my grandparents. I don't even know how my parents hooked up with them. There was a small shul in walking distance. They invited my grandparents for Shabbat dinner, too. See, Tal—your family is not the only one who invites complete strangers to their house!"

I smile. "Let's go downstairs."

Ruthie and Shifra follow me to the basement. I pull them both into the guest suite and close the door. Then all three of us plop down on the bed and start talking at once. I tell them about my visit to the Rockefeller Center, the Metropolitan Museum of Art, and the tour of NBC studios and Carnegie Hall, but what Shifra and Ruthie want most to hear about is Gabbers. They start peppering me with questions.

"So? Did you get any more clues?" Shifra asks.

"I told you, I hardly saw her—"

"But the ride," Shifra interrupts. "She must have said something during the four-hour drive."

"Definitely," I say, grinning. "Gab, gab, and more gab."

Ruthie looks at me expectantly. "Well?"

I shrug. "Honestly, I kind of tuned her out after a while."

"So what did she do in the city?" Ruthie asks.

"Went to see her old friends."

"Did you meet any of them?"

I shake my head. "But one morning my mom asked her if she and her friends wanted to join us for lunch, but Gabbers said she had an appointment."

Ruthie's eyes widen. "What kind?"

"Didn't say. She just said she had to check in with someone"

"That's weird," Ruthie says.

Shifra taps her finger on her forehead. "I bet it was with her shrink."

Ruthie agrees. "Maybe she has ADD and needs her meds."

"Did she talk about her family?" Shifra presses.

"Barely. She talked about *Miriam's Song* and all her ideas and on and on and on."

Ruthie lies back on the pillow. "That's disappointing. I was hoping for some juicy tidbits."

I try to think of something Gabbers might have said that would be interesting. "Oh! She did mention that her parents might come to the production."

"Now that's intriguing," Shifra says. "All the way from Texas just for a school play?"

"Maybe she considers this her *magnum opus*," I suggest.

Ruthie raises her eyebrows. "Her what?"

"It's Latin for masterpiece," I reply. "Gabbers is really into this production. Big time. That's all she talks about."

"It just doesn't add up," Ruthie says. "I mean, she danced with the New York City Ballet, right? She performed professionally. Why would our school production be such a big deal?"

"It's obvious," Shifra says. "Because it's Jewish! She's never done anything like this before."

"I say we google her to see if we can dig up some info," Ruthie says, getting up to look in my mirror.

"You mean cyber-spying?" Shifra asks.

Ruthie examines her perfect complexion in the mirror. "Exactly."

"I don't know. I prefer the old-fashioned method. Observation and deduction."

"Okay, Sherlock," Ruthie says. "But that method hasn't gotten us very far."

"What are you looking at?" I ask Ruthie.

"I'm having second thoughts about my haircut."

"Oh, please! You'd look good with it shaved."

Ruthie turns her head side to side. "I heard that the best wigs are made from Chinese hair because it's the most straight and shiny. Liora could probably make some good money selling her hair."

"Have you heard from Liora?" I ask hopefully.

Ruthie's shakes her head. "Not even a text."

"Me neither," Shifra adds. She joins Ruthie at the mirror.

"I'm sort of dreading going back to school tomorrow," I admit.

Shifra tries to console me. "You know Liora. She is incapable of staying mad very long."

"Define very long," I say.

"It's a new semester. We're back to production rehearsals. Liora will come around, you'll see."

"Besides," Ruthie chimes in, "she'll get tired of eating lunch with Hannah."

Later that night, before I go to bed, I check my e-mail one last

227

time. My heart jumps when I see Liora's message.

Yes. I forgive you, even though it still hurts. Hope you had a great vacation. BTW... I got a rabbit!

I am so relieved. My body feels lighter. Must be all that guilt melting away.

I get into bed feeling hopeful about tomorrow. Then I start to wonder. Did she get the rabbit instead of the laptop?

"Girls, please stop shaking the tambourines!" Gabbers shouts over the noise.

The entire production cast is crowded into the art room for Miss Markus' Big Idea: that we each decorate personal tambourines in honor of Miriam the Prophetess who led the women in song after crossing the Red Sea. I'm standing at a long table between the two 'Miriams', Malki and Rina Sneiderman.

"I know you're excited to get started, but I just need a few words with y'all first," Gabbers announces.

A few words. That's unlikely.

"Before you start, please remember the spirit of Miriam. Let her guide you, inspire you," Gabbers continues. "Don't just copy your friend or make any old design. Let the tambourine reflect your uniqueness!"

She closes her eyes and breathes in deeply. I look over at Ruthie and try not to laugh.

"Imagine..." Gabbers says in a hushed voice. "Imagine you are in the midst of slavery and oppression, and yet, you are certain that redemption is near. One night, you are told to flee from your oppressor. You must leave Egypt quickly! And yet, you make time to grab your musical instruments. This is what Miriam did. She anticipated God's miracle."

I've heard this story a dozen times, but the way Gabbers tells it, I must admit, gets my attention.

She claps her hands. "So, thanks to our wonderful art teacher, Mrs. Clark, you have plates of jewels, fabric, sequins, glitter, ribbons, and paints to design your tambourine." Gabbers reaches behind her to turn on the CD player. Lively music fills the room. "Okay, girls, go for it!"

"This is so cool," Malki Sneiderman says. "Miss Markus is so creative."

"And nice," Rina adds, shaking the purple glitter glue. "Talia, you're lucky to have her staying with you."

I don't comment.

"I'm going to write Miriam in Hebrew on mine," Rina says, eyeing her tambourine.

"Hey, I was going to do that!" her sister replies. "Never mind, I'll write the Hebrew word for song. And I'll paint it the color of the sea."

Gabbers is making her way around the room, giving little pep talks. Pretty soon the art room is buzzing with excitement. Everyone seems to know what to do. I keep staring at my tambourine, unsure of how to decorate it. I never was very crafty. I'd rather do a paint by numbers... hey, that gives me an idea.

I dip the brush in the blue paint. Carefully, I write 18—my birth date and a lucky number in Hebrew. Each Hebrew letter has a number value. The Hebrew word for life is *chai*, and it has two letters. The first letter is equal to 8 and the second letter is 10. Add them up and you get eighteen. A beautiful number. It shimmers in my mind. Funny how the number 1 by itself is so lonely, but along comes great 8 and it becomes lucky!

"That's original," Malki says, picking up my tambourine. "I like it."

"Thanks," I say. "I'm going to make a circle around it using the word *chai*."

"I wish I were good in math like you," Rina says. "I think something happened to that part of my brain after birth."

"Are you joking?" I say, cutting a blue ribbon.

"No. Malki and I were preemies."

"Speak for yourself, Rina," Malki says.

"You're not good in math, either," Rina says.

"Better than you."

"Nice to know you guys argue once in a while," I kid them.

"This isn't arguing!" Malki says.

"Yeah," Rina adds. "We're just teasing."

I watch Liora across the room. She hasn't said much to me today. At lunch she had her nose in a book. Maybe she's waiting for me to take the lead. I decide to go see her while my tambourine dries.

Liora's tambourine is a wash of beautiful peach, purple, and pink. "Looks like a sunset," I say to her.

She nods. I stand there while Liora ties on purple ribbons.

I clear my throat. "Want to come over after school tomorrow?"

"I've got stage design," she says flatly.

"Oh." I watch Maya Rubin paint musical notes on her tambourine. "What about this Shabbat? There's the Club—"

"I'm staying at Hannah's. Thanks anyway."

I feel myself getting mad. What does she want from me? I said I was sorry.

"So, I'll see you, though," Liora says, as if she's trying to make me feel better.

"Why are you staying *there?*" I whisper.

Liora looks at me dead-on. "Because she asked me. And the Shabbat Club is at her house."

I glance at my table and see Hannah talking to Rina and Malki.

"Besides," Liora says, cutting the ends of the ribbons, "you always have a ton of guests."

I almost choke. "They're not my *friends.*"

Liora shrugs. "I know, but my mom thinks your mother has her hands full."

I want to scream. How does Mrs. Clark know that? She doesn't even live in our community. "So... you actually thought about staying at my house?"

Liora ties the ribbons. "Well... yeah, kind of."

"Five more minutes!" Gabbers calls over the music.

Liora has struck my sore spot. I have no idea what to say. "See ya, Liora," I mutter and walk back to my table.

I feel Hannah's eyes on me. "What are you all huffed up about?" she says.

I shrug. "I don't know what you're talking about." I check to see if the paint on my tambourine is dry.

Hannah looks at my design. I can just feel a critical remark brewing.

"Do you think they wrote numbers in Miriam's time?" she asks.

"That's not the point, Hannah. Anyway it's not just a number," I say. "Eighteen means life. Miriam saved Moshe's life. Get it?"

"Only you would think of that one," Hannah replies.

"Yup. That's because I'm a one and only."

"Hey, that's funny," Rina says.

"Must be lonely being an only," Hannah says with fake sympathy. Ouch.

"My sisters drive me crazy, but I think it would be ten times worse if it were just me," she continues.

"I agree," I say, proud of my comeback.

Gabbers turns off the music and calls our attention. "Girls, I am absolutely overwhelmed by the creative energy in this room."

Here she goes again.

"Can't you just feel it?" she asks, looking around the room, her hand over her heart.

Ruthie holds up her pink-polka-dotted tambourine, its turquoise ribbons streaming down, and calls out, "Amen!"

The next second everyone is doing the same, and the room is filled with the shaking of tambourines. Gabbers' smile is as wide as the Red Sea.

Thirty-One

For the first time since Gabrielle Markus landed at our house, she ate somewhere else Friday night. Malki and Rina Sneiderman's parents invited her for Shabbat dinner. I guess that's not too surprising since the twins got the starring role in *Miriam's Song*. Still, I am a little surprised how chummy they seem to be with Gabbers. I knew it would only be a matter of time before people starting asking her over, especially now that she's running the production. Suddenly, everyone knows Gabrielle Markus! Last Shabbat morning after services, she was surrounded by a bunch of mothers. They all wanted to meet the wonderful young lady their daughters having been talking about. Yes, everyone seems to love Miss Markus.

So with Gabbers gone, you'd think that Mom would just chill and enjoy a little peace and quiet for one Friday night, as in *family* time. Fat chance. Instead, she wore herself out cooking for ten guests. Six of them she hadn't even met before, so at the table we had to do all that getting-to-know-you stuff. One lady was considering becoming Jewish. As you might imagine, she had a zillion questions, and Dad took his time answering every single one.

Luckily, Mom let me eat at Ruthie's for Shabbat lunch. Any meal at Ruthie's house is an experience. Ruthie's brothers pop up and down, play with their food, drop their spoons, and make a lot of noise. Ruthie's parents have Shabbat guests once in a while—mostly their kids' friends. They invite normal people who they actually know.

And, they talk about the funniest topics at their table. I don't mind sitting squished with Ruthie's parents and their six kids in their small dining room in their cluttered house. In fact, I've come to like it.

After lunch, when we were hanging out in her room, I asked Ruthie how her mother manages to stay so calm even when there is chaos all around.

Ruthie shrugged. "It's just her nature, I guess."

"My mom seems pretty uptight compared to yours," I said. "She always wants everything perfect."

Ruthie laughed. "There is just no way things could be perfect around my house. I think my mom just kind of... surrendered. A long time ago. You know what I mean?"

I considered Ruthie's words for a moment. "My mom does too much. Now she stopped traveling and gets Fridays off, but she still can't slow down."

Ruthie's eyes widened like a light bulb just went off in her head. She jumped up from the beanbag chair.

"What?" I said.

"I remember overhearing my mom tell her sister to slow down."

"So?"

Ruthie lowered her voice. "She wanted to have a baby. She'd been married three years."

"And?"

"And her doctor told her to chill out, too."

"But what did your aunt do to slow down?" I asked, my hopes rising.

"I think she went on a vacation, for one thing." Ruthie snaps her fingers. "Oh yeah, and she got acupuncture treatments."

"What's that?"

"Some kind of ancient Chinese medicine."

"And what happened?"

Ruthie smiled. "Amanda Leigh. My cousin. I guess acupuncture did the trick."

I considered Ruthie's information. "I wonder if my mom knows about those treatments."

That night, I looked up acupuncture on the web. It sounded

pretty weird, not the kind of thing my mom would go for. She's very practical. Basically, the acupuncturist pokes certain areas of your skin with long, skinny needles. That's supposed to release blocked energy which leads to a cure, or relief of your symptoms. I looked through the long list of ailments acupuncture is used to treat—just about everything from headaches to insomnia. Then I saw the word I was looking for—*infertility*—which I happened to know means not being able to have a baby. That's the word Mrs. Siedel, our teacher, used when we learned about the Torah story of Sarah and Abraham. When the disguised angels came to visit Abraham, they told him that his wife would have a baby in a year. Sarah, who happened to be 90 years old at the time, was in the tent listening. When she overheard this unusual prediction, she laughed. (Wouldn't you?)

Mrs. Siedel said that Sarah knew she was infertile and that having a baby at her age would be impossible. There probably weren't any acupuncturists around in the desert where Sarah and Abraham lived, but it turns out they didn't need one. A year later Sarah gave birth to Isaac (whose name means laughter). God worked a miracle.

The biblical Rachel also had to wait a long time until God granted her wish for a baby. And while I'm thinking about it, so did Hannah from the Bible, who lived during the time of the First Temple. She gave birth to Samuel after crying and praying her heart out. I'm pretty sure my mom has offered a lot of prayers over the years. I've said my fair share, too. What's left to do? Wait for a miracle?

This reminded me of something else I learned in Torah class: we're not supposed to rely on miracles. We pray, and then take action. That was it! An action plan. I decided then and there to start a personal campaign to get my mom to slow down and relax. In other words, I've got to be more helpful around the house and try to lighten her load. I'll serve the meals and let her sit down for a change. And then, somehow I have to get her to an acupuncturist.

Thirty-Two

Rehearsals, rehearsals, rehearsals. Gabbers has been working us hard the first couple weeks of January. Funny thing, I don't hear many complaints from the cast. In fact, most of the girls really like Gabbers, which, according to Ruthie, is why they are perfectly willing to work as her slaves. (Get it? Egypt?) Ruthie is always making funny remarks during dance rehearsals, but Gabbers doesn't seem to mind. Ruthie also has no qualms about throwing out a personal question. (Hey, Miss Markus, are you going to be here next year?) Of course, she's allowed to do this because Gabbers is not her guest and Ruthie's mom isn't on privacy patrol like mine.

At this afternoon's rehearsal, everyone is all excited to see Miss Markus' dance solo. I hope it's more interesting than those yoga poses I've seen her do. She shows up wearing a black long-sleeved leotard, a lavender wraparound skirt, pink leg warmers, and ballet slippers. Only she could get away with that outfit around here. Her hair is pulled back in a long braid.

Gabbers stands in the center of the stage. "Hi, y'all!" she says cheerfully. "Let's do a quick warm-up and get right to work."

I take my usual spot on the hard piano bench. The dancers all take their places on the stage. Gabbers leads them through a stretching routine. She lifts her arms. "Stretch toward the sky…" Then slowly she bends forward, putting her head to her knees. Ouch. Glad the musicians don't have to do that.

Maya starts tuning her violin while I sit at the piano rubbing my cold hands together. "Miss Markus gave me her dance music last week," she whispers to me.

"Miriam's Song?" I whisper back.

Maya nods. "It's so *sad*."

Ten minutes later, Gabbers tells us that she decided that in her dance she would represent the Jewish woman.

"She is me and you, your sister, your mother, your aunt, your grandmother—each praying for redemption." Gabbers pauses, her face serious. Then she spreads her hands out wide. "Yet while she prays, she is oblivious to God's tiny miracles." Gabbers stops and just stares across the empty auditorium.

"That's pretty deep," Ruthie says, breaking the silence. "Deep like the sea."

Gabbers pops out of her trance and nods, apparently missing Ruthie's pun. "My dance is an interpretation of this idea—that we pray for big miracles without seeing the hidden ones."

"Miss Markus?" Rina Sneiderman asks. "What are we supposed to be doing while you dance?"

"Okay, so at the end of the tambourine dance, I'll exit stage left. Dancers, y'all sit down in back with your legs to one side." Gabbers motions for the dancers. "Let's try it now."

The girls run to the back of the stage.

"Remember to keep your tambourine quiet and your body very still," Gabbers says as she helps each girl get into position. " W h e n the lights dim, the two Miriams take their places at the opposite corners of the stage." She guides the twins to their spots. "Rina and Malki, you'll recite the last lines of the play together. That's when I come out." Gabbers walks to the center. "Spotlight is on me, the future. Maya begins the violin solo. After my dance, the lights go up, the recorded music starts, and every cast member gets her tambourine and dances onto the stage."

"Everyone?" I call out.

"Absolutely!" Gabbers says. "Talia and Maya, the chorus members, the stage crew—I want this auditorium rockin'!"

Maya looks at me and shrugs. This is not what I signed up for.

Ruthie squeals. "This is gonna be so good!"

"Can we try the dance now, Miss Markus?" Maya asks. "It's getting late."

Finally—the moment we've all been waiting for.

Maya pulls the bow across her violin, which makes a sort of crying sound. Then Gabbers starts to dance. Her body moves like liquid in slow motion. She stands on one leg while the other leg is straight up in the air. She darts across the stage, leaping, spinning, bending, twisting, her arms perfectly coordinated. Her lavender skirt twirls. Every movement is in sync with the music. I can tell she is totally into the dance, like she's unaware of everyone watching.

I become one with the dance.

Gabbers finishes, standing straight on her toes, her arms reaching forward, like she is trying to touch something just out of reach. Then the music stops. Everyone seems to be holding her breath. Then we start to clap.

"That was so awesome!" Ruthie cries.

"Go, Miss Markus!" the girls cheer.

Her face is flushed. "Thank you," Gabbers says breathlessly.

"And I totally got it," Ruthie says. "I could see the sadness and pain in all your moves."

"Definitely," Esther Grubner calls out.

"You don't think it was too sentimental?" Gabbers asks, twirling her braid.

"Not at all," Ruthie assures her. "It was very contemporary."

Excuse me? Pain and sadness? Contemporary? I must have missed something.

Gabbers turns toward me and Maya. "The music was superb! Let's give Maya a hand, everyone."

Maya bows.

"You were great," I tell her.

"Thanks, Talia."

"Okay, girls," Gabbers calls. "Whaddaya say we take the whole thing from the beginning?"

It's ten o'clock PM, and I'm just about to turn out my bedside lamp, when I smell the popcorn. What is it about Gabrielle and popcorn? Is it a Texas custom to have buttered popcorn every night? I decide to pay her a little visit.

"C'mon in," she says, when I knock on the door.

She is sitting on the bed wearing her black yoga pants and a gray t-shirt that says *Greenwich Village* across the front.

"Hey there." She holds out the popcorn bowl. "Want some?"

"No, thanks. I already brushed my teeth."

I try not to let my eyes wander around the chaos in her room, but she picks up on it right away.

"Excuse the mess. I've kinda been in a creative frenzy. I'm not being a very good role model."

"I don't mind. If it weren't for Doris on my back, my room would look the same."

"Don't worry, I'll get it all cleaned up before Doris comes."

Gabbers stuffs a handful of popcorn in her mouth. I'm just about to ask her about the popcorn habit when I notice the noodles piled near her closet. Not the noodles you eat, but the kind you use in a swimming pool. Long, skinny, blue ones.

"What in the world—"

"Oh shoot, you saw 'em!" Gabbers says, jumping up from the bed. "I wanted to surprise you!"

"Surprise?" I look at the noodles and then back to Gabrielle. "I don't get it. Are we going swimming in the Red Sea?"

Gabrielle throws her head back and howls. "That's funny!" She runs over to the noodle pile and grabs one, then starts waving it up and down. "Remind you of something?"

"Um, not exactly."

"Think water." She grabs another two. "Here. Try it."

"Try what?"

"Wave the noodle up and down."

I take a noodle in each hand. "Like this?"

"A little slower. Watch." She stands across from me and waves the noodles in slow motion. "Now imagine the dancers all lined up facing each other, waving these blue noodles up and down while the sea parts."

I can't help smiling. "Oh, I get it now! That's pretty creative. How did you even think of it, and where did you find all these pool noodles in the middle of the winter?"

Gabbers gets that wild look in her eyes. "I happened to be glancing out your kitchen window into the backyard when I saw one noodle near the pool. It looked kind of funny with the pool all covered over and snow on the ground, like someone forgot to put a bit of summer away."

She starts talking faster. "And that made me think of the ocean, and suddenly I got this mental image of the girls waving them in the air and I knew I had to have them, so I went back to the recycling store and sure enough they had a whole bin full of noodles!"

She tosses the noodle back on the pile. "I'm gonna bring them to the next rehearsal. But I want it to be a surprise."

"I'll keep it a secret," I say, aching to tell Ruthie and Shifra, not because they're going to get excited about shaking noodles, but because it's funny that Gabbers *thinks* they'll be so excited.

Gabbers give me a funny look, as if she suddenly noticed that I'm wearing my pajamas. "What time is it anyway?"

Before I can answer she looks at the clock radio. "Oops. I was supposed to call my mom back half an hour ago." She tosses the noodles on the floor.

"Oh. Well... I just wanted to say... that your dance today was incredible."

"Well, thank you!" She curtsies. "I really do appreciate that. I know dancing isn't your cup of tea."

"Yeah, but you really looked good. I mean, I'm not sure if I got the whole interpretation, but I think you're going to steal the show."

"Oh, I hope not. Between you and me, I think the twins will. They are really something. Natural actresses." She spreads out her hands. "They give off this certain aura, a kind of synergy. You know what I mean?"

I nod, even though I have no idea what she's talking about.

"Are your parents going to visit you?" I ask.

Gabbers waves her hand. "They hate cold weather. But, I'm hoping I can convince them to venture out of their comfort zone to

239

see our show."

"I probably don't have to tell you that they are welcome to stay here."

"Thanks." She sits back down on the bed. "Somehow I can't imagine that happening." She picks up her cell phone and starts flicking it open and closed.

I wait for her to say more, but she doesn't.

"Well, I'd better go to sleep now," I say, heading toward the door. "Good night."

"Oh, Talia?" Gabbers asks. "Will it bother you if I play my guitar softly?"

Yes. It will.

I shake my head. "I don't mind."

Thirty-Three

"Do I look alright?" I ask, standing in front of the entryway mirror.

"Stunning," Mom replies.

"You don't have to exaggerate." I turn sideways and smooth my black velvet skirt that Gabbers said I should wear in the show.

"Okay," Mom says, "you look spectacular. It's time to leave."

"This white blouse makes me look like a waitress. What was Gabrielle thinking?"

"It's called formal wear," Mom says. "I believe the female musicians in the Boston Symphony wear black and white."

I step closer to the mirror. "It makes my face look even paler."

Mom sighs. "Try pinching your cheeks."

I turn around. "Can I wear blush?"

Mom opens the coat closet. "No. You look fine." She grabs her coat and her car keys. "Come on, it's getting late. Gabrielle wants you there at five o'clock. Put your coat on. It's very chilly.

"How about lip gloss?" I try.

Mom zips up her leather coat. "Fine."

I can't believe production day is actually here. These last couple weeks Gabbers has been insane. I was actually worried about her. I think Mom and Dad were, too. She turned into one of those wind-up toys that keep going in circles. Except she never wound down. Shifra says that Gabbers is in a manic phase. I think she is just completely consumed with making *Miriam's Song* the greatest show on Earth. And it looks like she'll get her wish. We sold every single ticket, thanks to the front-page article in *The Jewish Journal* featuring Gabbers' professional dance portrait from the New York City Ballet. Ruthie was right—Gabrielle Markus is a draw.

"I hope this snow stops soon," Mom says in the car on the way to the performance. "We've still got an hour and a half until the show." She glances at me. "Nervous?"

Yes.

I shake my head. "Not me. Gabrielle is the nervous one."

Mom blasts the car heater. "That's true."

"I think she'll be relieved when it's all over," I say, wiping the fogged window with my hand. "I know I sure will."

Mom pulls into the school parking lot. "You're not the only one."

I look out the window and see Liora and Hannah getting out of Mrs. Clark's car. Ever since the math team disaster they've become good friends, which is something I just can't understand. Shifra says Liora is subconsciously trying to get back at me. I don't think it is subconscious at all.

"I'll see you after the show," Mom says as I open the car door. She blows me a kiss. "Break a leg!"

When I walk into the auditorium, I almost get knocked over by Ruthie who is skipping up and down the aisles with the other girls following behind her.

"Hey, Tal, come join us!" Ruthie shouts over the singing..

I wave. "What's happening?"

She skips away and doesn't answer. Looks like they've all caught Gabrielle's mania.

I spot Gabrielle on stage standing next to a pile of blue noodles, her arms moving all over the place. "No, no. Over there!" she cries to Liora.

Liora is pushing a cardboard pyramid across the stage. "But you just told me to put it on the other side," she says, sounding pretty frustrated.

I decide to take my place at the piano. Maya is warming up on the violin. With her honey-colored skin and light brown hair, I think she looks much better in the black-and-white outfit than I do.

I take off my coat. "Did I miss anything?"

"Everyone is completely hyper!" Maya says. "Miss Markus keeps changing her mind about the scenery." Maya tightens a violin string. "I think you and I are the only ones who aren't nervous."

Speak for yourself.

"Yeah, well, it can be contagious, you know."

Maya looks around at the pandemonium. "I can't believe we're actually going to pull this off."

"Girls! Girls!" Gabrielle calls to the dancers. "Quiet, please!" Gabrielle's face is all flushed. She looks stressed out. Once everyone calms down, she says, "I appreciate your excitement, but we really need to pull together now. It's time for costume changes and makeup. Then I want all cast members on stage for last-minute details."

Gabrielle looks down from the stage at me and Maya. "Where are the rest of the ensemble members?" she asks in a panicky voice.

"They're on their way," Maya answers.

"Okay, well... why don't you two rehearse what you can?" she says, then runs backstage.

Maya says to me, "I didn't want to tell her they are stuck in Boston traffic."

"Good thinking." I set up my music. "Let's practice 'Looking Back,' since we're more likely to mess that one up."

For some reason, while I play the piano, the number 2 starts bouncing around my brain. My thoughts get carried away. *The animals went two by two, double trouble, even-steven, you and me, two Miriams.*

"Not so fast," Maya says, putting down her bow. "That first section is supposed to be much slower. Remember?"

"Sorry. I got distracted." I stare at the music, trying to focus on the notes. Then that nervous feeling starts swirling in the pit of my stomach, but it is not my performance I'm feeling nervous about. It's Gabrielle. Something just isn't right.

At 7:05 PM, the lights dim and the murmuring of the audience stops. Maya draws her bow across the strings and the auditorium is filled with the rich sound of her violin. The curtain goes up. The stage is dark. A spotlight falls on Rina, the old Miriam. She wears a white scarf on her head and a long blue tunic.

In a clear, strong voice she says, "I have lived a full life. I have seen our redemption from Egypt. I have traveled the desert with my people. I have witnessed God's miracles. I am the daughter of Yocheved and Amram, sister to Moses and Aaron, mother of Hur, ancestor of King David. My name means Bitter Sea. I am Miriam."

My heart is pounding. I start to play and the choir sings along. *Looking back, looking back, one can see meaning in the path.* They sound beautiful.

When the choir finishes singing, the spotlight moves to Malki. She's dressed like the young Miriam, her hair in two braids.

"My parents fear the evil decree of Pharaoh," she says, "that all Hebrew baby boys shall be cast into the Nile River. Father's plan is to separate from my mother so they will have no more children. I must beg Mother and Father not to let Pharaoh win. I believe my father's decree will be harsher than Pharaoh's, for my father will forsake the future daughters of Israel as well as the sons. Though I am a just a child, I know the God of Abraham, Isaac, and Jacob will not forsake us. I am the daughter of Yocheved and Amram, sister to Aaron. I am Miriam."

The center stage brightens and the slave dancers come on. Shanie accompanies them with hand drums. Sitting at the piano, I look back at the jam-packed auditorium. Everyone is mesmerized by the dance.

The next scene is young Miriam with her mother and father. Gabrielle was right; Malki is perfect for the part. During rehearsal, Tamar, who plays Miriam's father, couldn't stop cracking up when she says to Katya (who plays Miriam's mother): "We can no longer live as husband and wife!" Now, she delivers that line very convincingly.

"You will give birth to Israel's redeemer," young Miriam says to Yocheved and Amram.

Later, when baby Moses is born, the spotlight makes his cradle glow. Elyse Stein plays the flute while the choir sings a Hebrew lullaby. Very cool.

This is the first time I've gotten to see all the props and scenery.

The riverbank looks so realistic, right down to the reeds in the water and Pharaoh's palace in the distance. (I'll be sure to compliment Liora and the rest of the stage crew.) Malki stands at the riverbank and sings a beautiful solo.

My little brother I watch over you,
Still believing my dream will come true.
Watching that no harm should befall,
As you float toward that palace wall.
You I shall not leave,
To our God I will cleave,
Redeem us, my God, I pray.
Redeem us, my brother, one day.

Here comes Hannah as Pharaoh's daughter, dressed like an Egyptian princess. I'm sure she's thrilled to be wearing so much makeup and jewelry. After the princess discovers baby Moses in the water, her handmaidens dance in celebration. They wear white belted tunics and ankle bracelets. Gabbers found some cool Egyptian-like music for this dance. I can't believe the girls learned all those fancy moves. The choir chimes in with, *"Moses! Moses! That will be his name."*

So far no one has forgotten her lines, and I haven't made any mistakes on the piano. I guess all those rehearsals really paid off. My nervousness disappears and the music just flows through my fingertips as Yocheved sings, *"You are a Hebrew child, my son."*

Now the stage darkens again. Elderly Miriam stands in the spotlight and says, "We left quickly that night. The time for redemption was near. How we would be saved, I did not know. That we would soon praise God for a miracle, I was certain. In anticipation of this, I brought my tambourine and encouraged all women and girls to do the same."

The entire ensemble starts to play, as the choir sings "Expect Miracles," my favorite song in the entire production. Then the stage dims. The dancers split into two lines facing each other and wave their pool noodles up and down. A blue spotlight shines on them. We hear the sound of a roaring sea. Then acoustic music starts slowly. The dancers form an arch with the blue noodles. Out come the two Miriams holding their tambourines. The girls lift the noodles in the air and shake them, which gives a really cool effect.

Malki and Rina cross the sea and wait at the other side. The music builds to an exciting tempo. Then, two by two, the girls take turns running under the arch, tossing their noodles aside as they come out.

Finally, Gabrielle makes her dramatic entrance wearing a white, flowing dress. She lifts a tambourine and shakes it in the air. That's the cue for the musicians to start playing "Miriam's Song". The other girls pick up their tambourines at the back of the stage. The scenery quickly changes to show the dry land. Gabrielle leads the girls in the tambourine dance. Amazingly, they seem to get it perfectly this time. The audience starts clapping along with the beat.

When the dance finishes, the audience cheers. Gabrielle runs off for a quick costume change. The girls take their places at the back of the stage. The lights dim and each Miriam stands alone in a spotlight at opposite ends of the stage. Together, they recite their last lines: *Daughters of Israel, the spirit of Miriam resides within you. Remember the Exodus from Egypt each day. Stand up for what you believe. Pray for redemption. Anticipate miracles. Lead our nation to a better place. Sing Miriam's song!*

I take a deep breath, then smile at Maya as she lifts her violin. She pauses for a moment, and then begins to play the beautiful piece. All eyes are on Gabrielle. She's now wearing a stretchy black dress with a white sash, giving her a modern look. Her hair is slicked back in a low ponytail. As soon as she begins to move, the audience murmurs. With the costume and lighting, she is absolutely breathtaking to watch.

She runs toward the young Miriam, reaching out to touch her, but can't because of some invisible wall. Gabrielle covers her hands with her face, then dances toward the old Miriam, again reaching, and yearning to come closer, but some force pushes her away. Gabrielle stretches her hands out toward the heavens, like she is praying. Her face looks so sad that I swear she isn't acting.

Then she gracefully lies down on the stage floor, as if she is going to sleep. The violin changes to a more joyful sound and the girls gently tap their tambourines with the beat. Gabrielle wakes up like she's heard some good news. The choir starts to sing "Miriam's Song," and Gabrielle joyfully spins and turns and leaps across the stage. All

I can say is *wow*.

When Gabrielle bows, the audience begins to cheer. I look around and everyone is giving her a standing ovation. So I get up from the piano bench and start clapping along with Maya and the rest of our ensemble. Gabrielle motions for the dancers to join her for a bow. Then the two Miriams and the rest of the cast line up beside her.

Liora comes out from backstage bringing roses for Gabrielle. The applause strengthens. Then the music starts playing and everyone is hugging each other and jumping up and down. All the girls in the choir run on stage and grab their tambourines.

So do I, along with Maya, Shanie, Elyse, and Jessica. Ruthie grabs my hand and Shifra takes the other. Everyone is dancing and singing across the stage. The audience is going wild. I look out and see girls dancing down the aisles. I don't feel silly at all. It's like I'm part of a big, happy family full of sisters.

Gabbers got her wish; this place is rockin'!

Thirty-Four

I know it was really nice of my parents to host the cast party after the show, but I didn't realize it was going to be so… well, fancy. I mean, popcorn, soda, candy, and cookies would have been just fine. Instead, there are waiters walking around carrying trays of hors d'oeuvres. The dining room table is filled with French pastries, a chocolate fountain, and a carved melon overflowing with fruit chunks. In the center of the table is an ice sculpture of a tambourine! Seems like Mom got carried away. Of course everyone is complimenting me left and right and having a great time, but I still feel self-conscious because I'm starting to realize how much things cost.

"Your house is so cool," Hannah Finkelstein says to me as she bites into a chocolate-covered strawberry.

"Thanks," I mutter, pouring myself a glass of punch.

"With this space, you should have more parties."

Leave it to Hannah.

"That's my parents' department."

Hannah looks up at our staircase. "If I had a house this big, I'd make it party central. How many bedrooms do you guys have?"

"I lost count," I say sarcastically. I gulp the punch. "I'd better go see if my mom needs help. Have fun!"

I dash into the kitchen to escape Hannah and the rest of the crowd only to find Mrs. Brody, my principal, talking to Mom.

"There she is!" Mrs. Brody exclaims. "A marvelous performance,

Talia."

"Thank you."

I catch my mother looking at me with raised eyebrows.

"And thank you for all the support you gave us," I add.

Mrs. Brody beams. "Well, it has been a pleasure. This result was beyond my wildest dreams. What a blessing it is to have Miss Markus."

"Hey, speaking of the star…" Mom looks at me. "Have you seen her?"

"Not since I left the auditorium," I say.

"She's probably still signing autographs!" Mrs. Brody exclaims.

Mom says, "I didn't get to wish her a mazel tov."

"How about I go look," I offer, not wanting to get cornered by my mother and my principal.

I walk through the crowded dining room, then the entryway, and then into family room, but don't see Gabbers.

Someone taps me on the back. "Yoo-hoo!"

It's Shifra. "These brownies are sooo good!" she says, holding out a little plate. "Want one?"

"I ate too much already," I say, patting my stomach. "Have you seen Gabrielle?"

"No, but Liora was looking for you."

I instantly perk up. "Really?" I wasn't even sure she'd come to the party.

Shifra bites into a brownie. "Mmm. I saw her heading downstairs."

"Maybe Gabrielle is there, too. Be right back."

I dash downstairs to the basement. Sure enough, there are Liora, Ruthie, Malki, and Rina playing foosball.

"Hey, Talia, great party!" Ruthie calls as she spins. "Score!"

"Anyone see Gab—Miss Markus?" I ask.

"I don't think she's here yet," Malki says. "I saw her talking on her phone as I was leaving school."

"Hope she doesn't miss all the good desserts," Rina says, dropping the foosball.

"She's probably recovering," Ruthie says. "Did you see the mob after the finale? They were practically hanging on her!"

I walk over to the foosball table, hoping Liora will say something. I watch her play for a moment, but she doesn't say a word to me.

"Oooh, great move," Rina says to Ruthie.

"Liora?" I say before they start the next round. "Shifra said you were looking for me."

Liora stares at me, blinking. "Oh, right. Remember that blue fleece jacket I lent you?"

It takes me a second to remember. "Uh… yeah. I still have it."

"Good." She twirls the rod. "I need it back."

I swallow. "It's upstairs. Should I get it now?"

Liora fakes a smile. "That would be great."

When Gabrielle finally arrives at the party, the girls in our entryway start applauding. Ruthie breaks out into *"Three Cheers for Miss Markus!"* and the others join in.

Gabrielle looks a bit shocked when she sees the crowd and the catered food. "Thank you, everybody. Thank you!"

"There you are!" Mom says, rushing over to her.

"Naomi… this is so nice," Gabrielle says. "Sorry I'm late—"

"Come, have a drink. Wait till you try the chocolate mousse." Mom takes Gabrielle's arm. "And there is someone I want you to meet."

Watching Gabrielle as Mom leads her through the crowd in the living room, I get the feeling that she doesn't really want to be here, which is weird, because she seems like such a party girl. Something is different tonight.

By eleven o'clock, everyone has gone home and my house is quiet. I crawl into bed and turn off the light. I'm so tired, but it's a good kind of tired, like I accomplished something big. Even though I didn't want to be part of the ensemble at first, I'm really glad I did it. Dad said that Zayde would have been proud of me tonight. I could tell Dad really meant it.

Do you ever wonder if your dead relatives know what you're doing down here on Earth? Sometimes, when I am playing my grandfather's piano, I pretend that I am giving him a concert. (I've never told anyone that before.) It makes me feel connected to his memory. I even talk to him. That's why I got kind of ticked off at Gabbers when she asked me if I ever felt my grandfather's presence when I played. It was just too personal a question for me. At least at that point, when I didn't know her very well.

But do I really know her now?

You'd think that with all the talking she does I would know a lot more about her past. For instance, is her grandfather alive?

I feel myself getting sleepy, so I quickly mumble the bedtime prayer, *Shema Yisrael*... A minute later I am drifting away.

I wake in the middle of the night needing to use the bathroom. (Probably drank too much punch.) I stumble out of bed and attempt to open my eyes. The clock says 2:22 AM. Well, what do you know? Number 2 is haunting me tonight.

When I come out of the bathroom, I hesitate before getting back in bed. Did I hear something? I open my door and peek out. No light coming from Gabrielle's room. Guess that's a good sign. Still, I have this weird feeling.... That's when I hear the sound again.

I step into the hallway and listen closely. It sounds like... someone crying. I move closer and press my ear to the door. I'm right. I can hear her crying in there. At least I think it's *her*. My inner alarm sounds.

Without even thinking, I knock. "Gabrielle?" I whisper. I wait for a few seconds. Nothing.

"Gabrielle? Are you okay?"

She doesn't answer. Now what am I supposed to do? I gently turn the knob and open the door a bit.

"Gabrielle?"

A soft gray light comes through the window blinds. Gabrielle is sitting on the floor against the bed with her knees pulled to her chest. She's wearing her yoga pants and a baggy sweatshirt. She doesn't look at me.

"Is everything all right?" I say, even though it seems like a stupid thing to ask. I'm not sure she even heard me. "I don't mean to intrude..."

Gabrielle looks up, startled. The light coming through the blinds

251

casts a shadow on her face. I can see her swollen eyes.

She tries to speak. "I... I think..." She seems to have trouble catching her breath. "I'm just... having... a hard time right now."

"Did something happen?"

She stares at the window. I look there, too, half-expecting to see someone, but there's just a sprinkling of snow in the moonlight.

Gabrielle sniffles and wipes her eyes. "I'm not doing well."

"Are you sick?"

She shakes her head and then starts crying again. The back of my neck gets warm. I really don't know what to do. Should I just say good night and go back to bed?

"Do you want me to get my mom?" I ask gently.

"No, no. Please. Don't bother her. I just have to calm down. See, I have this problem..." She puts her hands over her face.

I stand there in the dark waiting for some explanation. Mainly, I just want to know if she is okay.

"I have a problem with my moods," Gabrielle continues. "They go up and down."

Who *doesn't* have a problem with moods?

"And, now... I'm really down."

I try to think of something to say that will make her feel better. "But everything went so well today. You were amazing."

"That's just it," she says, her voice hoarse. "It was all too much. I've been running on empty. I gave my heart and soul... now it's all over."

"Oh." I must sound really clueless. "So... you're disappointed?"

I wait for her answer, but she just keeps crying.

"I kind of felt that way after my Bat Mitzvah weekend," I offer. "I'd been looking forward to my party for so long and all my relatives were here and after it was over, I felt let down."

She hangs her head between her knees.

I guess that wasn't the best analogy. I certainly didn't get as upset as Gabrielle seems to be right now. Oh, I wish Shifra were here. She'd know the right thing to say.

Gabrielle stands up. "I'm sorry you have to see me like this—"

Then she stumbles in the dark.

"Maybe I should get my mom—"

"*No*. I don't want to disturb her." She puts her hand on the desk chair and steadies herself.

"Really Gabrielle, I know she wouldn't mind. She even—"

"I just have to calm down." She looks at me with a desperate expression that makes me feel scared. It's like she is a completely different person. "Could you just keep me company... for a few minutes?" Her words come out choppy, like she's in pain.

"Sure."

I hesitantly sit down on the edge of her bed. The quilt is still pulled up; she hadn't gone to sleep yet.

Gabrielle rubs her forehead. "My parents didn't come."

So *that's* what the matter is.

"I know it seems silly," she says softy. "But it was pretty important to me."

"Texas is a long way from Boston," I reply.

She shakes her head. "It's not that. They're just not happy with my choices. That's all. They think I'm crazy for leaving the ballet company." She takes a deep breath. "And, they think I've gone overboard with being Jewish."

"Oh."

I wonder if I should tell her that it's pretty common for parents to feel this way about their newly religious kids. I hear a lot of these kinds of comments from our Shabbat guests. It seems funny to me that parents would get mad at their children for practicing Judaism, but what do I know?

"You could send them the DVD," I suggest, trying to sound more cheerful. "I know they'll be impressed."

"And tomorrow is my birthday."

It takes a second for her statement to register in my brain. "Really? But you didn't say anything—"

"It's just another reason they probably didn't want to come."

That makes absolutely no sense to me. "What do you mean?"

She sighs. "It's been a sad day for twenty of the past twenty-three years."

There are those 2s again. The digits flash in my head. I have this feeling that Gabrielle does have a secret after all.

"Your birthday is sad?" I ask incredulously.

She walks to the dresser across the room. Then she turns around and walks back to the bed, and then turns around and walks back to the dresser. I watch her pace back and forth. She is really making me nervous.

"My parents have let the sadness strangle them," she says. "I mean, you'd think after all this time they could celebrate their children's birthday joyfully."

Gabrielle seems like she is talking to herself more than to me. Wait... Did she just say, *children's* birthday?

"I thought you were an only child," I say.

Gabrielle stops pacing. She stands in the middle of a patch of moonlight on the rug.

"I am... but I wasn't always."

I feel a tugging in my chest. I know my mother would not like me asking, but I really think Gabrielle wants to tell the truth.

"What happened?"

Her words tumble out like she's been saving them up for years.

"I had a twin sister, Lily, and we both got the flu when we were almost three, only her case was worse and she died on our third birthday, February 9th. My parents never got over it, and tomorrow Lily would have been twenty-four."

The air in the dark room suddenly changes, and I find it hard to breathe. I think of the twins, Malki and Rina, the two Miriams. Of course. It all makes sense now.

"That is awful, Gabrielle," I say softly. "I'm really sorry that happened to you."

"But it isn't so awful for me," she replies. "I was three! I barely remember her."

Her remark takes me by surprise. I feel a chill. "You don't remember her at all?"

Gabrielle waits. Then the tears come again. She stands there by the window, sobbing. "No, I don't," she cries. "But... my soul remembers. That's for sure."

I feel tears push at the back of my eyes. I can't even speak.

"For the longest time, I've felt like part of me was missing." Gabrielle taps her chest. "Like there's this space I have to fill. A very lonely space." She walks over to the bed and sits down beside me. "I never used to know what to say when people asked me about my family. At first, I'd tell them that I had a twin sister in heaven. Then, after a while, I began to wonder if I was still a twin." She takes a deep breath. "My parents kept the photographs of Lily hanging on our family room wall—the two of us together dressed in matching outfits. They even kept her toddler bed with the Winnie-the-Pooh blanket and her stuffed panda bear. I grew up while Lily remained frozen in time."

She gazes toward the window. "I knew my parents could look at me and know what Lily would have looked like, except..." Gabrielle stops. Her voice gets higher. "Except, at some point, I started believing that they wished Lily had lived instead of me."

Her words hit me in the heart, and I suddenly know that what Shifra said was true. I slowly move my hand and rest it on top of Gabrielle's. We sit there in the dark, not saying anything for a while.

"You're very lucky," she whispers. Gabrielle turns toward me. "But maybe you don't even know it yet."

I'm not sure what to say. Does she mean because I have a big house and two happy parents who celebrate my birthday each year?

"I always wanted a sister," I confess, maybe to show Gabrielle that my life isn't so perfect either.

She nods. "One doesn't have to be a lonely number, Talia. Unless... unless you started with two."

Thirty-Five

My toes are frozen. I think these ice skates are too small. Mom bought me them last year just before the annual school ice-skating party, and here I am again, still slipping and sliding instead of gliding. I shuffle along, sticking close to the railing just in case. One of these days I'll learn to skate better.

There's Hannah Finkelstein in the middle of the rink showing off her spins. Hannah's little fan club (which now includes Liora) is skating around her.

"Beep, beep!" Malki Sneiderman shouts, skating right past me, then turning around into a sharp stop.

"Hey, watch out," I say, grabbing the rail.

"You're a slowpoke," Malki jokes. Her cheeks are all rosy. "Is Miss Markus coming tonight?"

"I doubt it. I bet she needs to protect her precious dancer legs."

Malki starts gliding alongside me. "I bet she's good at skating," she says. "Figure skaters take ballet, you know. Are you gonna join the dance club, Tal?"

After the production last month, Mrs. Brody hired Gabbers to run a dance club for the rest of the school year. It turned out to be quite popular. And even though I admit the dances she choreographed were great, I have no intention of putting on ballet shoes.

"Sorry. I've got too much homework."

Malki speeds up. "Aw, you're such a nerd."

"Thanks," I say, wobbling along.

The music changes to my favorite song from the Judah Brothers, "*Jerusalem Dreams.*" Maya Rubin had them perform at her Bat Mitzvah party last summer. Her dad has some connection to the music business.

"Hey, there's Ruthie!" I say. "At the rink entrance."

Ruthie waves to us. She's wearing a hot pink sweater and an ivory skirt and black leg warmers. She starts skating toward me.

"Looking good, girl!" Ruthie says, patting me on the back.

"Yeah, as long as I don't move!"

Ruthie grabs my hand. "Come on. Stop hanging on the sidelines. Take a risk for a change."

"Excuse me—" Suddenly I'm moving much faster than I want. "Ruthie, slow down!"

"Take it easy," Ruthie coaxes. "Just push off and glide. Right, left, right, left."

Malki zooms off. "See you guys at the refreshments."

Ruthie and I start passing the other girls, dodging in and out. Then she pulls me toward the center.

"No way!" I cry. "Let go, I'm going to—"

Fall.

That's exactly what I do. Smack on my bottom. Ouch.

"You okay?" Ruthie helps me up. "Sorry."

My feet slip out from under me and I'm back on the ice. I see Hannah skating toward me. Oh, great.

"Are you hurt?" Hannah asks, coming to a quick stop. I think she's actually sincere.

"Uh no," I say, getting onto my hands and knees. "Just practicing my falls."

"That's exactly what my skating teacher taught us," Hannah replies. "You can't avoid falling once in a while, so you might as well learn how to get up."

"That's about the truest thing I've heard you say," Ruthie snips.

I grab onto Ruthie's elbow. Hannah offers me her hand. Between the two of them I manage to stand up.

"Thanks."

Hannah asks, "Want to learn how to go backwards?"

I brush the snow off my jacket. "Next time."

"Those are high-quality skates," Hannah remarks. "Fancy shmancy."

"And they don't keep me up," I reply, suppressing the urge to tell Hannah to keep her mouth shut.

"Hey, check out Liora," Ruthie says, pointing to the center.

I look over and see Liora skating like a pro. When did she learn to do that?

"Those are front crossovers," Hannah says, switching back to her know-it-all voice. "I taught her."

Ruthie and I stand there watching Liora while the rest of the crowd skates by. "She looks great," Ruthie comments.

"We've been practicing a lot," Hannah says, swiveling backwards. "Well, see you guys later for pizza." She skates off toward Liora.

This new information spoils my fun Saturday night. As if it wasn't bad enough that Liora is sleeping over at Hannah's, now she's taking skating lessons with her.

"Let's practice," Ruthie says, taking my hand again. "We can learn to do that."

"Get real," I sigh.

Maya Rubin whizzes by us. "Hey Tal!"

I wave back at her, then trip on my toe pick. I feel the wet ice through my gloves.

"I think I've had enough," I say to Ruthie as she pulls me up for the second time.

"But I just got here."

"I need a hot cocoa break," I say. "Go ahead—skate."

Ruthie puts her hands on her hips. "You sure?"

I nod. "I'll catch up with you later."

Ruthie skates off in the opposite direction.

I shuffle toward the rink entrance, relieved to make it without falling again. Then I wobble over to the refreshment table and take a cup of hot cocoa and a chocolate donut. Comfort food. I park myself in the bleachers and watch the skating party. I spot Ruthie and Shifra speeding around the rink. Liora and Hannah are still showing off in the center. They look like they're having the time of their lives.

Why do I feel so miserable?

I sip my hot cocoa. For some reason I think of Gabrielle. I wonder what she is doing tonight. Ever since she shared her secret with me, things have been different. She doesn't seem quite as annoying. I can't say exactly why. I mean she still chews my ear off and pops popcorn every night and plays those folksy songs on the guitar when I'm trying to study, but I guess it doesn't bother me as much.

I have to admit, I'm proud of myself for not breathing a word about Gabrielle's twin to Ruthie and Shifra. After all this time wondering about Gabrielle's past, I finally have the scoop. I knew Shifra would have eaten it up; only I didn't have the heart to reveal the story. I mean, I guess everyone has the right to hold her own stories inside until she decides to let them out.

After Gabrielle told me about her sister, I thought about it a lot. I decided that it is much better to be an only child the rest of my life than to have had a sister who died. I didn't mention this to Gabrielle, but when I was little I used to have an imaginary twin sister named Tova. I'd even insist my parents make a place for her at the Shabbat table. I hadn't thought about Tova in a long time, that is, until Gabrielle told me her story. I happen to know quite a bit about twins because after Tova faded, I developed an obsession and started reading a lot on the subject. Did you know that twins often make up their own language? Wouldn't that be cool? I also read about twin sisters who were separated at birth and found each other as adults. They had each married someone named Steven, and both worked as book illustrators!

I see Liora stepping out of the rink. She spots me in the bleachers and waves. Surprisingly, she heads my way.

"Hey," she says, pulling off her mittens. "Why aren't you skating?"

I lift my cocoa cup. "Needed warmth."

"Speaking of warmth," she says, "did you bring a donation for the Boston Children's Shelter?"

I suddenly remember the hat, glove, and scarf set I left on the kitchen counter. Liora is charge of the winter clothing drive.

"Sorry, I left it at home. Can I bring it to school Monday?"

"Actually, Hannah and I are bringing the collection over tomorrow."

"Oh." Strike one.

"You could drop it by her house in the morning," Liora suggests cheerfully.

"Okay. I'll do that." Then the question just pops out of me. "I hear Hannah's been giving you skating lessons."

"Yeah, I never thought I'd be any good. It's a lot of fun. You should learn."

Her suggestion doesn't go over so well. "I don't think I could take Hannah as a teacher."

Liora crosses her arms. "You know, Talia, Hannah isn't so bad. In fact, she's pretty nice when you give her the chance."

I roll my eyes. "I've known her since first grade."

Liora frowns. "You don't know her. Yeah, she can be annoying sometimes, but that's just because she says what is on her mind. And guess what? That's not such a bad thing."

"Oh, so you call insulting people a good thing?" I regret my words as soon as they leave my mouth.

Liora raises her eyebrows. "At least Hannah tells the truth. Which is more than I can say about you."

I feel tears sting the back of my eyes. "I said I was sorry!"

"You're just jealous because I'm friends with Hannah now," Liora announces.

She's right.

"No," I say. "You're just trying to get back at me by getting all chummy with Hannah."

Liora sighs. "You just don't get it, do you?"

"Get what?"

"People change. Friends change," Liora says, like I'm stupid.

"I know *that*."

"Well?"

"Well what?" I say.

"So, I'm friends with Hannah now," she says matter-of-factly. "For real."

I let this news sink in. "So… are you still mad at me?"

Liora bites her lip. "A little."

"It's not fair to hold a grudge," I scold.

Liora turns her attention to the skaters. "You're right."

I didn't expect that response. "So?"

Liora looks at me. "So I'll let go of my grudge against you, if you let go of your grudge against Hannah."

I feel a surge of anger. Is that what this is all about? I'm just about to jump up and storm out of the rink when I look down and remember I'm wearing these stupid skates.

Liora extends her hand. "Deal?"

Suddenly my heart softens. I miss Liora.

"Deal," I say, shaking her warm hand.

Thirty-Six

Ruthie's mom is on bed rest. Her doctor said she was in premature labor and suffering from exhaustion. I didn't even know exhaustion was a medical condition. (In that case, I better be careful during school finals.) Mrs. Braitman still has six weeks to get through until it's safe to deliver the baby. I marked April 14, the week before Passover, on my calendar. The digits add up to 5, which is a good sign, because she is due May 5, and 5 is a girl, at least in my brain.

Ruthie has to come home right after school every day to help out with her brothers, which means she misses dance club with the infamous Miss Markus. When Gabbers heard the news, she got all the girls in the club to say special Psalms for Mrs. Braitman. Then she asked each girl to commit to saying one Psalm each day for six weeks. When Ruthie told me this, I thought again about Gabbers' secret. I was really tempted to tell Ruthie. But then I thought that getting her thinking about a dead child wouldn't be such a good idea.

Ruthie blames her brothers for their mom's situation. "They are so wild," she said to me over the phone. "They mess up the house, they don't go to bed, and they fight all the time."

I sympathize with Ruthie. I wish I could think of a solution, other than shipping her brothers off to a relative's house. The doctor said they have to get household help, so Ruthie's grandmother from Kansas might come stay with them for a while. She is supposed to be good at handling the boys.

Of course, my mom has already organized a rotating schedule of volunteers from our neighborhood to make meals for the Braitmans. That's one of the nice things about our community. We really take care of each other during hard times. All this has gotten me thinking again. Will I ever be someone's big sister?

Meanwhile, Mom hasn't slowed down one bit, as far as I can tell. The Schumacher Hotel is back in full swing. Last week we hosted six ladies for the Boston Jewish Singles weekend. Since Doris was sick, I had to make up all the beds. The six ladies plus Gabbers had a chat fest that drove me nuts. Do I really want to hear about how hard it is to find a nice Jewish man over forty?

Mom says it's a big mitzvah to help someone find a marriage partner. "So now you're in the match-making business?" I said sarcastically, which Mom did not appreciate. Lately, I seem to just blurt out what ever is on my mind, especially when I'm talking to Mom. Everything she says grates on my nerves. As soon as I decide to try to be more understanding, Mom does something to make me explode.

Now that we're into March, I'm aching for spring, but outside there are still mountains of dirty snow. At least I have my favorite holiday to look forward to next month. Every Passover we go away to a kosher resort in Puerto Rico with my aunt Dayna, Uncle Jeff, and their three kids. Last year, my cousin Abby and I got our own connecting room. The hotel is gorgeous and right on the ocean, with two tropical swimming pools and an awesome water slide. We have a private room for our family seder, and my grandparents and other relatives usually join us. The food is amazing and I don't have to lift a finger. I know Mom loves that part, too. After serving so many meals during the year, she finally gets to sit down and be served! Now that's what I call freedom from slavery.

There is so much fun stuff to do at the resort. When we were little, my cousins and I went to the kiddie camp. Once, all the kids put on a circus and I actually swung on a real trapeze. Now, I'm looking forward to the teen activities and meeting other Jewish kids from all over the world. Just thinking about all this is getting me excited.

And then... an idea starts to grow... a sensational, five-star idea!

Maybe my parents would let me invite Liora to come to Puerto Rico for Passover, and just maybe her parents would agree. I'll have to stay on their good side first, and then find the right time to ask.

"So let's hear your Purim costume ideas for the masquerade party," Ruthie says as we sit around our dining room table Sunday morning. We are filling Purim baskets to give to the nursing home. Purim is my second favorite Jewish holiday. We celebrate the heroine Queen Esther who saved her people from Haman's evil plot about 2000 years ago in Persia.

"My costume is a surprise," says Shifra.

"Oh, come on," Ruthie moans.

"No, really," Shifra replies. "You won't even recognize me." She wraps pink cellophane around the basket.

"I'm being a candy machine," I say. "So bring change."

Ruthie laughs. "Awesome idea. I still don't know what to be."

"How about a fashion model?" Shifra suggests.

"No one will know I'm dressed up."

"Very funny, Ruthie," Shifra says. "Maybe you should team up with Miss Markus. I heard she's going to be a hippie."

"I thought she'd be a ballerina," Liora says, sticking a label onto a finished basket.

"I don't think she wants to prance around the school in a tutu," Ruthie says. "A hippie isn't a bad idea, though."

"You could wear that tie-dye peace shirt you bought at the Gap last summer," I add. "Remember?"

We continue to toss out costume ideas as we finish up our share of the Purim baskets.

"What a beautiful job you girls have done!" Mom exclaims when she comes into the dining room. "I thought we'd drop off the baskets Purim morning after the megillah reading," she says. "Can any of you join us?"

"Count me in," Ruthie says.

"Me, too," adds Shifra.

Liora starts putting on her jacket. "Sorry, Mrs. Schumacher, but I'll be giving out Purim packages in my own neighborhood."

"Oh, of course," Mom replies. "Thanks so much for making the drive today. We'd love to have you over for Shabbat some time. It's been too long."

Liora smiles at me, and for a split second I see the expression of my old friend again. In that moment I know for sure that all is forgiven.

I also know for sure that Mom is in a good mood. She loves when I have friends over for community service projects. So, after they leave, I decide it would be a good time to ask about the Passover trip. I wait until she's actually sitting down and having her green tea in the kitchen. She's got the New York Times spread out on the table. Hey, when did she get those reading glasses?

"Mom?"

She looks up and smiles. "Hmm?"

"Can I talk to you for a minute?"

She takes off her glasses. "Sure. Do you want some tea?"

I shake my head and then sit down at the table. I look out the kitchen window and see patches of brown grass peeking out beneath the melting snow. Okay, it's now or never.

"Mom, I have a big favor to ask you... do you think it would be possible for Liora to join us for Passover? I haven't said anything to her yet. Obviously her parents have to be okay with it, but I wanted to check with you first."

Whew.

Mom stares at me for a moment. "You must have been reading my mind, sweetheart. Your father and I have been meaning to talk to you about that."

My heart swells with hope. "You mean you had the same idea?"

"Well, not exactly. But I would like Liora to join us, it's just that..." Mom pauses and rubs her forehead. "I know this is going to disappoint you, but your father and I want to do something different this year."

"Like a different hotel?" I ask.

"No. Like making Passover here."

"Staying home?"

"Yes. For a change. Do you realize that we've never made Passover in this house?"

"So?"

"We want you to have that experience. Liora could join us."

I feel a panic rising. "What about Aunt Dayna and Uncle Jeff and Grandma and Grandpa?"

"I'm talking about hosting everyone. Any relative who wants to come. We'd have a Schumacher reunion. Doesn't that sound nice?"

"Mom, are you crazy?"

"Talia, please."

"I don't want to stay home. We go to the hotel every year."

"That's exactly my point." She sips her tea.

I can't believe this. No ocean, no beach combing, no snorkeling. I need to take a different tactic.

"Mom, you deserve a rest! My friends tell me how much work it is… the cleaning, the food shopping, the special dishes, all the cooking."

"Talia, really. Listen to yourself. Doris will help us with the cleaning. And Gabrielle—"

"Gabrielle! Is that it?" I throw my hands up. "You're staying for Gabrielle?"

Mom looks at me sharply. "Lower your voice."

"Mom, really. I don't mind if she comes along. I'll even share a room with her if I have to—"

"That is very generous of you, but right now you are sounding rather spoiled."

I cross my arms and frown. I hate that word.

Mom sighs. "And I suppose it is our own fault. We wanted to give you wonderful Passover memories—"

"You did! And I can have even more good memories this time with Liora."

"We want you to have the memory of preparing for Passover, just like your grandparents and great-grandparents did. Memories of sitting around the seder table in our own home with all our relatives, not just the ones who can make it to Puerto Rico. We're afraid that the eight days of Passover have turned into one huge vacation, and not the spiritual experience it should be."

"What's wrong with a vacation?"

"Nothing. And we will take a vacation another time. But, Passover is a *yom tov*, Talia. A holiday first."

"I'll go to the classes this year," I plead. Dad and Mom always bugged me about not going to the guest rabbi's lectures.

"We can do fun things together in our neck of the woods," Mom replies, ignoring my comment.

"Like what?" I demand.

"We could go to Newport or Cape Cod during the middle days," she suggests.

"It'll be cold."

"Passover is later this year. We might get lucky."

I feel tears well up. "I just don't get it, Mom."

"There is another factor as well," she says.

I sniffle and look at her expectantly.

"This year Rabbi Gordon is bringing in several Russian Jews who have never been at a seder. We'd have the chance to host—"

"So that's what this is about!" I yell. I feel like my heart just burst open. "You can't say no, Mom. You have to be the perfect hostess! That's the real reason, isn't it?"

I see the shocked look on Mom's face, but I don't stop. "You and Dad fill up this house with guests so everyone will say how wonderful we are—"

"Talia! That's enough."

I stand up. "No, Mom, it's true."

"You don't know what you're talking about."

"I'm sick of it, Mom. I really am." Mom looks hurt now, but my heart has become hard like Pharaoh's. "You don't care about me or my privacy or the fact that I might want time alone with just my family or my friends."

"Whoa, just what is going on here?" Mom reaches for my hand and I yank it away. "What's this all about, Talia?"

I shove my chair against the table. "You're taking away the trip I look forward to all year!"

"I think you should calm down. When you can talk to me in a civil tone—"

"I don't want to calm down!"

Then I hear Gabrielle ask, "Is something wrong?"

I turn around and see her in the doorway, staring at me, looking clueless. Why does she have to butt into my business?

"Yes!" I say to her. "There is. *Everything.*"

"Excuse us," Mom says, moving toward me. "Talia, go to your room and—"

I don't let her finish. I run past Gabrielle and out of the kitchen.

I stomp up the stairs, and it takes every ounce of resistance to keep myself from yanking down that dumb Chagall painting in the hallway.

I fling myself on my bed and cuddle with Snowball, my stuffed kitten. Snowball's matted fur reminds me about all the times I used to beg my parents for a cat or dog. They always refused, saying that animal allergies are very common and one of our guests might be allergic. Ugh. Our whole life revolves around guests. Why? Why does my mother have to go so overboard?

I consider protesting by going on a hunger strike, but I remember that Purim is almost here and Mom makes delicious hamentashen, not to mention all the yummy stuff we'll get from our neighbors. Instead, I elect the silent treatment.

A while later, there's a knock at my door. I don't answer.

"Talia?"

Oh, it's Gabbers again.

"Yeah?"

"Can I come in?"

Well, there's no reason to give *her* the silent treatment. "Okay, but proceed with caution."

Gabrielle shuts the door behind her. I look over from my bed. For once she doesn't start talking.

"Sorry about the yelling," I mutter.

"And I'm sorry about intruding on you and your mom. I should have just walked on by." Gabrielle steps over my clothes strewn across the floor and sits down at my desk. "It's just that you sounded so upset, and my first instinct was to see if I could help."

"Thanks," I say. "But you can't."

"Are you sure?"

For a split second I try to imagine how I might get Gabrielle on my side, but I don't want to drag her into this. "I'm sure."

She nods. "I guess everyone has their ups and downs. I should know."

I wonder if she is feeling better. We never talked about that night after the play. It's almost as if she forgot it even happened.

"Well, then… I have some news to share," she says.

I sit up in my bed. "Good news, I hope?"

Gabrielle squints. "Well? I suppose it is how you look at it. I think you'll consider it good news."

Maybe she's engaged to Jared Samuels!

"In June I'll be moving on to Israel," Gabrielle announces.

It takes me a few seconds to respond. "Really?"

I realize my surprise might be taken for excitement, so I try to think of something to say. "I mean, that's great. You've never been there before, right?"

Gabrielle shakes her head. "I'll be starting a crash course in Hebrew next week and continuing when I get there."

"What made you decide to go?"

"I'm entering a women's study program in Jerusalem. It's geared for those who didn't grow up religious. There's so much I want to learn about Judaism. And what better place than our Holy Land?"

"You're going all by yourself?"

"Not exactly. I know two girls from New York who will be there. And, best of all, my wonderful teacher and spiritual adviser from the Living Torah Center will be a guest teacher!"

I vaguely recall hearing something about this woman when Gabrielle first arrived.

"You're going to love it there," I say. A funny feeling swirls inside me. I'm not sure if I'm glad or sad.

"I hope so," she says. "It's hard to start over again, but it seems like the right time for me."

"Will you come back?" I ask, surprised at my own question.

"To Boston, you mean?"

I nod, unsure of which answer I want to hear.

She looks up at the ceiling. "I have no idea. Whatever God has in store for me, I'm ready for the adventure."

"Did you tell my mother?"

Gabrielle nods. "She's the one who helped me with the planning."

I feel the sting of being out of the loop. Why doesn't my mother tell me anything?

"What about Mrs. Brody?" I ask.

"She knows, but I haven't said anything to the girls yet."

"Well, everyone at school is really going to miss you," I say. And that's the truth. "You're very popular."

Her green eyes beam. "Thank you. And I'll miss them. It's been an amazing experience. I never thought I'd enjoy teaching dance so much. And who knows where it will lead? I've toyed with the idea of a starting a dance company, choreographing dances based on biblical stories, or opening my own dance school one day. Maybe I could write plays for community productions…" She waves her hand. "Well, there I go, getting carried away again."

I can't help smiling. "You *do* get carried away."

Gabrielle stands up. "That's what makes life interesting," she says. "Don't you think?" Then she does a little ballet curtsy.

I think that is exactly what happened with my parents and their hospitality.

The next morning Mom leaves for work, and I don't even say goodbye to her. I just stare into my bowl of oatmeal as she walks out the door. Maybe tonight I'll have a chance to see Dad and talk some sense into him. If Dad changes his mind about the trip, then Mom probably will, too. I bet I can even get Doris on my side. Wait till she hears how much cleaning and scrubbing she's going to have to do to get our kitchen ready for Passover.

On the way to school, Ruthie reminds me that we're having a guest speaker during last period, which means gym class is cancelled. Too bad. I'd much rather play basketball. Ruthie agrees, although Shifra told her the speaker is a famous lady from Israel. "Speaking of Israel…" I say excitedly, but then stop.

Ruthie glances at me. "Yeah?"

Gabrielle didn't actually say not to tell, but then I decide that she'd want to be the one to tell everyone the news.

"I can't wait to go back," I say.

"What, are your parents planning a trip?"

"Possibly in the summer, but nothing for sure."

Oh, gosh, why did I say that?

The rest of the morning I have this sick feeling in my stomach, like I'm dreading something, but I don't know what. At lunchtime, I help out with the decorations for the masquerade party, but I just can't get into the holiday spirit. Purim is in three days and it is supposed to be a time of joy. That is the last thing I feel right now. I keep seeing my mother's face last night when I yelled at her, like a freeze-frame that won't go away.

"Why are you so quiet today?" Liora asks me as we hang the streamers in the school hallway.

I don't want to tell Liora about the fight with Mom. "I'm not feeling so well."

"Oh, no. You can't get sick before the party," she says, taping one end of the streamer.

"It's not that kind of sick." I hand her a purple streamer. "I'm just in a mood."

"Oh. Well, I guess that's better than being sick." She puts her hands on her hips and stands back to admire the colorful streamers. "There. How does that look?"

"You've got the magic touch," I say.

"I have the magic medicine for a bad mood, too. Come on."

I follow Liora to her locker. She reaches in her backpack and pulls out a small tin wrapped in pink cellophane. "I know it's a little early. Happy Purim," she says, handing it to me. "It's chocolate fudge. I made it myself."

"It's not the sugar-free carob kind, is it?" I joke.

Liora laughs. "No. One hundred percent junk food."

"Yum. Thanks," I say, feeling better already.

During last period all the seventh and eighth grade girls gather in the auditorium for the program. I strategically find a seat in the back next to Liora and Ruthie, in case the speaker is boring. That way I can play with my calculator or doodle in a notebook and the teachers (sitting up in front) won't even notice.

"What's going on?" Ruthie whispers.

I shrug. "Don't want to talk about it." I guess Liora said something to her about my mood.

"What? Are you having fifty guests for the Purim meal or something?"

"Just about, but that's not it."

"Something with Gabrielle?"

"Never mind. Okay?" I glance at her. Ruthie looks hurt. "I'll tell you later," I say.

Then her face brightens. "Call me tonight."

"Girls, may I have your attention, please?" Mrs. Brody calls, tapping on the microphone. "We are so fortunate to have Dr. Zahavah Jaffe in Boston this week. Professor Jaffe is a motivational speaker, writer, and professor of Biblical Studies at Tel Aviv University. Her topic today is: Finding Your Life's Mission."

I was all prepared to daydream, but there is something about Professor Jaffe that captivates me. So I decide to listen for a change.

The speaker adjusts the microphone at the podium. "Girls, it is such a pleasure to be here. Even though I find your city a bit cold for March, it warms me up to see so many lovely young faces. I look around the room and see our future Jewish mothers and leaders."

Professor Jaffe has this rich Israeli accent and wide, welcoming smile, the kind that you know isn't fake. She wears a beautiful blue head scarf, which gives her a rather exotic look. She begins by telling us that we each have a unique mission in life, and part of the fun is figuring out just what it is. On our Jewish journey we're supposed to find out what our special mitzvah is—the Torah commandment that has a particular meaning to us. Once we figure that out, we will get a clue to our life's mission.

Even though Professor Jaffe is speaking to a room full of about sixty girls, she makes me feel like she is talking just to me.

"When I was your age, I never thought I'd end up traveling around the world speaking to women and girls about living a purposeful life.

I was a shy bookworm, after all."

Professor Jaffe mesmerizes us with the story of how she ended up where she is today. "So you see, we have to pay attention to the signs God gives us. Pay attention to the people who are sent into your lives. Don't sleep through the journey, girls!"

I look over at Liora. She seems totally into the professor's talk.

"Why is it that one mitzvah comes so easily to one person, but is so hard for another?" Professor Jaffe asks us. "Let's take prayer, for example. We are supposed to serve God through prayer, yes? For some of us, this is natural, pleasurable, and even easy. And for others, well, they'd rather sharpen a whole box of pencils than read the book of Psalms."

This gets a laugh from everyone. I can relate to that idea.

"So you girls know that it is a mitzvah to celebrate with the bride and groom at their wedding, right?" she continues. "Now that's a fun mitzvah, isn't it? To make the newly married couple feel happy? An easy good deed. You basically tear up the dance floor."

Mrs. Jaffe pauses and looks around the room.

"I know a woman who has taken this particular mitzvah to heart. Her name is Leah. She helps brides and grooms who have no parents, or those with difficult financial situations, to make a beautiful wedding. She finds them a hall, musicians, a caterer, even a bridal dress. This special lady created a whole organization to collect funds and resources just for this purpose. Amazing, huh?"

Professor Jaffe tells us more inspiring stories. I glance around the room. No one is dozing off or texting friends.

"Sometimes, a person has a special reason for devoting energy to a certain mitzvah. Maybe someone who recovered from cancer might feel drawn to the mitzvah of visiting and caring for people who are sick. You girls are very young, I know, but not too young to start thinking about this. What mitzvah means the most to *you?*"

Hmm. That's a question I never thought of.

"Remember the Torah story of our patriarch and matriarch, Abraham and Sarah, yes? Of course you do. Since you were little girls your teachers told you about Abraham and Sarah's tent, how it was open on all sides so they could welcome guests in the desert from any direction. Am I right?"

Mrs. Jaffe recounts the biblical story of the three men who come to visit Abraham on a hot day in the desert of Haran. The visitors are really angels. God has sent them because Abraham wants so badly to have guests even though he is in physical pain. Each angel has its own purpose: to heal Abraham, to warn him that the wicked city of Sodom will be destroyed, and finally, to announce that ninety-year-old Sarah will have a baby.

Ruthie nudges, then whispers to me, "See, there's hope for your mom."

"Very funny," I mouth.

"And Abraham washes their feet and tells them to hang out under his shady tree. Then he and Sarah go about serving the guests delicious food," Professor Jaffe continues, "but they're angels! They don't need any food. Did you girls ever wonder about that? I mean, what's going on here? You may have heard the Jewish saying from the Midrash: 'More than the host does for the guests, the guests do for the host.'"

Professor Jaffe pauses and looks around the room. I think of Gabbers. I hear my mother's voice in my head. *Our house is an open house.*

"You know, I have taught this Torah story to students many times," Professor Jaffe says thoughtfully. "A few years ago, I was teaching it to a group of newly religious women. I pointed out how this story is used as the quintessential example of the mitzvah of *hachnassat orchim*—welcoming guests—what we call Jewish hospitality."

That weird feeling in my stomach returns. My palms start to get sweaty.

Mrs. Jaffe leans on the podium. "I'm sure you all learned this in kindergarten—Abraham and Sarah were gracious hosts and we should be like them, too! You remember this?"

Our house is an open house. Is this some kind of joke? I half-expect everyone to turn around and stare at me, but no one does.

"Well, there was one woman in my class, Brenda was her name, who had been married for ten years," Professor Jaffe says, "and she was very sad that she didn't have any children yet. When she learned this Torah story, she saw something in it that I never did. Brenda saw the angel's message that childless Sarah would have a baby as an inspiration for *herself* to bring guests into her own home! Girls, I'll never forget Brenda's words to me. She said, 'Dr. Jaffe, if I can't fill my home with children, at least I can fill it with guests. And who knows, maybe in the merit of doing the mitzvah of hospitality, God will bless me with a child.' "

My heart starts to pound. Professor Jaffe is still talking, but I can't hear her anymore. I suddenly stand up. My knees feel shaky. I start inching my way past Ruthie and Liora.

"Where are you going?" Liora whispers.

I don't answer.

I hear Ruthie say my name as I quickly walk to the back of the auditorium, and then through the exit. I run to my locker and grab my backpack and coat. I glance back to see if anyone is following me. Then I head down the empty hallway and out the school doors.

The cold air outside slaps me in the face. I feel like an invisible hand is pushing me ahead and up the street. My legs move faster and faster. I try counting my steps. I know I could get in trouble for leaving school early without permission, but I don't care. I just keep walking and walking, passing house after house, until I know where I have to go.

I see the downtown train approaching just as I run up the platform steps. It stops and the green door opens, just as if it were waiting for me. I flash my student card to the driver, then sit down on the cold seat. The train starts to move.

How could I be so stupid? How could I not have known? Doris was right. I am spoiled. I only think about myself. How could I not see my mother's mission? I was too busy complaining. Too busy sulking about being an only child. What about Mom? How did she feel all this time? She's the one who can't have another baby.

I stare out the train window. My own words haunt me. *You and Dad fill this house with guests so everyone will say how wonderful we are.*

I'm so sorry, Mom. Now I understand. Why couldn't you just tell me?

A half hour later, I get off at Government Center. I quickly walk the few blocks to the State Street Bank building, which towers over the others in the Boston skyline.

"Talia Schumacher," I tell the guard at the front desk. "I need to see my mother, Mrs. Naomi Schumacher."

In the elevator I try to catch my breath. I push number 4. I stare at the numbers on the buttons. I don't see any colors.

I step out of the elevator knowing I will find her. I walk past the maze of office cubicles.

I hear her voice.

"Talia!" Mom practically jumps out of her desk chair. "What are you doing here?"

Her smile vanishes as I approach her office. I see the alarm in her eyes, but I can't even talk.

She steps closer. "What happened, baby?"

I throw my arms around her. She smells like cinnamon.

"Talia, are you okay? What is it, sweetie?"

I let my tears fall.

"Mom... I'm so sorry. I really am. Please forgive me."

She holds me tight for a while. Mom takes my hand and sits me down in the oversized leather chair by her desk. Then she shuts the office door.

Thirty-Seven

If my life were a Hollywood script, I'd be writing about how Mom found out she was having twins.

Well, at least she's trying acupuncture these days. I have Gabrielle to thank for that, in addition to her convincing Mom to take up yoga. (Mom always thought yoga was too slow.) I've noticed her starting to chill out. And that's a good thing. The past five Fridays she's come home early. Not bad. And best of all, we've decided to start a new ritual: Happy 8 Day. Basically, on the eighth day of every month, we'll do something special together like going out for ice cream or getting our nails done.

Maybe someday one of our guests, claiming to be a psychic, will announce that Mom is going to have a baby. Wouldn't that make a cool story? I guess there is still hope—who knows? I sometimes wonder what God has in store for me and my parents, and how much our actions and prayers have anything to do with it. I wonder if I'll figure out what my special mission is, like Professor Jaffe talked about. I guess it's all part of the mystery of living on this planet. Either way, I'm looking forward to the adventure, baby sister (or brother) or not.

The only new baby in the picture is Aviva Braitman, Ruthie's first sister, born on May 5, her exact due date. We were all doing high-fives in school. Did I pick it or what? Since Ruthie is so into fashion, Gabrielle thought it would be great to buy Aviva her spring wardrobe. So, Gabrielle took me and Shifra shopping and we picked out armfuls of frilly baby clothes. You should have seen Mrs. Braitman's face when we delivered the huge gift bag.

Next news flash: Liora joined my family for our first Passover at home, along with my relatives, a bunch of Russian guests, Gabrielle, and, believe it or not—Hannah Finkelstein. Funny thing, it was actually Gabrielle's idea to invite Hannah. Since I wanted to stay on good terms with Liora, I caved. I have to admit that Liora was right—Hannah isn't so bad after all. Maybe Liora tamed her, or maybe I just got more tolerant, but the three of us ended up getting along.

Gabrielle totally got into the Passover preparations. When she found out about my disappointment over not going to Puerto Rico, she set her mind to making it the best Passover ever. At the seder, Gabrielle gave pillowcases filled with heavy blocks to the younger kids and had them carry the sacks on their backs. Dad pretended to be Pharaoh and barked orders for the kids to work harder. And Gabrielle "whipped" them with one of those blue noodles!

Then, as we all took turns reading the Haggadah, Gabrielle acted out the part about the Four Sons. Liora, Hannah, and I couldn't stop giggling. Then, when we came to the description of the Ten Plagues that were brought upon ancient Egypt, Gabrielle surprised us with plague bags. In no time my little cousins were throwing hail (ping-pong balls), plastic frogs, and grasshoppers all over the table. You should have seen the look on the guests' faces, especially when Gabrielle handed out oversized sunglasses for us all to wear for the plague of darkness.

By the time we got to the actual meal, the guests were all singing Russian songs at the top of their lungs. Hannah turned to me and said, "Gosh, Talia, your seder really rocks!"

So, although the Boston weather wasn't anything like Puerto Rico, and I didn't get to swing on a trapeze, my entire family was together under our roof. And that felt good. Mom was right—now I have a different Passover memory. I bet our Russian guests will always remember *their* first seder at Hotel Schumacher.

If my life were a Hollywood script, I'd get to report that I won first place in the state math contest. I didn't. Neither did Meyer Feingold. The test questions were really hard and the competition stiff. Without

Hannah and Liora by my side, I felt more nervous and alone. What was almost as bad as not winning was that I tied for ninth place with Meyer! Not even my lucky number eight could save me. To top things off, *The Jewish Journal* put our pictures on the front page with the headline, *Hebrew Academy 7th Graders Tie*. Ruthie, Liora, and Shifra all thought it was hilarious. Ha, ha. What journalism school did that reporter go to? Hannah couldn't resist teasing me. "So, Talia, did you two study together?" I wanted to crawl in a hole.

If my life were a Hollywood script, Gabrielle would become my adopted big sister and stay for good. Not.

In the beginning of June, Gabrielle took off to Israel. Our school made her a going-away party and the dance club surprised her with a performance choreographed by Ruthie, the new Dance Queen. Gabrielle got all choked up and gave a real mushy goodbye speech. Then Malki and Rina Sneiderman presented her with a book on famous Jewish women and a framed picture of her performing "Miriam's Song." I saw the twins hug Gabrielle, and I wondered if she ever told them about Lily. I am proud of myself for keeping that secret inside me.

Mom says there's a Jewish custom to accompany your guests part-way home after they leave your house. This basically translates to seeing them to the door and walking them outside a little way. In Gabrielle's case, Mom insisted that we all drive her to the airport. If my life were a movie, there would be a tearful scene at the airport, "Miriam's Song" playing in the background, while I tell Gabrielle how much I will miss her. I would apologize for being a reluctant host.

But it didn't happen that way. Instead, we got stuck in terrible traffic on the way to Logan Airport and had to rush our goodbyes so she wouldn't miss her plane.

Gabrielle managed to snap a few pictures with us, and then she gave Mom and me a big hug while Dad parked the car. Of course Mom told Gabrielle that she was welcome to visit us any time.

"I hope y'all will visit *me!* You know, 'Next Year in Jerusalem!'" she said, quoting the phrase we sing at the conclusion of the Passover seder.

Mom and I stood there watching as Gabrielle pulled her pink

suitcase toward the security line. Then she stopped for a moment, looked back, and waved at us before moving ahead.

Mom sighed and said softly, "I hope she continues to heal."

Mom's surprising words were like a missing puzzle piece. And that's when I knew why Gabrielle came here and why she was moving on. She needed to find something to fill that lost half—so she could be whole again.

Thirty-Eight

June 18th. Last day of school today. I practically skip all the way home. Boy, am I ready for summer. Thanks to Dr. Janas, I get to spend a week at MIT Math Camp. Then Shifra and I are off to the Jewish Girls Retreat in upstate New York. After that, Mom and Dad are spending a week on Martha's Vineyard—by themselves. I get to stay at Liora's house for a change. Can't get better than that.

"Hey, Doris," I say, walking through the front door. The house smells like pine. "I'm done," I call, dropping my bulging backpack. "I'm officially an eighth-grader! Eight is great!"

Doris appears at the top of the stairs waving a dust cloth. "Congratulations to you, princess." She blows me a kiss. "I buy you chocolate chip cookies. Go see in the kitchen."

I love Doris.

"And I left a mail package for you, too. On the table."

When I see the Israeli stamps on the brown paper package, I know right away it's from Gabrielle. I unwrap the package, wondering what in the world she would send me. Israeli chocolate, perhaps?

Inside I find a necklace—a delicate silver chain with a silver number 1 dangling on the end. On the top there's a tiny Hebrew letter engraved: an *aleph*, which means 'one'. Wow.

Dear Talia,
I thought of you when I saw this. I wish I had it to give when you

won first place in the math contest. Guess what I learned? One is not a lonely number. Every day in our prayers we say, Listen Israel, the Lord is our God, the Lord is One. God is One, Talia. We even sang this at the Passover seder! The letters in the Hebrew word for One add up to 13. I learned there are 13 attributes of God. Add 1 and 3 and you get 4. There are 4 letters in the Hebrew name for God! I just thought that was kind of cool and that you would appreciate it. Be proud of who you are, Talia, and thank you again for sharing your home with me.

Love,

Gabrielle Markus

I slip the necklace around my neck, and then walk over to the mirror in the front hallway. I'm surprised that I have to blink a few times before I can see my reflection through the tears. The necklace looks great. It's a unique gift—a good conversation starter, as Mom would say. *Thanks, Gabbers.*

I remember the guests we'll be hosting tonight for Shabbat dinner. As always, Dad will ask me to introduce myself at the table. I think I'll try something slightly different this time.

"Hi," I say out loud, smiling at my reflection. "I'm Talia Schumacher, the One and Only. Welcome!"

YM BOOKS

For Jewish Girls, by Jewish Girls!

YM Books is a division of **YALDAH.** YALDAH is dedicated to providing a safe space online for Jewish girls of all backgrounds to express themselves and connect. We hope to inspire girls to embrace their Judaism with pride and become leaders of the future. YALDAH shows girls that using their talents and determination, they can make their dreams come true!

Visit our website, **www.yaldah.com** for articles, games, shopping, and updates on new books and programs for Jewish girls!

One is Not a Lonely Number
THE MOVIE!

If you loved the book, you'll love the movie!

In Summer 2011 the Jewish Girls Retreat produced the movie version of One is Not a Lonely Number. It features drama, dance, and choir performed by the campers of JGR, and is professionally filmed and produced. This 90-minute film is excellent for girls of all ages and backgrounds.

To order the DVD visit www.JewishGirlsRetreat.com/store.

ABOUT THE AUTHOR

Evelyn Krieger, the oldest of six children, grew up in Detroit, Michigan. As a child, she entertained her friends with imaginative stories and dance performances. In fact, the inspiration for her first poem came in the middle of the night when she was just eight years old. Evelyn has been writing ever since, and her essays and stories have won numerous awards. After studying ballet seriously, and earning her master's degree from Harvard, Evelyn worked as a reading teacher and private tutor. Today, she is a writer, learning specialist, and a homeschooling mom. Evelyn lives in the Boston area with her husband and three children.

To connect with Evelyn and her latest writing, visit her blog at

www.evelynkrieger.net.